BEWERE THE NIGHT

OTHER BOOKS BY EKATERINA SEDIA

The Secret History of Moscow
Paper Cities: An Anthology of Urban Fantasy (editor)
The Alchemy of Stone
Running with the Pack (editor)
The House of Discarded Dreams
Heart of Iron (forthcoming)

BEWERE THE NIGHT

EDITED BY

EKATERINA SEDIA

PRIME BOOKS

BEWERE THE NIGHT

Prime Books
www.prime-books.com

ISBN: 978-1-60701-252-8

To those who cannot keep one shape

TABLE OF CONTENTS

INTRODUCTION

After editing *Running with the Pack*, I was a tad apprehensive about taking on another shape-shifter anthology. Sure, it's more than just werewolves, I reasoned, but how many variations on a theme can there be? The metaphor was, to me, obvious: violence and wildness, the human's animal nature hidden by a thin civilized veneer . . . a theme as old as storytelling.

As it turned out, I should never have worried. The imaginations and inventiveness of the contributors amazed and delighted me. Their stories were richly diverse, both in terms of were-creatures and the themes they represented. Were-hummingbirds and were-socialists, failing families and immigrant resilience, stories set in the present, past, and future, a variety of cultures and influences, from China to Mexico to Hollywood. The protagonists of these stories are just as diverse: from children to old astronauts to mountain climbers to actors, all have singular stories and unique perspectives on their human and animal natures.

As for my assumption about the meaning of shape-shifter stories, my concept was wonderfully broadened: these stories are not always (or even mostly) about humankind's inner animal nature. They are often about longing and wistfulness, the desire to be something we are not, to regain some aspect of ourselves that we've lost without ever actually possessing it, the yearning for something we cannot quite remember.

Some of the stories are recognizable as traditional tales of werewolves or animal wives; some take on the now-familiar tropes of urban fantasy. Others are singular: were-jellyfish; an entire city infested with a strange malaise; lycanthropes in an STD clinic . . . I could never have imagined!

The stories were chosen for their individual beauty and for their many differences of viewpoint, for their novel flights of imagination, or for their radical twists of the familiar tropes.

I invite you to enjoy these stories, one by one, to give each the room to breathe and unfold and to show you what's inside. Some are funny and some are scary, but all are beguiling. Each of them will delight you with its love of language and of storytelling. They offer unique perspectives on shape-shifters and were-creatures, and I only hope that your notions of these strange beings will be challenged and expanded as much as mine were while editing this collection.

And most of all, beware: these stories might transform you!

Ekaterina Sedia
December 2010
Grenada/New Jersey

THE THIEF OF PRECIOUS THINGS

A.C. WISE

Their shadows are crows.

They are two men, standing at the mouth of an alleyway, watching the night with dark, guarded eyes. Their long, black coats flap in the wind, and their shadows have wings. They have feathers and beaks and claws.

When the moon reaches the apex of the sky, they crush their cigarettes against the bricks. Their shadows break into a dozen birds each and take flight.

They have been waiting for her.

She is a fox-girl, running swift over the close rooftops. Up here, the world smells of dust and feathers. Fresh-washed laundry hangs from obsolete radio relays, satellite dishes, and cell phone towers, which sprout like mushrooms atop every building. Sheets and shirts flap in the wind, flags to mark her passing.

Her paws—black as burnt wood—fly over shingle, tile, brick and tar. The birds follow, floating on silent, star-lined wings. She stole something from them, something precious. They want it back.

When the roof ends, there is nowhere else to run. She jumps, changes in mid-air, and lands on two feet on the cracked pavement. The smells between the buildings are wet—all puddles, garbage, and food left to rot. She longs for the dry smells of the world near the sky. Neon turns the alley the color of blood. She is on four paws again, running.

The fox-girl can almost remember what she stole. She remembers a stone on her tongue. Images tumble through her mind: an unearthly blue glow, a chair, leather straps around her wrists, a needle in her arm. There was a woman, a human woman, and she buried something under the fox-girl's skin. It burns.

Sheltering against the side of a dumpster, she snaps fox-teeth at her own flank, tastes blood, and spits fur and flesh onto the wet ground. Something catches the light, gleaming in the patch of bitten-free skin. It is a small square of plastic, patterned with silver.

She stole it from the men in the tower; she can almost remember why. The crows want it, the humans want it; it is precious. She picks it up between careful teeth, and tucks it in her cheek.

A door opens onto the alleyway, spilling yellow light and the scent of noodles and cooked vegetables. A young man stands framed against the light, holding a bulging, plastic bag full of wasted food. Her eyes meet his, but before he can speak, four and twenty black birds fall from the sky.

The crows fold their wings tight, diving for her eyes. She whirls, snapping and snarling at the storm of feathers. The precious plastic thing scrapes her gums raw. She leaps, twists—a war dance. She is all fox now, her animal heart beating hard inside a cage of burning bones, wrapped in fur the color of coal.

"Hey! Leave it alone!"

Amidst the chaos of wings, she hears the young man drop the swollen bag of trash. It splits, spilling new scents into the alley—meat and sauce, cooling in the night air.

He runs to her side, arms beating the feathered whirlwind. She could slip away, now that the birds' attention is divided. A sharp beak draws blood from his arm, and he cries out. He is nothing to her, this young human, but she stays.

The crows are distracted, and she leaps, snatching a bird from the air. Her jaws close, crunching hollow bones. Liquid shadow slides down her throat, tasting of primordial tar, tasting of the decayed flesh of a million dead things from the beginning of time.

Twenty three birds lift, wheeling in the sky. They scream, and fall together again at the far end of the alley, coalescing into shadows where two men wait and watch with hard, dark eyes.

One man is missing a piece of the ragged blackness spread beneath him, cast by the alley's light. His eyes meet hers, full of pain and surprise. He limps as he and his brother walk away.

A hand touches her back. The young man's voice is soft. "Are you okay?"

She's still postured to fight. Instinct snaps her teeth; the man yelps and pulls away. She tastes blood—his and hers—mingled with the lingering taste of crow-shadow oil.

She changes and lifts her head. She is a woman now, naked, crouched on blood-colored pavement that remembers the rain. She is bleeding, shaking, and tired to the bone.

The young man stares at her, open-mouthed, wide-eyed, cradling his wounded hand. She tries to speak, fails, and spits blood and plastic into her palm before trying again.

"Sorry," she says.

She collapses, but not before closing the precious, stolen thing that the crows and the humans want tightly in her hand.

She wakes on a pallet in a strange room. The scent of noodles, cooked meat, and vegetables, has sunk deep into the walls. A thin blanket lies draped over her. When she shifts, its rough weave catches on her torn skin.

The young man from the alleyway enters carrying a tray holding a bowl of water, a bowl of soup, and a roll of gauze. He sets the tray down and backs away. His hand is wrapped; two spots of crimson have soaked through the white.

He could have run, too. He could have left her in the alley on the blood-colored ground. Why bring her here? Perhaps she reminds him of someone.

She sits up, letting the blanket fall, and reaches for the gauze. He watches, wide-eyed, as she licks the wounds she can reach with her tongue, and cleans the ones she can't with water from the bowl. The young man is too frightened, too stunned, to look away.

After she wraps the last of the bandages, he shakes himself and hands her a shirt from a pile draped over the back of a chair. She catches his scent—sweat, laced with pheromones, but mostly with fear.

The shirt is clean. It reminds her of the wind on the rooftops. She pulls it on. Only now that she has covered herself does the young man blush, as though his skin has just remembered shame. He looks away.

She reaches for the soup and drinks, swallowing until she almost washes away the taste of crow-oil and shadows and blood. The young man looks back at her as she sets the bowl down; she smiles—a fox-grin.

"What's your name?" he asks. He watches her as though he believes she will bite him again, or worse.

"I don't know." As she speaks them, the fox-girl realizes the words are true. "I don't remember."

She lifts the plastic square, which she held tight even as she slept, letting the young man see.

"I stole this. Do you know what this is?"

Fear flickers through his eyes. "I think so."

He perches on the edge of the pallet, body rigid. He doesn't meet her fox-eyes straight on, but looks at her from the side.

"My name is Yuki. If you don't have a name, what should I call you?"

She shrugs. She isn't interested in names, only the patterned plastic in her hand.

"Ani. I'll call you Ani."

The way he speaks the name makes her look up. He holds the name on his tongue like it's a precious thing, one he's afraid of breaking. The name has a physical weight; it changes the air in the room and leaves it tasting of ghosts. That he has given her this name frightens her. Once she had a name that meant something. Names have power, and this heavy name, fallen from his lips and soaking into her skin, might change her if she lets it. Maybe it already has.

She pushes the thought away. "Tell me about this." She holds up the stolen plastic again.

"It's a computer chip, from before the war. Everyone used to have them, but now they only exist in tower." He points to the window. "I used to deliver food there, but not anymore."

Ani looks. The tower glitters. A thousand windows catch the setting sun and turn it into a column of living light twisting up from the scrub-brush of the city surrounding it.

"I carried a stone on my tongue," she says.

"What does that mean?"

"I don't know." She closes fox-eyes. "Except sometimes, I do."

She remembers.

Before the glass tower there was a tower of stone. It is nothing like the glittering tower outside Yuki's window. It has no windows, but it is open to the sky, and it rustles with the sound of restless wings.

In the central courtyard, a line of men with cold, hard eyes stand on a raised platform. If the fox looks straight ahead, she can only see their shoes. Even if she changed, they would still look down on her. She is less than nothing in the Crow Lords' eyes—all foxes are. So she stands with her head held high, just to show them she can.

Above the hard-eyed men, hundreds of crows line the tower's edge. The fox-girl holds her tail erect; she does not show her throat; she does not bow.

"Why are you here?" one of the Crow Lords asks.

"I've heard you need a thief. I'm the best there is."

She meets their eyes, bird and human both. Her tongue lolls, a fox-grin. She speaks truth.

Powerful and ancient as they are, there are places no Crow Lord can go. They were tricksters once, but they've forgotten the old ways, or let them go. Fox-girls were born to steal, and no fox-girl is quicker or cleverer than she.

"Cocky child." Another Crow Lord speaks, and the fox-girl turns to him. His eyes are cold, harder than those of his brothers, filled with contempt.

"You must learn your place," the Crow Lord continues. "I will take your name to teach you respect."

Every fox-girl earns her name. It is a battle, hard-won with teeth and claws, with wit, and cunning, and quickness. But with a thought the Crow Lord rips her name away, leaving a hole where a thing she can't even remember anymore used to be. The hole fills with ice; it slows her blood and threatens to stop her breath. She shivers as though at winter's deepest cold.

The Crow Lord steps down from the platform and crouches. She could reach his throat, tear it out. The cold spreading from the place where her name used to be keeps her from doing anything at all. He laughs—a sound like rustling wings.

He grabs her muzzle, forcing open her jaws. Her needle-sharp teeth are so close to his skin, but she cannot close them while he holds her.

"I could snap your neck," he says in a voice like feathers brushed against fur. "I could rip your lower jaw from your skull and leave you broken and bleeding on the floor."

With his free hand the Crow Lord takes a smooth stone from the pocket of his long, black coat. He places it on her tongue. She expects it to be cold—and maybe it is—but it also burns.

"Your name belongs to me until the moment I choose to return it, if I ever do."

He lets her go. She wants to retch. She wants to whimper and yip, but she won't give him the satisfaction. He watches her with hard, empty eyes. She does not look away. The shadow of a smile lifts the edges of the Crow Lord's mouth.

She knew when she walked into the Crow Lords' hall that this could happen, but she came anyway, because no other fox-girl would. When the Crow Lords fly, her sisters lower their eyes. They keep their places, the places the Crow Lords give them. They whine and show their bellies. And if the Crow Lords' sharp beaks seek their lights and their livers, they hold their teeth, and whimper as they die.

So for the sake of her sisters, she refuses to look down. She needs to show the crows that at least one fox-girl is not afraid. She bares her teeth, trapping a growl at the back of her throat. A name is a small price to pay.

"What would you have me steal?" she asks, and she does not say, *my lord*.

"The humans in the tower are trying to resurrect their old magic, their circuits and wires. This time they are trying to infuse it with Crow Lord magic. They have forgotten their old ways, and they have forgotten their place in the world. They seek to steal from the oldest and the highest. We would have you steal from them what they stole from us first."

"Then it is done." The fox-girl grins, showing sharp teeth.

She will steal this precious thing for them, not because they asked her to, not for their favor, but because she *can*.

⬥

Ani wakes with the moon and stars still bright in the sky. Even now, shadows and oil linger on her tongue. She slips from the bed, and tiptoes past Yuki, who lies snoring on the floor.

The night air is cold, raising goose bumps. It hardens her nipples, making them stand out against the fabric of her borrowed shirt, fabric so thin that it shows the thatch of hair between her legs—dark as burnt wood.

A man waits beside the dumpster with its peeling paint. The chill in the air dampens the smell of rotting food. A rat squeaks its fear at Ani's approach, turning tail and running. Ani faces the hard-eyed man, waiting for him to speak.

"You took something from me," the Crow Lord says.

There is pain in his voice where she expected cold anger. She meets his eyes, which are crow-black and hard, but not as hard as before. The moonlight throws his shadow over the cracked pavement. Ani sees the jagged hole where her teeth tore part of that shadow away.

She can taste him, even after a day and a night, she can taste him. He tastes like the sky, like the wind and the stars. He tastes like freedom.

With a suddenness that stuns her, Ani understands. It's no wonder the Crow Lords look down on her kind. The entire world is a blanket spread beneath them. They speak with the dead; they know each current of air by its secret name. Humans read their flight to auger the future, and everything that walks the earth, or swims the seas must look up to them.

Ani understands, and she hates the understanding. She wants to vomit up his shadow—feathers beak and all—and force him to take it back, covered in her bile. But she can't. It's in her blood; it beats in her heart. It is part of her.

"You took something from me first," she says, thinking of the stone and her name.

"You walked into our house." Light shines in his eyes. Is he the one who placed the stone on her tongue? All Crow Lords look the same.

"He is my brother." The Crow Lord reads her mind. "All Crow Lords are brothers."

As all fox-girls are sisters, she thinks. But she is different now. There is crow-shadow in her blood; she has no name—or rather she has a name given to her by a human man.

She is part anger, part defiance, as she was when she walked into the Crow Lords' tower. Yet now she is something more. She has tasted crow-shadow and human blood. She looks at the jagged shadow on the ground.

"I could eat more," she says.

The Crow Lord's eyes widen. The memory of shadow tastes of power, *his* power. She wants to turn away, but emptiness gnaws in the pit of her stomach—

a craving for freedom. The world has been still too long, crows above, foxes below, and men somewhere in between. She growls, a low animal sound.

The Crow Lord doesn't move. She catches his scent—cold wind, silver stars, and empty sky as black as her fur.

She threads fingers through the Crow Lord's hair—dark as feathers—and pulls his face close. She kisses him, lip bruising lip in a hungry kiss. It tastes like freedom.

Sharp, white teeth nip fragile skin. The Crow Lord tries to pull back, but the fox-girl holds him tight, licking his broken lip with her long tongue before she lets go. Her eyes glow, fox-fire bright in the dark, and she whispers, "I could eat more."

Yuki brings her white rice and strips of cooked meat, which Ani wishes he had left raw. There is something so earnest and sweet about Yuki. She thought she understood the world of men, but he is different. The more she doesn't ask of him, the more he gives. In time, will he learn to read her mind? Will he feed her meat, bloody and raw, and let her lick red juices from his fingertips, flavored with salt from his skin?

He watches her as she eats rice and meat with her bare hands, looking for someone beneath her skin. Ani—the name comes back to her, weighing heavy in the air between them.

"Tell me about her," the fox-girl says.

Yuki looks up, startled. His eyes are the color of good, clear tea, shining in the sunlight falling through the window. For a moment Ani wants to taste them. She imagines Yuki's tears would be just like that hot, strong drink. She imagines they could wash away even the taste of shadows and oil and blood.

Ani sees the question of how she knew to ask about a girl die on Yuki's tongue. He shakes his head and turns away, looking out the window at the glittering tower rising above the waking city.

"Her name was Ani," he says, which she already knew.

The fox-girl looks at the tower, reflected in Yuki's gaze. The thousand glass eyes that make up its infinite sides are formed of all the things that people have lost, left behind, and given up by going inside.

"She worked in the tower. When they ordered food, she was always the one who met me at the door to take the delivery. She smiled at me, every time. Sometimes, when she gave me my tip, I think she put in a little extra, even if her co-workers were cheap, so it would seem like more. It's stupid, but I thought I was in love with her."

"What happened to her?"

"I don't know." Yuki sighs. "She called me . . . the last time she called, she sounded scared. She didn't order any food. She couldn't catch her breath, and it sounded like she was crying. I think her hands were shaking, because the phone kept moving away from her lips and back, her voice going in and out like the wind.

"Then she was gone. The people in the tower stopped ordering food. I called every number in their directory and asked about her, but every person I talked to told me they'd never heard of her. I'm afraid she might be dead."

Ani can't bear to tell him that the name of the girl he thought he loved tasted like ghosts when he first spoke it aloud. She sets aside the empty bowl and picks up the plastic chip marked by her teeth and stained with her blood. She traces the frozen quicksilver patterns.

A memory shivers across her skin, fleeting and quick. In a moment of stillness, she might even catch it.

"If I could get you inside the tower to look for her, would you go?" she asks.

"Yes." Yuki looks like he might cry, spilling good, hot tea down his cheeks. "But how could you get me inside?"

Ani grins. "I'm a fox-girl."

Ani sits on Yuki's pallet, while he sleeps on the floor. Her knees are drawn up to her chest, her arms wrapped around them, her mind seeking after the fragment of memory buried under her skin.

Yuki's dreaming helps. He is dreaming *his* Ani, dreams strong enough to conjure her into the room. Fox-Ani remembers the girl, remembers where she has seen her before. She looks at the rising spire of glass through Yuki's window, and remembers being inside.

She remembers.

The city's nighttime glow falls through a thousand panes of glass. It patterns the floor so she walks through pieces of light, like fallen leaves. Her bare feet pad, silent as paws. The hallways are empty; all the humans have gone home for the night. They are so confident, or so few, that they don't even bother to leave guards behind.

The fox-girl winds along the hall until she find a door leading deeper into the tower's insides. She drops four paws onto the ground for a moment before rising on her hind legs and bracing her front feet against the door. She puts her muzzle to the lock, licks it once to bind it to her, and calls a high, sharp yip into the keyhole. Crow Lords may know the secret name of the winds, but fox-girls know the way to make any door open.

She changes again, two feet on the ground, and twists the knob. She steps into one of the few rooms inside the tower without windows. The room is lit by the glow of machinery, the salvaged scraps of humanity's one-time glory. Some screens shed an eerie luminescence. Others are cracked, broken, long fallen into disuse and disrepair. Outside, the tower is beautiful. At its heart, it is rotten and sad.

A shadowed form moves, illuminated by the half light. It is a woman with long, black hair. The fox-girl has stayed so quiet that the woman doesn't hear her, doesn't turn.

From the set of the woman's shoulders, hunched protectively forward, the fox-girl recognizes a kindred spirit. This woman is a thief, too, creeping through the shadows after dark, snooping where she shouldn't. The fox-girl slips up behind her, places her teeth next to the woman's throat, and breathes hot against her skin. Even in girl form she could tear through this soft, human throat before the woman could scream.

"Hello," the fox-girl whispers.

The woman doesn't scream, but she goes tense, her body rigid against the fox-girl's naked flesh.

"Who are you?" The woman's voice is almost steady. There is only the faintest tremor, matched by the faintest whiff of fear sweat prickling her skin. The woman's fingers tense on the keyboard in front of her, skritching softly. Now that she has been caught out, the fox-girl wonders, will the woman fight or flee?

"I have no name, not anymore. I came here to steal what you stole from the Crow Lords," the fox-girl says. She sees no harm in honesty; there is nothing the woman can do to stop her.

The woman surprises her with a sound like laughter. The fox-girl can only see part of the woman's face, a half-moon, tinted blue in the monitor-light.

"If I turn around, will you bite me?"

The fox-girl steps back, and lets the woman turn. The woman looks at her, takes in the fox-girl's nakedness, and the corners of her lips lift in a bemused smile. She shakes her head, as if at a wayward child. The fox-girl suddenly feels young, foolish, and she bares her teeth. But she holds her ground, waiting for the human woman to speak.

"Do you really think we could steal from the Crow Lords?" the woman asks. "Think about it, and look at this place. We're just starting to rebuild, re-learn everything we've lost. How could we take anything from them? We have no magic of our own. That's why we built all this." She waves her hand at the machines around them. "And look where it got us."

War. The fox-girl nods, but says nothing aloud. The tower, beautiful on the outside, isn't a stronghold. It's only the gathering place where the shattered remnants of humanity have come to try to put back together what their greed tore apart.

The fox-girl sees now what she should have seen the moment she walked into the Crow Lord's tower. The Crow Lords, tricksters still, are playing a long game, setting humanity and the fox-girls against each other in the hopes they will wipe each other out. They didn't send her here to steal; they sent her hoping she would be captured, tortured, broken, the secrets of fox-girl magic ripped from her skin. They sent her here to make her less, and make the humans more, tipping the balance just enough to start another war.

"What were you doing here?" The fox-girl points at the monitors behind the woman, speaking to hide her shame.

"Trying to wipe out the old programs before our people can unravel them. These machines did us no good the first time. I don't want to see she same mistakes made again."

The fox-girl grins, sudden and quick in the half-light.

"I think I can help you. Can you get me the chip out of one of those?"

The woman looks at her askance, but after a moment she turns and opens a panel beneath the desk. As the woman digs within the machine, nimble fingers working, the fox-girl wonders if her trust is bravery or stupidity. She decides on bravery, holding on to the image of the woman as a kindred spirit, a fellow thief.

"What's your name?" the fox-girl asks. She doesn't think humans earn their names the way fox-girls do, but she would still like to know.

"Ani."

The woman straightens and holds up the thing she has dug out from the heart of the machine. Blue radiance slides across a pattern of frozen quicksilver printed on a small square of plastic. She holds it out to the fox-girl, but the fox-girl shakes her head.

"I want you to cut me open and stitch it up inside my skin."

Yuki turns, snorting in his sleep before moving on to another dream. The fox-girl remembers the chafe of leather against her wrists, the prick of the needle going into her skin. She remembers the look of fear and doubt in Ani's eyes, the salt-tang scent of fox blood, a moment of hot pain, then drifting into the dark.

She glances down at the chip in her hand, flecked with rust-colored flakes. She remembers everything now. She meant to change the programming, re-write it with her being, imprint her memory on its quick-silver patterns and give it back to Ani: a fox-girl virus, thief quick, spreading throughout the human machines and bringing the tower crashing down.

She meant to infect the humans themselves, instilling them with defiance against the Crow Lords, starting a war of her own. She turns the chip, studying it in the light. But now, she is different. The fox-girl she was, all cocky anger and defiance, lives only in the chip. The self that came out of the tower has changed, gentled by eyes like tea, illuminated by a human thief in a tower, and darkened by a crow shadow that tastes like oil on her tongue.

Something brushes against the window, a feathered wing. Ani opens the window and leans out. The sloped roof isn't so far that she can't catch hold as she turns her back to the tower and wiggles out into the cold night air. She pulls herself up, nails scrabbling on the tile, and then she stands on four paws on the roof. Eleven crows circle against the stars before dropping to join the shadow of a man whose eyes are no longer as hollow and hard as they used to be.

The light in his gaze speaks of fear. He doesn't belong with his brothers anymore, as she no longer belongs with her sisters.

"You took something from me." He echoes his words from the night before. "I want it back."

Ani cocks her head, ears alert, eyes bright.

"Give it back!" He lunges for her. His voice breaks, becoming a crow's call.

She sidesteps, and eleven ragged birds rise into the air, maddened by pain. His shadow swarms, but doesn't dive, doesn't strike. His birds beat at her with their wings, and she feels the answering stir of shadow-slick feathers under her skin. She tastes oil at the back of her throat. She can read his mind now, a Crow Lord trick.

He wants her to take away the pain, and he hates himself for wanting it. He wants to roll, like her sisters, whine and show his belly. He hates what he has become, but even more, he hates what he has been. He wants—he needs—to feel her teeth in his skin.

Ani jumps, catching a shadowed bird. She holds it gently between her jaws, a precious thing. He doesn't fight her. Above her, ten crows scream their confusion and speak their divided minds. She bites down, exquisite needle teeth piercing feathers, bone and skin. The shadow slides down her throat. She savors it—Crow Lord power running through her veins.

A truth beats in time with her heart, one half-felt in the moment she tasted the first piece of his shadow, but fully realized now. She owns him. This Crow Lord is hers, and it doesn't matter that she is on all fours on the ground; he can't look down on her, not anymore.

Ten birds coalesce beneath the man crouching on the red roof tile, holding himself against the pain. He looks up, and his eyes aren't hollow, and they never will be again. They shine, heavy with tears.

Ani pads forward, burnt-black paws hushing over the tile. The Crow Lord doesn't move. He whines a little in the back of his throat; he raises his head, baring skin. It is not a crow gesture; it is a fox gesture—submission.

She licks his throat, but doesn't nip. He lowers his face. Her long tongue cleans his cheeks, tasting his tears. Salt mingles with the shadows and blood as she swallows them down. When he stops crying, she sits back on her haunches and looks up at him.

"I'm going into the tower," she says. "Tomorrow. Tonight, I'm going hunting."

She turns, tail blurring in the moonlight. She jumps, changing before she hits the ground. Two feet land, then four paws run over the broken asphalt. She glances back, grinning, tongue lolling, devouring the night air.

"There's blood on your mouth," Yuki says, waking her.

Ani looks up. Yuki stands over the pallet with a tray of plain rice and steamed vegetables. She sits up and the sheet slides away, revealing naked skin. She pushes a hand through her tangled hair, and then licks her lips clean. Blood flakes onto her tongue, cold and dry.

Yuki looks at her sadly, but he doesn't turn away anymore. She isn't his Ani, and it breaks his heart.

"I could be," Ani says, reading his thoughts. "I could be her." She rises, and takes the tray from him, setting it down. She takes his hand. His skin is cool, and she presses it to her breast, over her heart. Her nipple is hard beneath his palm.

"There," she whispers. "Can you feel it? She's inside my skin."

Ani is hungry. The fox in her, the crow in her, she struggles to hold onto to them, because part of her knows she is still changing. Before Yuki can pull away, she digs her nails into his hand, holding it against her sleep-warm flesh. She catches his hair with her other hand, pulls him close. She tastes his mouth. Unlike the Crow Lord, he doesn't respond. Like the Crow Lord, she tastes his tears. They taste just as she imagined.

Ani lets go. Yuki's eyes are infinitely sad.

"What do you want from me?" Yuki's voice is hoarse, heavy with salt.

She reads his mind again. He is thinking about the old tales of fox-maidens seducing young men and stealing their souls. Like the fox-girls who roll over for the crows, Yuki is ready to roll over for her. He thinks he has lost everything that matters, and that there is nothing left to care about anymore. He tried to help her, and she threw it back in his face—taking the last thing that was *his*, the last thing that matters, his kind heart.

"I'm sorry." Fox-Ani means the words, and they surprise her. She is a fox, a thief. She bows to no one, not even the Crow Lords. She takes what she wants because she *can*, but looking at Yuki, all she wants to do is give.

"I'm sorry. I'll take you into the tower, if you still want me to. Then you'll never have to see me again." She smiles—a true smile. Strangely, she doesn't feel weak, laying her words at his feet, showing her throat. She feels strong.

"Put on some clothes," Yuki says. "Let's go."

Inside, darkness swallows the stairwell. A scent pulls her up, a thread of pain. Fox-Ani changes, shedding clothes like skin. Four paws hit the ground, and she sprints up the cold metal steps, her nails clicking as she runs. Yuki's labored breath follows behind.

She stops in front of a metal door, halfway up the tower, and presses her paws to either side of the lock. She speaks her fox-word, a high, eerie sound that echoes in the silence, then she changes again, standing to open the door with human hands. She hears Yuki coming up behind her, still breathing hard.

They step into the hall. The glow of the city spills through the windows, dappling the floor in fallen-leaf patterns of silver and blue and neon-red. Ani walks through them, barefoot, and the light slides across her skin.

"Here." Yuki holds out the fallen robe she left behind in her sprint up the stairs. Ani slips it on, a skin over her skin, and belts it tight.

"It's this way." Ani beckons him down the hall, memory and scent guiding her back to the room filled with half-broken computers.

Outside, she pauses. She opens her mouth, about to tell Yuki to go back. She knows, without a doubt, what they will find inside. She can smell it—strength and pain. He shouldn't have to see this.

As though reading the words on her face, Yuki lifts his chin, defiant. Tea-colored eyes shine in the dark.

"Open it."

Ani doesn't bother to change. The door is unlocked and she pushes it open. The first Ani, the real Ani, is waiting inside for them.

She rises stiffly from the bank of computers. Fox-Ani braces herself, but behind her, unprepared, Yuki gasps. Human-Ani's left eye is swollen shut, the skin around it deepened with purple bruises, fading to sick yellow. She holds one arm against her side, wincing in pain as she steps forward. A hairline fracture in her rib, Fox-Ani thinks. She can smell sickness, infection, a wound improperly cleaned and struggling to heal.

Still, the human Ani's eyes are bright. They defy any offer of sympathy. She holds her chin high, and speaks through cracked lips, her voice almost without inflection.

"They found out I helped you and tried to kill me. I escaped. I've been hiding out in the ventilation system and the basement. There's so few of them in the tower now, they can't cover enough ground. If I keep moving, they'll never find me."

Ani takes a labored breath, and Fox-Ani winces.

"I've been waiting for you to come back. Every night, I sneak up here and wait."

Fox-Ani nods and swallows hard around a sudden thickness in her throat. She reaches up and unknots the leather cord she has tied around her neck, carrying the silver-patterned chip. Ani's eyes gleam, and she holds out her hand, but the fox-girl pulls back.

"Don't touch it, unless . . . unless . . . " She takes a deep breath, and forces herself to look Ani in the eye. "You have a choice. I can destroy the computers, bring the whole system crashing down. But if you touch this chip, you'll be infected with my memories, with the fox-girl I used to be. You can help me spread the disease, bring war to the Crow Lords one human at a time."

Behind her, Fox-Ani feels Yuki stiffen, understanding her betrayal. The real Ani's bruised face doesn't change, her eyes still shine and she lifts her chin a little higher.

"No more war."

Fox-Ani nods. "Then you should leave now. I'll come find you when it's done."

She turns, unable to bear the human woman's eyes any longer. If she saw anger there, she would understand, but there is only a kind of sadness, and the fox-girl feels young and foolish again. How is it that she, who walked the earth for ages before the first humans ever raised their heads to look up at the stars, could be so much less wise than them?

The fox-girl hears the humans retreat, footsteps soft on the carpeted floor. She counts them along with her breath and her heartbeats, waiting until she can't hear them anymore, and kneels. She opens the panel beneath the desk, seeing where the chip fits back into the computer. The next time one of the humans tries to access something from the chip's memory, the essence of everything she was will infect the system, wipe it clean.

A sound that isn't a sound makes Ani's head snap up. Crow Lords—she can feel them coming, she can smell them on the air, a scent like oil and shadows and blood. She snaps the panel closed and rises, running for the hall.

Ani climbs, spiraling up into the dark. At the top of the stairs, she steps out onto the roof. Crows fall from the sky, screaming at her. Ten of them, whose taste she knows, throw their bodies between her and the bodies of their brothers, fighting beak and claw. She beats his brothers back, snapping with human teeth, trying to gather the birds belonging to her Crow Lord.

All around the edges of the roof, men with hollow eyes watch her while their shadows do battle. Only one does not have hollow eyes. His eyes are full of fox-light. He trembles.

Her gaze fixes on him, ignoring the feathers that snap against her skin and the beaks that draw blood.

"Trust me," she whispers.

Ani holds up cupped palms. She can feel hot, sticky blood, running down her skin. She won't fight the Crow Lords, not here, not now, not like this. Her war will be a quiet war, infecting the Crow Lords from within as she would have infected the humans. One of her birds lands, awkwardly in her out-stretched hands. She draws it close and holds it against her heartbeat. Then she lifts it to her lips.

Across the rooftop, the man with full eyes twitches. His Crow Lord shadow melts between her lips, sliding down her throat. He surrenders. The nine birds remaining flock to her. She opens her arms wide, opens her jaws, and devours them all.

When she has swallowed the last of her Crow Lord's shadow, Ani screams at his brothers. "I'm one of you now! Your Fox Brother, your Crow Sister."

The Crow Lords shriek their rage. They slash at her with beak and claw. Twelve birds lift, swirling around one of the hollow eyed men at the corner of the rooftop. They coalesce, and his shadow lies long beneath him. He steps forward.

"We still have your name." His chuckle becomes a crow-caw. Ani answers with a fox-grin.

"I don't need it anymore."

She turns towards her Crow Lord. He is on his knees now, but he raises his head. His eyes are full of light. Even though he is shaking, she feels his shadow inside her, stronger than ever. He knows her name, and he will whisper it to her in the dark. His eyes are a promise. It is all she needs.

He grits his teeth, and speaks. "Trust me. Jump."

She drops four paws onto the ground and runs for the edge of the roof. She leaps, trusting the shadow beneath her skin. She falls and the city streaks towards her from below. In the screaming wind, her shadow shreds, tatters, and spreads impossible wings. She soars.

She bares fox-teeth, laughing, and tasting the stars. She is free, and she is alive.

After an eternity of flight, of devouring the moonlight and drinking the world, she touches down. Four paws come to rest on dirty asphalt in an alley that smells of rotten food. Red neon spreads puddles of light beneath her feet. When she rises to stand on two legs, she is clothed in a coat as black as a crow's wing. It hides her torn and bloodied skin.

Yuki steps out of the doorway where the fox-girl first saw him, the human Ani behind him. She looks smaller away from the glow of the machines, half-broken by all that has been done to her.

Fox-Ani closes her eyes and places her hand to her mouth. She tastes the stone, Crow Lord magic, smooth and cool on her tongue. It has been there the whole time, but she can touch it now. She pushes it onto her palm and opens her eyes, holding out her hand.

Ani looks at her, questioning. "What is it?"

"Forgetting. If you want, you can start over again."

Ani considers a moment, then holds out her hand. The Fox-Crow-Girl tips the stone onto the human woman's palm. The woman considers it a moment, weighing it, then slips the stone into her pocket.

"Thank you."

She turns away. Yuki moves after her. "Ani! Wait!"

The human woman turns, a sad smile moving cracked lips, pulling bruised flesh tight around her eye. "That's not my name anymore. I'm no-one, now. A ghost."

She turns again and walks away. This time Yuki doesn't try to stop her. Fox-Ani steps close and slips her hand into his, pressing warm skin against skin. "I'm sorry."

"Don't be," he answers, but she can feel the sorrow rolling off him. The air around him smells like tea and tears. "I never really knew her. I only had an image of her in my head that I wanted to love. Now there isn't enough of her left to know."

"Maybe she'll come back one day."

"Maybe." Yuki shrugs. He turns to look at Ani, his tea-brown eyes clear. "What are you going to do now?"

"Run. Fly." She lets go of his hand and whirls, changes, a blur of fur and feathers, then she is a girl again.

"Thank you for everything." Her voice is soft in the neon tinted dark. She means the words more than she has ever meant any words before. Though it was the Crow Lord's shadow she devoured, Yuki has changed her, too.

"We'll see each other again," she says. "If you want. We can eat noodles on the rooftops, up under the sky. The world is going to change soon. I'll tell you what it looks like from above."

A smile touches Yuki's lips, shadowed with pain, but still a smile. "I'd like that."

He lifts his hand to wave goodbye, and she is flying, fox and crow and girl, lifting up above the city to taste the light of the stars.

THE POISON EATERS

HOLLY BLACK

I trust that your bonds are not too tight, my son. Please don't struggle. Don't bother. You're soft. All princes are soft and these cells are built for hardened men.

It is a shame that you never met your grandmother. You are very like with your tempers and your rages. I imagine she would have doted on you. How ironic that father tried her for being a poisoner. Right now, especially, Paul, I imagine irony is much on your mind.

The morning of her execution she had her attendants dress her all in red and braid her hair with fresh roses. Wine-colored stones cluttered her fingers. There are several paintings of it; she died opulently. It was drizzling. I was to walk her to her tomb. It was something like a wedding processional as she took my arm and we went together, down the steep steps. The place was dark and stank of incense. My mother leaned close to me and whispered that I looked splendid in black. I remember not being able to say anything, only taking her hand and pressing it. Outside, the rain began to fall hard. We heard the shrieks of the assemblage; aristocrats don't like to be wet.

My mother smiled and said, "I bet they wish they were down here where it's dry."

I forced a smile and made myself kiss her cheek and bid her farewell. The masons were waiting at the top of the stairs.

My mother and I were not close, but she was still my mother. I was a dutiful son. I had commanded the cooks to put the sharpest of my hunting knives beneath the food they had prepared for her. I wonder if you would do that for me, Paul. Perhaps you would. After all, it cost me nothing to be kind.

See this cup? A beautiful thing, solid gold, one of the few treasures of our family that remain. It was my father's. He had a cupbearer bring him his wine in it, even as his other guests drank from silver. I have it here beside me, just as you filled it—half with poison and half with cider, so that it will go down easy.

I have a story to tell you. You've always been restless, too busy to hear stories of people long dead and secrets that no longer matter. But now, Paul, bound and gagged as you are, you can hardly object to my telling you a tale:

Sometimes at night the three sisters would sleep in one bed, limbs tangling together. Despite that, they would never get warm. Their lips would stay blue and sometimes one of them would shake or cramp, but they were used to that. Sometimes, in the mornings, when women would bring them their breakfasts, one might touch them by accident and the next day she would be missing. But they were used to that too. Not that they did not grieve. They often wept. They wept over the mice they would find, stiff and cold, on the stone floor of their chamber; over the hunting dogs that would run to them when they were out walking on the hills, jumping up and then falling down; over the butterfly that once landed on Mirabelle's cheek for a moment, before spiraling to the ground like a bit of paper.

One winter, their father gave them lockets. Each locket had the painting of a boy inside of it. They took turns making up stories about the boys. In one story, Alice's picture, who they'd taken to calling Nicholas, was a knight with a silver arm, questing after a sword cooled from the forge with the blood of sirens. At night, the sword became a siren with hair as black as ink and Nicholas fell in love with her. At this point the story stopped because Alice stormed off, annoyed that Cecily had made up a story where the boy from her locket fell in love with someone else.

Each day they would eat a salad of what looked like flowering parsley. Afterwards, their hands would tremble and they would become so cold that they had to sit close to the fire and scorch themselves. Sometimes their father came in and watched them eat, but he was careful to never touch them. Instead, he would read them prayers or lecture on the dangers of sloth and the importance of needlework. Occasionally, he would have one of them read from Homer.

Summer was their favorite time. The sun would warm their sluggish blood and they would lie out in the garden like snakes. It was on one of those jaunts that the blacksmith's apprentice first spotted Alice. He started coming around a lot after that, reading his weepy poetry and trying to get her to pay him attention. Before long, Alice was always crying. She wanted to go to him, but she dared not.

"He's not the boy in your locket," Mirabelle said.

"Don't be stupid." Alice wiped her reddened eyes. "Do you think that we're supposed to marry them and be their wives? Do you think that's why we have those lockets?"

Cecily had been about to say something and stopped. She'd always thought the boys in the lockets would be theirs someday, but she did not want to say so now, in case Alice called her stupid too.

"Imagine any of us married. What would happen then, sisters? We are merely knives in the process of being sharpened."

"Why would father do that?" Cecily demanded.

"Father?" Alice demanded. "Do you really think he's your father? Or mine? Look at us. How could you, Mirabelle, be short and fair while Cecily is tall and dark? How could I have breasts like melons, while hers are barely currants? How could we all be so close in age? We three are no more sisters than he is our father."

Mirabelle began to weep. They went to bed that night in silence, but when they awoke, Mirabelle would no longer eat. She spit out her bitter greens, even when she became tired and languid. Cecily begged her to take something, telling her that they were sisters no matter what.

"Different mothers could explain our looks," Alice said, but she did not sound convinced and Mirabelle would not be comforted.

Their father tried to force Mirabelle to eat, but she pushed food into her cheek only to spit it out again when he was gone. She got thinner and more wan, her body shriveling, but she did not die. She faded into a thin wispy thing, as ephemeral as smoke.

"What does it mean?" Cecily asked.

"It means she shouldn't be so foolish," said their father. He tried to tempt her with a frond of bitter herb in a gloved hand, but she was so insubstantial that she passed through him without causing harm and drifted out to the gardens.

"It's my fault," said Alice.

But the ghostly shape of Mirabelle merely laughed her whispery laugh.

The next day Alice went out to meet the blacksmith's apprentice and kissed him until he died. It did not bring her sister back. It did not help her grief. She built a fire and threw herself on it. She burned until she was only a blackened shadow.

No tears were enough to express how Cecily felt so her eyes remained dry as her sisters floated like shades through the halls of the estate and her father locked himself in his study.

As Cecily sat alone in a dim room, her sisters came to her.

"You must bury us," Alice said.

"I want it to be in the gardens of one of our suitors. Together so that we won't be lonely."

"Why should I? Why should I do anything for you?" Cecily asked. "You left me here alone."

"Stop feeling sorry for yourself," said Alice. Lack of corporeal form had not made her any less bossy.

"We need you," Mirabelle pleaded.

"Why can't you bury yourselves? Just drift down into the dirt."

"That's not the way it works," Mirabelle told her.

And so, with a sigh of resignation, gathering up the lockets of her sisters, Cecily left the estate and began to walk. She was not sure where she was headed, but the road led to town.

It was frightening to be on her own, with no one to brush her hair or tell her when to sit down to lunch. The forest sounded strange and ominous.

She stopped and paid for an apple with a silver ring. As she passed a stall, she overheard one of the merchants say. "Look at her blue mouth, her pale skin. She's the walking dead." As soon as he said it, Cecily knew it to be true. That was why Alice and Mirabelle would not die. They were already dead.

She walked for a long time, resting by a stream when she was tired. After she rose, she saw the imprint of herself in the withered grass. Tears rolled over her cheeks and dampened the cloth of her dress, but one fell where ants scurried and stilled them. After that, Cecily was careful not to cry.

At the next town, she showed the pictures in each of the lockets to the woman who sold wreaths for graves. She knew only the first boy. His name was Vance—not Nicholas—and he was the son of a wealthy landowner to the East who had once paid her for a hundred wreaths of chrysanthemums to decorate the necks of horses on Vance's twelfth birthday.

She started down the winding and dusty road East. Once she was given a ride on a wagon filled with hay. She kept her hands folded in her lap and when the farmer reached out to touch her shoulder in kindness, she shied away as though she despised him. The coldness in his eyes afterward hurt her and she tried not to think of him.

Another traveler demanded the necklace of opals she wore at her throat, but she slapped him and he fell, as if struck by a blow more terrible than any her soft hand should have delivered.

Her sisters chattered at her as she went. Sometimes their words buzzed around her like hornets, sometimes they went sulkily silent. Once, Mirabelle and Alice had a fight about which of their deaths were more foolish and Cecily had to shout at them until they stopped.

Cecily often got hungry, but there was no salad of bitter parsley, so she ate other leaves and flowers she picked in the woods. Some of them filled her with that familiar cold shakiness while others went down her throat without doing anything but sating her. She drank from cool streams and muddy puddles and by the time she reached Vance's estate, her shoes were riddled with holes.

The manor house was at the top of a small hill and the path was set with smooth, pale stones. The door was a deep red, the color berries stained eager fingers. Cecily rapped on the door.

The servants saw her tattered finery and brought her to Master Hornpull. He had white hair that fell to his shoulders but the top of his pate was bald, shining with oil, and slightly sunburnt.

Cecily showed him the locket with Vance's picture and told him about Alice's death. He was kind and did not mention the state of Cecily's clothing or the strangeness of her coming so suddenly and on foot. He told servants to prepare a room for her and let her wash herself in a tub with golden faucets in the shape of swans.

"If you kiss him once, then I will be able to kiss him forever and ever," Alice told her as she dried off.

"I thought you liked the blacksmith's apprentice," Cecily said.

"I always liked Nicholas better." Alice's ghostly voice sounded snappish.

"Vance," Cecily corrected.

Servants came to ask Cecily if she would go to dinner, but she begged off, pleading weariness. She planned to doze on the down mattress until nightfall when she could steal out to the gardens, but there was a sharp rap on the door and her father walked into the room.

Cecily made a poorly-concealed gasp and struggled to stand. For a moment, she was afraid, without really knowing why.

He pushed back graying hair with a gloved hand. "How fortunate that you are so predictable. I was quite worried when I found you had gone."

"I was too sad to be there alone," Cecily said. She could not meet his eyes.

"'You must marry Vance in Alice's place.'"

"I can't," Cecily said. What she meant was that Alice would be mad and indeed, Alice was already darting around, muttering furiously.

"You can and you will," her father said. "Every thing yearns to do what it is made for."

Cecily said nothing. He drew from his pocket a necklace of tourmalines and fastened them at her throat. "Be as good a girl as you are lovely," he said. "Then we will go home."

The earliest memory Cecily had of her father was of gloved hands, mail-over-leather, checking her gums. She had been very sick for a long time, lying on mounds of hay in a stinking room full of sick little girls. She remembered his messy hair and his perfectly trimmed beard and the way his smile had seemed aimed in her direction but not for her. "Little girls are like oysters," he told her as he pried her eyelids wide. "Just as a grain of sand irritates the oyster into making nacre, so your discomfort will make something marvelous."

"Who are you?" she had asked him.

"Don't you remember?" he had said. "I'm your father."

That had upset her, because she must be very sick indeed to not know her own father, but he told her that she had died and come back to life, so it was natural that she'd forgotten things. He lifted her up with his gloved hands and carried her out of the room. She remembered seeing other sick girls on the hay, their eyes sunken and dull and their bodies very still. That, she wouldn't have minded forgetting.

Cecily thought of those girls as she drifted off to sleep in the vast and silky bed Master Hornpull provided for her, cooled by the twining limbs of her ghostly sisters.

The next day, Cecily's face was painted: her mouth made vermillion, her eyelids smeared with cerulean, her cheeks rouged rose. They had brought pots of white stuff to smear on her skin but she was already so pale there was no need. Cecily waved the servants off and pinned up her hair herself. She wasn't very good at it and locks tumbled down over her shoulders. Mirabelle assured her that it looked better that way. Alice told her that she looked like a mess. Mirabelle said that Alice was just jealous. That might have been true; Alice had always been a jealous person.

In the parlor downstairs, Cecily's father grabbed her elbow with one gloved hand and spoke through a broad, forced smile.

Vance was nothing like their made-up stories. He was short and slender, but handsome just the same. They danced and Cecily was conscious of the warmth of his hands though the fabric of her dress and the satin of her gloves, but she was even more conscious of the tender glances he gave to a small, curvy girl in a golden gown.

"He would have liked me," Alice crowed. "I am exactly the kind of girl he likes."

"Maybe you should have thought of that before you—" Cecily started, forgetting for a moment that she was speaking to the dead. Vance turned toward her, face flaming and lips spilling apology.

But when the priest asked Cecily to take Vance in marriage, she was named as Mirabelle. She repeated the words anyway.

"Does that mean Nicholas is mine?" Mirabelle whispered, her ghostly voice filled with surprised delight. He was her clear favorite in the stories. Cecily had made the boy in Mirabelle's locket too bookish for her tastes.

"Vance," Cecily corrected under her breath.

"Kill him already," Alice hissed. "Stop mooning around."

And, indeed, Vance was leaning toward Cecily to seal their vows with a kiss. She pulled back at the last moment, so that his mouth merely brushed

THE POISON EATERS   33

her veil, then tried to smile in apology. As she turned to depart the ceremony with her new husband, she saw her father in the crowd. He nodded once in her direction.

At the party following the wedding, one of the guests remarked to Cecily how good it was that her father was taking an interest in society again, after falling out of favor with the King.

"He seldom talks to me about politics," Cecily said. "I did not know he was ever a friend of his Majesty."

The woman who had said it looked around, seemingly torn between guilt and gossip. "Well, it was when the King was only the youngest Prince. No one expected him to take the throne, because his father was so young and his two older brothers so healthy. But illness took all three of them, one after another, and once his Majesty was on the throne, your father was well favored. He was given money and lands beyond most of our—well, you know how vast and lovely your father's land is."

"Yes," Cecily said, feeling very stupid. She had never wondered where these things came from. She had merely assumed that there had always been plenty and there would always be plenty.

"But after the Prince was born, your father fell out of favor. The King would no longer see him."

"Why?" Cecily asked.

"As if I know!" The woman laughed. "He really has kept you in another world up there!"

Later, she went to a large bed chamber and changed into a pale shift that was still, somehow, darker than her skin. She stared at her arms, looking at the tracery of purple veins, mapping a geography of paths she might take, a maze of choices she did not know her way out of.

"You look cold," Vance said. "I could warm you."

Cecily thought that was a kind thing to say, as though he was more interested in her well-being than in her vermillion-painted mouth or the sapphires sparkling on her fingers. She didn't have the heart to stop him from taking her hand and pressing his lips to her throat. Lying beside his cold body afterward reminded her of sleeping with her sisters before they were only shades. The chill touch of his skin comforted her.

In the morning, the whole house wept with his sudden death. Alice and Mirabelle wept too, because although he was dead, he did not live on as they did. They could not catch his spirit as he passed.

She rode in a fast coach with her father and Liam was dead before word reached the household of Vance's burial. The second boy was much easier than she expected. At this wedding, her name had been Alice. In their bedchamber, he'd barely spoken; only torn off her gown and died. There was no time to steal out to the gardens. No time to bury her sisters.

Cecily's father was so pleased he could barely sit still as they pressed on to the palace. He ate an entire box of sweetmeats, chuckling to himself as he watched the landscape fly by.

He had brought something for her to eat too, a familiar mix of herbs that she left sitting in their bowl.

"I don't want them," she said. "They make me sick."

"Just eat!" he told her. "For once, just do as you are bid."

She thought about throwing the bowl out of the window and scattering the herbs, but the smell of them reminded her of Mirabelle and Alice, who barely smelled like anything now. Besides, there was nothing else. Cecily ate the herbs.

She could still taste them in her mouth when the carriage arrived at the palace. She half expected to be clapped in irons and as she passed whispering courtiers, Cecily thought that each one was telling the other a list of her evil deeds.

We first met in the library. I was tall and plain, with pock-marked skin. Yes, I'm the prince in this story. Did you guess, Paul? Cecily later told me that when I first smiled at her, I still appeared to be frowning. What I remember was that she had the blackest eyes I had ever seen.

"This is your betrothed, Cecily," Cecily's father told me.

"I know who she is," I said. She looked very like the picture I had been given. Most girls don't. Your mother certainly didn't.

That afternoon, Cecily washed the dirt of the road off her clothing and went to walk in the gardens of the palace while her father made the final arrangements. The gardens were lush and lovely, more beautiful, even, than those of her father. Plants with heads full of seeds, large as the skulls of infants, lolled from thick stems. She touched the vivid purple and red fronds of one and it seemed to twitch under her fingers. The lacy foliage of another seemed like the parsley plant of her salad. Crushing it produced a pungent, familiar scent. It was like the breath of her sisters. She bent low for a taste.

"Stop! That's poisonous!" A gardener jogged down the path, wearing steel and leather gloves like those that belonged to her father. He had hair that flopped over his eyes and that he brushed back impatiently. "You're not supposed to be in this part of the garden."

"I'm sorry," Cecily stammered. "But what are these? I have them in my garden at home."

He snorted. "That isn't very likely. They're hybrids. There are no others like them in all the world."

She thought of the woman at her wedding telling how her father had once been close to the king. He must have taken cuttings from these very plants.

She began walking, hoping she might leave the gardener behind and be about her burying business. He seemed to misconstrue her wishes, however, pacing alongside her and pointing out prize blooms. She finally managed to put off a lengthy explanation of why the royal apples were the sweetest in the world by pretending a chill and retreating into the palace.

That night there was a feast in Cecily's honor. She sat at a long table set with crisp linens and covered with dishes she was unfamiliar with. There was eel with savory; tiny birds stuffed with berries and herbs, their bones crunching between Cecily's teeth; pears stuffed into almond tarts and soaked in wine; even a sugar-coated pastry in the shape of the palace itself, studded with flecks of gold.

"Oh," Mirabelle gasped. "It is all so lovely."

But Cecily realized that no matter how lovely, it disgusted her to bring the food to her mouth. She looked across the table and saw her father in deep conversation with the king, not at all behaving as if he was out of favor.

That night, Cecily left her room and went out to the garden. Her walk with the gardener had revealed where he kept his tools and she stole a spade. With her sisters fluttering around her, Cecily looked for the right spot for them to rest. In the moonlight, all the plants were the same, their glossy leaves merely silvery and their flowers shut tight as gates.

"Be careful," Mirabelle said. "You're the only one of us left."

"Whose fault is that?" Cecily demanded.

Neither of them said anything more as Cecily finally chose a place and began to dig. The rich soil parted easily.

That was what I saw her doing as I walked out of the palace. I had been looking for her, but when I found her, digging in the dirt, I almost didn't know what to say.

She saw me standing there and crouched. Her fingers were black with earth and she looked feral in the dim light of the palace windows. I don't think she knew it, but I was afraid.

"Please," Cecily said. "I have to finish. I am digging a grave for my sisters."

I thought she was mad then, I admit it. I turned to go back to the house and get the guards, thinking that my plans were in shambles.

"Please," she said again. "I will tell you a secret."

"That you have come to kill me?" I asked her. "Like you killed Vance and Liam?"

She frowned.

It was then that I told her the part of her story she did not know and she told most of what I have said tonight. I will summarize for you, Paul. I know how tedious you find this sort of thing.

When he was a prince like yourself, my father had hired hers to kill those before him in line to the throne. He was very efficient; no one doubted but they had merely fallen ill. Mother told me this much before her death and I told it to Cecily.

Apparently, it was my birth that made Father send Cecily's father to the country. It made him uncomfortable to look at his own son and to consider the sort of son he had once been.

As I got older, however, he grew increasingly certain I was planning his death. He wrote to Cecily's father and coaxed him from retirement. Her father had a price, of course—Liam and Vance—some grudge avenged. I have forgotten the details. It doesn't matter. Our engagements were arranged.

"How did you find out?" Cecily asked when I finished speaking.

"My mother taught me to go through Father's correspondence." I had not expected her to be both the poison and the poisoner and I found myself studying her pale skin and black eyes for some sign that it was true. I leaned toward her unconsciously and something about her smell, sweet as rot, made me dizzy. I stepped back abruptly.

"I will make this bargain with you," I said. It was not the bargain I had planned to make, but I tried to speak with confidence. "Kill my father and yours and you may bury your sisters in this garden. I will keep them safe for as long as I shall reign and I shall make a proclamation so that the garden remains the same when I am no more."

She looked at me and I couldn't tell what she was seeing. "Will you bury me here as well?"

I stammered, trying to come up with an answer. She was smarted than I had given her credit for. Of course she would be caught and slain. Men were coming now from the baronies, I was sure, to avenge the murders of her two husbands.

"I will," I said.

She smiled shyly, but her eyes shone. "And will you tend my grave and the graves of my sisters? Will you bring us flowers and tell us stories?"

I said I would.

Cecily finished the graves for Mirabelle and for Alice. Each girl curled up at the bottom of the pits like pale sworls of fog and Cecily buried them with her hands.

I wished that she was a normal girl, that I might have taken her hand or pulled her to me to comfort her, but instead I left the garden, chased by my own cowardice.

The next day, she put on her wedding gown, long white gloves, and dressed her own hair. At the wedding, she was called Cecily, and she promised to be my good and faithful wife. And she was. The best and most faithful of all my wives.

There was a feast with many toasts, one after the next. The king's face was red with drinking and laughter, but he would not look at me, even when he drank to my health. As a dish of almond tarts was passed, Cecily rose and lifted her own glass. She walked to where her father and the King sat together.

"I want to toast," she said and the assembled company fell silent. It was not the normal way of things for a bride to speak.

"I would thank my father, who made me, and the King, who also had a hand in my making." With those words, she leaned down and took her father's face in her hands and pressed her lips to his. He struggled, but her grip was surprisingly firm. I wondered what her mouth felt like.

"Farewell father," she said. He fell back upon his chair, choking. She laughed, not with mirth or even mockery, but something that was closer to a sob. "You crafted me so sharp, I cut even myself."

The King looked puzzled as she turned and took his hand in hers. He must have been very drunk, now that he thought himself safe from me. Certainly he wore no gloves. He pulled his fingers free with such force that he knocked over his wine. The pinkish tide spread across the white tablecloth as he died.

They shot her, of course. The guards. Eventually she even fell.

Yes, I suppose I embellished the story in places and perhaps I was a little dramatic, but that hardly matters. What does matter is that after they shot her I had her carried out to the garden—carefully, ever so carefully—and buried beside her sisters.

From each grave bloomed a plant covered in thorns, with petals like velvet. Its flowers are quite poisonous too, but you already know that. Yes, the very plant you tried to poison me with. I knew its scent well—acrid and heavy—too well not to notice it in this golden cup you gave me, even mixed with cider.

In a few minutes the servants will come and unbind you. Surprised? Ah, well, a father ought to have a few surprises for his only son. You will make a fine King, Paul. And for myself, I will take this beautiful goblet, bring it to my lips and drink. Talking as much as I have makes one thirsty.

I have left instructions as to where I would like to be buried. No, not near your mother, as much as I was occasionally fond of her. Beside the flowers in the west garden. You know the ones.

Perhaps I should take the gag from your mouth so that you might protest your innocence, exclaim your disbelief, tell your father goodbye. But I do not think I will. I find I rather appreciate the silence.

GO HOME STRANGER

JUSTIN HOWE

Thank you for your recent visit to our island. We hope you found everything you desired. As with all vacations, you believe your memories will fade with time. We guarantee they will not.

Maybe it is better to embrace what you have done. Embrace what you are. Respectability infects us all at times. Even now it is compelling you to forget what you sought and bury the memories, push them aside, and bury them deep.

If only it were so easy. Revelation is always hard to face, and fear is often the first response to a glimpse of our own reflection when the veneer is stripped away and ultimate objectivity stumbled upon. We do not always like what we are. Take heart. Know that what you were is no longer. Who and what you are now is simple.

You are a monster.

Do not fear this. Do not flee it. Do not believe it is punishment. Shed what you were, become what you are. A desire has been satisfied. Only it was not yours.

It was ours.

Remember the friend who first spoke of us? They spoke about our island and whispered of moonlight and the embrace of warm bodies. Their words rose from them like the scent of an orchard: inviting, promising, a heaven close enough to touch.

This friend spoke and you listened. Curiosity infected you like a virus. It grew over days and weeks, a persistent desire that intruded into all your thoughts. Palms, sand, and the rolling blue surf stretching as far as the horizon, an island getaway, exactly what you deserved. We promised succor to a wound within you never until now acknowledged. An image of moonlit beaches and bodies. Reward. Desire. Satisfaction. Weren't these what you sought?

A jet brought you here, and as you dove beneath the waves and lazed upon the sand, you remembered your friend's words. The visions they described.

Paradise. Curiosity became fever. But had you noticed your friend's slow decline? How they withdrew from social life until they disappeared entirely? Or did your desire overshadow your concern?

Your friend once sat where you sit now. Their thoughts mirrored yours. They too sought to forget. But they could not.

Quietly, as a lover sneaking across the sand, you approached one of the hotel's staff.

At first they refused. They warned you away. Yet they would not tell you *why*. Their evasiveness only heightened your desire. You mistook their reticence for greed.

You named a sum, for your kind believes truth may be purchased. They gave in, and pocketed what you gave them. They told you to be outside on the road near midnight.

Do you remember the warm breeze that rustled the palms as you stood in the dark with the resort compound behind you and the air ripe with the scent of blossoms? The toads chirped in their ponds, and your heart leapt at the cough of a jeep's approaching engine.

Besides the driver, a taciturn native with a cataract clouding one eye, there were others. Like you, they had come from far away, following the half remembered words of a whispered conversation. Like you, they sought an end to their desires. Yet, despite all you had in common, you avoided eye contact. The jeep carried you deeper into the swamps and up into the hills to where the trees bowed overhead, their leaves bending down to brush against you like tongues. The headlamps illuminated a clearing. Your pulse quickened. Great stone steps climbed to a rock bluff overlooking the water.

The moon was rising from the sea, massive and white, breaching the surface and climbing to the sky.

The dancers welcomed you. The fairest the island had to offer. They emerged from the darkness, promising to fulfill your desires.

The dancers beckoned. They danced a step away and then another, each step a promise, a suggestion. To witness it meant you must follow. They climbed ever higher into the starless night, drawing you up the steps towards the moon that captured and tethered your soul.

Remember the sight? Remember the song of the waves and the glow upon the water? At first you believed it but a reflection of the moon, until it dissolved into fragments, each one a luminous swimmer that heaved itself out of the water. The surf roared and in the foam churned those swimmers. The dancers brought you to the precipice. You could go no further. At the edge you glanced down to where the swimmers waited. Did not one of them call you by name? In those transformed features, bulbous and phosphorescent as undersea corals, did you not recognize that friend you had so long ago forgotten? Did they not beckon and invite you into the water with them? And as they embraced you beneath the watching eyes of the dancers, did panic make you forget that this is what you wanted?

Call us inhuman. Call us monsters. Yet it was you who came here seeking only to satisfy your desires by consuming others. How are we worse for using this to our purpose? Do not believe you are now other than what we are. We are not something you may simply set down and leave behind. What we are resides inside you now. Growing. Metastasizing. And the words will come soon. The ones your friend spoke to you. You now will tell another.

As you sit, returning to the drudgery of your previous existence, you should give thanks. We have given you more than you desired. Satiety is a lie. Desires never die. They can only be satisfied like hunger until they return. We have freed you from this cycle and cut you loose from your bonds.

Speak of us, but know you will be misunderstood.

Transformation. Permanence. You simply found more than you hoped for. The life you led is over. Already our purpose grows. When the next full moon rises, the water's call will be too strong. Do not fight this.

Embrace it.

Flee the familiar. Go home stranger.

THE HEAVY

CHERIE PRIEST

⸻

"Everyone already thinks I'm a goddamned hippie," Mark bitched.

He gulped another swig from his Heineken and knocked his knuckles against the bar.

Josh threw back the last drops at the bottom of his glass, shrugged and signaled the bartender that yes, please, he'd like another double-dose of Jack. "If you didn't want any help, you should've shot it yourself."

"I *did* shoot it myself," he insisted. "And where's your friend? He's late."

Josh glanced at the ancient, nicotine-stained clock that hung crookedly above the roadhouse door. "He's got another five minutes."

"This is stupid," Mark said for the twentieth time. "It's going to turn out the thing that got those goats was just a big damn dog. And my wife's going to kill me."

"What for? You're not paying him anything."

"You said he doesn't charge up front?"

"He don't charge at all. He just fixes things."

"Why?" Mark asked.

Josh cupped his hand around his freshly refilled drink. "Because sometimes, things need fixing. And that's what he does. The Heavy fixes things."

The jukebox lit up on the one side that still lit up, and "Bad to the Bone" began to play. Mark checked over his shoulder, wondering what dumbass was too new to know that A-13 wasn't really Lynyrd Skynyrd anymore.

He didn't see anyone he didn't recognize, so he turned back around and shifted on his stool. "Why do they call him that?" he asked.

"The Heavy?"

"Yeah. How come?"

Josh made a grin with the half of his mouth that wasn't wrapped around the lip of his glass.

Before the song's first verse was over, the hinges on the door gave their signature squeal and the street lamp out in the parking lot poked its edges into the room, but just barely. Something big was blocking it.

"Holy *shit*," said Mark.

The man in the doorway turned sideways a notch to let himself in.

He was not quite as big around as he was tall, and he was six foot five if he was an inch. His bullet-shaped head was perfectly bald except for the chops that sprouted a wild retreat from his topmost chin. From the neck of his metal head T-shirt to the tips of his motorcycle boots he wore black over every last inch; and covering up the whole of his massive frame was a coal-dark trench coat that was bigger than a bedspread.

He tossed Josh a nod of recognition, and he stomped toward the bar. It wasn't an angry stomp; it was a stomp of sheer mass. The big man pointed at a bottle behind the counter and the bartender picked it up and started pouring.

While he waited for that drink, the Heavy approached Josh and Mark with his hand outstretched.

"Hey there, buddy! I hear you've got a problem." His voice was quick and friendly, and so was his handshake. He angled his bulk against the side of the bar, skipping the stool and letting himself lean.

Mark was speechless, so Josh got the ball rolling.

"Well, first off, by way of getting fancy—Mark, this is Kilgore Jones. Kilgore, this is Mark," Josh said. "He's the man with the problem."

Kilgore nodded. He'd heard part already. "The man with the goats. Or the ex-goats, as the case may be."

"Oh, I've still got goats," Mark assured him. "Not as many as we started with, but we've still got them." He waved his empty green bottle at the bartender, who popped the cap on another one and handed it over the counter, along with Kilgore's drink.

Kilgore took it and downed it in one swallow. "All right. Fill me in on the facts, and I'll tell you if I think I can help," he urged. "It might be you've got a bad dog, and if that's all it is, I'm still happy to lend a hand. But Josh thinks it might be worse than that."

Mark blew a sad, honking note down the bottle's frosty neck. He braced his feet on the stool's rungs and twisted them there while he spoke. "I guess I should start with the goats," he said. "I don't give a damn for goats. They're bad-tempered, ugly little things, and they smell like shit. But I lost my job at the Caterpillar plant, and my wife got this idea."

"The goats were your wife's idea?"

He bobbed his head. "Hell yeah, they were. Do I look like a man who needs organic soap in his life?"

Kilgore shook his head, and a row of tiny silver hoops in his left ear jingled together. "No sir, you do not," he said. His oddly boyish face stayed composed and serious.

"Well, I've got it now—by the metric assload. I didn't know thing one about goats, but Elaine did a bunch of reading, and a few days later she came home with a pair of Saanens. It was my job to clean and repair the barn, and it was her job to milk the residents—because God help me, *I* wasn't going to reach down underneath one."

Mark curled his fingers around the beer. "And anyway, now we've got goats, and we've got a website, and we've got soap, and lotion, and yogurt—and just about anything else you can comb, curdle, or cook that comes out from a goat's undercarriage. That was three years ago. And now I'm the vice president of Signal Valley Farms, which is to say I shovel goat shit and do what Elaine tells me. She's the president, since it was her idea."

The Heavy mentally jotted all this down and asked, "When did the trouble start?"

"A few weeks ago." Mark took another hard draw on the beer and nearly choked himself with it. He looked into Kilgore's face and didn't see a guy who was about to bust out laughing.

He just looked interested, and a little concerned.

So Mark cleared his throat and made a face that implied acid reflux, and he continued. "I found a couple of the goats all torn up. I figured someone's dogs got out, you know? Or if they weren't somebody's dogs, then maybe coyotes."

"Maybe," Kilgore said.

"Once we lost another couple goats, I started checking them out good before I buried what was left. And I'm telling you, it looked like they'd been . . . I don't know. *Gored*, or something."

"Gored? Like by a bull?" Kilgore frowned.

Mark shook his head. "Naw, more like a baby unicorn. They were punctured, but the holes were too deep to be teeth." He held up his hands, trying to indicate his best guess. "It was like they'd been jabbed with something sharp, maybe the size of this bottle's neck."

"And how many have you lost now?"

"Eleven. The thing got one more last night."

Josh elbowed Mark. "Tell him the rest," he said.

"The rest?"

Mark stared at his bottle. "I shot it."

"You shot it?"

"I shot it," he said again. "But it didn't die."

"Ah." Kilgore said. "Does that mean you got a good look at it?"

"Not a *good* look. And the look I got . . . I don't know what I saw."

The big man kept his somber face on and didn't push too hard.

"You want to tell me what it looked like?"

"You're going to think I'm nuts."

"Bet you I won't." But that wasn't enough to make Mark talk, so Kilgore added, "Look, man. I've heard some crazy shit in my time, and a surprising amount of that crazy shit has turned out to be true. So I'll tell you what. I've got stories that would make you think I'm as nutty as a tree full of squirrels. I'll tell you one of mine if you'll tell me yours."

"Deal," Mark said. "Go on. Surprise me."

"All right, I *will*. Two weeks ago I was up in Knoxville, and I got stuck in an attic with a pair of vampires who were righteous pissed to see me."

"Wait. Stuck . . . ?"

"Now, I'll grant you it was faster getting down than going up—I fell through the floor and landed on a table downstairs, which hurt like a sonofabitch. But that was after I ran one of them through with a sharp chair leg, and I poured some of Reverend Sam's finest blessed H20 down the throat of the other."

"Blessed . . . ?"

"You heard me. What'd Josh tell you about what I do?"

Josh beamed, and Mark acted queasy. "He said you fix unusual problems."

And finally, Kilgore laughed. It was a merry sound, sharp and genuine. It matched the way he talked. "I do indeed fix unusual problems—mostly the weird ones that no one else'll touch. So if you think I'm going to poke fun at you, you've got it all wrong. You can tell me what you saw, and nothing you can say will send me running. Lord as my witness, I promise you that."

Mark gave up. "All right," he said, shaking his head left and right, and trying not to taste any more of his stomach in his mouth. "All right, I'll tell you what it was."

He picked at the label on his bottle and dropped it down on the counter with a clank. And then he said quickly, "It was a big black shape with glowing red eyes. There, are you happy?"

"Happy? *Hell*, no. Big black shapes with glowing red eyes are pretty far down on the list of things that make me happy, but I'd appreciate it if you could be a little more specific. Can you tell me what kind of big shape?"

Mark thought hard. "It was big, but low to the ground. Maybe it would've been waist-high on me, but it was long. It had a big head and a humped back."

"There you go, now you're talking. Keep going. Tell me about the eyes. Red and glowing, I've got. What else can you tell me?"

"It was dark," Mark said slowly. "And I couldn't see too clearly. They were close to the ground, like it's something that holds its head low. And I hit it broadside with at least two pumps from the shotgun, but it ran off and came back for more the next night."

Kilgore pursed his lips, and it made his whole face look small. He leaned himself away from the counter and stood up straight. "I believe you," he declared. "Now tell me, how far away from here is this farm of yours, and would you like to see something done about your problem tonight?"

"Tonight?"

"How many more goats can you afford to lose?"

Mark snorted. "I'd be happy to see the whole batch of them tossed off a cliff, but Elaine'll have my head if I don't put a stop to it. Besides, what if it don't stop with the goats or the dogs? What if she's out feeding the things, and it comes after her? Or me?"

"Exactly," Kilgore said. He adjusted his coat and cocked his head toward the door. "Josh, you know where this farm is?"

"I do."

"Then you're riding with me."

Signal Valley Farms sat in the shadow of Signal Mountain, Tennessee, and it was only a few miles away from the derelict roadhouse where Kilgore Jones had joined the party. As he drove his semi-black, beater Eldorado around the mountain, his passenger tinkered with the radio and groused about the knobs.

Josh punched the round handle and said, "You need a new one."

"That *is* the new one. You think they came with cassette players in '67?"

"You're a real dinosaur, man."

Kilgore smiled, but it was a grim little smile. "You said the turn's coming up?"

"It's right here. Right over there, I mean. Look, see? There's a sign."

The edge of the right headlight clipped a low-swinging sign with a picture of a goat and some purple flowers. Kilgore turned the long car slowly, and its tires chewed against the gravel. The unpaved road turned out to be a driveway, but it was a long driveway and it made a dead end at a ranch-style house with one light burning.

They parked up near the house.

Josh and Mark milled nervously while Kilgore rummaged through his trunk. He produced a battered book with a burgundy leather cover, a fistful of stakes that should have lined a garden, a pump water gun with loudly sloshing contents, a digital camera, and a pair of six shooters. Then he lifted out a small flashlight and checked its batteries.

"I told you, I shot the thing already," Mark said.

Kilgore methodically packed a camo-green duffel bag with everything except for the guns, which he popped into the holster he wore under the trench coat. "I heard you, and I believe you. But I'm willing to bet you didn't shoot it with bullets like these."

"What are they, silver or something?"

"Silver-plated," he said. "It works just as well, and I ain't made of money. I'm not saying these'll work or anything; hell, I don't know what you're up against here. But not much can stand up to this assortment. And oh yeah, this." He reached back into the trunk and pulled out a machete as long as his arm. The light of the trunk's half-dead bulb glinted against the shiny, sharpened edge.

Josh did a good job of appearing unimpressed, but Mark went green. "Is that a magic knife or something?"

"No magic here," he said, then changed his mind and patted the side of the bag. A rectangular square showed in outline through the fabric. "Except my mom's old Bible."

"What are you, some kind of preacher or something?" Mark asked. "Is that why you do this?"

Kilgore shouldered the bag and shook his head. "Almost exactly the opposite, my friend. I do this because I'm *not* a preacher. Now if you'll kindly point me at your barn, I'll get myself to work."

"It's back over there. You see the roof, through the trees?"

"Yes, I do."

"All right. There's the barn over there, and behind it there's a little run-off that turns into a creek when it rains. Watch out for that. It's none too deep, but it'll trip you up if you don't see it."

Mark reached out a hand and Kilgore took it and shook it. "I want to thank you," Mark said. "I appreciate you coming out like this. Is there anything I can do to help you, or anything you need?"

"No sir. Just you and Josh here go in the house and stay there, and don't come out—no matter what you hear. You two understand?"

"Sure do," Josh answered for them both.

And when they were safely inside, Kilgore looked into the distant sky. He saw the outline of the barn roof, and as he began to walk toward it, he started his mental checklist. He kept his voice to a whisper. It wasn't the world's quietest whisper, but it wasn't supposed to be.

If he was too quiet, nothing would hear him.

"Probably not a vampire," he said. "It would've sucked the goats dry but not torn them up. Might be a demon. But usually they get other people to do the sacrificial killing. It's not much of a birthday present if you've got to buy it yourself. Chupacabra, maybe?" He'd never met one, but that didn't mean they didn't happen. "Never heard of a goatsucker this far north."

The barn was barely more than a sharp-shadowed shape, squatting low and square along the ground. Within it, a few odd bleats of curiosity gabbled and small hooves shuffled back and forth. The smell of straw and shit wafted from underneath the locked and barred-up door.

Kilgore held his head against it. "Everybody all right in there?"

"*Na-aa-aa-p,*" somebody answered.

And something else answered, too—from over in the gully. First it was just the sharp, out-of-place pop of a branch, and then there was another rattling, the hard clack of two rocks coming together as if they'd been stepped on.

Kilgore pulled his head away from the barn door and reached for the gun that hung under his left armpit. He was a practical man, and he saw no good reason to ramp up slowly.

Another big twig broke, and another knocking set of rocks sounded like footsteps to The Heavy. "Josh, Mark. That'd better not be *you.*" But the pace of the motion told him it wasn't made by anything two-legged. There were four feet . . . moving at a sharp and regular clip.

He revised his guess. Not feet, perhaps. "Four . . . hooves?"

He listened for the firm, approaching patter. The creature was tracking around back, to the right. Kilgore tracked around to the left, keeping the barn between him and the thing that was crawling out of the gully.

The Heavy kept his eyes on the ground and his ears on the edge of the property, at the line where the creek run-off turned and flowed through a row of trees. His squint told him where to tiptoe past the building's corner and how to miss the watering trough. His ears detected a wet snuffling sound and the hard, knocking clatter that, yes, sounded like hooves.

As Kilgore circled the barn, the thing circled too, intrigued enough to follow but not bold enough to charge.

"Here, critter-critter," he called softly. "Come on out and get me. I'm just a slow, fat man. I'm easy pickings for a bad old thing like you, and I'm a *real* hearty meal. Are you hungry?"

He narrowed his eyes and peered through the night.

"Come on, now. Come out and let me get a look at you."

Around the back of the barn there was a covered storage area that came up to Kilgore's thigh. He put his left hand down on it and tested the wood. It might hold. It might not. But he was running out of barn and he was going to have to make a stand someplace. The platform was as good a defensive position as any.

He stopped his retreat and lifted one large leg. "Shit," he mumbled, and he said it a couple more times as he hauled himself up. But then he stood, and the storage lid held. It didn't want to. It bowed and creaked underneath four hundred and fifty pounds of man plus all his supplies.

Kilgore dropped the duffel bag and unzipped it, all the while trying to keep quiet so he could listen.

Around the corner, something big was tracing Kilgore's scent trail.

The Heavy pulled out his Bible. It was way too dark to read so he stuffed it into his belt, and the book bent against the strain . . . but he liked feeling it close. He held up the gun and aimed it down at the corner where the inquisitive snuffling was coming up fast. Mark had been right. Its head was low to the ground.

He shouldered the bag again.

It was too dark to see anything with real certainty, but near the earth there was motion in the nighttime blackness. Something blocky congealed, creeping snout-first from behind the edge of the building.

One dull red eye sparked into view. It blinked and the scarlet dot flickered, and focused, and turned to face the man on top of the storage box lid.

The second eye came around, and behind it came a high set of peaked shoulders.

The eyes locked on Kilgore and they brightened with greed.

"What . . . a werewolf?" he asked, knowing this guess couldn't be right. The shape was all wrong, the joints and muscles were strung together differently.

It snorted and scraped its hooves beneath its body.

The suddenness of its momentum almost took the Heavy off guard, but not quite. This wasn't his first rodeo, so to speak, and his trigger finger answered the charge with three rounds fired quickly and directly at those vicious little eyes.

The thing screeched a piercing objection. The bullets knocked the creature away from its path and it shook itself like a dog but it didn't go down. Instead, it went forward—head set low and body set barreling—into the storage bin.

Two boards busted outright, and combined with Kilgore's exceptional weight, this was enough to buckle the whole structure.

He tumbled down and off, falling and rolling over the edge and onto the creature, which grunted and tried to turn around in time to bite.

But once he got rolling, Kilgore was hard to stop, especially when he tucked his head down, pulled up his knees, and let the momentum take him. There was too much mass and too much inertia; nothing short of a gorge or a brick building could slow him down.

As it turned out, he happened to be rolling toward a thickly overgrown gully.

His body steamrolled over tall grass and skinny sapling trees. It bounced where appropriate and jolted to a rough and terrible pitch over the edge of the gully and down only a couple of feet to the V-shaped bottom . . . where he wedged himself to a stop.

He lowered his arms and shook his bullet-bald head.

Above, and around the curved path he'd mowed or flattened with his accidental retreat, the clattering quick clop of four hard feet approached. It wouldn't be long before the creature saw the man or smelled him, or simply followed the trail of the trampled foliage.

At least, thank God, Kilgore thought, wasn't stuck. But his leg was pinned underneath him, and his ribs were aching from the turbulence. He sat up and retrieved his leg. He'd dropped one of the guns, but he had both hands free—and he used them to pat himself down for a damage check.

His ass was numb. His knee was torqued. His right wrist was starting to swell. A dozen other assorted bumps, bruises, and scrapes made themselves known with a low-grade hum of pain.

None of it was so bad that he couldn't get up.

The twisted knee made a loud pop when he bent it, but then it felt better so he kept on crawling to his feet. Somewhere along the way, his bag had come unzipped and the contents had scattered; he'd lost some of the stakes, and the water gun had broken, leaking its contents all along his path. But he still had a light he was afraid to use, and he still had that second gun, which remained in its holster.

And his Bible was still stuck in his belt.

When he placed his hand on the rocks at his waist in order to make that final pull to bring him upright, he found his machete.

Something in the way the blade shifted caught the moonlight and gave him away. No sooner had he snared it and braced himself for trouble, than trouble came galloping between the trees that remained.

The creature knew these woods, too. It knew where the gully was, and even though it couldn't see much of the man who was standing in it, it could see that enormous knife glittering in the skim-milk glow of the half-covered moon. And it wasn't much afraid of knives.

Then again, it had never been struck with a knife that was flung by a man who weighed nearly a quarter of a ton.

The blade sank deeply into the soft tissue between the beast's jaw and shoulder, and again Kilgore's ears rang with the monster's ferocious squeal; but now the squeal sounded wet. Something was broken, and something was bleeding. No cry should sound so choked and damp.

The beast turned away from the edge of the gully, not quite fast enough to keep from dropping one leg over the edge. It scuttled and scrambled, and it did not fall over the edge—for which Kilgore offered up a quick prayer of thanks. Whether or not the creature was injured, The Heavy didn't want to end up trapped in a trench with it.

With a labored groan and another pop of his knee, Kilgore heaved himself up over the gully's edge and flopped down onto the low, angled ground.

The skittering scuff of the monster's hooves limped out ahead of him, back toward the barn.

"Sure," Kilgore said to himself. "Sure, you're hurt." If this monster was anything like others he'd encountered, it needed to feed and feed quickly if it was going to recover.

Running was damned hard, in the dark, on a trick knee—but The Heavy got a slow trot underway, and he hated it. He hated chasing anyone, or anything. Over the years, he'd developed a tactic for monster fighting, and that tactic did *not* involve a whole lot of dashing around.

He was big and he knew it. It was easy to look slow and soft and vulnerable. It was easy to draw the predators out to him.

But the damned monster was loping toward the barn, and toward the frantically chattering goats locked within. Kilgore did his best to lope faster.

He burst out of the vegetation with his remaining gun held firmly upraised and cocked. The object of his chase beat its head against the barn door, ramming it again and again, and squealing with each impact. The machete was still protruding from its neck, being farther jammed with every head-butt.

Kilgore tried to roar, "Oh no you don't!" but he was winded, and it came out in a raspy cough.

The creature turned. It scratched one front hoof into the dirt like a bull preparing to charge.

And Kilgore didn't waste any time unloading three more shots into that rolling, bucking shadow the size of a bear.

While it shuddered and shrieked, The Heavy drew his Bible with his free hand. It snapped up out of his belt, and he held it up over his heart like a shield.

He approached the creature with swift and measured steps. It was dying. Nothing man, beast, or other made a noise like that unless it had glimpsed the light on the other side and felt the Goodness of it burn like lava. It writhed and whimpered, and it splattered Kilgore with hot, gushing sprays of blood as black as oil.

"In the name of the Father," it spun around in the dirt, throwing a death tantrum. "And the Son, and the Holy Spirit," Kilgore told it as he came up close and brought the gun down. "*I unmake you.*" One of the hateful red eyes glowered up from the paste-like mud.

Kilgore fired into the eye because it was the only thing he could see well enough to aim for, and the fire there winked out.

The creature quivered. One of its legs twitched, scraping a mindless reflex.

The Heavy exhaled a huge breath and backed away. He knew, and the deep-bitten scars in his calf could attest, that there was no such thing as "too careful."

Keeping one eye on the carcass, he rifled through his bag and pulled out his flashlight. "Now let's see exactly what the hell you are, Mr. Goat-killer." His thumb caught the sliding switch and the bright white beam cut the night so sharply that for a moment, the man was blinded.

When his eyes adjusted, he followed the circle of light down to the gruesome mass of bullet-broken bones, torn hair, and hooves. And that's when he saw the tusks. "Tusks? This is . . . " He used the edge of his steel-toed boot to nudge the pulpy skull. "A goddamned were-pig. Were-boar. Were . . . son of a bitch."

The corpse shifted by slow, nearly imperceptible degrees, sliding around in the muck and losing the edges of its hulking shape. Kilgore reached back into the bag and whipped out the digital camera. He readied the flash and framed the shot. He caught the image just in time.

A moment later, the thing collapsed into an unrecognizable pelt.

TUSK AND SKIN

MARISSA LINGEN

—◆—

The research station was just as Peter had imagined it: small, cozy, remote, bright. The snow reflected in all the windows in the daytime and cast a glittering pall on the night. The station was immaculately clean, except for the lab, which was filled too full of instruments and computers.

"There's a lot to keep track of," Jens Olafsen, the research head, told him. "We send backups off every night. Can't afford to lose the data. Temperature, acidity, salinity—" He grinned, teeth white in a sunburned face. "But you know all that."

Writing for *Green Traveler*, Peter did. He had never been to Greenland before, but environmental scientists were much the same in the Sahara and Katmandu. Different flora and fauna and weather, same recycled-fiber, isolated good cheer. Peter felt he already knew Jens and his wife and partner, Lotte. Even their sled dogs felt familiar crowding under his hands.

Their servant was unexpected, and strange. "Anna is Tuniit," Jens explained. "Maybe the last one. Certainly one of the last. They were an ancient people when the Inuit first arrived here, say nothing of white men. The Inuit think they're frightful primitives, but Anna's bright enough, civilized."

Bright enough, Peter noticed, to handle the sweeping and the laundry, but Jens had forbidden her to go anywhere near the lab equipment. Perhaps that was unfair—perhaps the giant, sallow woman was incurious, uncomfortable with novelty. She was the only native Greenlander whose eyes had not widened at the sight of Peter's dark skin. But perhaps Jens or—more likely—Lotte had prepared her.

It took Peter a few days of experimenting with his cameras to get a sense of the lighting he could really be comfortable with. There was no sense to bringing home substandard photos of Jens's walruses, and the landscape shots might do if he needed filler, or even if he could write another article for a different market—though heaven knew it as hard enough to interest hard-core environmentalist backpackers in the plight of the Greenland walrus, much less anyone else. The Inuit, it appeared, were not much given to cozy chalets and pictur-esque hamlets. The Inuit had not focused on the tourist trade.

As he puttered around the research station with his cameras, trying not to get underfoot, Peter found his eyes drawn more and more to Anna. For such a large woman—at least two inches taller than his six-foot-one, and broad to match—she moved lightly. The planes of her face and the club of her black hair intrigued him.

But when he offered to help her dry the dinner dishes, she gave him a flat, displeased look. "I know what you want," she said in clear English, "and I'm not hired for *that* kind of help."

Peter stammered and retreated, professing his innocence, but he thought of his grandmother, cleaning white people's houses so his mother could go to college and then to medical school, and he was ashamed of himself.

The next day Jens took Peter on the sled, down to the bay where the walrus herd basked. Jens warned him not to stray too close to the walruses. "They move much faster in the water," he said, "but they can hurt you well enough on land, and not even mean to. I'm experienced with them; you're not. Stay well back. That's what telephoto lenses are for. And besides that, we're trying to keep them from getting the idea that humans are safe. With the hunters out there—their instincts and natural behaviors will be their best protection."

Jens carried a small crossbow for tagging and tissue samples—a new devel-opment, he'd said, and far safer for walruses *and* humans than using anaes-thetic to tag them. He still wandered much closer between the sunning beasts than Peter would have felt comfortable, even without the warning. Jens always seemed to know which way the walruses would shift and when to leap clear. Some of Peter's pictures were of just walruses, but others showed the parka-swaddled form of the man who studied them, moving with sure-footed wari-ness among them. He looked forward to more shots over the next few days.

But Jens was shaking his head the whole way back to the research station, and when they got in, he cornered Lotte immediately.

"The herds were mixing," he told her.

"What?"

"That's incredible!" said Lotte, and she switched to Danish, where she could more rapidly question him about the walruses' behavior.

The next morning, they told him with some regret that this unusual occur-rence needed Lotte's attention, and he would have to stay behind.

"Sorry, Peter," said Jens. "The sled will only take two, and it's important to Lotte's work."

"Of course. I understand. I'll just fix up my notes, putter around here. I can take your noon ocean readings, if you like."

Jens glowed. "That would be most helpful, thank you."

So Peter watched Jens and Lotte speed off with the dogs. He got a raised eyebrow from Anna when he went back into the house, but when she saw he was going to leave her alone, she relaxed into the day's duties.

Peter wandered restlessly as soon as the readings were finished. He wished he hadn't taken so many landscape shots in his first days there—the column was already half-written, and there wasn't much else for him to do.

On a whim, he started poking around the boxes and cabinets in the lab. Some held instruments he'd seen in use all over the world. Others were unique to the Arctic, and still others appeared to be overflow for the pantry—tins of peaches and boxes of crackers in neat rows.

One huge box in the corner contained a deflated Zodiac raft, neatly folded. Peter saw something whitish in the corner, where the raft had curled upwards. He pushed it aside in idle curiosity, then stopped short.

It was a walrus tusk.

Pulling the folded raft out, he unearthed the other tusk, perfect gleaming ivory. They nestled on a bristled, dark brown surface. It smelled musky and pungent. He pulled that out, too, gasping: the skin of an adult walrus, whole.

Surely Jens and Lotte couldn't be poachers, ivory-smugglers! Peter thought. But what else could it be? There would be no scientific reason to keep a carefully intact walrus skin in a box under a raft. And what had they treated it with? It smelled fresh and had hardly dried around the edges.

Footsteps in the doorway made him look up. Anna was staring down at him where he crouched on the floor, her expression blank.

"Do you know anything about this?" he demanded.

"Yes," said Anna. She stooped to gather up the skin. She draped it around her shoulders, a tusk in each hand. "It's mine. Thank you for finding it."

She turned and walked away. Peter, biting his lip, followed her. "Look, I want to respect your culture and all that, but you can't go around killing walruses! It's not permitted. Jens took it from you for a reason."

Anna paused at the front door, walrus skin flapping heavily around her. She did not look at him. "He took it to make me his slave. Now I am free."

"What?" Peter stepped outside, shivering against the Arctic wind. Anna headed down the hill at a half-run, and as she ran, the cold made him tear up, and his vision blurred. Peter blinked and squinted. The walrus skin flapped— the tusks shifted—

Anna slid into the water, a walrus.

Peter watched her swim off. When he could no longer make her out among the waves, he went back inside and closed the door. He sat at the kitchen table drinking cold tea and hoping that Anna would return and explain everything before Jens and Lotte got back.

He had no such luck.

Lotte came in first, shining with triumph. Jens followed on her heels, but he was the first to notice Peter's expression. He stopped, a questioning quirk to his eyebrows.

"I found a walrus skin and tusks," said Peter flatly. "Anna took them and disappeared into the water. It looked—it looked like she turned into a walrus."

Lotte thumped into the chair beside him, collapsing into it as though she could go no further. Jens seated himself more slowly, moving like an old man. "She got free?"

"Yes. Out into the water. You don't sound surprised."

"We took her walrus skin," said Jens, rubbing his eyes. "Of course we knew."

"Is it—some spell? Some shamanic trick?"

"It's how she was born," said Lotte. "There aren't many left with two skins."

"You know *others*?" said Peter.

"Not personally. Just rumors. Anna wouldn't say if she knew where her relatives were."

"I wish she wasn't out there," said Jens. "Damn! We try to protect the walrus population from human interference, and now this! It's an appalling level of human contamination!"

"But she's *not* a human," said Peter dazedly. "She's a—like a walrus selkie. A walkie."

"She's human enough," said Jens. "We've lived with her these years. Walruses don't scrub floors, no matter what happens to their tusks."

"Humans don't survive a plunge in the North Atlantic without gear, no matter what they do with a walrus skin."

"Whatever she is, she doesn't think like a normal walrus," said Lotte. "The contamination in their behavior patterns is inevitable if she stays. How will we know if the herd mixing would stay or break up if she hadn't come? What if she teaches them behaviors that ruin their chances of survival because they don't have the options she has? It's really quite impossible. Surely you must see that."

"What are you going to do about it?"

Jens sighed, rolling his shoulders. "Attempt to find her and talk her into leaving, I suppose. If we can't find her in human form and take her skin again."

Peter's stomach roiled. "That's how you did it last time? You stole her skin to trap her?"

"We had to keep her away from the walruses, once we knew what she was," said Jens.

Peter found himself at the center of a storm of activity he had no idea how to stop. Whenever he tried to object, Jens and Lotte assured him that they knew more about protecting the walruses than he ever could. That Anna could not be allowed to contaminate them.

"How will you know when you've found her?" he asked them desperately. "What if you mistake another walrus for her?"

"You must not have had the skin long enough to see the markings," Jens explained. "There are white streaks on her back. No walrus has them."

"What if you can't get her to come with you voluntarily?"

"Walruses are very susceptible to anaesthetic," said Lotte, loading her crossbow. "We will do what we need to do."

Peter shuddered. "How do you know that the walrus herd isn't full of others like her?"

Jens smiled patronizingly. "Peter, Peter. Surely you aren't suggesting that all walruses have human forms."

"Well, no . . . ."

"I'm sorry you stumbled upon this," said Lotte. "But we'll handle it. Wait here until we get back. Then we'll take you for some more photos on the other side of the bay. Photos of real walruses, not humans!"

Peter didn't want to stay in the station by himself, nor to leave Anna without aid, whether she was in her human or her walrus form. He bundled up as heavily as he could and set out after the dogsled on foot.

By the time he reached the bay where the walruses had congregated the day before, he was sure he'd frostbitten at least two fingers. He kept expecting Lotte and Jens to pass him going home, with Anna in tow—but no, he reminded himself, only two could ride the dogsled at a time, so someone would have to walk. Would they pack Anna's skin on the sled? Would they be able to catch her with her walrus skin off? Would they have to use the anaesthetic? Was it dangerous to her?

He paused at the crest of the hill. Jens and Lotte's bright parkas stood out among the brown backs of the walruses down on the beach. They were picking their way among the torpid creatures. Some of the walruses were watching them, eyes half-lidded but still alert.

Peter spotted her, or thought he did—but then there was another white-marked walrus, and another. Which was Anna? Would Jens or Lotte be able to tell the differences in the markings? Or were some of them simply spotted with bird guano?

"Anna, watch out!" he shouted. Jens and Lotte were not particularly near any of the white-marked walruses, but that was probably safer for Anna—she could maybe make it to the water before they could find her and shoot.

Instead, the walruses moved suddenly, in groups more coordinated than Peter would have expected of non-verbal beasts. He watched, unable to move or speak, as the walruses, marked and unmarked alike, thundered over Jens and Lotte, trapping them, forcing them to the ice, then down into the half-frozen sea.

Peter cried out, but the sodden parkas disappeared under the swells.

The walruses all swam off: the males in one direction, the females in another, and the small, mixed group of marked walruses on their own, straight for the sea. He could have sworn one or two of them waved their tails at him as they went.

Peter stared down at the water for quite some time.

The whining of the sled dogs brought him back to awareness of how cold he was, and how dark it was getting. Peter gathered the dogs and headed back to the station to make the necessary calls.

A SONG TO THE MOON

RICHARD BOWES

This is the early nineteenth century part of Manhattan. Normally on such a night in a quiet cul-de-sac in the West Village you'd be able to see the full Dog Day moon hanging right over the low buildings.

But tonight outside the Cherry Lane, that tiny old theater, banks of klieg lights blot it out. You'd hardly think those still in town would be willing to come out of their air-conditioned apartments. However a crowd chokes curving, ancient Commerce Street on this muggy night in a torrid August.

We didn't get intense publicity but with a cult that's not necessary. All it took were brief notices in *Time Out*, a bit in the *Village Voice*, mention on internet sites, especially L-ROD the Luna-Related-Obsessive-Disorder blog. The message was: Thad Ransom live!

Just that slogan, this place and time. The crowd started to line up in the afternoon. The theater only seats one hundred and eighty-three and those first in line were let inside an hour ago.

Many others, old theater devotees and a lot of young people, are still in the street waiting for a glimpse of a legend, a touch of lunar magic.

People with a certain edge who have been in the city since mythic times remember a very young Ransom at a tiny café on Cornelia Street in an unknown writer's first play on a night very much like this one. He was transformed before them, his eyes got huge, his face awe-struck as he described the crash of an airplane.

For others Thad Ransom is a screen icon, famous for moments like the one where the camera a slides past a crowd of onlooker's in *The Kindness of Wolves*.

For a few seconds a face caught by the lens sharpens into a muzzle, the eyes gleam, the viewer tries to catch another glimpse and can't. It's the first sight of a serial killer.

Theories abound as to what tricks were used to produce that effect. But insiders know the scene was intentionally filmed at a certain moment on a certain night. And many believe that live on nights like this is the only way to see our kind perform.

Cops, emergency medics, and bartenders will tell you that a full moon brings out the beast. But all they have is anecdotes. Ransom is the proof, as am I in my way.

I should be inside but I feel the tension they call Moon Itch stirring inside me and need to be out here tonight. So I stand in the doorway of the old apartment house across the street from the Cherry Lane. In tight black slacks and a black turtleneck, wearing light make-up I'm ready to perform. A ritual is about to take place and I am the priest and also the priestess.

New Yorkers are ever on the watch for celebrities and some have noticed me. "Josie Gannon" I hear them murmur as they stare like I'm the Sybil or a shaman.

My book, *The Why of Were,* makes me an L-ROD expert gets me on TV as a talking head when Lunar-Related-Obssessive-Disorder gets discussed. And Ransom aficionados know I'm embedded in his story. When we were both new in this city, I was the androgynous roommate.

Edia, his first New York girl friend, died of an overdose and can't be here tonight. Random and Selka, his first wife, parted under unfortunate circumstances. He stabbed her on a certain night of the month. It wasn't a really serious wound and she didn't press charges. But she also won't be showing up.

Wife Two hasn't been heard from lately. On parting she said, "It's waking up every day figuring out how long it is till the next full moon and wondering who he's going to be when it happens."

Before and after each of them I was best girl, therapist and pillow boy. I think of myself as a shaman: a woman with the strength of a man and a man with the insight of a woman. But after all these years I wonder if this is love, obsession or the absence of an alternative. At times it feels like he and I are the only true examples of a breed.

Channeling our ability or affliction is the skill. A shiver goes through me and I let my face shift from older woman to young boy, from girl to old man. For all their fascination the fans are afraid to approach me and that I think is only right.

Some members of the crowd and I share a tension, a discomfort in our skin as the time slips close to midnight. A face here and there flickers, a body appears to be fluid. The Moon Itch real or imagined is almost palpable. Many are impatient, some think this is a last chance to see Thad Ransom, the great shape shifter.

Then from a sound system in the theater lobby comes a crystal clear soprano: Dvorak's water nymph Rusalka laments to the silver night goddess her hopeless love for a mortal. Our show tonight is called, *A Song to the Moon.*

On cue, hand drums are heard around the corner and the crowd turns. A voice proclaims, "You know who I am. I'm the thunder at twilight and the cry at the gates."

And there amid a phalanx of young, black-clad players is Thad Ransom, six foot four with a shock of white hair, half man, half mythic creature, all actor. At this moment the voice is Barrymore's, the eyes could belong to an intelligent coyote. But the haminess is all his. Ransom's managed to become a man notorious for being notorious.

A camera and a boom microphone follow him. Another camera is inside the open door of the theater. He is the subject of a documentary which explains the venue, the lights and the hour.

As I step forward the young players see me, reach out and get me through the crowd. Some of our company are actors, a couple are musicians. Some are just shape shifter wannabees but tonight there are gleaming eyes and bared teeth in the group.

I notice that especially in Tomlinson, called Tommy, the company bad boy and favorite, the one who reminds everyone of the young Ransom. Tommy's bouncing on his toes.

A couple of punks in the crowd bark, someone howls and Tomlinson answers with a long howl of his own. I'm used to danger but I wince at how the crowd plays with moon-driven actors.

A young actress Mary Kowal, puts her army around Tommy. Ransom kisses me on the cheek and sweeps me with him. He turns at the lobby door and says to the crowd, "I am the fear every factory owner feels when he finds himself awake in bed in the hours after midnight."

Great stuff: 1940 Broadway socialism. This being the crowd that it is many besides me recognize the lines from the Kaufman and Hart comedy *Sat On A Wall*.

In act one the daughter of a dull, rich family brings home a Greenwich Village artist named Pierce Falkland. His specialty is huge murals of heroic workers and farmers. In the second act Falkland paints his greatest work on the living room wall and turns their world upside down.

A young John Garfield played it originally on Broadway. Clark Gable, of course, did the movie with a lot less socialism and a lot more kissing.

On the night of a full blue moon almost forty years ago young Ransom as Falkland blew the minds of the second string critics sent to view a revival of that rickety comedy. "Pure Animal Power!" one of them wrote.

Tonight, for a few moments, the white hair and the years are wiped off his face and he is the young stage radical. Ransom and I have planned and discussed tonight's show for months. But this is unrehearsed and spontaneous. With such an actor at such an hour it's impossible to predict what will happen.

The crowd, the people looking down from apartment windows applaud. A few howl. At times I wish the Food and Drug Administration would speed up the approval of drug therapy for Luna-Related-Obsessive-Disorder, not for the actors but for the fans.

A camera tracks us as Ransom and I go through the lobby and down the center aisle of the Cherry Lane. The curtain is up revealing an unadorned stage. The house lights remain on for this performance.

The audience turns to watch us. Our players stop in the standing room at the back of the house.

After this we'll play larger venues—big old theaters, concert halls, open meadows in parks. The Cherry Lane is a choice both sentimental and artistic; an evocation of Ransom's past, a chance to capture a performance in an intimate setting.

Ransom turns his back to the audience and stands motionless facing the rear wall. The cultists all lean forward in their seats. Behind them our players are a shifting background of black clothes and moving faces.

I sit on a stool stage center. When the music stops, I lean forward and slip into a favorite dual roll as man of learning and priestess of the moon.

"As I speak the clocks have moved past midnight."

Someone down front gives a little yip and someone in back answers. I ignore this.

"In the wild, the hunt for food is all consuming," I tell them. "Some of us have bits of that obsession, especially on a night like this. In the hunt the ability to choose your physical form is a huge advantage and some of us retain traces of that.

"We are a society addicted to turning problems into excuses and letting cable TV news define our character.

"They whisper that we are a menace. But in my entire career I've have seen just five full lupus transformations and all of them were in hospitals, jails or both."

As I speak, the audience murmurs. I feel my body mass shift, my face crinkle. Without a mirror or monitor I know that my face is half man of learning/half woman of magic.

Ransom turns slowly, faces the audience, steps forward. "My father," he says softly, "would have looked the way I usually do if he'd lived as long as I have and gave up crew cuts." This part he has rehearsed.

"Thaddeus Taylor Ransom preached hellfire in the fields. He'd done a bit of college, University of Nebraska, before he went off to war. Got wounded and frostbitten in the Battle of the Bulge. Won a Silver Star, two purple hearts, maybe lost a few things.

"But my father believed that God in that very time gave him what Dad called his visions and the voice to tell us about them."

Ransom's delivery is slow and steady, growing hypnotic just like his father's must have been. "He could describe the sun at midnight and the red eye of Satan. His family was Presbyterian but that church wouldn't hold him when he returned. Instead he discovered The Children of the Fire, an apocalyptic sect. In your moment of spiritual need the Children were there with the comfort of a guaranteed fiery death.

"My father became a preacher. He was a charismatic, a hands-on healer." When Thad reaches this point his face has become stark with burning eyes as its main feature. "He preached on Sundays. And sometimes in church it could seem like he was burning the world down.

"Often, though, he saved the most intense moments for his family. That was my mother and two sisters and me."

Here Ransom's voice rises. "And at certain times, nights like this one, he would gather us in the living room and run something like this, 'The Lord's Great Eyes, God the Father's great eyes are upon us. His fiery gaze is upon us. It burns into your chest, into your heart, into your soul!'

"One of those nights, he woke me up, just me. I must have been ten, maybe eleven, dragged me out in my pajamas to a pasture where there was a pond and baptized me under the moonlight. I'd been baptized years before in daylight and in church.

"But this time he had a pair of torches he'd made with rolled paper and tar. He submerged me in the water, pulled me out by the scruff of the neck and held the torches so close they singed my hair."

"THE UNION OF WATER AND FIRE IN ONE BODY," Ransom yells, his eyes are huge as plates. "MY SON WILL NEVER REST EASY IN YOUR SERVICE, GOD OF FIRE."

And at that moment Ransom is as big and as terrible as that father was to that little kid. I can hear the audience gasp, see their fear.

Then the voice softens; the eyes get a little sad, a bit pensive, become no larger than anyone's. "He collapsed in the pulpit one ordinary Sunday morning six or seven years later and died in the ambulance on the way to the hospital. Over time a bullet fragment had worked its way into his heart.

"Six months later my mother married a member of the congregation, a man who owned a Buick dealership. My sisters were regular kids. Maybe I was the old man's only legacy.

"When I was eighteen I left town for state college. I ended up in the Drama

Department. They say acting and preaching are related skills. At the end of sophomore year, needing more space between my family and me, I left home and ended up in New York."

He sits on a stool. The audience nods: Ransom's upbringing was extreme but lots of them came here from situations into which they didn't fit. And more than a few get a bit turned inside out by the light of the moon.

I look up and smile. "My launching on the lunar path was a bit less dramatic.

"It was on a fine, warm night when I was maybe four. My Irish grandmother was taking clothes down from the line on the roof of the apartment building in Boston where she lived.

"Grandmother hadn't really decided who or what I was—never did I think. They'd named me Joseph but were already calling me Josie. It's a slippery name that over the years has come to be as much a girl's as a boy's.

"She pointed up at the moon and recited that ancient appeal to the goddess of the night sky. It was invented for protection against the creatures that mean us harm and walk in the silver light:

"I see the moon and the moon sees me
God bless the moon and God bless me"

"Was it also a prayer for those beings who are its worst captives, the women and the men ensnared in the lunar cycle? Could my grandmother sense that in me?

"It was part of the folklore of every nationality long before it became Lunar Related Obsessive Disorder and got discussed on TV and the internet.

"But if it's a disease where is the virus? If it's a mental disorder where are the conclusive studies? And if the moon's role is a delusion, why are there nights like these?"

I hear my voice at a distance. My face moves on its own. The lunar priest and the woman of science flicker there and a camera catches them.

As I finish Ransom is prowling the stage. "I came to this city the usual way," he says, "knowing nobody and nothing and almost immediately fell in with the perfect wrong crowd. A girl I met took me to an acting class at the New School."

We are into an old routine, one I can almost watch myself do. "I saw him the first time sitting in that acting studio all legs and hostility," I say. "Afterwards we talked and walked. It was late in the lunar cycle on a summer night with nothing in the sky but the Dog Star. Even without the moon he was intense. His eyes never blinked. He ended up crashing in the same pad I was staying at."

"I'd never met anyone like Josie," says Ransom. "But I figured this must be how people were in the big city. Josie explained a few things about my life. I realized there was nobody else like Josie—except me in lots of ways.

"I don't know if going to Central Park in the dead of night a couple of weeks later was his idea or her idea."

Laughter follows. "It was yours," I say, "For several reasons I expected life to include some danger. And thought anyone we encountered would find you as scary as I did. So I went along."

Remembering that night I begin to relive it. I can smell the grass, feel the night breeze. As I return to that night I can feel myself change and see him become young again.

"The wonder of that place at midnight is you can forget the city," he says. "Our senses sharpened. We moved in shadows, dodged police patrols, and walked to the north end of the park. The Harlem Mere at two a.m. had the Harvest Moon shining on the water. There was a waterfall and lone cars with their lights on high-beam speeding along the drives: the only other sound was the wind rustling in the trees."

"Our heads touched the sky—without acid," I add. And I am there. We recited Shakespeare "Oh, swear not by the moon, the fickle moon, the inconstant moon . . . " We sang, "Oh Moon of Alabama" *A capella*, we sing a few choruses about finding the next whiskey bar, the next pretty boy. For us the Cherry Lane stage disappears.

Ransom says, "Our senses grew more acute. We realized that a certain rustling in the bushes was not the wind and that it was following us. There was a moment of silence like someone or something was going to attack."

I told him, "NOW WE HOWL!" And just as on that night our eyes narrow, our jaws jut forward. We move downstage screaming. Our company lining the back of the theater joins in.

I feel the audience gasp and pull back in their seats as we two come forward wild eyed. I hope the cameras got every bit of it. I remember to hold my hand up. The noise stops.

"It was kids up to no good—like us," Ransom says. "We chased them howling first then laughing. Next day I remembered it like a dream and had to talk about it to keep the details from slipping away.

"But maybe a week later, this guy stopped me on Bleecker Street and said my eyes were insane. He was Sam Shepard and his first play was going to be up that weekend at Caffe Chino on Cornelia Street. He wanted me in it. That was my first time in front of a paying audience."

As Ransom speaks his face relaxes but not all the way.

"My initiation was a lot less dramatic than Thad's," I say. "You can grow up in a city and stay very unaware of nature. But when I was eight we lived in a leafy part of Boston. There were hills and big old mansions that were now, many of them, divided up into apartments, into duplexes. But the yards were large and unfenced; the hills looked out on ocean and sky.

"Old Yankees in the neighborhood worked in their gardens by moonlight. They lived in houses they'd grown up in, planted vegetables and talked at night on their porches. They drove model A's, had coal furnaces and got ice delivered by a man with a horse and cart just as it had happened when they were young.

"They followed ritual: Memorial Day and Fourth of July and Harvest Moon and at Halloween they had pumpkins with candles inside them on their porches.

"Instinctively I understood the power of a certain grain in the blood."

That old neighborhood decades ago is where I am. I feel smaller. The face of the kid Joseph/Josie wide-eyed but guarded is my face as I speak.

"My parents often seemed very young. They had been actors, people of the theater who settled down but not entirely. My mother wrote for a local TV show *Boston Common*. On five mornings a week it was songs, the news, dramatic pieces (her specialty), a segment for kids.

"Sometimes she took me with her when she brought scripts over to the station. Old friends she'd acted with worked on the show. They greeted each other with kisses. She'd be flushed with excitement. I never thought to see if it was the full moon.

"My parents always wanted me on the show and I always said no. Maybe some part of me understood where I was going and wanted to delay the trip as long as I could. When *Boston Common* got cancelled after a few years my mother was devastated, lost.

"By then I had other concerns. At that time boys swam, showered, took group physical exams naked. As a small child I'd just seemed undeveloped and got teased. With the onset of puberty it grew obvious that I had a cock and a cunt as well. I was taunted, kicked, taken to doctors.

"Drug treatment was suggested, surgery. I didn't want to change and my parents, who knew a little about being different, didn't insist. They moved to another part of the city enrolled me at a school where I got excused from gym and swimming class.

The secret scared me but left me feeling superior to others. Danger and lust got intertwined.

"My parents still dabbled, did readings, took small parts in plays. My father was in a production of Shaw's *The Devil's Disciple* done in late spring outdoors in the Public Gardens.

"I went with a couple of fellow outcasts from our high school drama department. The full Flower Moon rose over the trees. By then I knew all the names and phases and was aware of what was up with my parents. I felt my body grow fluid and knew what I was meant to do.

"The next year I was a page boy in *Henry the Fifth*, not a big stretch. Shortly afterwards I was Yum Yum in *The Mikado*. We opened the night of Green Corn Moon and I was sensational.

"Sex was a tense game. I had so many ways of disappointing partners. My freshman year of college I got picked up at a party by one of the boys who'd tormented me back in the old neighborhood. He didn't recognize me. I showed him what I had. His eyes widened in recognition.

"Then I showed him this," and on the stage of the Cherry Lane my face is the Gorgon Medusa's. It's my way of telling the audience we're past the pleasant introductions. They recoil but don't turn to stone.

Ransom has disappeared from the stage. I stand motionless, getting back my face and body. Drums beat out in the lobby and then in the house. Ransom comes down the center aisle. His hair is in golden ringlets; his face gleams. Behind him the chorus twirl, buck, roll their eyes back in their heads. They chant:

"Dance now
dance again
when Bacchus
mighty Bacchus
leads us"

They are the wild maenads, the women, some played here by guys, who have followed Dionysius all the way from Asia to ancient Thebes. Several have leather drums on which they maintain heartbeats that will go on as long as the performance does. Two others hold aloft on sticks a light-reflecting silver disk: the full moon.

Euripides' *The Bacchae*: maybe everyone sees herself in every great play. But those who follow the silver goddess are close to this one. Order—Pentheus the righteous young king of Thebes—confronts Chaos—Dionysius god of wine and frenzy.

The chorus sings and dances:

"With my drum that
the god made for me
dancing for him
with my leather drum"

All are supposed to be wild-eyed. But tonight some are barely under control.

Intentionally, we are playing with fire. Tommy is the worst, twirling, smacking into others on the crowded stage. He's the company pet. Random lets him get away with too much. I catch Tommy's attention, stare right into him. He subsides.

At Lincoln Center many years ago there was the legendary production in which young Ransom played both Pentheus and Bacchus. Tonight he stands at the back of the stage and announces:

"I am Bacchus. I am Dionysius
I am a god the son of Zeus"

His eyes are wide and blazing as he goes on to speak of his anger at the city and its ruling family—relatives who have disowned him and plans for vengeance.

In Greek drama, actors take multiple roles. With my back to the audience I wear a crown and am Pentheus; young, arrogant, full of hubris, speaking to what he thinks is a lunatic, ordering him imprisoned.

"Lock him up in the stable
If you like to dance, dance there"

And all the time the chorus goes on chanting quietly, the drums beat. The silver disc shines on the stage.

Minutes later Ransom, young and severe, wears the crown and is Pentheus his face rigid and imperious. Tommy is a messenger describing the packs of maddened Bacchantes which include Pentheus' own mother and aunts, destroying villages, tearing wild beasts and cattle apart:

"Ribs, hooves, flying asunder"

Pentheus demands to see this for himself. Now I am Dionysius all golden hair and glowing face. I dress him in woman's robes and lead him up the mountain while the chorus around us snaps their teeth like mad dogs. The night, the drums begin to take me. My eyes lose focus.

"Make the drums roar
and the hounds of madness
bay at the moon"

Then we are all supposed to exit except for Mary Kowal who remains onstage. Tomlinson passing by suddenly turns and bites her on the shoulder. She cries out, shoves him away. This is not acting and I hear the audience gasp. For a heartbeat everyone on stage stops. For a moment it seems that we might all start tearing at each other.

I know Ransom is being dead in the wings. He lies stretched out on the floor, mouth gaping, an expression of horror on his face. I've seen it many times.

It's up to me. I grab Tomlinson, look right into his wild, staring eyes with all the authority of a priestess and the madness of an actor with forty-five years on the New York stage.

"Don't waste this last chance, Tommy," I whisper. His eyes focus and the troupe leads him off. Onstage Mary Kowal as a messenger describes how the Bacchae, maddened, fell upon Pentheus. Agave, his own mother, tore her son's head from his body believing he was a lion.

In the wings we form up in a tight group, pick up dead Pentheus and emerge onto the stage. And now I am Agave marching back into Thebes. In triumph I hold my son Pentheus' bloody head by his mane of hair, his jaw flapping open. Foaming at the mouth I sing:

"I caught him myself
This savage beast
Without weapons or net"

And the chorus chants:

"And the drums
Let the drums
Praise Bacchus
For this deed"

Slowly Agave understands what she's done. I stare with a face like a mask of horror. The drums cease. Suddenly the lights go down. One spot remains, shining on the silver disc above us. I stand shaking, catching my breath.

The players who carried Ransom and blocked sight of his body while I held up his head put him down and escort him off silently.

My Moon Itch has begun to ebb. The lights come back up. I am alone on the stage.

There is applause. But I shake my head. This isn't over.

"Euripides wrote," I say, "when people had begun to forget the time when woman and god and man and beast weren't as separated and distinct as they are now. But his was a time when all humans male and female were tied by nature to the cycle of the earth, were servants to the phases of the moon.

"They still understood what seems a terrible alien disease to us now and that sometimes it was best to let that beast run."

Again there is applause. Ransom and company are behind me on the stage. It goes on for a while. We take our bows after which we're supposed to make our exit up the center aisle. Instead Ransom holds up his hands.

He looks drained, old. He puts his arm around Tomlinson's shoulder and around Mary Kowal's. "There's a story theater people tell about a great actor playing a great part. He comes off stage to tumultuous applause and storms to his dressing room in a black mood. 'You were stupendous' they say, why are you so unhappy?'

" 'I was incandescent,' is his answer, 'AND I DON'T KNOW WHY.' "

Ransom shakes his head, says in rich actor tones, "Ah, the mystery of ART! But what if you do know why your performance is terrific and the reason why isn't you? What if you're the drum and not the drummer, the brush and not the painter? What if you're a tool intended to give everyone a glimpse of ourselves as we are by nature?

"Descended from hunters of flesh, born to a hunter of souls, I've become a hunter of applause. I'm as surprised as you by some of what happened here. But each night the earth will take a small bite out of the silver goddess. In a week's time it will be sliced away and Josie and I and young Mr. Tomlinson and even Mary Robinette Kowal will be very ordinary actors indeed. Try to remember that when the moon is full," he tells Tommy. "You'll not get nearly as many second chances as I was given."

I've heard him say much of this on many different occasions. But it's one of the reason why, when he holds out his arm, I take it and walk with him up the aisle. A camera backs up before us.

People rise applauding and he smiles his way into the narrow lobby and out onto Commerce Street.

Outside all is quiet. By arrangement with the block association, the Klieg lights are off. The crowd is largely dispersed. The moon has disappeared behind the houses. Cameras follow us to the curb then stop.

A driver opens the back door of a limo. We kiss the kids good-bye, promise we'll see them all tomorrow, make sure Mary will have the shoulder looked at, and escape before the fans can get to us. The cameras don't follow any further. We'll see them tomorrow also.

Ransom and I settle into the back seat and I give the directions home. Yes. We are roommates again—*un folie aux deux*.

The energy of the moon has flowed out of us. The wolf sleeps after it has fed. I sink into the seat. "I hope they got the footage they wanted," I say.

Next month we do this at the Chandler in L.A. In October under the Hunter's Moon it's the Colonial in Boston. We're booked two years in advance. The documentary, the long farewell tour—we're showing them how it's done.

"Tomlinson was out of control, tonight," Ransom says. He sounds tired and old. "Much as I like him I'm afraid Tommy's got to go."

"He reminds me of you at his age," I say. "And he gave you the chance to make that speech."

"What he did was unprofessional."

"Hmmm. Remember the binge you went on after you walked out on Edia?"

"I remember waking up from a week-long blackout."

"And discovering you'd signed on to play Cyrano de Bergerac in a former tin can factory in Jersey City."

"The nose was great. You said so yourself."

"They'll find a medical cure for Tommy's problem. We'll be the last of our kind."

But Ransom's asleep and I take his hand. When I first saw him I knew he was dangerous. But it's what I was used to. It's easy to entice and easy to anger when you offer the mixed bag that I did. Now we are as you see us.

On my iPod, Dvorak's Water Nymph sings to the moon of her troubles. I think of her as a creature caught between worlds—like me as a child. I want to tell her that I've seen over eight hundred moons both silver and blue come and go. And I look forward to seeing some more.

IN THE SEEONEE HILLS

ERICA HILDEBRAND

My name is Claire.

Four months ago, Jules told me she was a werewolf. We were already sleeping together. She should have known better, but I should have been more careful.

Lycanthropy, unless you're born with it, is debilitating. Contracting it is easier than you think, even when you're just experimenting with some rough play in the bedroom.

It's all in the bite.

I went to the clinic—not just any clinic, *the* clinic, if you're connected enough to find it—to get tested. The clinic's only open at night, catering to the sensitivities of their clientele.

The test was just a smokescreen, my way of trying to cross paths with the Seeonee Pack.

I sat by myself, reading a pamphlet on lycanthropy. Jules had sworn to me it wasn't a disease, but she'd been born with it. She could control it. I couldn't. So, every full moon, her pack pumped me full of sedatives and muscle relaxants to keep me from changing. The Rothschild Pack ran a pharmaceutical company.

The clinic's pamphlet talked about smells and instincts, about tapping into the primitive brain of the human psyche, all neatly arranged in bullet point factoids.

A nasty mechanical smell drifted from where the vampires sat, reeking of preservatives and rotten fruit.

I closed my eyes and focused on smells coming from the other side of the clinic instead, smells that reminded me of childhood trips to my grandparents' farm: muddy creek water and cedar wood shavings. Comforting and familiar. The smells of a pack.

A clean, earthy smell came closer. Cinnamon, woodsmoke, and a November breeze. The plastic cushions of the bench shifted as someone sat beside me.

I opened my eyes and flinched when I saw how close she'd sat. She was early twenties, same as me. Her auburn hair had that short, tousled, bedhead look that I was pretty sure had taken an hour to style. Her amber eyes reminded me of white wine. Moon earrings jingled from her lobes, matching the long necklaces that draped over the cleavage her spaghetti-strap top displayed.

Her face dimpled with a devil-may-care smile and I instantly felt small and pathetic by comparison. She was gorgeous. I realized I was staring. My face heated with a blush and I instinctively looked away.

"Hi. You're all alone. I'm Ginny Donnelly; would you like to come sit with us?" She gestured to the group from whom the earthy smells emanated.

"Please," I said, and introduced myself.

"We're the Seeonee," she said. "Named so for *The Jungle Book*."

"Never read it," I said. I hoped I didn't show reaction, even though my heart skipped a beat. I'd found them.

She tilted her head to one side, hair and earrings tumbling in the appropriate direction. "Really? You should. It's one of my favorites."

Her pack stood as we approached, and they all pressed in around me, touching my shoulders, shaking hands. Ginny pressed me forward to the only packmember still sitting, a pregnant woman of about fifty, golden trinkets interwoven in her salt-and-pepper hair.

"Mae is our pack leader," Ginny said. "Her obstetrician works here."

She turned to Mae. "Mom, this is Claire."

"A new friend, Geneva?" I detected a note of criticism, but Mae reached her hand out and pulled me down next to her on the seat. "I smell you're new to the wolf magic. Thankfully you don't look harmed."

Catching lycanthropy was normally a violent act, like being impregnated by way of rape, the pamphlet in my hand had told me.

"N-no, nothing like that," I said. "It was an accident." Should I be so nervous? What happened to a lone wolf when she encroached on a pack's territory? The Rothschilds had kept me in the dark.

"Who infected you?" Ginny asked, sitting down on my other side.

Jules had instructed me to be honest with them. About anything except the plan. "My girlfriend."

There was a subtle shift in Ginny's posture. "What's her name? We might know her."

"Um," I said, "Julia Straus."

Mae and Geneva didn't know her, but they asked the others. A boy with spiked hair nodded. "Yeah," he said, "I've heard of her. She's with the Rothschild Pack."

Mae grumbled beside me. "Oh, them."

I looked at Ginny, feigning ignorance.

"They're a territorial rival of ours," she explained. "They've recently been encroaching on Seeonee hunting ground."

I absently watched the vampires across the room, not wanting to betray that I already knew that. My ears and nose, however, were busy sifting out the individuals of the Seeonee beyond Ginny's clean autumnal scent.

"Does that make me a Rothschild?"

"Nah," Ginny said, patting me on the back. I roused at the touch but stayed quiet. "You're free to do as you want."

Was I crazy? Why had I agreed to do this?

I was only dimly aware of a gothed-up vampire hissing at me from across the room.

"Never mind them," Mae said quietly. "We don't associate with that kind."

I didn't lower my gaze from the vampire staring back at me; a cold oily feeling poured down my spine. I'd never been a confrontational person, but I didn't break eye contact with him, not until I heard the nurse call my name, crisp and clear.

When I stood, Ginny stood with me. "Can I go in with you?"

I nodded. We went into the back room where a nurse in scrubs took my height and weight, blood pressure, and a blood sample.

Ginny took out a length of looped string from her pocket and we played Cat's Cradle while we waited, sitting cross-legged on the exam bed. She wore her sleeves over her palms, the same way I did with the cuffs of my hoodie, and I liked that about her.

No, I told myself, *don't get sappy*. The Rothschilds had told me these people hated anyone who wasn't a natural-born. I didn't know why Ginny was being nice to me, but it didn't matter. I wasn't here to make a friend.

"So, you come here often?" I asked.

She laughed. "A pick-up line? I'm disappointed."

I blushed furiously. "No, that's not what—"

"I know," she said, amused. "It just sounded funny. Yes, this is our one-stop shop for healthcare. We have to put up with the awful vampire smell but at least this way we can take note of which ones are in our territory. So, your mate let you go alone?"

"What?"

"Julia. She didn't come with you to the clinic," she said. Her expression turned serious.

"She's not my mate," I said, suddenly defensive.

"But you said she's your girlfriend."

"Well, yeah. Sure, I guess."

"Oh," she said, and avoided my gaze. "I'm sorry, I just assumed. I guess it's a lupine thing. Sometimes I forget it's not human nature to mate for life—I mean, you have to admit, people are flakes."

"I guess," I said. I suddenly hated that she was being nice to me.

When they came back with my test results and started explaining options and lifestyle changes, I didn't understand why it hit me so hard. Maybe I'd held out some fool's hope that this test would tell me it was all just a false-positive. That I was normal after all. I don't know. All I knew was that Jules had done it to me. By accident, but it happened all the same.

I questioned helping the Rothschilds take over the territory. They hadn't told me what I was supposed to do, exactly, except that I had to be among the Seeonee when I changed for the first time.

I had a week to get used to the idea.

My name is Geneva.

I carry in my veins the last legacy of Ireland's wolves since Oliver Cromwell's campaign of slaughter destroyed the packs all those centuries ago. We Donnellys aren't strictly Irish, not anymore. Donnelly blood mingled with the American timber wolf and eventually the pack changed its name from Donnelly to Seeonee. I'm third-generation. Also, my mom's Italian.

Even though a Donnelly bite can infect, we protect people who live in our territory. That includes culling the number of infected weres in the area, lest they run around spreading mayhem.

The problem started when Mae got pregnant, around the time my dad died, and her wolf magic went dormant. It only made sense that our rivals would try to murder the Seeonee's alpha in her vulnerable state. We had a choice. We could spend nine months wearing ourselves out, worrying that at any moment we'd be attacked, wage fights and risk vampiric infection or death.

Or we could kill a human.

The human community would respond with all the fury of modern technology and send all of us—including our enemies—underground. I'd argued long and hard over the implications of the humans hunting us and our cousins the wolves, but it was all for nothing.

Mae suggested that if we could get an outsider to do the deed, we wouldn't have to sacrifice any pack members as the culprit. We had no control over vampires, but we could dupe a hapless infected werewolf, serve them up to the humans and rid ourselves of a potential troublemaker all at once.

It was the will of the pack. That's why, against my better judgment, I went to the clinic in search of a patsy.

And I hated myself for finding Claire.

The clinic gave me some pills. Some sort of suppressant that was nowhere near as strong as the Rothschild sedatives—which I was no longer taking. At the next full moon, the change would hit me no matter what.

A few days later Ginny, who'd gotten my cell number at the clinic, called and asked me to meet her for lunch. We met at a sandwich stop.

"Lost your appetite, I see," she said.

I picked at my salami but otherwise didn't eat. "Must be nerves," I said.

"No, it's those pills they give you."

"What the hell else can I do?" I asked, suddenly irritated. "You're natural-born, I'm infected. It's different for me."

I'd been reading as much on the subject as I could get my hands on. Jules had, of course, loaned me some books, but she was natural-born too and couldn't understand any more than Ginny could.

"I'm afraid," I said. "The nurses said it's going to hurt worse than anything I've ever felt. They say I'm not going to be able to control it."

With three days until the full moon, the lunar cycle was already twisting my insides, making me snap easily. I had no idea what I'd be like if I wasn't on the pills. Feral, maybe.

"Your hormones are all misaligned," Ginny said. "Those drugs are messing with your emotions."

"You natural-borns can control it, right? The change?"

"It's hard to explain." Ginny munched on a potato chip before continuing. "We feel the pull of the moon just as the tides do. But we don't go mad. And aside from the moon, we can change whenever we want." She shrugged. "It's easier if you've got other wolves around. A pack to submit to."

"I'm afraid," I said again, and hell if I didn't mean it.

She reached over the table and took my hand in hers, offering a little smile. "I already talked to my pack and they agreed to help for your first change. We'll go into the woods, somewhere private, don't worry."

I shrank back and the wolf behind my eyes flattened its ears in embarrassment. I didn't want a bunch of calm, collected werewolves watching me totally lose it. I'd never be able to look them in the eye. But this was what Jules had asked me to do.

Ginny tilted her head to the side. "You can trust me."

I don't even know you, I thought. But the wolf inside me wanted to say yes, trust her. Could instinct tell me if I was going to get hurt? Could instinct protect me?

"Fine," I said with a sigh. "Let's do it."

"Good. You couldn't be safer, I promise you that. Here, I brought you something." She took an old Rudyard Kipling paperback out of her satchel and put it on the table between us.

On the bus ride home, I read about the wolves of the Seeonee, who called themselves the Free People and protected the jungle's laws. I imagined Ginny's family being like that. Whatever the Rothschild Pack had planned, if it was supposed to hurt these people, I couldn't do it.

Jules *hurt* me. She *gave* me this, put this on *my* shoulders. I didn't want anything more from her. I didn't want to contribute to whatever she was planning.

So I called her that night and backed out.

When I tried to sleep, later, I heard distant howls with my increasingly sensitive ears. They sounded so sad.

Behind my eyes, the wolf responded to the terrible yearning brought on by the sounds. I wanted to empty my lungs and cry out yes, I want to join you.

Outside my window, the moon waxed.

I sent Claire a text the next morning letting her know where to meet me. Then I spent the day arguing with Mae, asserting that we couldn't use Claire for our scheme. But my mom had already found us a victim, currently bound and gagged in her garage.

The plan was to take Claire and the victim into the woods, let Claire change and then ravage him. As an infected she wouldn't remember the event, and we could make up whatever story we liked.

But she wasn't just a nameless werewolf to me, not anymore. She was alone and frightened. One more victim of a pack that didn't take care of their own.

I'd started hating myself for even considering the plan. Of course I wanted to protect my mom, but the more I thought about it, the less I wanted to kill anyone. And I didn't want to do it at Claire's expense.

I hung up with Mae just before dinner time, when Claire was due to arrive at my place. I had invited her to spend the night with me, afraid that she might change early. The first change had a general twenty-four hour window, but any more specific than that was a guessing game and I could tell she didn't want to be alone for it.

I didn't share any of this with Mae, who wanted me to keep an eye on Claire and bring her to the Seeonee meeting at tomorrow's full moon.

I'd baked a ziti dish but I was too conflicted to have much of an appetite. Claire only poked at hers, too. She wore her dark shoulder-length hair down, smooth as silk. Her dress flattered her figure and she pulled off a casual, girl-next-door charm even when she was obviously nervous about the full moon.

I knew I couldn't put her in harm's way.

We sat on my balcony after dinner and sipped coffee, looking out at the hedgerow and the patch of woods beyond.

"I can open a bottle of wine," I offered.

Claire shook her head. "I already feel strange. I don't want to risk lowering my guard or anything."

I nodded and we sat in silence for a time, swaying idly in the wooden porch swing I'd hung from the supports of the upstairs neighbor's balcony.

"I don't think I should be around the Seeonee when I change," she said in a quiet voice. She bit her bottom lip and I couldn't help but stare at her mouth, the softness of her skin.

"That's a good idea," I said. We could avoid the Seeonee. They could just kill Mae's victim, deal with the consequences themselves, and leave us out of it.

She gave me a sidelong glance, her dark eyes suspicious. "Why do *you* think so?"

I sipped my coffee. If I told her the truth she'd disappear on me. "I just think it's prudent. Why do you?"

Claire hesitated before answering. "I don't want anyone to get hurt."

It dawned on me then that there was a chance she'd be able to harm me. The Rothschild Pack carried the blood of the red Eurasian wolves. A bit smaller than me, but we would be on par as predators. It was too much to hope for her to remain conscious through the ordeal.

"I don't see how I can live with this," she said, picking at a loose thread on my sleeve. I was very aware of her proximity.

"This is what you are now."

"But I've got some sort of sickness. Isn't that what you think? That I'm going to be one of those monsters, the kind that terrorize London in the movies?"

I bit my tongue. It *was* close to what I thought.

"I don't see how you can be so hypocritical," she said. "Natural-borns are the ones who give people this sickness in the first place."

A growl threatened to rise in my throat. I realized I felt the moon's pull, too. "So you're just going to go through life believing you're a victim?"

"I wasn't *born* this way."

"*I* was. I've been one all my life. That isn't my fault." I took a deep breath, and my nostrils flared as I inhaled the natural perfume of her skin. "It's just who I am."

Instead of answering, Claire leaned towards me and pressed those soft, pretty lips against mine. Desire fluttered deep within me. I wanted to touch her. But I couldn't do this, not until I was sure I could protect her.

Abruptly I stood and went in through the open patio door—putting some distance between us—and set my cup down on the kitchen island. I turned the faucet on.

"If you have kids," I called over my shoulder, desperately wanting to change the subject, "they'll be natural-borns like me. That isn't so bad."

I plunged my hands into the cold water and splashed my face and neck until my roiling blood calmed and my shallow breathing steadied. The water only momentarily cooled the heat of my skin.

I toweled off, waited a moment, took a deep breath and when I heard no response I returned to the balcony. "Claire, listen. I'm sorry. I—"

Claire was doubled over, clutching her stomach with both arms and her face twisted in pain. I rushed to her and put my hand on her back; the muscles beneath her thin dress shivered. I cursed.

It was starting.

"Come on," I said, and pulled her to her feet. She needed to be in the natural world for this. I took her through the apartment, hoping I could get her down the stairs and out into the hedgerow. Halfway out the door I thought to grab my digital camera. Claire cried, moving slowly from the pain. I dragged her across the lawn, sparing a quick glance to make sure no one saw us, then pulled her into the forest. At the first clearing I dropped everything and stripped off her clothes, thinking she'd not want to ruin them.

Her skin rippled from the spastic changes underneath.

As I yanked her dress off, two loud pops of bone and tendon—sickening sounds, even when you're used to it—signaled the shift of her shoulder joints.

"It's all right," I said.

She writhed on the ground, crying and begging me to make the pain stop. My heart tripped; I wanted to comfort her, but I couldn't. I set the camera to start recording, checked the angle of the shot and balanced it on a maple branch. She'd need to see this. Through the viewfinder I saw her snout elongate and the fur grow. I stripped off my own clothes.

Her pheromones filled my nose with wafts of pine boughs and pumpkin seeds and something else, something I hadn't noticed before when her human scent masked it, something that grew pungent when she changed.

Some sort of drug.

The change came easy to me so close to the full moon. My shoulders dislocated and rolled forward, my nose popped, my insides burned with the familiar fire. It hurt, but I was used to it and I had control. Claire didn't.

The wolf magic consumed me as my vision blurred and diminished, focus going to my ears and nose. Claire's transformation was nearly complete. She was not quite a common wolf; her fur was thicker, richer, and ruddy.

I put my big paws on the leafy ground and stood straight and tall. I was a daughter of alphas, and the wolf magic raged within me as I watched Claire, my instincts howling: *Infected. Dangerous. Stranger.* I moved forward, intending to press her into submission. She was smaller than me and I smelled fear and anger and insanity brought on by the drug. Still beneath the drug she smelled, to my surprise, natural.

Once she shook off the pain, Claire focused on me with fangs bared and lunged for my throat. She only caught ruff and as I recoiled she caught my leg in her teeth and a lightning bolt of agony ran up my foreleg. I lashed out in reflex and latched onto the fur at her throat, forcing her to the ground.

Despite her fury, she was disoriented and confused, though her snarls could have woken hell itself.

I held her there for what seemed like hours.

As she metabolized the drug and eventually grew docile, I wondered whether my family had engineered this unnatural aggression in her.

She whined and I finally let her be.

We sniffed each other, as is the way of wolf introduction, and she bent her head and nuzzled my injury by way of apology.

I watched the video recording of my change for the third time. I didn't remember any of it.

I sat curled up on the floor of Ginny's bedroom in a borrowed robe, fresh from a much needed bath, my back against her bed. I winced at the ruthlessness of the two wolves—us, me, that's actually *me*—on screen, and rubbed my throat with a shaky hand.

My body ached everywhere. The wolf behind my eyes was thankfully silent.

"How long were we like this?" I asked, my voice hoarse.

"Just the night," Ginny said, sitting across from me with her back against a wall, hair disheveled from her shower. She'd bandaged her arm in gauze.

"I don't know what to say. Your arm—"

"Will heal," she said, and glanced at the clock on the nightstand. The sky outside glowed pink with the coming dawn. "I have to get you out of here before tonight. The Seeonee will be angry."

She'd told me about the drug she'd smelled, what had sent me into a rage. She'd also told me about her pack's plans to make me murder a human.

"Ginny," I said, but I turned my head and buried my face against her comforter. I wanted to tell her the truth. She'd already had the chance to kill me, and to trick me, and she hadn't done either.

I heard her come closer, felt a hand on my arm and when I lifted my head she sat beside me. Wordlessly she pulled me against her and I laid my head on her shoulder.

And I talked.

I told her about my infection, about Jules, about the Rothschilds' plan to overthrow the Seeonee, about my role in it. I guessed they'd administered the drugs when they sedated me at full moons, testing on me, planning all along to make me go insane and hurt someone. I opened up to her about my fears of dealing with it alone, about what a mistake I'd made in agreeing to help with the Rothschilds and how horrible I felt.

"If you hate me," I said, "I understand."

After a moment of tense silence, Ginny said, "Likewise."

Then she stiffened against me.

"My mother," she said. "That's who they wanted you to attack. She can't change while pregnant. That's why they feralized you with drugs."

"Well," I said, sitting up straight, "I won't be there to do it. You told me the drugs got flushed out of my system."

She nodded, "You smelled clean, after."

I touched her bandaged hand. "I didn't . . . didn't *give* you anything, did I?"

At that, she looked at me with her Chardonnay eyes and flashed her dimpled smile. "No." Then she assumed an Irish brogue. "If anything, I pray you swallowed some honest Donnelly blood and put your spirit to rights."

I laughed with the relief of broken tension.

She laughed, too.

And then she kissed me.

She hesitated, as if unsure. After my surprise subsided, I nudged my lips against hers. Accepting that as permission, she kissed with renewed fervor, parted my lips with her tongue and drew me into her lap.

I ran my hands through her disheveled wet hair and traced the features of her face with my lips, moving towards her neck. She opened my robe and slid her hands in, cool against my warm skin, sending electric shudders along my flesh.

I pulled back long enough to peel off her shirt. Straddling her, I slid my hands down her breasts, drawn to her body warmth. Her hands caressed my ribs. I shivered as her hands slid lower, tracing my hips. Her thigh pressed up between mine.

Ginny rolled me and laid me down on my back, parted the robe and pressed her breasts and stomach down against mine. She nudged my head to the side and wrapped her lips around my earlobe as her hand slipped between my thighs, her hair spilling across my face, our heartbeats pressed against each other.

I panted, clinging to her shoulders. Her breath trembled against my ear and then she was inside me, eclipsing all other sensation. Body heat radiating against mine, her careful rhythm built a slow mounting pressure within me. I moaned into her shoulder.

The sensation crested, then faltered, lingering.

"Claire," she whispered. A sweet nothing carried by her breath, but so genuine. I knew what it asked. *Let me take you.*

I surrendered. The mental barrier dropped; the sensation blossomed and exploded within me. The world fell away.

When it passed, she held me, fingers exploring the contours of my body. I'd never dreamed I would feel so safe at the hands of a wolf.

After a moment, I took a deep breath and said, "Can I touch you now?"

She smiled, nipped at my throat. "What's your hurry? You're mine now. Think I'm letting you go anytime soon?"

My heart swelled. I answered with a kiss, long and slow.

I laid my ear against the spot between Claire's breasts and listened to her heartbeat, letting it lull me. She dozed on the carpet, her fingers tangled in my hair.

I recognized then and there, watching her sleeping, that I wanted her as my mate. There wasn't a doubt in my mind. I didn't care that she wasn't a natural-born; she had smelled perfectly natural to me.

In the afternoon I returned to idle stroking along her skin. She eventually squirmed and made little half-asleep noises. I set my mouth to work rousing her as pleasantly as I could, her legs parting as she realized what I was up to.

Suddenly alert, her nails dug into my shoulder blade. "What time is it?"

"Who cares?"

Claire opened her dark eyes, but they slid closed again as I pressed a palm to her cheek and she turned her head to kiss my fingers.

Then she started to sit up. "The full moon."

I rested my hand on her chest. "You changed last night. Don't worry. It won't happen again so soon."

"But the Seeonee think I'm going to be there," she said. "And the Rothschild Pack knows I won't."

I froze. "You told them you weren't going?"

Her expression turned worrisome and I reminded myself she wasn't to blame for this.

She said, "I told them. What if they send someone else?"

"What are their plans, exactly?"

"I don't know. They kept me in the dark."

I started to disentangle myself from her limbs and the blankets. "I should get to them," I said, glancing at my clock on the nightstand. We'd been lying here all day. Evening approached.

Claire sat upright, wincing. She was probably still sore from her change last night. "I'm going with you."

"Better if you didn't," I said, pulling on my underwear. "I haven't talked to my pack yet. They think you're coming to play our scapegoat."

"I'm not going to let you face this alone," she said.

I opened my mouth to speak but a loud crash interrupted. I flinched. Someone kicked in my front door and just as quickly, footsteps sounded in the living room. I pushed Claire to the floor behind me, but as soon as the shadows appeared in the bedroom doorway something stung my thigh and I looked down at a tranquilizer dart.

The dart, the room, and the advancing figures spun out of focus as the ground rushed up to meet me.

They'd found me. I didn't expect them to come after me, but they had. Ginny landed beside where I lay, unconscious, and I threw myself over her to shield her from the red wolves that stalked into the room on their hind legs. Peter stood in the doorway with a tranquilizer gun. Peter, alpha of the Rothschilds.

Worse, Jules was there, too. I recognized her instantly: curly dirty-blond hair, firm short figure. She was only a few inches higher than five feet and, even so, she was strong. She'd had to quit rugby after she'd broken the clavicle of a woman twice her size.

The wolves came towards me. I didn't know what to do. I didn't have the instinct for this sort of thing. They grabbed my arms with their padded hands, hauling me to my feet. Naked, I shivered.

Lamplight glinted off Peter's glasses as he scanned the room. His short gray beard gave him a wolfish appearance even in his human state. He motioned to the wolves.

They pulled me along after him. One of them stooped and lifted Ginny, throwing her over its shoulder. Peter rummaged through Ginny's satchel until he found her cell phone.

"What are you doing?" I demanded.

"Breaking up your little love nest," Jules said, arms crossed. "You left me for *this*?"

My nostrils flared. "I left you because you used me," I said.

Jules jabbed a finger at my unconscious lover. "Like *she* isn't? You're just an infected to her." She stepped forward and pain registered on her face, if only briefly. "I'm sorry. I never should have let Peter talk you into this. But once this is over, we'll talk."

"Once *what* is over?" A chill crept up my spine as I watched the wolf carry Ginny out the door. I started to struggle but the other wolves manhandled me to a less mobile position. "What are you doing to her?"

"As much as I'd like to, I'm not doing anything. We take the Seeonee territory tonight." She sniffed at me. "You've already changed."

"If you hurt her, I'll—"

"You'll what?" Jules spread her arms, inviting me to explain. "You'll what, Claire?" She stepped towards me and touched my chin with her fingertips. I didn't have the freedom to recoil. "Don't you see how they were planning to use you?"

I did. Ginny had come clean with me about that. But that was Seeonee scheming. There was no way Jules could know. "You're lying," I said.

"Why would I lie to you?" Her hand moved from my chin and stroked my cheek.

"I don't know what you're talking about." I stiffened as I tried to turn my head away, and she dropped her hand.

"Then you're a bigger fool than Peter took you for." She took a step back. "The Seeonee were going to use you for murder and let the humans kill you for it."

I blanched. How did she know?

I didn't have time to think about it. Jules pulled a hypodermic out of her pocket and removed its plastic sleeve. The red wolves tightened their grip on my arms and one grabbed a fistful of my hair. Another held out my wrist.

The wolf inside my head snarled. "What is that?"

"A new batch of cocktail," she said.

She came at me with the needle but I struggled. The claws in my hair tightened and pain lanced up my spine. Jules grabbed my face and brandished the needle in my field of vision.

"You can hold still and let me administer this," she said with an undercurrent of a lupine growl, "or you can keep up the shenanigans and I'll jam it straight into your tear duct. Which will it be?"

Terrified, I held still. She grabbed my wrist, tapped the veins there with the back of her fingernail, and stuck me. The fluid spread up my arm like ice water.

Tingling followed the numbness and the wolf howled inside my head, trying to claw its way out. Every muscle cramped. I started to faint, but shook my head violently to clear my vision. The change was coming again, the pain still familiar from last night. "Why are you doing this!"

Jules waggled the empty syringe at me. "Test subject."

My skin crawled from beneath, as though she had injected me with a hive of angry bees. My legs faltered and the red wolves dragged me along as they followed Jules out of the apartment. I wanted to vomit. My head spun. Tingling spread to the rest of my limbs, my mouth watered and my vision tunneled. I forgot where I was.

Next I knew, I was dropped on my knees in the gravel of the driveway. I did retch, and felt a little better afterwards, except the drug was making my heart race and spots clouded my vision. I heard Jules's voice, painfully loud in my ears. "Did you make the call?"

The plastic click of a shutting cell phone was as harsh as a gunshot.

"Yeah," Peter said. "They barked my ear off. Pretty convincing, to their credit."

Footsteps on the gravel crunched like a coffee grinder. I wanted to cover my head but my arms wouldn't move. My shoulders, still aching from last night's disjointing, popped again and I blacked out as they readjusted.

"They'll come right to us," Peter said. I strained through the blurry vision and saw him crouch down beside Ginny. He stuck a needle in her arm. There were more wolves in the parking lot, at least a dozen that I could see.

Jules walked over to me, straddled me, and draped a loop of chain around my neck. I growled a deep, horrible sound at her and it shocked me that I'd made such a noise. I looked down at my hands, but black paws had replaced them. The pain and rage faded.

I was *conscious*. The change had come, and I was still conscious. This wasn't the same drug as before.

Jules tightened the chain and pulled my head up, but I felt her finger pressed against my nape, under the chain, to prevent it from choking me. She bent to my ear.

"I know you can hear me," she whispered. I couldn't see her and I tried to struggle, but she put a knee between my shoulderblades and yanked my head higher. "I know you can, Claire, so listen to me."

A car pulled up with a blaze of headlights. The doors opened and Mae got out, along with two of the Seeonee, who dragged out a fourth person in chains. He was a scruffy man, bruised and beaten, but he wore designer jeans and a nice jacket. His eyes widened when he saw us.

I tried in vain to sniff for Ginny, but Jules's quiet, urgent voice distracted me. "I told you I wasn't lying. I knew what Mae was planning to do with you because Peter told me. Just watch."

Peter sauntered to the car and, to my astonishment, kissed Mae. He put his hand on her swollen stomach. "How's our son?"

Mae's hand covered his. "Doing fine, sweetheart."

"Peter?"

The voice belonged to the shackled man.

"Peter, what's going on?"

"I'm sorry to do this to you, David," Peter said, putting an arm around Mae's shoulders. "But you're only human, after all."

I could hear David's panicked heartbeat.

Jules rested her other hand, the one that gripped the chain, atop my head. I thrashed but she was strong enough to hold me still. "That's the man you're supposed to kill," she whispered.

Mae appraised me with a glance, then nodded and asked, "How is Geneva?"

"Ready to wake up with a bad temper," Peter said. He glanced at his wristwatch. "When's the rest of your pack due?"

"Any minute."

"Good. Get your perfume ready," said Peter. He stripped out of his suit. The two Seeonee that had come with Mae did the same. One of them handed her the car keys.

"Remember," Mae told them, "These are our new packmembers. We can't have an all-out war. Attack only the dissenters."

"Including the Donnelly girl," Peter added. A shadow crossed Mae's face when he said that. "Do whatever's necessary to kill her when she comes after your alpha." He put his hands on Mae's stomach again. "We've got a new heir, combining the bloodlines."

I bristled. So, that was their plan all along. Unite the packs with deception, kill anyone who didn't accept it. We'd *all* been duped. I snarled, and when Mae caught sight of me she flinched. She said to Jules, "Is she feralized?"

"Yes," Jules lied. "She'll kill David like you want, as long as he's in her path when I unleash her." At that, the smell of David's sweat soured.

"Good," Mae nodded and turned back to Peter. "Good."

Howling sounded in the woods. I felt the immediate urge to answer, but Jules tightened the chain to prevent me. Peter stepped back from Ginny; she stirred and started spasming.

Mae stood back as Peter and the others changed. While they shifted, Jules bent and whispered quickly in my ear. "This has been in the works for a while, and I won't follow an alpha who lies to the pack. When I let you go, do whatever you think is right. But know this—the fight is coming." She hesitated. "I'm sorry I exposed you to this. I'm trying to make it right."

She stroked a hand down the side of my furry neck. Then she slipped the chain off and I heard her begin her own change, clothes ripping.

I did the one useful thing that occurred to me. I filled my lungs, reeled my head back, and howled.

Other howls responded, closer now. I strained to listen and heard them brushing against undergrowth in the woods. I howled again. A dozen gray wolves charged from the hedgerow into the gravel lot and bodies of red and gray clashed in growling whirlwinds beneath the brightness of the full moon. I couldn't tell which were loyal to the alphas and which were loyal to the packs.

Peter, now a huge red wolf with a dark muzzle, watched me. His fur twitched once, and half a heartbeat later he bolted for David, who'd been handcuffed to a parked car and was trying desperately to get away.

A small red wolf darted past me and hopped on Peter's back, biting at his face and snarling like a demon.

I ran to Ginny, who had changed and gnashed her teeth like she had gone mad, spittle flying from her mouth. She was bigger than me, the gray wolf. Her injured foreleg was still bandaged. I nosed towards her but she snapped at me and I backpedaled and then she saw Mae, the only human standing.

I smelled something foul and swiveled my ear towards Mae, hearing a hiss of aerosol. Mae sprayed something from a small perfume bottle. I bared my teeth at the rotting stench of vampire odor, but I was able to control my predatory urge to rush her.

Ginny wasn't.

She charged Mae. I blocked her path. I didn't want to hurt her but she snapped at my throat and got a mouthful of fur as I flinched away. I didn't want her to hurt *me*. I caught her on the injured foreleg and bit through the bandages; she yelped in pain and kicked me loose.

She rushed at Mae again.

I jumped on her back, letting instinct lead me, and clamped down on the back of her neck with my jaws. *Please*, I begged silently, *please stop*.

I held her with my teeth as the battle raged around us. Wolves stalked towards us but never reached us, either blocked by another dogfight or engaged in one by Jules's supporters.

Ginny raged beneath me like a gray hurricane, but I clamped down harder and prayed that she'd snap out of it. She was stronger than me but her leg was lame and I'd pinned her.

I had no idea how long the drug-induced rage lasted. I tried to think back to the video recording of last night. It hadn't lasted long, had it? Seemed like hours now.

My jaw ached, threatening to lock up. Ginny settled down and I must have dropped my guard because she wrenched free and spun on me, black lips peeled back from deadly fangs. I wasn't quick enough. She bit down on my throat and rolled me onto my back. Her growl vibrated against my neck.

She had me. I closed my eyes and waited for the inevitable crush of my windpipe. Or was it the jugular first? I clung to the memory of last night's tenderness. I wanted that to be my final thought in life. Joy, not pain, not betrayal.

The sounds of fighting faded around me, as did Ginny's growling. I squeezed my eyes shut.

Instead of oblivion, the jaws lifted and a wet nose pressed against my face a moment later. I wasn't dead. I squinted one eye open.

The gray wolf licked it.

When I regained consciousness, I had my jaws around a red wolf's throat. Was I fighting or asserting dominance? Not knowing frightened me.

The red wolf smelled like pine boughs and pumpkin seeds. *Claire. Oh, God.* I pulled away immediately and searched for signs she was all right. She seemed to be.

I scanned the area. Were we in danger? I smelled Seeonee, but other wolves too, and blood, and anger. A large black-muzzled male lay bleeding out beneath the shadow of a parked car. A human lay slumped and bleeding against the same car.

In the distance I saw another car's taillights receding and heard the boom of an accelerating engine. The stink of vampires faded in a whiff of car exhaust.

Claire nudged me to my feet, though my foreleg threatened to give way beneath me. She sniffed at my face and I smelled a mixture of worry and relief on her. She was a wolf but . . . she seemed aware. She wasn't impeded by her infection at all.

One by one, wolves—all except the dead—shifted back to human form, the moon's demand sated for another month. When I shifted back, I wobbled and sat in the dirt, my head swimming. Claire wrapped her arms around me and squeezed me so hard it almost hurt.

Almost.

I sat in the waiting room of the clinic while Ginny got dressed in the medical wing. The doctors had checked her thoroughly; she'd been so pumped full of drugs.

Jules came back from speaking with the toxicologist and sat on the plastic chair beside mine with a sigh. "Peter's dead and hell if I know where Mae ran off to. If we catch her, she's dead. But that's really Geneva's call."

I didn't know what to say. My first reaction was to protest talk of execution, but the world and its rules were different for me now.

"David is still alive," Jules added. "Infected. But if he wants our drugs, he's welcome to them. I doubt we'll see the human backlash Mae and Peter dreamed up."

"I've had enough of your drugs to last a lifetime," I said.

She nodded, not meeting my gaze. "But that's what I can offer you." She reached into the pocket of her torn jeans and pulled out a prescription bottle. "If you want them."

"More sedatives?" The wolf inside me bristled.

"No," she said, balancing the bottle on the armrest of my chair. "What I gave you tonight. Clarity of the natural-born. I can't take back what I did to you, but I can . . . I can make it easier."

"Thanks," I said quietly, not sure what else to say. I watched the others—Seeonee or Rothschild, in human form I couldn't tell them apart—filter out from the exam rooms. They looked tired, and sad. They stayed close together, like they were waiting for something.

"I am so sorry for everything," Jules said. She scrubbed her face with her hands, looking exhausted. "Jesus, what a day."

"Jules?"

"Hm?"

"Thanks," I said, and meant it. I squeezed her shoulder in gratitude and stood, going into the back of the clinic. I wasn't content to wait anymore.

Ginny came out into the sterile hallway. She smiled at me, that dimpled smile, and I couldn't wait the length of the corridor. I ran to her and threw my arms around her, claiming her mouth with a kiss. She wrapped her good arm around my neck and tangled her fingers in my hair.

"I had a feeling you were coming for me," she said.

"Jules has these pills," I blurted out. "She's going to offer them to infected were-wolves, to keep control during the change and I . . . I was wondering if . . . but I won't if you don't want me to pretend to be—" She gently tugged my hair, bit her bottom lip in a wicked grin, and I stopped rambling. "If you're going to be a Seeonee wolf," she said, "you might as well do it properly."

I smiled at that. I pushed her through the nearest door and when we were alone, she lowered her good hand to my hip and pulled me against her.

"Good to know you're not an elitist," I said.

I flicked off the fluorescent light and let our hands and noses and mouths take over in the ensuing darkness. My mate's scent bewitched me and I breathed it in: cinnamon, woodsmoke, and a November breeze.

THE SINEWS OF HIS HEART

MELISSA YUAN-INNES

Rachel Feng missed the funeral, but she still got to see her dead cousin while she was stuck in the back of a Chinese taxicab.

Cho, the deceased cousin, or at least his identical twin, signaled her from a white Range Rover in the right-hand lane of Harbin's main highway.

Rachel clutched her burgundy faux Prada handbag. Her damp fingers slipped off the cheap leather. This could not be happening.

On the other hand, a lot of weird crap had unrolled lately, from Rachel's newfound love for steak tartar to Cho's alleged funeral scheduled five hours from now. She'd recognize Cho's bulbous nose anywhere. It ran in the family and dominated Rachel's otherwise delicately-featured face. At least her nose wasn't cocked to the left, the way Cho's had remained after one too many fist fights.

Cho took a hard right and bumped to a stop on to the side of the road, which looked too narrow to handle a Range Rover, but a cyclist swerved around him like this was business as usual.

Rachel knocked on the Plexiglas separating her from the taxi driver. "Pull over, please," she called in English. He didn't turn around. All she could see was his well-trimmed, graying hairline, the weathered back of his neck, and the cigarette tucked in the corner of his mouth. She rummaged her brain for the correct Mandarin and finally dredged up a "Stop! Please!"

She pressed the lever to roll down her taxi window. Humid smog smacked her in the face. A woman's voice said, in English, "Please do not touch any button" and the window began to roll back up again.

"Stop! It's my cousin!" she yelled back in English, and through the glass, she called, "Cho! Is that you?" She jammed her arm into the remaining window gap, but when the glass kept rolling upward, she yanked her hand back and hammered on the Plexiglas taxi divider instead. "Let me out!"

The taxi crawled a few more feet on the highway. The woman's voice said, "I'm sorry. We have not yet reached your destination." Rachel had read somewhere that, since the 2008 Olympics, Beijing drivers used portable translators in their cabs. Too bad the translation only seemed to work one way. She craned her neck to stare out the back window.

Cho popped his door open and jumped out of the vehicle. She recognized the tilt of his head and the way he kicked the pavement, although he'd grown a little potbelly over the past fifteen years and he wore a camouflage hat and matching jumpsuit, like he was in the military.

It was him. Why the heck had she flown down for his funeral when he was alive and driving a Range Rover? Her aunt had said he'd been mauled by a tiger, which sounded so 18th century anyway. Maybe it was all an elaborate plot to get Rachel to fly from Canada to China? Or, more likely, Rachel was hallucinating after traveling for 24 hours?

She ripped open her wallet and grabbed some Chinese cash. She waved it at the driver and yelled, "Take it!"

He finally met her eyes in the mirror and rolled down the divider. "No," he said.

Something about his expression made her hesitate for a second. The whites around his dark irises. The lift of his eyebrows. Then she figured she must be getting heat stroke in the confines of this greasy little cab. She left the money on the seat and yanked on the door handle.

"Wait!" he said in Mandarin. "It's dangerous. You shouldn't be meeting a ghost."

She nearly laughed. She'd heard about Chinglish, that weird combination of Chinese + English = charming nonsense. But with her rusty Mandarin, she could make up Chinglish out of her own head. She opened the door.

The driver muttered to himself, but he finally wove his way on to the highway shoulder and popped open the trunk. She seized her luggage and wheeled it toward her cousin as fast as her running shoes would take her.

It was Cho. For sure. She spotted the scar under his left eyebrow from when he fell skateboarding, showing off in front of eight-year-old Rachel and her sister before their family emigrated. He'd developed a red nose and broken veins on his cheeks. Her aunt had never mentioned booze, but no doubt it had played a role in any alleged tiger mauling.

"Cho. I thought you were . . . " Dead. But the words locked in her throat. She felt all wrong in China, a Chinese girl who could hardly speak Chinese. She wished again her family could have come with her. She tried again. "It's good to see you, cousin." Nervousness bubbled in her stomach. A burning pain lodged behind her heart, even though she too young for heartburn. She pressed her hand to her heart. Her body seemed to rebel lately.

"Come on. I'll show you the tigers," he said.

"Tigers?" He spoke English with a Mandarin accent, so maybe she'd misunderstood him. Or maybe "tigers" was slang for how he talked about his family, the way English people would talk about bearding the lion in his den. "I'm on my way to, ah, see your mother and everybody else here." She showed him the printout of the funeral home information. He stared at the paper blankly. She was so punch-drunk tired, she wanted to say, *You're supposed to be dead. What happened to you?* Instead, she said, "Can you take me there? Do you want to come?"

"Come," he repeated, and jumped back into the Range Rover. He must have been lighter than he looked, because the vehicle didn't sink under his weight at all.

She hesitated for one more second. "Cho. Can you take me to see Auntie—"

"Come," he repeated, and revved his engine.

She tossed her own luggage in the back before she climbed beside Cho and dialed Auntie's number. It rang five times before it switched over to voice mail.

Meanwhile, Cho took the first exit off the highway and the signal faded.

Rachel cursed and texted Auntie instead. It slipped through the ether. "Cho picked me up. See U soon."

Auntie immediately texted back, but before Rachel could open it, the signal died again.

Rachel shoved her useless phone in her shorts pocket. "Do you have a phone?"

Cho lit a cigarette held between his lips while he held the wheel steady using his knees. Just when Rachel felt like lunging for the wheel and driving herself, the tip of the cigarette glowed orange, the smoke curled around his face, and Cho grabbed the wheel in his left hand. He said, "No."

Man. Who didn't have a phone in this day and age. "How far is it, anyway?"

Cho shrugged. "Nothing's far in Harbin."

Rachel squinted at the road signs, but most of them were in Chinese. All Rachel knew about Harbin was that it was located in the northeast corner of China, it was famous for its ice festival, and Cho's family had moved there almost ten years ago. Rachel had downloaded a map of the city, but Cho seemed to be taking the back roads and she couldn't read the calligraphy. She said, "Is this the way to the funeral home?"

Cho smiled around his cigarette. "Trust me."

After twenty-four hours of traveling, she really wanted to. She rolled down the window and closed her eyes.

The smoke curled in the cab, haloing Rachel's face, but somehow the tobacco didn't stink as much as it usually did. Muggy air drifted in from the window. Surprisingly, the weather in Harbin in August didn't seem all that different from Toronto.

A ghost, she remembered the taxi driver saying, but she pushed the thought away and flickered in and out of a dreamless sleep. At last, she woke up with a dull headache and a dry mouth. The moon rose behind clouds, but the sun still glittered in their rearview mirror. At least it was cooler, but hours must have passed.

This ain't no funeral home. She cleared her throat. "Cho. Can we stop for something to eat?"

No response. They hit a pothole and Cho steadied the wheel.

She reached for his sleeve, but he moved away before she made contact. She realized they hadn't touched each other, not even an air kiss. Which was okay—who knew how to greet a cousin you hardly remembered and never visited—but still.

"Cho? Food? Supper? I'm kinda dying here."

He didn't even look at her.

She unearthed an airline packet of pretzels in her bag and sipped her water. Soon the bottle would be empty and she'd have to pee. Either he'd let her out or she'd have to fight for the wheel. She laughed a little at the thought.

"Not long now," he said.

Rachel ran her hands over her arms. She'd waxed them before her trip, but the hair grew back thicker and faster, just like her girlfriends used to warn her before she started shaving her legs. Only, for the first time, her arm hair glinted orange, as if she'd hennaed it. So in the past two months, Rachel had transformed from the typical Chinese girl with minimal body hair to a ginger beast who paid regular visits to the esthetician but somehow couldn't make time to see a doctor to figure out whassup. Just one more sign that her life and her body careened out of control.

Rachel said, "I'm going to have to stop soon. Seriously." But her eyelids sagged again and she stretched out her legs, stifling a yawn.

Cho turned on the radio. Even though it was in Chinese, she understood words here and there. Like something about the full moon and were-tigers.

Cho changed the station to a hard rock station where a guitar wailed almost as loudly as a man yelled about his ex-girlfriend.

"Wait." Rachel pushed herself upright. Her shoulder ached from resting against the jouncing window. Her brain still rested in the foggy state between sleep and wakening. It felt like the worst hangover of her life. "What was that about *were-tigers*?"

Cho pushed the cigarette to the other corner of his mouth using only his lips. "Superstitious bullshit."

"I want to hear it." She fumbled for the radio buttons.

Cho pushed her hand away. It was the first time he'd touched her. His hands felt so cold, they hurt her skin. Like ice.

Like death.

Rachel rubbed her hand warm again. The guitar shrieked a solo above her pounding heart. She said, "What's the big deal?"

Cho snorted. "Nothing to know. You Westerners have your werewolves. We have were-tigers. Only old mothers believe in them." He smirked. He glanced at her. In the darkness, his eyes looked like obsidian.

"That's kind of cool, though," said Rachel. "I've never heard of them." She pulled out her iPhone, but it still showed no service. Too bad. She wanted to Google about were-tigers and take her mind off her increasingly creepy cousin.

"Next you'll be believing that our family is related to the tigers."

Rachel glanced at him sidelong. "Why would I think that? I think we're a lot closer to monkeys. Charles Darwin and all that."

Cho puffed on his cigarette. While Rachel waved away the smoke, he shrugged and said, "No reason. No one believes what the old mothers say, always crying about evil spirits roaming the earth."

Rachel stared at her phone. The battery showed only one bar power. She must've played too many tunes. "Do you mind if I plug it in?"

"Be my guest."

The converter for her phone charger fit in the Range Rover's socket, but the energy lines never perked up on her phone. And then Cho killed the music and said, "We're here."

Seconds later, Rachel looked up from her phone and smelled cat urine and dust.

Cho accelerated past a faux Chinese temple decorated with a banner sign in Chinese characters. A smaller sign staked into the ground declared this the HARBIN TIGER REFUGE.

"What the—" Rachel said. The hair on her head and yes, her arms prickled with danger. Evening had fallen around them like a shroud.

Cho reached toward a box mounted on his visor and pressed a button. A metal gate clanked open. He gunned his way through it.

Rachel said, "Cho. This isn't funny." In the distance, concrete barracks carved black outlines against the sky.

Above the thrum of the engine, an animal snarled.

Not just any animal. A tiger.

Rachel's heart nearly stopped.

"Get me out of here." Goosebumps rose on her arms. When she ran her tongue over her teeth, they felt too large and sharp for her mouth.

Cho pressed the gas pedal even harder. "No one wants to be here."

"Then why are you—"

A tiger answered. The most eerie sound of her life: a moan rose into the night air, sounding almost human yet thoroughly alien.

Rachel fumbled with the door latch, but she knew it was too late. Like the dumbass heroines in horror movies, she had just stumbled into the equivalent of facing down a murderer armed with nothing but cheerleader pom-poms. If she didn't break her bones jumping out of the car, a tiger would still maul her.

Cho had to be a foot taller and forty pounds heavier than her. She wished she had a gun.

She heard a snarl, the angry sound of a very large cat, and she had to work hard to control her voice. "Cho. I don't know if this is a game to you or what. But if you don't turn this car around, I am going to call Auntie and she will have your head."

He eased off the gas and puffed on his cigarette. Thank God. Her grip loosened on the door handle. Stupid Cho, still playing games even though he was thirty years old and he should know better.

The cigarette tip glowed a speckled red in the darkness. Smoke billowed out of his nose. Then he said, "Too late. The tiger already got it."

Rachel couldn't scream. The breath huffed in and out of her lungs in short, uneven breaths.

A low growl, almost subterranean, seemed to vibrate their vehicle. Cho accelerated into the darkness, toward the concrete barracks, "Stupid. They said the tigers aren't even good hunters. They take forever to kill a cow when a tourist pays for us to give them one."

"Are you telling me you're dead?" she asked in too high a voice. She lowered it. She smiled even though her lips and hands trembled. "Look. Cho. We're family. I came here for your funeral, okay? Let me go."

He huffed out a laugh, closing his lips around the cigarette. Then he ground the butt into the ashtray and hit the gas. "Yeah. You're family. Only family blood can save me now. A life for a life. Sorry, cuz."

This was what she understood: he wanted to kill her.

The barracks were only fifty feet away.

Thirty feet.

Twenty.

She could hear the tigers snarl. She could hear them pace. She could smell them, the sharp scent of urine, the heavy overlay of feces, and the stinging undercut of bleach, thoroughly foreign and yet somehow familiar.

She refused to die.

She refused to let this fucker, dead or alive, cousin or ghost, drive her to her doom.

She grabbed the base of the gear shift, under his fingers.

His hand closed over hers. His flesh felt cold and implacable.

Her fingers splayed open involuntarily, as if he'd shocked her with icy electricity.

She clenched her fist around the gear shift and tried to downshift. If she stalled the car, she might be able jump out without killing herself.

"An eye for an eye. A life for a life," said Cho. He plucked her fingers off the gear shift and crushed her hand in his arctic grip.

Tears sprang to her eyes. Only the terrible cold of his hand muted the pain.

"You had it easy in Canada. Now you might as well do some good, saving my life. Or afterlife." He chuckled, a hollow sound that frightened her as much as the tigers huffing in the background.

She didn't understand his blather, but she grasped the basics: he intended to kill her.

And he didn't have control of the gear shift.

She swung her free hand toward the gear shift and knocked it out of gear.

The engine whined. More importantly, the Range Rover suddenly slowed.

Cho swore and released her hand.

She laughed wildly and groped for the door handle,

He smashed his fist into her ear.

Pain.

She heard sobbing and realized it was coming from her own throat, but the sound seemed dampened beneath ringing in her ears.

Her right hand still flailed in the air, searching for the door handle, but between the tears in her eyes and the tinnitus, she was trapped for a few crucial seconds while he got the Range Rover under control and pulled up to the tigers' lair.

The bunker was actually a series of cages, like wire condominiums, one abutting the other, each holding a tiger or two or three.

A dozen pairs of eyes fixed on the Range Rover, glowing green in the headlights. Pacing tigers paused to evaluate the intruders. Sleeping tigers lifted their heads.

Rachel could hear them breathing. Some of them made funny, stacatto breath sounds.

One of them snarled. A short, angry rasp that rent the air and temporarily overrode the ringing in her ear.

Rachel caught her breath. The pain in her ear subsided a little. Cho said, "We don't feed the tigers a lot. Costs too much. Poachers can sell tigers for the cost of a bullet."

"So they're hungry," Rachel said stupidly. She wiped the tears out of her eyes, smearing them across her face.

A tiger moaned, a mournful and eerie noise that straightened Rachel's spine and made sweat pop out of her pores.

"Yeah," he said. "Don't worry. I'll take you to the one who killed me. She was fast."

Rachel grabbed the door handle and launched herself out of the vehicle.

She'd take her chances with the tigers.

Cho cursed, but she was already running, flying as fast as she could, away from the tigers, away from her crazy cousin. Back to the gate, which was illuminated by large fluorescent lights.

Night air plastered itself to her body. Her left ear still felt blocked. But she sprinted onward, even though she heard Cho curse and rev up the engine once more.

The Range Rovers headlights advanced on her, illuminating the road ahead of her as if he wanted to help.

The motor growled louder. And louder still.

Rachel came down hard on the side of her right foot, twisting her ankle. Pain lanced up to her knee. She fell on both hands and knees, screaming at the latest agony, but also furious at herself.

This was it. She might as well wear a sign that said "KILL ME, CHO! LET ME HELP YOU OUT!" She crouched there on skinned knees and bloodied palms, waiting for the Range Rover to mow her down.

Instead, she felt the full moon shine on her back.

Rachel had never felt the moonlight before, but tonight, it felt like a coolness washing over her body, a subtle hum in the air.

A blessing.

She felt her face recalibrate, the nose lengthen into a snout.

Fur sprouted out of her skin.

She could smell dirt and diesel and fear. She could detect traces of poultry and other game animals. She could feel the muscles lengthen in her shoulders and legs and her chest broaden.

A tail broke out through her hind end. Somehow, that was the most painful part.

She screamed again, half in terror and half in jubilation. Her brothers and sisters gnashed their teeth and roared in their bunker.

Rachel Feng. Were-Tiger.

Cho roared behind her, scant meters from her tail.

Rachel began to run. Slowly at first, but gathering speed, her paws pushing into the pavement, her legs springing into the air.

Her ankle gave a starburst of pain every time she landed on it, but she tucked the pain deep inside her and raced off the road.

She wove around the sparse trees. The Range Rover bounced after her, but she could her it slow down, crashing around rocks, grinding its gears.

Tiger Rachel smelled water. Real water. A pond. She veered south, racing toward the pond.

Human Rachel dimly remembered her grandmother saying that ghosts had trouble crossing water.

Human Rachel also thought water might slow down the Range Rovers.

One, two, three more leaps and—splash! Into the pond.

The cool water made her yelp with shock, but she waded into its depths. The muddy bottom soothed her ankle a little but slowed her progress. The pond was only about fifty feet across and no higher than her chest, tangled with reeds. Still, she picked her way to the middle of the pond.

The Range Rover bumped to the edge of the pond. Cho killed the engine, so now all Rachel could hear was the sound of her breathing and her limbs moving restlessly in the water.

Although the wind blew away from Rachel, she could still smell something putrid waft from the vehicle. Death. Putrefaction. She no longer doubted that her cousin had died and, for whatever reason, he wanted to kill her, too.

Cho called to her. "Rachel. Rachel." His voice sounded like honey, warmer than her grandmother and more alluring than a lover.

Involuntarily, Tiger Rachel moaned, a mournful, eerie return call, less controlled than a wolf's howl.

"Here, kitty, kitty," Cho said, in English.

She took a step toward him. Her paws splashed through the water before she stopped herself, breathing hard.

"I will take care of you," said Cho. "You don't have to worry any more."

Rachel closed her eyes. She swished her tail through the water, tracing a figure eight. Why was she so drawn to him?

"Kitty," said Cho again.

Rachel's ears rose toward his voice.

"Come with me or you will die and they will throw your body in cold storage with hundreds of other dead tigers. They will make tiger wine out of your bones and sell your meat in the caféteria. They will sell your whiskers on eBay."

Rachel's tail swished from side to side. Human Rachel remembered eBay.

"Come with me. I'll take you home."

Rachel took another step. Twenty more steps and she would mount the muddy banks of the pond.

Cho popped open the back door of the Range Rover. "It's big enough for you here. I trust you. I know you won't hurt me. I'm your flesh and blood. I love you."

The moon shone on his face, making him look pale and innocent. She took another step.

The wind shifted slightly and she smelled rotting flesh again.

Her mouth opened and she grimaced, forcing the smell into the cavern of her mouth so she could explore it.

Decay.

Betrayal.

She snarled. No, she'd never go back to this rotten man, this ghost, no matter how much his words seduced her.

Cho recoiled from her sound. Good. He was frightened. Perhaps he'd search for easier prey.

Instead, he reached into the back of his truck and pulled out a gun.

Rachel gasped a breath into her tiger lungs and ducked under the water. She didn't dare swim away. Any movement would help him track her,

Underwater, she couldn't hear his lulling voice.

Underwater, she couldn't breathe.

How long could tigers hold their breath?

One Mississippi.

Two Mississippi.

By the time she arrived at fifty Mississippis, she had to raise her snout above the water line.

A bullet zinged past her nose and splashed into the water.

She gasped and ducked underwater again. Human Rachel remembered Auntie bragging that Cho was an excellent shot. He could kill her.

Heck, the pond was so shallow that even a terrible shot could aim a dozen bullets in her direction and hasta la vista, baby.

But he wasn't killing her. Why?

He wanted her to get back in his Range Rover.

He wanted to present her to the tiger who'd killed him and let it kill Rachel.

He wanted to sacrifice her. Somehow, he thought it would help him, or at least his foul spirit.

She hunched her body close to the pond bottom and began skulking away from Cho.

The pond grew shallower as she worked her way to the opposite bank. Her ears poked out of the water. She heard the Range Rover paralleling her progress and retreated into the center of the pond.

A bullet zinged by her left whisker. She plunged into the water again.

When she surfaced, gasping for breath, she heard the Range Rover drive away.

Had Cho given up? It seemed unlikely. And yet Rachel took the opportunity to breathe deep the night air. Never had it smelled so sweet, even though her own death hung like a specter in the air. How could she escape from this concentration camp for tigers?

Should she bolt for the main gate? But how could she cross it, without Cho's transmitter? And even if she did escape, would she remain a tiger or revert to human once the sun rose?

All too soon, the Range Rover roared back toward the pond. Cho's laughter drifted toward her on the night wind. But instead of firing another shot at her or luring her with his voice, he killed the engine and leaned against the vehicle.

He lit a cigarette.

Rachel ducked underwater once more. When she resurfaced, the breeze wafted toward her and she smelled tiger.

She paused and sniffed again.

It was not Rachel's own changed body smell, but the ripe scent of a mature female tiger who had been caged too long and fed only a few stringy chicken necks in the past two days.

Cho could not cross the pond water. But a tiger could.

He had unleashed the killer tiger on Rachel.

Cho held his cigarette between two fingers and yelled, "See ya, cuz! No hard feelings!"

Rachel kept her ears and eyes above the water. She wanted to see how many tigers would come after her. Cho had said the female who killed him was very fast, but the others were inept.

She half-expected the tigers to ring the pond and then, at some feline signal, attack her at once. She probably still smelled human, at some level; she could still think in words, after all.

But she could see nothing except the Range Rover bleached by moonlight and Cho's eternally smoking silhouette.

She finally spotted something crouched on the ground. Even in this quasi-forest, with just rocks and the occasional tree as camouflage, she would have missed this hunkered figure watching her from about one hundred feet away.

"Get her!" Cho yelled suddenly. "Go on! Kill her and let me be!"

Still, the figure huddled close to the ground.

Rachel tried to remain still in the pond water. She would have run except she was lame and at least in the water, one of her enemies was held at bay.

Slowly, slowly the killer tiger wove its way to her. Not racing like a lion, or even stalking proudly like a housecat, but creeping close to the ground. Even Rachel's tiger eyes and ears could barely detect it creeping toward her, padding soundlessly on its paws, its stomach certainly brushing the ground. It wove from rock to tree to rock, making its way to her.

"Finally," Cho muttered.

Although Rachel knew she had to concentrate on the tiger, she glanced at her cousin, leaning against the Range Rover.

Rachel edged closer to Cho, even though it brought her closer to the killer tiger. Cho spat at the ground and laughed.

The killer tiger sidled closer. Fifty feet. Ten feet.

Rachel would fight to the death in this pond. Even if the end came very fast.

The killer tiger crouched at the mouth of the pond, partially hidden by the reeds. For just a moment, the killer eyes gleamed green in the moonlight.

Then it sprang silently at Rachel, mouth open, teeth bared.

At the same moment Rachel burst out of the pond. She landed in the reeds. Her ankle protested, but not too badly; Rachel had managed to land with most of her weight on her other three paws. She was learning.

Meanwhile, the killer tiger landed in the pond with a splash.

And Rachel raced toward Cho, who dropped his cigarette and fumbled for the door of the Range Rover.

The killer tiger snarled. Rachel heard it splashing in the pond.

Rachel sprang at Cho's throat.

He was a ghost, but he could touch Rachel, so he was solid and therefore vulnerable.

Cho managed to thrust open the door of the Range Rover, but Rachel's teeth cut into the muscles of his shoulder and he stumbled.

Cold. Cold flesh. It numbed her teeth. Her head ached. But she could taste her cousin's blood, ever so faintly. It maddened her.

He fought to enter the carapace of his car, but she sank her teeth deep and ripped the flesh off his back.

He screamed and fell on his back, pulled down by the force of her attack.

The hunter-tigress landed beside her, but Rachel didn't pause. She surged forward and sank her teeth into Cho's throat. Her teeth clicked together inside his flesh and she reared her head backward, lifting his body off the ground before his neck vertebrae snapped, the neck muscles ripped apart and his body flopped to the ground.

Rachel tore open his abdomen and swallowed the pink sausages of his intestines. She licked the urine out of his bladder like it was a fleshy chalice. She chewed his still-beating heart, the blood squirting out sideways.

She gorged herself until she could eat no more.

She opened her eyes and saw Cho's decapitated head. Its face was spattered in blood, but his open eyes and mouth were frozen in a rictus of horror.

And the killer tigress snarled.

Rachel backed away from Cho's corpse, hoping the tigress would consume Cho's easy flesh rather than attack Rachel again.

But the tigress ignored Cho's body. Instead, she fixed on Rachel with her eyes gleaming iridescent green.

And Rachel received a picture of tigers pacing in their cages, surrounded by mounds of feces and even dead tiger corpses the authorities hadn't bothered to clear away. She saw human hands wringing a deformed baby tiger's neck. She saw mounds of tiger corpses in a deep freeze, their eyes dull, their flesh collapsing, with only their black stripes to identify them.

And Rachel understood. The killer tigress would allow her to live only if Rachel helped these tigers.

Rachel tried to transmit a picture back. A picture of herself in her favourite red dress and heels and faux Prada handbag. She thought, "I'm not a tiger! I can't help you!"

The hunter-tigress sent more images. A giant green glass vat, filled to the brim with a clear liquid. Rachel couldn't read the Chinese characters, but the full-sized skeleton in the vat spoke for itself: an adult tiger. Tiger wine.

This was the tigers' fate. Unless Rachel stepped in.

Rachel huffed. It was the first time she tried to speak "tiger," but she wanted to convey her understanding.

"I'll try," Rachel thought, and moaned aloud.

When the moon disappeared and the sun rose, perhaps Rachel would remain a tiger, imprisoned in this tiger concentration camp or shot as Cho's second murderer.

Or, when the sun rose, Rachel might revert to human form and the killer tigress might kill her.

But if she didn't, Rachel could appropriate the Range Rover and dump its owner's body before maneuvering her way back to Harbin and negotiating an end to this tiger concentration camp. Rachel could let the tigers in and out of their cages, thanks to the keys hanging on Cho's belt. And if Rachel found a legitimate piece of land, somewhere the tigers could live and feed one day, in dignity . . .

The hunter-tigress walked away from Cho's body, back to the pond. She sniffed the water and began to lap it up.

Rachel joined her. The water tasted like algae and dirt and something entirely different: hope.

(NOTHING BUT) FLOWERS

NICK MAMATAS

Amber's two greatest obstacles, she decided, were her journal which she still wrote in every night, though she had no light and didn't bother checking what she had written during the day when she could actually see the pages, and the gasoline she used to keep warm when it got very cold in the tree house.

She was conflicted about using tampons instead of moss, even though the pack had all talked about it and consensed that the tampons were okay, so long as they were shoplifted. Nobody liked blood. And that put Amber on shopping duty, which led her back to the gas, which she actually had to buy after working the sign, and little notepads and pens. There was something sexist about all of it, she was sure—the boys got to spend more time in the woods and didn't have to think about her period except when one of them was horny for her at the wrong time, and they used most of the gas for direct action, which she was not enthusiastic about anymore.

Then there was the whole idea of even thinking about *obstacle*. And sexism. More symbolic thought bullshit. Amber wrote all this down in the dark of her platform—there was a big gibbous moon tonight but the canopy of the woods blocked most of it and the light pollution from the city. Amber decided that in the dark symbolic thought didn't count so much because she could never really be sure that the letters she wrote in her cramped hand would ever be legible to anyone, even herself.

The branches rustled and "Hey" said a voice and Amber said back, "Hey Berg."

"How did you know it was me?"

"You still smell of soap," Amber said. "In the dark, things are easier to smell. I'm sure you smell me."

He laughed, nervous. "Sorry about that." Berg, on his hands and knees awkwardly crawled over to Amber and nuzzled, finding her dreds, her neck. She wrapped her limbs, all four of them, around Berg's skinny torso, and then bit into his shoulder. First, playfully, but she didn't stop till after Berg yelped and tried to squirm away.

"That a no?" Berg asked.

Amber grunted.

"That a no-symbolic-thought thing?"

In the dark, Amber shrugged extensively enough that Berg could make out the gesture.

"I guess I don't get that part of it. Didn't you come here because of a theoretical realization? Zerzan? Jensen? *Species Traitor*?"

"You did," Amber said. Neither Berg nor Amber said anything for a minute or so after that.

"Amber?"

"I'm deciding."

Wind through the branches. Some shuffling around. You could almost hear the blood in their bodies, coursing.

"Okay." Berg surged forward and got fingernails to his cheek from it.

"Okay I'll tell you. Want to check out a copy of *Proletarian Worker*?"

"Huh?"

"It was a negative dialectic." She giggled. Redwood went on about negative dialectics all the time. The term had become a joke amongst the pack. "I was a socialist in school. Sold the paper every Saturday, went to demos and meetings all the time. Always tabling at the student union, sending around petitions, standing up in class and denouncing marginal economics or sociobiology or old Maoist professors for not being the Trotskyists. You know, the usual."

"Yeah, of course. *PW* is like blight. They were always trying to take over movements and coalitions and the paper was so awful."

"I know, I know," Amber said. "Anyway, one time we had this educational on black self-determination and one of the comrades during her talk mentioned that in Haiti during the slave rebellion of 1791 the battle flag of the rebelling slaves was a white baby impaled on a pike."

"Yeah . . . " Berg said.

"Yeah, so anyway, after the meeting—and you know it was all white people—everyone was all like, 'Yes, that's us. We can do that if we had to.' And half the comrades couldn't even get up on time to sell the paper on Saturdays at the park, and their dues were always late, and none of them ever did their reading and—"

"So? You sound like an MBA or a sorority sister planning a bake sale." Something flew at Berg. He jerked his head to the side and it flew past him.

"Shut up," Amber said. "No, it was just all the lies, all the posing. And I was doing it too. They were lying to themselves, to me, to one another. 'Yeah, kill that white baby and wave his ass around.' Could I do it? No, I didn't think so, and I didn't think any of the comrades could either. It wasn't authentic, we didn't *really* feel that kind of rage. That dead baby didn't belong to us—it was just a symbol of how everyone was going to be a hero of the revolution one day. So I quit. The party and symbolic thought. Well, the best I could."

"And then?"

"And then I met Salmon and he turned me on to primitivism and consensus politics and then after we both dropped out of State we came here and made a platform. I always loved nature, wasn't one of those boring 'political vegans', so it fit. We were both looking for something, Salmon and me, though he was further along of course. It wasn't horizontal recruitment. Anyway, after the electricity got cut off in his apartment, we took it as a sign—into the woods."

"Yeah."

"Yeah."

"But mostly with the honesty. I like that."

"Cool," Berg said. "So anyway, if we're not going to fuck, I guess I'll go fuck some shit up now."

"Okay," Amber said. "See ya."

"Coming?"

"No. I mean, yeah, go ahead. Trash that shit. I don't want to tonight. That's what's freedom all's about, right?"

Berg and Redwood and Salmon met at Berg's little lab—Berg had a survival tent covered haphazardly in leafy branches on ground level, a camp stove, and a pair of repurposed saucepans. Other things too. He'd come with them, just the month before. Sometimes it takes a bit for the shell of civilization to slough off, but for now he was allowed his technology provided he put it toward the ends of the movement. With Amber's gasoline and a few bars of shoplifted soap from a Dollar Tree, Berg prepared the napalm. The little pots made for an okay double boiler. Some water was heated in the lower boiler as Berg shaved the soap. Then, off the stove and onto a rock, quick *quick* before the water cools. The gasoline into the top boiler and then the soap—a 1:1 ratio. A drizzle of gas, a tiny tongue of soap. Stir with a thick twig. Some more gasoline, a handful of soap shavings sprinkled like mozzarella cheese through Berg's fingers. Stirring and stirring, the liquid grew viscous and thick. Twice more, three potfuls, six Mason jars. Rags dipped in spilled gas. Two jars to a man, held in pockets of military surplus jackets. Salmon had the matches; he kept them in his boot.

They walked to the lip of the highway without a word except for Redwood who said, "Don't fall down with this shit in your pockets," and they didn't. The highway was a target-rich environment. Berg and Salmon took off to the left though Salmon found the first fork onto a service road and walked down it. Redwood to the right. To the Ford dealership, rich with oversized trucks and SUVs. There were some Fusions too, but they'd burn like the rest. To a Starbucks, closed with chairs on the tables. And Redwood, always a bit madder than one should be and taller as well, to a gas station. Shell, those butchers of the Ogoni people, stranglers of the world. An open one, though no cars were at the pumps. Redwood went to the little booth and knocked on the Plexiglas. He had to bend down to make eye contact with the employee, a kid. High school. No stake in the system, even if he didn't realize it. Redwood had the words FUCK YOU scrawled in oil across his forehead, his cheeks, his nose. There'd be security camera footage and photos, but they wouldn't be published everywhere at least and the published pics would have to be airbrushed, Photoshopped, and some detail would be lost.

"I've got a gun under here," the kid said. Bored kids are always very interested in potentially getting to shoot somebody.

"You're going to shoot me for the privilege of staying in a cold plastic box pumping gas for rich bastards for your junk food money?" Redwood asked. "Here, I'll help you out with that." A lighter from his left hand pocket, the first jar, an oily rag through the hole in the top from his right, a casual backwards toss and Redwood started running because he heard the crash of broken glass, his long legs taking him out into the road. For kicks, Redwood lit the other rag, threw the second jar behind his back, and ran. Jellied fire spread across two lanes of blacktop faster even than Redwood's long legs could take him.

In the trees, Amber almost slept to the sounds of helicopters flying low, to the knives of spotlights sweeping through the forest, setting night birds to fly.

When Redwood wasn't around the next morning, the band decided rather quickly that of course he had been captured by the police and was now being held as a political prisoner in the county lock-up.

"What are we going to do?" Berg asked.

"What do you mean *do*?" Salmon asked.

"You know, contact sympathizers, hold a demo, do basic prison support work?"

"Ha!" Amber said, "that's herd thinking, not pack thinking." Salmon had told her something similar about a month prior, when she wondered if the crew couldn't liberate extra food during their Dumpster diving expeditions and deliver them to the homeless. *We're homeless*, Salmon had pointed out. *But we're a pack, not lone wolves and not a herd.*

"Well, what if the pigs come after us, if Redwood tells them about us?" Berg asked. Amber didn't know what to say to that. "You can't live a free life in prison, pretty much by definition. I mean if freedom were just an individual subjectivity, you could be 'free' taking English literature courses or interning at Google."

"So? We're out here trying to be free; we're not looking to free everyone else, or even anyone else," Salmon said. "In fact, you're going to have to face facts, we'll need a massive population crash in the first place to really experience freedom. It's civilization and its diseases and wars that'll bring that about. Our job is to survi—"

"Then why the hell did I napalm half a dozen Hummers last night?" Berg threw up his arms. His voice was birdy and shrill. "With that logic, the best thing I can do for the cause of human freedom is go to work for Exxon or Blackwater, I could—"

The boys argued. *Free free free.* It was all symbolic thought, Amber realized quickly enough, but underneath the rhetoric was something else. Monkey rivalry. Chest-bumping and displays. Or mating calls, birdsongs. But then the symbolic thought. After that comes the division of labor—we fuck shit up, you stay here. Then agriculture. Domestication of the wolves who comes too close to the fire. Stories of spirits in the wind, of dead ancestors. Scratch out a language on the sides of rocks. Better build a temple. And from there pharaohs and slaves, kings and peasants, CEOs and transfats and Twitter and smokestacks, and we're all prisoners of civilization. Now the only thing left to do is wonder whether the planet will die in a nuclear holocaust, or if the melting icecaps will drown the soldiers in their ICBM silos first. Amber wandered off, not to her platform, but just to go out deeper into the woods to be really human. What was that line—*Running on emptiness.* Get out there and be, and don't think about what "be" means.

Amber heard the police in the woods. They were easy enough to avoid. They stumbled over twigs and leaves, their communication devices crackled and whined. She didn't bother trying to divine their motives or outthink them. They were just other noises, loud ones to walk away from. Soothing ones beckoned and she found a stream and followed it, feet wet on the rocks, a careful leap over the branch-dams of the beavers. There were smells too, obvious ones. Plastic and cooked meat. Amber had eaten nothing but berries and mushrooms and the occasional hastily stolen Hostess Cupcake jammed into her mouth whole during the latest shoplifting spree. Her stomach growled.

There was a family—little Asian girl in purple with giant boots, white parents in colors they probably didn't even realize matched the environment. Khaki pants like the dirt of the clearing, green and brown tops. Camouflage by way of accident of demographics and fashion trends. They had tents, fancier than Berg's, and a camp stove, fancier than Berg's, and some solar power contraption that was probably also a stove but didn't seem to work right as the father was hunched over it, and the parents both had the white cords of iPod headphones hanging down their torsos. They were silent. The girl played with leaves, the mother was fuming about something with her chin high and hands on her hips. Amber realized that there should be four, not three. A boy, slightly older, cartoons on his sleeping bag. They weren't food, they weren't anyone she could talk to, they weren't threatening her with violence as the police did simply by existing and by marching through the woods with their sticks and their guns and their dogs, so she left the family behind.

The sun had moved into the orange of afternoon when Amber heard the yawp and the thrashing about that attracted her attention next. It had been hours, though she wasn't aware of the passage of time except when the shouting brought her back into the world of symbolic thought, and then only because it was so ironic. If there was anything at all left of humanity after tens of thousands of years of civilization and symbol-making that could be considered real and pure and true, it was a scream of fear. A boy's voice, broken like a girl's from shock and rage, and then there were echoes. Responses. A woman's voice shrieked, "Jeremy!" and the woods grew restive.

Amber had heard screams before. When Salmon had twisted his ankle. When Redwood and her were up on her platform fucking like wolves. The day before Berg had found the pack, when he was tramping through the forest shouting both parts of the fight with his father that had sent him into the woods with his camping gear and a dog-eared copy of *Future Primitive*. He screamed again when Salmon had torn it apart in front of his face. But this scream was different. It hadn't been swallowed up by the echoless trees and hills. The police were alive in the woods now, shouting again through megaphones and amplifiers. The woman couldn't stop shrieking *Jeremy!* The little girl was whooping too, like a bird.

Amber didn't even mean to walk toward the first scream—why would she? But she strode right into it. Not in a clearing, but in a tight clump of the thick-trunked trees, where the woods were dark. And she saw the boy. And the boy held a stick. And at the end of the stick was much of an eye. And just a foot or so beyond the tip of the stick was Redwood, his face wrinkled and brown like bark, a gouge where his eye had been, his lipless mouth open wide. He gasped when he saw Amber, and Amber's knees buckled from the stench of cooked meat. The boy dropped the stick and his smile and ran. Amber vomited into her hands. Redwood tried to talk but the scream was all he had. He keened, a lung pushing air through a scored and warped tube of flesh. In his remaining eye was a message. A glare. Amber noticed that his eyelashes, which she always liked because they were long like she was always told a girl's should be, were gone.

Amber had gone back for her journal, and that is what saved her. Despite the copter and the chain of police and volunteers—mostly portly militia types with barely legal firearms slung uselessly across their backs—marching in a long single file across the woods, she was huddled on her platform and missed. The boys had been picked up. Arson. Redwood was dead, or probably was anyway. There was nothing to keep her. The next morning she dropped from her platform, cut off her dreds with a sharp rock, and moved into town. There were enough crusties on the street to blend in with and she was a pretty girl, even with a haircut by hack. The city was easy. Dumpster dive behind the yuppie supermarket, wash in the library, spread for someone when it rained, and huff and write in her journal with her eyes closed. She showered a lot, standing in a puddle of black water, till she smelled like soap, smelled like Berg.

It was hard for Amber to get used to talking all the time, to street signs and clothing with logos on them. The world was a huge advertisement for itself, and it stank.

Amber spent most of her days outside the county courthouse in the part of town that was all pillars and thick slabs of concrete from the old days, and littered with the homeless and ratty fast food joints from the now. She was a protestor, though the sign she held up was incomprehensible. She chanted, with the few other people who had rallied around Salmon and Berg, "Free Berg!" was a popular chant, and someone on an acoustic guitar had come up with some new lyrics to the old Lynyrd Skynyrd song. They had destroyed some property, but not very much, and hadn't hurt anyone. Even Redwood had only hurt himself.

A thin man with significant sideburns asked Amber if she wanted to check out a copy of *PW*. Amber opened her mouth to tell him no when she saw the little Chinese girl, her knees high as she climbed the steps to the courthouse. She was on a leash and holding it was the mother. The father was there too, his hand clamped hard on the wrist of the boy who had once held a stick that had once been tipped with a man's eye.

"Yeah, please," she said.

The guy sidled up to her and opened to a two-page spread. "I wrote this article," he explained. "It's about how we, you know, reject anti-civ anarchism as fundamentally playing into the hands of the capitalists."

"Wow."

"Yeah, it's just giving up the fight. Individual acts of terror just bring state repression, *and* the fact is that we have seven billion people on this planet. If we all lived like hunter-gatherers, there would be a huge population crash. The only reason the bourgeoisie keeps the proletariat alive is because they don't want to do any work themselves, and—"

Amber grabbed the paper. "Thanks. I'll read it myself."

"Okay, well we have meetings too . . . " he reached into his messenger bag for a leaflet. Amber grinned inside. The local socialists were still a revolving door of stupid freshmen—she knew this shtick down cold.

"And that's a dollar, by the way." He tapped the edge of the paper. "What kind of socialist *sells* a newspaper?" Her eye wandered to the parking lot.

He nodded. "Yeah, well, see. The paper isn't free. We live under capitalism, after all, and the printing press isn't a worker collective, yet. Plus, when you just give out papers for free people don't read them. When they pay a dollar, and some people even pay *five* to support the movement—"

"Look asshole, I'm not paying you a fucking dollar!"

He tried to grab the paper back but he was weak and Amber strong. She darted away from him and grabbed his messenger bag. "Paper for the people!" Amber shouted, and she flung the bag in the air. It rained copies of *Proletarian Worker* and then she kicked the socialist right in the knee, making his leg buckle. The other protestors cheered and then the cops, always itching for a chance to use their truncheons, were on them, but Amber was already gone.

Amber wasn't worried. She wasn't hopeful either. She was wedged in the hatch area of the SUV, one much nicer than civil servants could afford, and whose hood was hot to the touch. Unlocked too. Careless parents, the parents of that Chinese girl, of the boy with the stick. Had Amber been thinking, she would have even thought herself clever for showering and taking care of herself these past few days—surely she would have smelled like rotten wood and ripe human and filled the vehicle with fumes otherwise. Stink lines rising from the top of cartoon garbage can. She took a deep breath. Nothing but flowers. Not even a thought. No thought, no obstacles. Amber was beyond good and evil now, beyond boredom and engagement for that matter. She had her journal and the moon was full even as the sun still stood over the horizon. Plenty of light, but even she couldn't read what she had written in her time living outside. There was something in those glyphs and strokes though, something older the words, older than symbols. Just what she had been wanting all along.

The family was sedate when they got in the car. The boy—Jeremy, but Amber didn't think things like "Jeremy" now—wasn't with them anymore. It didn't matter. The drive seemed long. The sun had gone down and the moon sailed away, as if Amber was being taken around the curve of the world, away from the city and into the woods. But the trees she saw out her window were slaves of lawns, Holocaust survivors forced forever to mourn for their brethren whose bodies made their own coffins. Homes. McMansions. The car parked.

The parents got out and collected the sleeping little girl from her car seat and took her away. The girl stared at Amber but didn't say anything.

Amber slid out of the SUV easily enough and landed on her hands and knees. Everything smelled wrong. There were sounds, real ones. A breeze and crickets, but false sounds were more insistent. Tinny laughter. The buzzing of lightning trapped in wire cages. Wind in walls. She loped toward the family's home and peered through the window when she reached it. They were watching TV, but it was all just flashes of color to her. She could smell them through the glass, smell how hot they were. Amber did have a final pair of symbolic thoughts before she threw herself through the window and took the child by the neck in her mouth and crunched, one last bit of culture before she finally sloughed off all that she had been like dirt on skin.

This is a fairy tale!
And I'm the hero!

THE COLDEST GAME

MARIA V. SNYDER

The screech of a small child being tortured woke Lexa. At least, that was what her alarm sounded like at four in morning. *I feel your pain, girlfriend*, she muttered under her breath as she swatted the clock before her roommate could growl.

Why? Why did I ever volunteer for the five a.m. shift? Lexa asked herself this every single Friday morning. The answer remained the same. *Because I'm an idiot and fell for Ben's bullshit claim that the morning shift is the most exciting. It wasn't.*

Grabbing her shower basket, she schlepped to the bathroom down the hall. Her choice of shower stalls remained the best thing about this time of day. *Ah, dorm life.*

After a scalding-hot shower, Lexa returned to her room. She dressed in the dark—jeans, sneakers, and a shapeless navy Penn State hoodie. Twisting her long brown hair into a knot, she tucked it under a navy baseball cap before leaving.

An early November fog blanketed the silent campus. Street lights reflected off the white mist. No one around—the only time Penn State's main campus was this quiet. It matched her gloomy mood.

She'd been in a funk since Lauren, her younger sister had been killed by a drunk driver over Memorial day weekend. It deepened when Jason, her boyfriend of three years dumped her in September. Now failing thermodynamics, Lexa thought she'd never see daylight again.

Lexa headed toward the Walker Building on the western edge of campus. At least she had her own key now. Last week Ben had forgotten his, and they had botched the forecast in their haste. A couple radio stations had complained. *What did they expect anyway? They were getting free weather forecasts from a bunch of student meteorologists after all.*

When Lexa cut through West Halls, a strange icy feeling slipped down her spine. The campus was relatively safe, but her imagination conjured up all those horror movies that Jason had dragged her to see.

Perhaps she should have arranged for a security escort—some jock doing his good deed for the day, but she'd never felt unsafe on campus until now. She dismissed her anxiety as a product of her overdramatic imagination.

Just before she entered the short cut between Irvin Hall and Jordan Hall a low anguished growl emanated from the shadows. Logic urged her to run. But she savored the feeling of fear for a moment. Since Lauren's death, she'd been going through the motions of living, trying to keep the painful storm of grief contained inside her. She felt nothing else.

Lexa lingered a moment too long. A black mass launched from the shadows. She fell back, banging her head on the cement as the heavy beast landed on her chest. In a flash, white pointy teeth dug into her neck. Burning pain squeezed her windpipe closed.

Black and white spots clouded her vision. Then the creature paused. It released her and bounded away as fast as it had appeared. She caught a glimpse of a four legged creature with gray fur stripped with black. *A big fucking dog.*

Blood gushed from her throat, soaking the collar of her hoodie. Dizziness and nausea swelled as she explored the ragged skin. A strange concern over the location of her cap floated through her mind before she passed out.

Unfamiliar voices woke Lexa. She squinted into a bright whiteness. The antiseptic smell matched the room's décor—curtains hanging from a U-shaped track on the ceiling, florescent lights, and cabinets with glass doors.

Lexa touched her neck. Bandages covered her throat. A sharp ache pulsed from underneath the dressing.

The curtains parted and a tall young man entered. He skidded to a stop in surprise. Large splatters of blood covered his ripped white Penn State T-shirt and dotted his white sweat pants. Lexa's first thought—college student was followed by—jock.

"You're awake," he said.

"Who . . . " Her voice rasped painfully.

"Don't talk . . . Wait." He dashed away, calling to another.

A nurse bustled in and Lexa wondered if nurses ever just walked or sauntered. The student trailed after her. Concern creasing his forehead, he raked his fingers through his short spiky black hair.

"What—"

The nurse cut her off. She sent the student to the waiting room before asking Lexa questions. Lexa explained about the oversized dog. It didn't take long.

"Was the dog foaming at the mouth?" she asked.

A vision of sharp teeth flashed in her mind. "No."

"We'll test for rabies just in case." The nurse clicked her pen and wrote on her clipboard. "Miss Thomas, you're in the Mount Nittany Medical Center's emergency room. You have a mild concussion and four lacerations in your neck. We put in sixty sutures, administered a tetanus shot, and contacted your parents."

She groaned. *Mom probably freaked.*

The nurse continued with a more scolding tone. "You're extremely lucky. One of the lacerations *exposed* your jugular. If it had been torn, you'd be dead."

Upset parents no longer seemed so bad. "How did I get here?" Lexa asked.

"A student found you and called an ambulance. He's been here all morning."

"Can you ask him to come back?"

"Sure. The doctor and the police will also be in to see you." The nurse left.

The police? Lexa searched for her phone. It was in a plastic bag under her bed along with her clothes. No baseball cap. Ignoring the fifteen text messages and three voice mails from Ben, she called her mother, and endured the hysterics. Calming her mother, Lexa noted the irony of how *she'd* been injured, but her mother needed to be soothe.

"No need to come, Mom," Lexa said for the seventh time. "I'm fine. It's a couple of scratches, and I'll be home in two weeks for Thanksgiving." Their first holiday without Lauren—hell with turkey and stuffing.

Finally, her mother agreed. Lexa read through Ben's texts. He'd teased her, assuming she slept in, but when she missed classes, his texts became more frantic. Avoiding another phone call, she texted Ben. Two seconds after she hit send, her phone vibrated with another message from Mr. Lightning Thumbs.

I'm coming.

She didn't have the energy to argue. Besides, she'd need a ride home. Lexa tossed the phone on the table. There was no one else to call. Her roommate, Bubbles the aspiring freshman beauty queen, wouldn't even notice her absence.

The curtain to her room parted, and the black-haired student entered. A wary concern lurked in his blue eyes as if he was afraid she would yell at him.

"Uh . . . the nurse said you . . . "

"Thank you for helping me," Lexa said. She gestured to the dried blood on his clothes. "Sorry about bleeding all over you. If the stains don't come out, I can buy—"

"Don't worry about it. I get blood on my clothes all the time."

"Really?"

"Man, that sounded weird." He crossed then uncrossed his arms as if he wasn't sure what to do with them. "I play hockey."

Her first impression of jock had been right. Plus only an athlete would have biceps that defined. "Are you one of Penn State's Ice Men?"

"Yeah, I'm—"

A police officer stepped into her room. "Miss Thomas?"

She nodded.

"I'm Officer Reed of the State College Police. I'd like to ask you a few questions." The officer addressed the hockey player. "You can wait at the nurses' station. I've questions for you, too."

"Yes, sir." He retreated.

"Are you sure it was a dog that attacked you?" Officer Reed asked.

"Yes. It was gray with black stripes. It was wide and solid, not tall. Big teeth."

He wrote a few notes in a small book. "Do you know Aiden Deller?"

The name sounded familiar, but she couldn't place it. "No. Who's he?"

The officer gave her a tight smile. "He called the ambulance."

"Oh." She made the connection. Aiden Deller was a senior forward, and one of the top scorers for the Ice Men. The nickname Ice Men came from the precise, emotionless way they played.

Officer Reed's next set of questions focused on Aiden and his timely arrival.

"It was an animal," Lexa repeated. "Ask the doctor who stitched me up."

"No need to get upset. I'm just eliminating all the possibilities. Dog attacks of this magnitude are extremely rare." He handed her a card. "Call me, if you remember anything else." Officer Reed left.

After twenty minutes, Aiden returned. "I overheard the nurses." He pointed at her neck. "They mentioned a dog?"

"You didn't see it?"

"No. As I told Officer Reed, I found you lying on the ground. Alone."

She shivered at the memory. "I don't think they believe me."

"What were you doing out that early?" he asked.

Lexa explained about her forecasting shift.

"Meteorology, that's cool."

"Most people think it's geeky." Including Jason. "What's your major?"

"Architectural engineering."

"Wow. I thought—"

"Jocks aren't smart?"

"No." She rushed to assure him. "I thought you'd be doing something sports related."

"Odds of me being drafted in the NHL are slim."

"But you score a hat trick every game, and last year, you had the best record in the league."

He raised his eyebrows. "Hockey fan?"

"Sort of."

Aiden waited.

Lexa felt self-conscience, but she couldn't let him think she'd lost her mind. "My ex-boyfriend is a big fan. He dragged me to all the home games the last three years, but I haven't gone this semester. Besides," she added to avoid sounding pathetic, "it's impossible to score tickets this season, and I don't want to be one of those fair weather fans."

He laughed at the weather pun, but paused as if surprised by his own response. "If you've sat through those three horrible seasons, then you're not at all like those filling the stands now."

A smile tugged. "It was painful to watch."

"It was painful to play."

"The new coach made a big difference."

Aiden sobered. "Yeah, Coach Hakim . . . who'd of thought a guy from Indonesia would know so much about hockey."

Lexa detected bitterness in his voice.

"If I sent you a ticket to tomorrow night's game, would you come?" Aiden asked.

"Of course, but—"

Ben arrived with two security guards in tow. "Can you please tell these goons that I'm allowed in here? I'm practically next of kin!"

Lexa grinned at Ben's disheveled appearance—mussed brown hair in need of a cut, flannel shirt untucked and two days of stubble. They'd been best friends since freshman physics. He was the first person she'd called when Lauren had died. "It's okay. He's my ride home."

He sputtered, but couldn't complain since the guards left. "What happened? Your text—" Ben noticed Aiden standing on the other side of her bed.

The two men sized each other like warriors preparing to battle. Stocky but not fat, Ben was shorter than Aiden, who was all lean muscles.

Lexa introduced them. "Aiden, this is my *friend*, Ben Bernstein. Ben, this is Aiden Deller." She explained Aiden's rescue.

"What were you doing out that early?" Ben asked him.

"Running."

"At four thirty a.m.?"

"Ben," Lexa admonished.

"I better go. Coach has a fit if we're late for practice," Aiden said. "Where should I send the ticket? Or should I send you two?" He glanced at Ben.

"One's fine. Ben hates hockey. I'm in 233 Runkle Hall."

Ben huffed. "I thought you hated hockey. too."

Lexa wished Ben would shut up. "You're thinking of horror movies."

"Uh-uh." Ben looked unconvinced.

Aiden said good-bye. Lexa felt suddenly fragile as if he had taken a part of her with him. Silly nonsense. She touched the bandages. What would have happened if Aiden hadn't shown up? Would the dog have killed her? At least she wasn't disappointed about surviving.

Ben kept her company until the doctor discharged her. With instructions and prescriptions in hand, she followed Ben to his Ford Ranger pick-up.

He slid behind the wheel and started the engine. "You shouldn't be alone. You can stay at my apartment tonight."

"And listen to the he-man women haters club while I try to get comfortable on your cushionless couch? Thanks, but no thanks."

"Hey, you're member, too, and haven't missed a meeting at the G-man." He pulled into traffic.

"I'm not passing up free beer and hot wings."

He gasped. "I should have suspected. You swore off dating women too easily."

Lexa laughed, but stopped as pain ringed her neck.

Ben glanced over. "Wow. That's the first time you've laughed in . . . months."

"Don't start."

"Fine. Humor me and stay tonight. You can have my bed."

"Bubbles is going home, and I have the room to myself."

"Are you sure it's not because you're hoping Mr. Knight-in-Shining-Armor delivers that ticket himself?"

"Don't be ridiculous."

"Just don't go all Florence Nightingale over him."

"You have that backwards. *I'm* the patient."

"You know what I mean."

"No, Ben, I don't know."

"He probably has a dozen girls drooling over him. I don't want you becoming Depressed Girl again."

"You're worse than my mother. It's just a ticket to a hockey game."

Yet the next day, a thrill of excitement rolled through her when she found an envelope under her door. Inside was one ticket to the game.

Lexa gawked at the packed stands. The Ice Pavilion's bleachers stretched along one side of the rink. It appeared as if every seat was filled.

She glanced at her ticket. Section C. Row 5. Just as she suspected, the seat was one of the best in the pavilion. Dead center and high enough to see over the Plexiglas.

Sitting next to a beautiful blonde, Lexa scanned the small roped-off area. Many of the seats remained unoccupied, but a few pretty girls and two older couples sat around her. *Ah, the girlfriend and parent section.*

The blonde gave her the once over. Lexa tucked a hair behind her ear, feeling inadequate in her navy turtleneck and jeans. Wearing Ugg boots, a pink Eddie Bauer sweater, and a sorority pin, the blonde was probably the homecoming queen.

"Who are you here for?" the blonde asked.

"Aiden Deller."

The blonde's thin eyebrows rose slightly. "That's surprising."

"Why?" Lexa demanded.

"Oh, no offense. He just never invites anyone. Even his parents stopped coming."

"Really?"

She gestured to the empty seats. "Most don't. Ever since the guys have been winning, they've ignored everyone. Hockey is all they care about."

Lexa watched the team warm up. A dead serious expression covered all their faces as they passed the puck with precise motions. She had heard the rumors, and the nickname, but to see them in action sent a chill along her spine. Aiden matched the other's mechanical movements, but when they circled to return to the bench, he met her gaze and winked.

Feeling a little better, Lexa asked the blonde who she was rooting for.

"Ryan Collins, but not for long."

"Why?"

"He's lost interest in life. Ryan's turned as cold as the ice he skates on. If you're smart, don't get involved with Aiden."

"Oh. No, I'm not . . . He just . . . " The game started, saving her.

With the blonde's comments fresh in her mind, Lexa paid attention to the Ice Men. Since she had seen them last, they had improved in every way— skating, passing, working as a team. Yet when they scored a goal, they didn't celebrate. No one raised a stick or smiled or slapped each other despite the crowd's roar.

Deep in the third period, Aiden scored his hat trick. He pumped a fist and smiled at Lexa.

The blonde leaned close to her ear. "Maybe you should stick around. Aiden's showing signs of life."

The buzzer signaled another win for the team. Spectators filed out as the players lined up to slap hands. Lexa debated. Should she go?

As the teams broke apart and headed off ice, Aiden caught her eye. He put his hand up in a stopping motion and pointed down as if he wanted her to wait for him. She nodded. He gave her a thumbs up.

A strange tingling on her skin caused her to look across the ice. Coach Hakim stared at her. His hard expression unreadable, but she sensed trouble in his gaze. She shivered, and pulled her jacket closer. When she risked another peek, the coach had disappeared.

The stands were almost empty when a familiar voice called her name. Jason and the girlfriend stood a few rows down from her. They held hands. *How cute*. She braced for the dagger of pain, but felt nothing.

"I thought you didn't like hockey," Jason said.

She shrugged. "It grew on me."

"Sure it did." His sarcastic tone suggested otherwise. "Don't you think this is a little pathetic?" He smirked.

"What is?"

"Coming here so you'd run into me, hoping I'd see you and regret dumping you."

The girlfriend giggled.

When they'd been dating, they'd always done what he wanted, and never did anything she enjoyed. She studied Jason and wondered how she could have fallen in love with him.

"Get over yourself, Jason. I didn't come here for you," she said.

"Yeah? Then why did you come?"

"Because I invited her," Aiden said. He held a hockey stick, and his hair was still wet from a shower.

Jason gaped and stammered.

"Ready to go?" Aiden asked her, holding out his free hand.

"Yep. I'm so done." Without hesitating, she took his hand. They left the rink as if they were a couple. From the moment she touched him, she felt as if they'd been a couple for years. That kind of thinking would only lead her in one direction, back into the valley of pain where she's been wallowing since May.

When they reach the parking lot in front of the pavilion, Aiden let go. "Sorry about that, but when I heard that son-of-a-bitch gloating . . . It was either that or I was going to punch him."

"And ruin another shirt for me? I couldn't handle the guilt."

Aiden laughed. He stopped next to a black Honda Accord and unlocked the trunk. Tossing the hockey stick in, he closed it. "I'm starving. Do you want to go get something to eat?"

Her heart danced in her chest, but she replied with—she hoped—a casual tone. "Sure."

"Great. Hop in." He opened the door for her.

So polite. She slid into the passenger seat.

He settled behind the wheel. "Almost forgot." Reaching into the back, he grabbed her baseball cap. "I picked this up after the paramedics left. Yours?"

"Yes. Thanks."

"You don't seem the baseball cap type," he said.

"I'm not, but it helps disguise me when I'm outside alone."

"You could arrange for an escort."

"I could."

He shook his head. "Do you mind if we go to Bellefonte for dinner? If I eat around campus, I get a bunch of drunk guys telling me how fabulous I am." He gave her a wry grin. "I don't mind being told I'm fabulous by drunk *girls*."

"It must suck to be famous," she said.

"Yep. Poor me."

Lexa laughed. For the first time in months her stomach growled with hunger instead of swirling with nausea. For the first time the thought of her sister didn't cause intense pain.

"Did you enjoy the game?" Aiden asked.

"Yes. But the players looked too serious."

Aiden kept his focus on the road. "Coach doesn't like us to celebrate goals. He thinks it's poor sportsmanship. Actually, he tells us to leave all our emotions in the locker room. He says pre-game jitters, anger, or just stressing over a test can all get in the way of our performance."

"That strategy is definitely working. No penalties, fights, plus the bonus of being undefeated."

"Yeah. It's nice."

She sensed a but.

"How's your neck?" he asked, changing the subject.

After dinner, Aiden drove her home. Before she opened the car door, he handed her a stack of hockey tickets.

"This isn't going to help my thermodynamics grade," she said.

"No problem, I got an A in thermo last semester."

"Of course you did. Can you turn metal into gold, too?" she teased.

"All the time. Except for my hockey skates, they're platinum—gold is too soft."

She stood there grinning like an idiot as he drove away. She knew it couldn't last, that he would leave her, too. At least when she hit bottom this time, it would be at full speed and cause major carnage.

Over the next five days, she saw Aiden every day. They either went to dinner after a game, or he helped her with thermodynamics. Officer Reed called her midweek to report that they had caught a wild dog on campus. He wanted her to identify it. Aiden skipped practice to drive her to the pound on Thursday afternoon.

"Won't your coach be upset?" she asked.

"Not for this."

"Why not?"

His grip on the steering wheel tightened. "Lexa, I need a favor."

"Sure."

"You don't even know what it is."

She shrugged. "Considering all you've done for me, it would have to be a crime for me to say no." She kept her tone light.

Instead of smiling, Aiden grimaced. *Uh oh.*

He stopped at a red light. Meeting her gaze, he said, "I want you to tell Officer Reed that the dog they caught *was* the one that attacked you even if it isn't."

"Why?"

"I'll explain later, although it's hard to believe. Christ, I don't believe it myself sometimes."

"But if it's the wrong dog, then the right one might attack—"

"Won't happen. I promise no one will be harmed again."

The light turned green. Aiden released Lexa from his intense scrutiny. Her emotions balanced on the edge, teetering toward the plunge. She touched her neck. Another turtleneck covered the bandages. The stitches would come out next week.

As the silence lengthened, she puzzled out the only logical explanation for his request. "Your dog attacked me."

"I don't have a dog."

A painful knot tightened her throat. "Did you see what attacked me?"

"No. Yes. It's complicated."

Shit. The bottom rose to meet her.

Aiden pulled into the pound's lot. "Please do this, and I swear, I'll explain everything."

Officer Reed met them in the lobby. "Ready?" he asked.

Lexa nodded. It was all she could manage. They entered the back room, and the dogs immediately started barking.

The volunteer seemed surprised. "Must be the uniform," he muttered.

The accused dog matched Lexa's description. The huge Mastiff had a black muzzle, and it had black stripes on a fawn-colored coat, which could be mistaken for gray in the dark. It growled, baring its sharp teeth when it spotted them. Its tail tucked under its body.

Without warning, a clear image from the attack flashed in her mind. This dog didn't match at all. The muzzle was too droopy, the ears weren't cropped, no white on its face, and it didn't have long whiskers. *Whiskers?*

Aiden stood behind her. His hands rested on her shoulders as if he lent her support. Officer Reed eyed him with interest. Conflicting emotions struggled for dominance, Lexa didn't know what to do. However, she believed Aiden when he promised no one else would be hurt.

"That's the one," she said.

"Really?" The volunteer scratched his goatee. "Normally, he's a real sweetheart."

"It's obvious he doesn't like her," Officer Reed said. "Case closed!"

Aiden kept quiet as he drove toward campus.

Unable to endure the silence, Lexa said, "You were going to explain."

"I will in Coach Hakim's office. You—"

"Take me home." The blonde at the game had been right, it's all about hockey. Aiden had probably been running with the Coach's dog that morning.

"But don't you—"

"No. I don't care. I just killed a perfectly good dog for you. We're done."

"But you *need* to talk to Coach."

Fear's icy fingers squeezed. "Are you kidnapping me?"

"No." He drove her back to Runkle Hall.

Returning to her dorm room, she plopped on her bed, feeling numb. Her phone rang. *If that's Aiden . . .* It was Ben. Disappointment stabbed. *How crazy is that?*

"I'll pick you up at four twenty-five tomorrow," Ben said.

"Tomorrow?"

"Campus weather. Remember?"

Barely. "Don't worry about me."

"I don't mind."

"I have pepper spray, and I need to do it myself. Like that old adage about getting back on the wagon."

"Getting back on the horse," he corrected. "Are you sure?"

"I'll be fine."

Except she wasn't fine. Not at all. She stood outside Runkle Hall the next morning, holding her phone in one hand and the pepper spray in another. Convinced a huge dog lurked in every shadow, she couldn't move.

"Lexa?"

She spun ready to push buttons when she recognized Ben. "Don't scare me like that!"

"Sorry."

"What are you doing here?"

He gave her a don't-be-stupid look.

She drew in a deep breath. "Sorry. Thanks for coming."

"I'm surprised Mr. Knight-in-Shining-Armor isn't here. You guys have been spending all your time together."

They headed west on Curtain Road.

"You were right about him," she said. "But you're not allowed to gloat."

"Not even a little?"

"Nope." After a couple minutes, she asked, "Do you know if there are any she-woman men haters clubs around that I can join?"

"Nope, but I'm sure my fellow he-mans won't have any trouble swearing off men."

The morning weather shift flew by. Lexa had an hour before her first class. She wasted time surfing the net instead of working on her thermo homework. Curious, Lexa pulled up pages on various big cats found in Pennsylvania, searching for one that matched the image in her mind. None. Remembering a neighbor who owned an exotic pet shop, she expanded to panthers and tigers. On Wikipedia, she leaned forward, clicking on the pictures of tigers to enlarge them. A wave of nausea hit her. *That's close.* Except the creature that attacked her wasn't orange, but gray.

Following a few links, Lexa found an article about a subspecies of the South Chinese Tiger which was rumored to have a slate-gray coloration called a Maltese Tiger. She swallowed as she peered at the artist's rendering. *Bingo.*

What was Aiden doing with a tiger? He had wanted her to talk to Coach Hakim. She read Coach Hakim's bio online. He was born in the city of Surabaya, East Java, Indonesia. He spent every free moment of his childhood playing hockey. In 1980, he started skating for the Hong Kong Tigers.

The team's name triggered a connection. Hong Kong was near South China. She read on. Hakim became head coach of the Tigers in 2003. After the Tigers won every single tournament in Asia, Coach Hakim was hired by Penn State.

When asked why Hakim moved half way around the world, he replied that he loved a challenge, and wanted to show Penn State fans that hockey was, "the coldest [coolest] game on earth." The brackets translated the Coach's meaning since English wasn't his first language. From what Lexa knew about Hakim's players, perhaps he had meant coldest.

She mulled over all the information. Did the coach own a Maltese Tiger? A tiger breed that has never been seen before? *The World Wildlife Foundation would freak.*

She startled when Ben tapped her on the shoulder.

"You missed thermo again," he said. "Do you want to copy my notes?"

"Uh. Sure."

Ben studied her. "Is Depressed Girl back?"

Lexa examined her psyche as if probing a sore tooth with her tongue. An ache for her sister flared, but nothing like the all consuming grief. "No. Depressed Girl is gone."

"That calls for a celebration."

"No time. I have to work on thermo for Monday's test or I *will* fail the class."

"I can help you with thermo. After all, I nursed you through meteorological instrumentation."

"Thanks. Where?" she asked.

He gestured to the weather center. "This place is a ghost town on Friday nights. We'll start right after dinner."

After Ben left, she searched a few more sites on Asian ice hockey and tigers. She uncovered an odd link to a write up about a folk legend popular in Java, Indonesia that claimed were-tigers existed. When killed by a were-tiger, a man would lose his soul. The victim couldn't reclaim his soul until he, in turn, killed another. Villagers in Java would watch the men closely, seeking the signs of soullessness—cold, emotionless, and without joy.

That description could easily describe the Ice Men. Which was ridiculous—another example of Lexa's overactive imagination. Besides Aiden hadn't acted like that at all. Without thought her fingers stroked her neck.

Even with thermodynamics to occupy her mind, Lexa felt Aiden's absence. It started with a sense of loss. She couldn't focus at all on Saturday night especially not during game time. Exasperated with her lack of concentration, Ben called it a night. They headed to the G-man to have the first men hater's club meeting.

During the week, the hockey team had a series of away games. Lexa ached and felt as though she had lost a limb. She wasn't Depressed Girl, but she couldn't sleep or eat or concentrate for more than two seconds. Her symptoms resembled withdraw.

Perhaps she had been too hasty in sending Aiden away. Athletes were loyal to their coaches. Maybe Coach Hakim's tiger escaped and Aiden had been trying to find it. Just bad luck she happened to find it first. Of course all this was pure conjecture. She needed to confirm the tiger's existence.

After her thermo class on Friday morning, Lexa hiked out to Coach Hakim's house. The team had an afternoon game at West Chester University and wasn't due back until late. Lexa circled his house, but found no evidence that a tiger lived there. He didn't even have a fenced in backyard. She returned to campus.

Instead of heading home, she entered the Ice Pavilion. She found Coach Hakim's office, but the door was locked. Peering through the translucent glass, Lexa couldn't see anything.

"What are you doing?" a deep male voice asked her.

She turned. Coach Hakim stood with Kyle Gant and Mike Miller, both defensemen behind him. He scowled.

"Uh . . . Shouldn't you be with your team?"

"I came back early. But I'm glad you're here, I need to talk to you." He unlocked the door and drew her inside, motioning her to the seat facing his desk.

The defensemen followed. They stood in front of the closed door as if guarding it. Lexa glanced around. Equipment, trophies, binders, stacks of papers, and posters of tigers decorated the office. *There's a clue.*

Hakim settled behind his desk, looking unhappy.

Fear bubbled up her throat. "Look, if this is about your pet tiger, I won't say a word to anyone. I promise."

He grunted. "Did Aiden tell you that?"

"No. I guessed. Isn't that what attacked me? What you didn't want the police to know about?"

"Sure. Let's go with that."

Confused, she said, "Is that what you wanted to talk to me about?"

"Not really. I'm more concerned about Aiden. He hasn't scored a goal since last Saturday night."

"Oh. What—"

"You're the reason, and we're going to fix it tonight." He stood. "Give me your phone."

"Uh . . . I'd better go. I've a class—"

"Kyle, take her phone. Keep her here until the team returns."

She jumped to her feet. "Hey!"

Even though she fought, Kyle confiscated her phone, shoving her back into the chair. When she stood again, he pushed her down and said, "Tape," to Mike who moved to grab the black roll.

"No," she said. "I'll stay in the seat." She met his gaze and true terror exploded in her chest.

Kyle stared at her with dead eyes. No compassion or emotion of any kind shone from his face. Mike's was also as cold as the ice they skated on.

Holy shit, they're zombies. Except they were in the peak of health. *Brainwashed.* She couldn't decide if that was better or worse.

She spent an eternity in that chair. They wouldn't answer her questions and she stopped asking when they held up the roll of tape. Every emotion, every horrible scenario ran through her mind until she was numb.

Hakim returned after dark. "Bring her."

Kyle and Mike each grabbed an upper arm and dragged her to the ice rink. The dark arena didn't bode well for her future. Four more players waited on the bleachers. Lexa recognized them all.

Coach Hakim sat on the bleachers. "Did you text him?" he asked Tim.

"Yes, sir."

"Good."

The door banged open and in rushed Mr. Knight-in-Shining-Armor. Too bad he was outnumbered seven to one. Aiden glanced at Lexa, but focused on his coach.

"Finish it Aiden or I will," Coach Hakim said.

"No. It can work." Aiden's voice held a note of pleading.

"You haven't scored a goal in three games. It's not working."

"That's only because we were apart. I scored four goals Saturday night when she was there."

"Can you tell me what's going on?" Her voice sounded as it should—petrified.

"Aiden attacked you," Hakim said. "He should have killed you, but his mother raised him too well."

"Kill me?"

"I lost control," Aiden said. "I'm sorry. I couldn't stand being . . . dead inside anymore." He gestured to his teammates. "Like them."

"If you don't kill her, I will have to kill you both. You know how it works," Hakim said.

Aiden closed his eyes for a moment. "Okay. I'll do it."

"Good. Go change."

Lexa watched Aiden walk away. He entered the locker room without looking back. Pure fear pumped through her veins. Panic jumbled all logic, but she managed to snag one coherent thought. Why would Aiden kill her? He wasn't dead inside. Not anymore. Was the Javan legend true?

"Will I come back like you?" she asked. "A soulless were-tiger until I kill someone?"

Coach Hakim peered at her in surprise. "How do you know?"

"Internet. Plus it's the only thing that fits . . . this."

A big gray tiger with black stripes stepped from the locker room.

"Sorry, but only men can survive the change. And they come back stronger and faster."

Mike and Kyle let her go, stepping away.

"Run," Hakim said. "Cats can't resist the chase."

Instead she backed up as the tiger . . . Aiden . . . neared. Powerful muscles bunched and he crouched just like a house cat ready to pounce. Her muscles liquefied in terror.

In a heartbeat, he launched. Roaring, Aiden landed on Hakim's chest. The others moved to their coach. Lexa didn't linger. She slipped out the doors and ran. Then stopped. She couldn't leave Aiden. He had the upper hand now, but the others could change into tigers as well. He'd be tiger food.

Think! She spotted Aiden's Accord in the lot and raced to it. *Please let the keys be inside.* Yanking open the door, she almost fainted in relief. His key ring glinted from the cup holder. Lexa jammed the key in the ignition and drove the car straight into the front doors.

The screech of metal and crack of shattered glass echoed throughout the rink. Four of them sat on Aiden. Two hovered over their unconscious coach. She aimed the car at the four. They scattered. She pressed the window button. The back one went down. Aiden sailed through the opening.

Throwing the car in reverse, she backed out, turned around and headed north on University Drive. They didn't get far. The front tires were flat, and the radiator was damaged. She pulled over near Jeffery Field.

Aiden hopped from the car and pawed at the trunk. She opened it. *This is insane.* Aiden reached inside and pulled out a duffle bag. He moved away, glancing back at her.

"I'm right behind you," she said. *Might as well embrace the insanity.*

They crossed the street, cut through the Intramural fields, and entered the Arboretum's grounds, stopping behind the Schreyer House.

Lexa puffed as she plopped on the ground. "Now what?"

Aiden dropped the bag in her lap. She unzipped it. Men's clothes had been packed inside.

Holding up stripped boxers, she said, "You don't seem the boxer type."

He growled with impatience.

"Okay, I get it. You're going to change back." She turned around. "And I think I get the other stuff too. You lost control, attacked me, but when you saw I was a girl, you stopped. Please thank your mother for me. Instead of getting my whole soul, you only got a portion—that's why I stopped being Depressed Girl and why when you're with me I feel so complete. And why, when you were away, I failed my thermo test. And, yes I'm babbling. Considering the circumstances I'm allowed."

Lexa sucked in a breath. "So your teammates are soulless and your coach must be the one who killed you. That's why he has emotions. Although he didn't seem upset about my future demise. And now they're going to hunt us down and kill us both. Unless we can figure a way to get the hockey team's souls back without killing anyone. And we need to stop Coach Death, but I don't think Officer Reed and the State College police can handle something like that. He seemed so happy to have found a wild dog. Imagine—"

"Lexa." Aiden wrapped his arms around her.

She leaned back against him. "What are we going to do?"

"Just what you said."

"How?"

"I'm going to do some recruiting."

◆

Aiden led her through the quiet campus. "Those six guys are Coach's favorites. But if we can get the rest of the team on our side—"

"Won't work." Lexa would never forget Kyle and Mike's dead stares. "They need souls."

"We're not going to kill anyone."

"Of course not. But . . . " An answer bubbled to the surface of her mind. "They can share."

Aiden stopped. "No. That's too much to ask. After this is all done, somehow you're getting yours back."

"No. I don't want it. I'm happy for the first time in years." Lexa realized she had assumed he felt the same. "Unless, you'd rather not be . . . I'm sure there are others . . . "

He drew her close. "I'd be an idiot to want anyone else. Look at what you've done tonight. Rescued me. Took the whole were-tiger thing in stride. You're awesome. I love being with you." He kissed her.

Her muscles melted again, but this time for a better reason.

Too soon, he pulled away. "We have to talk to the guys before Coach does."

"Not going to work. Talk to Ryan Collins' girlfriend. I'm positive she'd be willing to do anything to bring him back to life."

"Chelsea Belham? Really?"

Despite the late hour, convincing Chelsea was easier than expected. All she needed was to see the change in Aiden.

"I'm in. What's next?" Chelsea asked.

Lexa glanced at Aiden. "I haven't figure that out yet."

"I have. I thought of nothing else during that horrible week we were apart," he said. "It's an exchange of blood and saliva."

Chelsea drove them to Ryan's apartment in her silver BMW. He shared it with Doug Vett, a forward. When Ryan opened the door and saw Aiden, he grabbed him, pulled him into the apartment, and slammed him into a wall. Aiden crumpled to the floor.

Lexa and Chelsea jumped on Ryan, but he shrugged them off with ease. Doug Vett stood in the threshold of his bedroom. He didn't seem inclined to help, but he texted on his phone.

"Coach called," Ryan said in a monotone.

"Already figured that out big guy," Aiden said from the floor. He lumbered to his feet. "Wait," he said when Ryan moved. "Listen to me." Aiden rushed to explain.

"Coach said to hold them here until he arrives," Doug said.

Ryan blocked the door.

"I guess that's a no," Aiden said.

Chelsea hadn't moved since Ryan tossed her onto the ground next to Lexa. Her expression hardened into what Lexa would describe as bitch-mode. Opening her Prada handbag, Chelsea yanked out a thick nail file.

Figures. Although, a cell phone would have been confiscated right away.

Instead of filing her nails, Chelsea flicked her thumb and a blade shot out. Everyone froze in surprise. It was enough time for her to cut her wrist, stand, and cross to Ryan. She offered her bloody arm to him.

A predatory glint transformed his eyes into tiger eyes. Ryan clamped onto her wrist as if she was fresh kill. He sucked greedily.

Aiden pried Ryan from her. "Not too much or you'll kill her."

Ryan sank to the ground and put his head in his hands. Aiden knelt next to him.

Lexa wrapped a paper towel around a paler Chelsea's wrist.

"How long?" Chelsea asked.

Aiden said, "For me, it was pretty quick, but—"

"Chel?" Ryan glanced around.

The girl didn't hesitate. She threw herself into his arms.

One down, twenty-four more to go. Lexa glanced at Doug.

"Uh, Aiden." She pointed to Doug. He held his phone to his ear.

"Doesn't matter. Coach is already on the way," Aiden said. "We need to leave." He helped Chelsea and Ryan to their feet.

"Mary? It's Doug."

Aiden and Lexa exchanged a grin.

"Where can we go that Coach doesn't know about?" Aiden asked.

She felt her pockets. Despite all the running around, her keys remained. Holding up the key to the Walker building, she said, "This place's a ghost town on Friday nights."

The five of them crammed in Chelsea's BMW. They picked up Mary on the way.

It was a long exhausting weekend. Not all the players had girlfriends, and a couple weren't as understanding as Chelsea and Mary. Aiden and Lexa played matchmaker.

"I don't know about this," she said to Aiden as they waited for a potential girl. "What if they don't like each other, or have opposite personalities?"

"They won't afterward," Aiden said. "They'll be soul mates. It's what every single couple in the world hopes for, and only a tiny percentage achieve."

"But we're manipulating it with the tiger magic."

"We were manipulated. Do you have any complaints? Regrets?"

She stepped into his arms. "None."

The Coach remained a problem. And there was a game on Sunday afternoon. By that time, they had converted fifteen players.

"We play," Aiden said. "He's not going to do anything in public and we outnumber them. Once he sees we can still win, he'll back off. Winning is all he cares about."

En masse, they arrived at the Ice Pavilion. They met with a token resistance, but the ten remaining players didn't have the heart to fight. Lexa kept an eye on Coach Hakim during the game. He tried to prevent Aiden and the others from playing, but they ignored him. The team won seven to zero.

After that, the Coach cooperated. He even allowed the girls to travel with the team for away games. The rest of the players found soul mates. The Ice Men had thawed.

"Coach Hakim can't walk away scott free," Aiden said to Lexa after finals week. They were headed to the G-man to celebrate the end of the semester and an early Christmas with the he-man club. Ben hadn't been supportive of Mr. Knight-in-Shining-Armor until he realized Depressed Girl was gone for good, and Aiden wasn't leaving.

"Nothing's stopping him from going to another school and creating another team filled with soulless were-tigers. We all swore not to attack anyone, but Coach didn't."

She considered the situation. They needed something that would ruin his reputation to a point where no one would hire him. Jail time would be a bonus. The answer clicked.

"I love it when you have that evil gleam. Do tell," Aiden said.

"Child pornography."

"You serious?"

"Unfortunately. We can hack into his computer and download pictures and videos to his hard drive. An anonymous tip to Officer Reed would set it in motion. No one will touch a suspected pedophile, his career would be over."

"I'm not comfortable using kids."

"Me either, but they're already being exploited. The pictures and videos are there now." She considered. "Once everything with the Coach settles, the team can advocate to stop child pornography, do fundraisers, and maybe even shut down a few operators while we're at it."

"I hadn't thought of that."

"What else is a group of super-brawny guys who can change into tigers going to do during the off-season? Play baseball?"

"Gasp! Don't mention the B-word ever again."

When they parked at the G-man, Aiden pulled her close. "Forgot to ask. How did you do in thermo?"

Lexa grinned.

"You passed!"

"I failed. I'll have to take it again, and the F sent my GPA into the toilet."

"But you smiled?"

"It's only a grade. Not worth stressing over."

RED ON RED

JEN WHITE

—◆—

On the side of the track the eucalypts tremble. They are the earth's antennae, listening for something we cannot hear. The tops of the trees shiver delicately, sprinkling a permanent patina of red dust over everything. She is covered in it. It sticks to her like red Xmas glitter. She pushes brusquely past the trees, stamping along the track with her spade-like feet, her fat toes gripping the rubber thongs she wears, kicking the dirt up and back onto herself. She's relaxed. She doesn't care what she looks like. Who can see her here? Her plump middle flops over the waistband of her shorts.

Funny how in such a large, empty land there are crowds everywhere. People following her. Chasing her so that they can watch her big tits wobble. And she laughs, too, breathless and embarrassed. It's the only attention she ever gets.

But right now she's alone, and in order to celebrate that fact she sings. It's a throaty, tuneless sound, or perhaps it's a tune with different rules, different times. No matter. She sings for herself. To give herself pleasure. She relishes the thrum at the back of her throat. She can't get enough of it. She rolls the air around in her mouth like a boiled lolly, collecting spit, and pushes out the sound, thin and bubbling into the vast amphitheater she has chosen.

"You're asking for trouble," her mother said. "Everyone knows you do it, go bush. And anyway, you're nearly a grown woman. You should be staying closer to home. You're getting to that dangerous time when anything might happen."

Someone did follow her once, a kid from school. "Yah," he called, his voice high and strangled and thick with snot. He came up fast behind her and stood there with his fists at his waist, legs wide apart. "Yer no good," he screamed. "Yer a slut. Yer askin for it." If it hadn't been so hurtful she would have laughed. She, such a great ugly lump of a girl, asking for it? She could have died laughing.

He stood there, maroon-faced, opening his mouth wide to shout some more, baring his yellow teeth.

But he forgot, because all he saw before him was girl, that she was bigger than him. She turned, it was like some vast stone monument turning slowly, purposefully, and she began to run towards him with those heavy, stiff, log-like legs. He ran, too, but she caught him easily. He stood there, panting, staring at her, waiting to see what she would do. He wiped the snot from his nose with the back of his hand. She pushed him down on the dirt and put a foot on his back. "I can see up yer shorts," he sneered.

Back at school he yelled whenever he saw her. "Yer loved it. Yer know yer did." His mates cackled with glee. She stood there mute, with her impassive Easter Island stare, containing the pain.

And now, alone in the bush, when she sang her strange passion she always wondered if someone was following, listening.

That's what she thought it was that last time, when she crept out of the house, away from her mum's constant supervision, away from the rowdy good cheer of her six siblings. She was being followed, she knew it. How? Oh, by the density of the air around her, perhaps. Or the staccato flurry of birds' wings overhead. But, because of it she denied herself the pleasure of singing. Three times she stopped and waited for whomever it was to show themselves. The third time she was determined. She squatted there in the red dust and waited for an hour. Two hours. She panted slightly from nerves and because it was a hot, dry day.

And whoever it was watched her all that time.

After two hours a pale, heavy-jowled dog pushed through the undergrowth to meet her. It sat before her, cocked its head to one side, and smiled revealing powerful fangs. She could smell its breath.

"You stink," she laughed with relief.

It lifted one paw like a trained dog, a Hollywood Rin Tin Tin of a dog, and this appealed to her, even if it was artificial and manipulative. She thought it was cute. The dog stood and walked ahead a little, then stopped and turned to look at her as if to say 'Well, what are you waiting for?'

It wants me to follow, she thought, and it felt so nice to be wanted for anything that she forgot to ask herself why the dog had been stalking her, why it had watched her from the undergrowth for two hours. She followed, smiling all the while at the dog's cleverness and at her own willingness to do what it said. What have I got to lose after all, she shrugged. She enjoyed the delicate softness of the animal's tread, the soft, rhythmic padding of its four paws in the dirt. She followed the sound more than anything.

It was afternoon now, and hotter than ever. The sweat dribbled down her back and into her pink bike shorts and the crack of her arse. By late afternoon she had changed her mind. Now she thought it was silly. They were going nowhere, just further and further into the centre. "I'm going back, dog," she called.

The animal turned and snarled a warning. It was telling her that she had left it too late. She had come this far, she couldn't turn back. She realized suddenly that she had been following a wild beast.

She laughed a little, pretended still that it was just a game, and animal and girl continued on. She told herself that she could stop anytime. She was, after all, a human girl with certain powers of reason and intellect. He was only a dog. But they had already come such a long way, and she was drying out in the heat. She was a husk. Only the essence of her was left, the essential elements.

The shadows lengthened. The girl stopped. Even if she returned now it would still be the middle of the night by the time she reached home. She backed quietly away from the dog, intending to turn and run. But how could she have ever thought that her clumsy tread would be softer than this animal's? It knew instantly what she was up to and it sprang upon her.

It caught her by surprise. Otherwise she would have fought, pushed at his fangs, poked at his eyes. She knew how to fight. His teeth burst a major artery before she could even sort out in her tired brain what was happening. The blood pumped out of her in rhythmic spurts all over the T-shirt she wore. Chunks of gore slid down her arm. He had ripped a huge hole in her. She could feel strips of skin flapping open, and the air, cold now, on her torn flesh. She could see the cold yellow eyes of the beast. He sat beside her, watching, waiting.

And then she was in eclipse.

When she woke she felt the ground moving beneath her. The beast was dragging her by her right foot, so delicately that she could hardly feel it. But she could feel her throat. Dust choked the wound, irritating and scraping at it's rawness. Blood still dripped out of her and onto the earth. Red on red. It was a wonder she had any blood left. And the pain, it was so large that it was completely beyond her. She hadn't caught up with it yet, but she would.

Next thing, she was in a place between two rocks, a dark place, a cool place. It was like being in the shallows of the ocean, like a rock pool, only instead of water rippling around her, it was light reflecting and shimmering off shiny rocks. She was panting for water, or for air, she was not sure which. She sensed that she had been there already for a long time, days perhaps. She felt the pain now. She was turning inside out with it. Her skin was raw, new, it felt like it had been rubbed all over in sand. It went on for hours. The beast—she'd thought he was a dog but now she saw that she had been wrong—brought her small animals every so often, ripped in half. He offered their bodies up to her like bowls of chicken soup. He shoved them at her. She was thirsty. She lapped at the congealing blood.

"Oooh, oooh." He laughed as he watched her. "There, that's better," he said.

Surprisingly soon she was ready to stand, though the first time she tried her legs felt like matchsticks from lying down for so long. Her clothes were gone. It took her a while to get used to being naked. At first she dug under the sand to cover herself. She shivered, even though it was hot, at the thought of such complete exposure, and she spent a whole morning looking for her T-shirt. But a new power threaded through her and made her forget about stupid things like clothes. She had the strength now of something that had become other than what it was born. Her golden fur, flat at first and covered with a type of clear, gelid substance, glistened in the sun. She ran to see what running was like with four legs instead of two. The beast himself allowed her to wrestle with him, so that she could test herself. The muscles moved under her skin like small, lively animals. It was the first time she had ever enjoyed having a body.

She was grateful. She had wanted things to be different.

The beast taught her how to hunt and what the smells meant. He was wise, she could see it in the cast of his eyes. And if there was a certain smugness in the way he conducted himself, well, it was something she could forgive.

"That spicy stink," she said. "Like rotten meat dressed with exotic herbs. What is it?"

"They're the ghosts," he told her. "The flat-faced ones, the pearl-skins. They are what you used to be." She didn't ask what she was now.

Did her family know she was gone? she wondered. Did her mother realize that she had not returned? Did her brothers and sisters notice that there was one less of them? She suspected that any small space in the house due to her absence would have closed up almost immediately, like flesh cut cleanly, and left no sign of anything amiss. Her mother had warned her that something would happen to her if she kept going bush. Is this what she had meant?

They got along well enough, the two of them, the beast and she, until she attacked him one day. She made up reasons for it, like resentment, like she hadn't chosen this life. You can always find an excuse to fight. But, really, it was because she knew she could do it and get away with it. She had always been powerful and had always held herself back. Now she didn't have to any more, not even against him.

And that was all.

She had to prove it, test it. She brought him down and wounded him, and in her terror she fled. Weeks later she returned, but his smell was gone.

Without the beast she was utterly alone. But she was, by nature, and by inclination, a solitary being so she enjoyed it well enough, or at least it didn't send her half mad as it would have some. And if she needed company the dingoes let her sing with them of a night, though not too close, mind. She might have looked like them, but they could easily smell her difference. When she came near they backed away slowly and carefully. Their hair stood erect at the thought of her and of her kind. They thought she might jump them and eat their flesh, and she might have, too, if she were hungry or in the mood.

And that other, first life, that soft white larval stage of a life, moved further and further away. Sometimes, though, she dreamed of it and woke afterwards with a deep unease, for there was still something of that other, social creature in her. But it passed soon enough. She always felt better after she killed.

At times like these she haunted the edges of the human camps. She remembered their scents and their songs. They left a trail of smells wherever they went. The earth was crisscrossed with them like old scars never quite fading. She was drawn to them but she was appropriately cautious for she knew that, very often, you are drawn to that which can hurt you the most.

The smells were sweet and dark to her. Irresistible. She didn't hunt them, though, the humans. She knew that if you hurt one of them, you hurt the whole pack. They were too much trouble. She remembered that much. But she ate their companions, the dogs. The dogs smelled better anyway.

And every day she remembered less. Eventually there would only be the now, the continuous now. She would forget what a day was. She would forget that the sun would set until it did. Even now it surprised her and pleased her to see a fine sunset. And then to see the glittering stones far above her in the velvet dark.

That's what she was doing at the campsite that night. Bathing in its warmth, craving its painful comfort for reasons she had almost forgotten. Her nose twitched at the smells. She could hear high hooting sounds that had to be laughter, and the tinkling of bottles and cans, and she could hear car doors open and shut, and engines rev. And then she was on her belly, crawling nearer, dangerously near, for if they saw her, if they sensed what she really was, and how could they not with just one look into her beastly eyes, they would destroy her.

She was a mystery, and mystery must be contained.

She crawled closer, flattening grass, rustling past trees, her powerful muscled limbs pulling her closer and closer until someone came her way, almost treading on her. He wanted a piss. She ducked quickly into a shelter that was a little removed from the others, meaning only to hide herself until they passed. She stood there waiting and listening. It was dark, and in the gloom she could see a pattern of ordinary, everyday objects made sinister by the darkness and by her own faulty memory of their purpose. There were suitcases and a lamp, a folding chair and a low cot, and in the cot a young one. The young one was not crying, just playing with the ribbon on its woollen jacket. It was a very little one, so easy for her to carry, and she hadn't known what she was going to do until she was already slipping through the opening of the shelter and running from the camp with the baby in her mouth. The baby did not cry.

She tried to be gentle, but the act had to be savage. There had to be risk. There was blood, of course, mingled with saliva, and the baby's eyes turned blank like windblown fruit that's been pecked at by birds, but she brought the little one a fresh kill, just as one had been brought for her, and pushed it up to the little one's face. And the child sucked up the blood, her tiny pink tongue lapping, and her lids fluttering, and smiling up at her.

EXTRA CREDIT

SETH CADIN

Rubber wolf masks were on back order that year. Jedward found one hanging on a railing where the team used to race, and when he cut it down he was careful, like maybe the swaying made it alive. He almost chucked it in the cruncher on his way back to the dorms.

"Perspicacity," Karolin dictated up her own sleeve. From under the bunker's tall awning he heard her phone dial. He'd just listen a moment. Another moment. One more. She was talking about lunch, what she ate, and he felt strongly that he needed to know.

Then she said: "No, I left it at the chem lab," and Jedward knew what she meant. She had one too, because that year everybody did. And the gloves with the funny claws. When they were left in the sun too long, the ersatz fur stitched on over the wrists would turn from black to rusted brown.

"Hey, Kay." He shook an ant off his sleeve and extended his knuckles, which she brushed lightly with her own.

"Jeddy. You got one? Is it real?"

He turned the inside out to show her the label: Herkimer, genuine. "Found it," he said. "Know whose?"

He'd thought she might, but she had nothing to say. Her lip gloss smelled like the candles on his grandmother's mantle. She shook her head and sent a spray of light flying from the colorful glass-beaded tips of her many braids.

"I should turn it in . . . " he said hopefully.

"Give it here." She snatched it, her expression shifting from vacant to canny, though in the critical moment she snapped her gum.

"There's this bird you should hear—" What was he saying now, any old thing apparently.

She wasn't listening, not to him or any pointless birds. *Shut up*, he told himself, and went on, "It's just that it's really interesting because it can do all these—and it only sings at night, well morning really, but early, like thirteen hundred."

"A bird that sings in the morning," she repeated, absently, but still with clear enough disdain. "Can I have this or what?" She lifted the mask and shook it a little like a dead scalp. "Sure. I just found it anyway. I don't care." His arches flexed and he heeled off, squeezing his eyes shut against the reflected sprites from her braids dancing on the brick wall.

Extra credit meant extra access—clean and simple. Go over the blue line into the purple, and you could float there forever. One plus up over average got you an hour. That got you another plus, and so on. Jedward knew everybody in the labs very well, because the faces never changed. The masks did, of course; mostly wolves now, a few bats from last season, one unicorn with a saggy fabric horn. They dangled from fingertips or swung cheerfully from belt-loops, and their owners fiddled with them as the big glowing clock chucked through its daylight cycle.

After an hour at his station, he felt a padded hand grip the back of his neck. Plastic claws chattered over his skin, but he forced himself not to jump. Instead, he reached up swiftly to grip the glove, yanking it off and slapping it on the table. "Just sit and try not to be annoying."

Danny's bright evil grin, absent two bottom teeth, swung into view. His mask was wadded up and shoved into his front shirt pocket, which was at least two times too small for it, so bulging out like a shoplifted corsage. His fiercely combed-out puff of hair was now bleached out to red, striking against his deep brown skin. Jedward thought he looked like a clown. It was better than the horns from two seasons ago, anyway. The pointy ends always ended up tangled in branches when they'd gone hiking.

"Found a Herkimer," he said as they passed components and chemicals between them, tweaking each other's work. Danny was quick with sums and nimble-fingered, but he had no patience for plans, so Jedward set the pace and the tasks. "Kay Mendez took it, I mean I let her have it." He felt his face swell and blemish as he heard the suggestive way this came out of it. "I mean—"

"Yeah Jeddy, I know what you mean," Danny snorted at him. He jammed a wire against a Nano Pylon and soldered it without looking, too distracted by his own amusement.

Jedward wondered how far into Danny's brain he could get before they pulled him off, if he were to, for example, grab the hot soldering iron and shove it directly into his best friend's right eye. "It's not *that* funny, jerkface." Once he'd said it, he knew it would just make Danny worse.

But the red puff descended as Danny signaled his line-crossing with a quick nod. They'd never talked about it, but Jedward supposed it was obvious anyway. His loneliness felt like a hood, a sack on his head that everyone could see.

With deadly psychic accuracy, Danny changed the subject to an even worse one. "Are you going or what?"

Jedward stared into a beaker and tried to pretend he hadn't heard the question, but this time Danny wasn't going to fade on it. After a few hard elbows in the ribs he relented. "I still don't know, I'll just go if I do, or not, otherwise."

"Yeah obviously." Danny was almost done with his first board, somehow, though he never seemed to pay attention or care about his work. "You'll go or you won't, that is the question. What are you gonna do, start walking and see if you end up there?" Now he was the one who sounded irritable; Jedward knew he was personally offended by the very idea of indecision. "Just go. You're being stupid."

"So I'm stupid." Jedward sped up, fingers agile as he wove copper wires through leather pegs, and then stopped. "It's all stupid. You're stupid. I'm going home." He stood and kicked his chair back, though not so hard it would jostle someone else's station. "You finish that, you're better at it anyway."

That would help a little, make up for lashing out. Danny was relatively free inside himself, but he still had feelings.

There would be a label check at the doors. Wildhaus didn't throw chintzy parties. Sometimes a loser with a cruddy knock-off would crash in and flail around like a loon, pretending to be on the level, hoping nobody would summon the door guardians. More often, the maskless would creep in and clutter up the walls, hoping—for what exactly Jedward couldn't ken. To find a lost one like he had, maybe, but they'd never give it away. Of course, *Danny's* mask was always the best, the freshest pressing, and he always treated it like an old dirty sock, tossing it around and cramming it wherever.

Jedward wondered, lying under his thin, felty wool blanket, whether Karolin would even speak to him if not for the aura of Danny that followed him like a bodyguard. But she would, of course she would. She was a nice girl. She had a lot of growing up to do, that was all.

He crossed his arms in the dark privacy of his own bunk. *Look out for yourself for once,* he told the magic circle of Danny in his mind, and vanished it in a *poof* of smooth tan smoke. *I'm smarter than you think. I know how to beat the Herks.*

"Sure buddy, I'll go to the party," he said out loud, feeling good again at last. From the bunk above he heard Danny's head lift from his pillow and then drop again.

They always started at noon. Even the freshest faces couldn't peel off in time for moonup without some time to soak. Anyway there were streamers to hang, tall translucent towers of rapidly crystallizing sugar to press and mold into fantastic shapes, all the party details. It was a colorful year. Jedward was glad about that. Last season had been monochrome, which made his eyes feel like they were full of static. Danny had looked sharp in his checkered linen suit, though, that was true.

Eyes were all that was left by three. Soaked in, the masks began to ripple, and tiny silver-blue bubbles appeared at the edges where some skin was still left showing, spreading out over the backs of their heads and down their necks. *A rubberized hand feels like a suede bag full of sausages and sticks.* Jedward, creeping in from the gallery, was careful to keep a few feet of clearance all around him as two-legged, half-melted wolf-people snittered and worbled through the arches and into the den.

In the foyer there would be a messy hill of jeans and windbreakers looming up under a hanging rack of blouses and ties, with no one bothering to guard it. Jedward stepped through the spaces in the crowd and went there. As soon as he was alone, he touched his own face to reassure himself it was still real.

He had the new formulation in his bag. With nothing much else to do at night he'd always been up in the purple. He stripped out of his old jeans and pilly sweater and buried them, digging out a much nicer set before striding out confidently toward the wallflowers and poseurs he knew he would find leeching around the back gate.

"You guys looking for some fresh masks?" He smiled at them like Danny, like the whole world could just come right up and sit in his lap.

He sold out in less than fifteen minutes. Looping around front, he listened to his own boots crunching on the gravel and thought about the kids back there. Somebody had to look out for them, even if they *were* desperate and annoying, that much was clear. You could do anything to them, or with them, for that matter. Anybody could.

He saw Karolin and Danny when he was still out of earshot. They were hanging around the front arch, smoking through their masks and avoiding eye contact.

"It kind of sucks in there," he said by way of greeting as he reached them. "Why don't we just go out to the woods?"

Kay's mask distorted as she rolled her eyes beneath it, briefly giving her the appearance of a blanked-out zombie-wolfgirl. The plastic teeth already looked more like bone. It wasn't even the one he'd given her. "Jeddy, there are *bugs* in the woods," she said, barely patient with his foolishness. "And Tynesha brought those rum balls. And it's almost time anyway. We'd never make it out there. Your birdy girlfriend can wait, just come inside."

"Actually it's a juvenile male," he heard himself saying, and wished he wasn't. "Looking for a mate by showing off his repertoire."

"You always want to go," Kay told him, stubbing out her smoke and yanking open the Wildhaus door. "You always want to be somewhere else."

"It's not my fault most places suck," he said to the door as it swung shut with awkward slowness.

"Maybe it is." Danny sounded serious, but he smiled. "If you're the common denominator." He leaned on the wall and lit a second brown cigarette from the first. "You notice she said that while *leaving*."

"I like that she's not fake," Jedward said, because it was what he always said in his mind when practicing for this inevitable conversation. "She says whatever she's thinking and does whatever she feels like."

"Yeah, you know who does that? Assholes." Danny's anger, always flittering around his head, dive-bombed into the discussion again. "You just like it because you're all scrunched up on yourself. You go around like nothing means anything, like you'll wake up any time now. And it makes everybody think you think you're better than them."

Danny loomed up so close suddenly that Jedward was sure he was finally mad enough to actually hit him, and then for a second it seemed like maybe he was going to do something even weirder, but instead he fell back and sulked on the wall again. Nothing, Jedward realized. He just felt nothing at all.

"Something's going to happen, Danford," was what his mouth said this time. "You have to come and see."

The woods were cool and the color of glowing scallions. Fresh green leaves filtered the moonlight into tinted planes and striated beams, so every gap in the canopy became a projector and every flat surface an empty movie screen. Back at Wildhaus, the plastic wolf-people were probably gathering under the big skylight, waiting for the peak, the final hit that would take them over the edge. Into nowhere. Nothing. Another party. Another night nobody would remember, except who had the Herks to make it in. One plus up got you an hour. Everybody kept running in the same direction and nobody ever moved.

Not tonight. They could hear it coming from two miles off—a rumble, a rustle that gained bass until it became a steady throb. Danny grabbed his hand and stood too close, and Jedward could see the silvery-blue ripples starting to pulse and shine along the seams of his mask—where they would be, anyhow, if he weren't fully soaked now. Along the edges and between the lines, and the light was entirely unnatural, especially here, and then the wolf face stared back at him without Danny inside it.

But Jedward knew he was there, cheery and managerial, pulling the mental levers from inside. The paw on his arm felt warm again, articulated and alive, and the claws were real enough to lightly tear his shirt where they touched it.

The legs were basically the same, though bright red fur now ran down Danny's chest and belly and thighs. It wasn't quite thick enough to hide his genitals when he was standing, so with a very unwolflike gesture he plucked a few leaves and soft green stems from the bushes around them and wrapped them around his waist. They'd have loincloths on in Wildhaus, though some of them not for very long.

Jedward offered his arm again once his friend was covered, then on an impulse threw the arm up around Danny's fuzzy shoulders, feeling the new muscles tensing. Standing side by side, facing the road, they listened.

The rumble died away into a heavy quietness. Then a howl rang out, far off, and another answered it. Shrieks followed, coming closer as the Wildhaus partiers fled stupidly towards the woods, because that was what they always did before if the cops crashed in. Faster and stronger now, they reached the edge of the trees in just a few minutes, and Jedward hugged Danny closer as they heard crashing and stumbling all around them. Then another howl, this one taken up almost instantly by a pack that was clearly now unified and on the move. Jedward had sold two or three of his new masks to some of the stragglers, to hand out to their friends, so he figured the real wolves would well outnumber the plastic ones, since there were always more people outside than in.

Finally they saw one, and Jedward felt floaty with pride. It was beautiful, seamless and soft, flowing as it ran like a soft bead of black mercury with fur and white jaws. Nearby they heard plastic wolf-people trying to force unfamiliar, stiffened limbs to climb trees, and another shriek as someone fell from one. The black wolf that had just run by them pounced, but the Herks were thick and tough especially now, and its jaws could only pull away long gooey strands of furry morphic rubber, many of which snapped back onto the owner in warped crisscrosses and ugly lumps.

Danny, watching this, made the noise which Jedward recognized as a human laugh coming out of a mask-warped mouth. "Right," he said, muffled but clear enough, uncannily. He sounded relieved, as if he'd been a little worried his friend might have finally snapped. "Okay, it's funny. But these are good, really good. You can't even see that they're masks."

"That's because they aren't anymore," Jedward said, tightening his arm on Danny's shoulders in his excitement. "The masks are gone once triggered. One-use."

Danny's mask stared at him as the futile chaos of growls and shrieks and scampering around them in the dark woods continued. "Do you realize," he said finally, "how stupid rich we're going to be?"

"No." Jedward didn't mind; he knew this was how it would go. He'd been there too at first. Danny would come around, though. He would get it, and maybe Kay would too. Once she tried one, and maybe went on a run with him. Then she'd understand that he didn't think he was better than anybody. He just wanted things to be fair.

"No? Why? You . . . we made it, right?"

"Yeah," Jedward said. "But it's really one-use. One time. After that, it just happens on its own. Every full moon. For anybody that wants to."

Two more wolves ran by them, heads up with pleasure at the chase. They ignored Danny, who was funny and always remembered names. The masked who'd managed to get into trees were clinging and whimpering above, and Jedward knew some of them would wait there until morning rather than risk ruining their genuine Herks, not yet understanding that they were worthless now.

"I don't know, buddy, if you want us to make a living you might want to change the formula," Danny said slowly, doing math in his head and finding the brick wall at the end of the figures. "I don't think it'll work."

Jedward took a flashlight and a rope ladder from his bag and began sweeping it through the trees, looking for Karolin's beads shining in the white beam. She might be really scared, and if he helped her down, she might be really pleased.

"It's already working," he said.

THIRST

VANDANA SINGH

⇒

In the dream there were snakes coiling about her, dark and glossy as the hairs on her head, and an altar, and the smell of sandalwood incense, her mother's favorite kind. When her eyes opened she could not remember for a moment who she was. Even the familiar room, with the whitewash peeling off the walls and summer dust on the sill of the open window, the sag of the bed, the curve of the man's shoulders as he lay in sleep with his back to her—all that seemed imbued with remoteness, as though it had nothing whatever to do with *her*. Slowly her name came to her: Susheela, and with it the full weight of her misery returned. Her husband stirred in sleep, but he did not turn towards her.

Then she remembered (as she sat up very carefully so as not to wake her husband) that tomorrow was the day of Naag Panchami, the Snake Festival, and *that* was why the dream had come. The monsoons were late, and this was the hottest summer ever. Perhaps it would rain tomorrow. A Festival day rain would be a good thing. She slipped out of bed, bathed quickly using an inadequate half a bucketful of water and dressed in a pink cotton sari. An early morning hush lay deep over the house; the ceiling fans had wound down during the night (another power failure) and even the birds in the bougain-villea outside the window seemed reluctant to break the silence. As Susheela entered the kitchen she heard the creak of her mother-in-law's bed from the other end of the house, and the old woman's plastic slippers slapping the bare floor as she shuffled to the bathroom. Susheela's son was very likely still asleep in his grandmother's bed; she could see him in her mind's eye, fore-head beaded with sweat, plump hands closed into fists, cheeks flushed with heat, lips tremulous with the passage of some childish dream. For a moment she wanted desperately to see him and hold him, but she could not face the old lady just yet. Instead she put the tea water on to boil and turned on the taps so that when the water came (one precious hour in the morning and one in the evening) the buckets would begin to fill for the day's use. Now the tap only belched warm air; heat came in from the small window like the breath of a hungry animal.

She stood at the window, looking out into the courtyard and the untended garden behind it. The drought had reduced the back garden to a mass of dead, spiny shrubs dotting withered grass. Only the little harsingar tree stood proud, its young, leafy branches dotted with tiny orange and white flowers. It had survived on a daily cupful of water and her love.

Afterwards, as she rolled paratha dough for her husband's breakfast, hoping she would not (again) make him late for office, she heard the household stir; and the water came gurgling out of the taps. She felt the old hunger in her as though she was waiting for something. As the earth waits for rain, she thought, licking her dry lips.

She thought of the lake in the park, and—despite herself—the thin face of the gardener who worked there, and the way he said "namaste" so respectfully while his eyes looked at her in a way that dissolved all distance between them, all barriers of class and caste and propriety . . . She really shouldn't go there so often. But Kishore loves it, her mind said rebelliously, and she thought of how her little boy loved to walk under the trees and watch the parakeets eat the neem berries. She would make up stories for him about imaginary people who lived in the ruins around the lake and ate nothing but milk-sweets all day. The park was on the way to the vegetable market that came up in the late afternoon like a miniature city on the sidewalks, complete with towers of jewel-toned purple eggplants and cascades of coriander leaves and citadels of fat, shiny little onions. The market was her excuse for surreptitious visits to the lake in the park, with her boy (poor, innocent boy!) as chaperone and protector. Sweat rolled off her temples; she dabbed at it with the free end of her sari and thought of the translucent coolness of the lake, the lips of the water against her bare toes. I am a cursed woman, she thought to herself with a shudder. My mother-in-law is right, the water draws me and draws me, to what other thing but death. Curses do run in families. She thought of her own mother, and her maternal grandmother, and she resolved that today she would not go to the lake, even though that would make Kishore cry.

In the end she broke her promise to herself, as she had done many times before. In the dry, breathless heat of the day, Susheela felt as though the air in her lungs had turned solid. She went blindly about her tasks, cooking and serving lunch, piling the steel dishes noisily in the sink for the servant boy to wash when he came in the evening. The grandmother took Kishore off for his afternoon nap. Susheela collected the kitchen leavings—potato peels, turnip ends and scraps from lunch—into a battered tin and went up the short driveway to the front gate. Dead leaves crunched under her feet. Piling the refuse by the side of the gate, she waited for Muniya, the milkman's ancient cow, to come meandering down the lane.

The lane shimmered in the heat. The three shisham trees in the garden stood very still, their small, round leaves drooping. Behind her the house crouched like a yellow cat. Plaster flaked off its front, revealing an under-flesh of burnt red brick. Susheela leaned on the gate. A breeze, no more than a breath, stirred the dead leaves on the trees, smelling of dust. But Susheela smelled—or imagined she smelled—water.

Suddenly she made up her mind. She crept into the still, dark house and saw with relief that the grandmother had fallen asleep with Kishore. The two lay together like exhausted children, damp with sweat, the old lady's arm protec-tively around the boy. I have not been a good mother, Susheela thought. Her eyes burned with tears. She went out into the bright and dusty afternoon.

In less than ten minutes she was at the iron fence, with the rusty, indeci-pherable Archeological Survey of India sign leaning over the entrance. She paused for a moment, looking around her a little apprehensively. A bicycle-repairman sat nodding under a tree with his paraphernalia around him, but there was no one else about. She let herself into the gap in the fence where there had once been a gate; inside, tall neem trees made deep shadows. A clerk or two lay sleeping in the shade. Then she saw the gardener, sleeping, his turban spread out over his face. The bullock that had been pulling the lawn mower lay beside him like a white, humped mountain, chewing cud. Susheela crept soundlessly to the lake's edge.

The lake itself was small, more like a large pond. The edge was paved with stone, brown and weathered with age; at one end there was the old ruin with crumbling steps leading down into the quiet, green water. What ancients had built and frequented the place Susheela did not know, but it was tranquil here, under the neem trees. The water had receded with the heat of summer, but there was enough to allow a few fragile blue lotuses to bloom in the shade.

She leaned against a tree trunk, savoring the peace. Then she slipped a slender brown foot out of her embroidered shoe, over the sun-warmed stone paving into the water. She felt the cool silk of the water on her foot, and a tremendous longing arose within her, a desire to feel the water lick the dry heat from her body, to envelop her in its fluid embrace . . .

Some small sound jolted her back into herself. She withdrew her foot hurriedly from the water, wiped it on the stone. What had she been about to do? A bead of sweat ran down her cheek to the corner of her mouth. Then she saw that there was something in the water, making ripples as it swam towards her. A turtle, perhaps—or a snake? She leaned forward, peering. In the emerald depths, apparitions of pale fish scattered as the thing came closer. It was a snake—a cobra.

Just as she identified it she saw a stone skimming over the water, falling a few feet short. The snake dived and disappeared.

Her skin prickled. The gardener was standing beside her.

"They say it is good to see a cobra the day before the Snake Festival," he said. He wiped the sweat off his face with his turban. "It means rain. But better not to let the Naag Lords get too close, *behen*. Would you like some flowers? Amaltas blooms, yellow as sunlight, lovely tied in your bun, against your neck . . . or would you prefer . . . a delicate twig of harsingar?"

She edged away nervously. For a moment she imagined his fingers on the nape of her neck.

"No, I don't want anything," she said shortly. He was looking at her without any shame, as though she were a woman of his own class, not a respectably married housewife. But respectably married housewives didn't wander about parks alone.

"If ever there is anything you need . . . I will be happy to serve you. But tell me, where is your little boy?"

Oh why hadn't she brought Kishore? She looked around her, terrified, and was reassured to see a young couple enter the park, holding hands surreptitiously. Some of her fear abated.

"I have to go," she said, drawing herself up. The gardener put his palms together, accepting her dismissal, his gaze licking at her face. "*Achha, behen-ji,*" he said. Yes, sister. He watched her leave. She was conscious of the movement of her hips, the slight swing of her arms, the dust she raised with every step. She did not draw breath until she was out in the lane.

She had grown up off-balance. All her life she had carried inside her an empty space that disturbed her center of gravity, that drew her to the sheltering closeness of trees, walls, wilderness. Nothing she had done in her life—not her studentship, not marriage, not even the birth of her son—had assuaged that emptiness, that feeling of the earth waiting for rain. She was still waiting.

In her childhood the Snake Festival had been special. It was the one day she had always understood to be her own. Here in this small town where her husband had grown up, Naag Panchami would be marked only by a visit to the temple and prayers to the gods to prevent death by snakebite. But in her hometown of Ujjain, tomorrow, there would be special ceremonies and processions in the streets . . .

In her parents' house, every Festival day, the child Susheela had helped her mother arrange flowers and sweet offerings on the kitchen altar. Dressed in silks, Susheela had sat with her brother on the flower-strewn floor, watching as their mother lit the oil diyas. In the flickering light, her mother would become remote and solemn, chanting the ancient Sanskrit phrases: homage to the snakes of the earth. Homage to the snakes in the rays of sun, the tree-snakes. Homage to the snakes of the waters, homage to them all. The names of the Snake lords were then recited: Anantha, who supports the earth in his coils, Vasuki the king, who rules their fabulous, gem-studded underworld city. Takshaka, Muchilinda, all the greater and the lesser lords. They bring us life, her mother would say; they foster fertility and renewal. They bring also death. They are in the fire of Agni and in the primeval ocean.

Her mother would turn from the altar to her children and take the child Susheela onto her lap. Then the stories would come, wondrous tales, fierce or sad; about the Snake divinities speaking to gods and mingling secretly with humans; about their exquisite underwater palaces, where they kept the knowledge and wisdom they had accumulated, waiting until humankind was ready for the gift. As her mother spoke her hands would rise and fall in smooth and sudden gestures, and the stories, built thus of words and hands, would come to life in the fragrant air. Her mother's urbanized Hindi would give way to the sing-song village dialect she had spoken as a girl. Even as a five-year-old, Susheela was aware that what was being passed on to them on these occasions was meant particularly for her; that her brother, sitting wistful-eyed across from them was in some inexplicable way, excluded.

But the most wonderful thing about it all was that the three of them were sheltered for a while, in a cocoon of mystery and ceremony, from the mundane, silent bitterness between her parents. Her father kept away from them during Naag Panchami, leaving them to an unfamiliar peace. As she grew older, it became increasingly clear to Susheela that the undercurrents of ill-feeling in the house, the raised voices (mainly her father's) behind locked doors in the night, the misery, guilt and yearning in her mother's eyes—were all her fault. Her father treated her with a distant regard; his love he kept for his son, expressing it with his eyes whenever he looked at the boy, unaware that the boy feared him and longed to escape.

Coming home from school—she remembered how it felt to enter the dark, polished hallway, the high-arched ceilings—how the house diminished her. The respite of the garden and the parakeets in the guava trees, the three harsingar trees (her favorite kind) bright with tiny flowers ... And then quite suddenly she was grown up and her marriage arranged with a stranger she had met only three times. He had come once for tea in the garden, and later they had walked together, chaperoned by her mother and aunts. She had lost her reserve, pointing out to him the trees and flowers and her favorite shady spot under the jamun tree, and he had impressed her with the way his hands touched the blossoms, the ripe fruit, so gently for such a big, quiet man. She had wanted him to touch her like that . . .

For the five years of her marriage the Festival had brought her nothing but shadows from the past, and a small remembrance from her brother. Only this year—this year was different. The intensity of the old dream, the tightness in her chest, the feeling of breathless anticipation . . . Entering the dim stillness of the house, Susheela found herself longing for her son. But he was still asleep in his grandmother's bed. She wanted to hold him forever because she feared that she would not hesitate to leave him for the nameless hunger that was in her.

In the late afternoon, when the heat had abated a little, Susheela's husband came home from work. His name was Prakash, but she couldn't think of him by his name, only by the way he made her feel, a mixture of bewilderment and yearning. Kishore ran up to him at the doorway, calling "Baba!" in his high voice. The child had sulked all afternoon when she told him they were not going to the park. Finally she had made him a paper boat and told him he could play in the washing-up water. Now he held out the damp boat to his father. A brief smile broke the serious cast of her husband's face, accentuating the lines that made him look older than he was. He glanced at Susheela quickly, noncommittally, and went into the back to wash his hands, leaving in his wake a faint odor of musty offices and old ledgers. Standing in the silence and heat of the dining room, with the silver teapot and the array of delicacies arranged on the table, Susheela felt suddenly bereft of hope. How had she come to this?

Once she had almost loved him. Not at first—she remembered sitting terrified before the nuptial fire under a canopy of marigolds in the front lawn, with this man that she hardly knew. Her father had died the previous year. She had left the large suburban bungalow, the luxuriant garden that had been her refuge, and her mother, alone, serene now after years of unhappiness, but with a haunted, fragile air about her—all that, for the life of a senior accountant's wife in a strange town. Still, in the beginning, her husband's gentleness had won her over. He had been loving and attentive, filling her with a joyous, incredulous relief, allaying her fears that her married life would be as dreary and bereft of happiness as her mother's had been. She had started to fall in love with him, with his patience, his long, contemplative silences, and the inexplicable, endearing seriousness with which he took his work. But then, quite soon after the birth (nearly painless) of their son, everything had changed. Her husband suddenly began to avoid her as much as was possible, and sometimes she had caught him giving her peculiar, wary, sidelong glances that she could not fathom. It had disturbed the healthy, animal joyfulness of motherhood.

He had evaded her questions, meeting her pleas, tears and anger with a pained silence. Finally she had come to accept that things would stay this way between them. Four years later he was still the kind, quiet man she'd known, but he had kept his distance; he no longer looked at her much, even when they (infrequently) made love.

The evening wore on—dark fell and mosquitoes came swarming in through cracks in the shutters. The power was still out so her husband lit candles in the rooms that cast large, tremulous shadows. The air was thick as a blanket.

There was a sudden loud crash in the house, and the sound of water splashing. Her mother-in-law screamed, "Susheela? Arrey Susheela! Look what your son just did! Don't cry, my darling . . . "

In the kitchen, which was lit dimly by a candle, Kishore stood soaked to the skin in the washing-up water. The bucket lay overturned on the floor. He was crying noisily, holding the soggy remains of the paper boat. As Susheela picked him up, her mother-in-law shook her head. "It's the curse on your family!" she said. "Drawn to water—and to death! He had climbed into the bucket with his boat. He would have drowned if I had not come in just then. My poor boy, what will become of him!"

"Let her be, Ma-ji," her husband said. He was standing in the doorway. He gave Susheela a quick, shy look. When she came towards the door with their son he laid his hand on the boy's dripping head.

"Susheela?"

He spoke her name tentatively, questioningly, but her eyes were already filling with tears. She stepped past him with her burden. In the bedroom she stood Kishore on the bed to dry him down and change his clothes. "I'll make you another boat tomorrow," she told him, glad that the semi-darkness hid her tears. Curses did run in families . . . She remembered her brother's escapades to the pond at the end of their street when they had been children, and how their father had scolded him as he stood dripping and half-naked on the polished floor of the hall. Nothing he said had made a difference to the boy; the next afternoon he would be gone again with the servant children, diving and splashing in the pond among gleaming green lily-pads, coming reluctantly home in the evenings through the dining room window, all aglow with his adventure, swearing her to secrecy . . .

The power came back suddenly. Susheela blinked in the light. The ceiling fans began their laborious circumlocutions, and the still air began to move. Her son laughed, jumped off the bed and went to find his father, holding out his little arms like airplane wings.

Late that evening, after the servant-boy had finished doing the dinner dishes and been dismissed, Susheela stood alone in the kitchen, finishing the day's chores. She could hear the low sound of the TV from the drawing room. In the small bedroom that her son shared with his grandmother, her mother-in-law was singing some old, half-remembered lullaby. In the storeroom, above the bins and sacks of grain, the gods gazed at Susheela from the altar—a brass statuette of Vishnu the Creator, reclining under the sheltering hood of the great serpent Ananth; Krishna with his flute, a meditative Buddha and a print of Lord Shiva. She cleaned the altar of dead flowers, lit an incense stick and watched the smoke curl up to the rough, white-washed ceiling.

One more task remained. She filled a steel bowl with cold milk, put the rest of the milk into the small fridge, and took the flashlight. She had watched her mother do this every night for years in their home in Ujjain. Now, with her mother gone, the ritual gave her comfort. She went into the silent, moonlit courtyard behind the house, staying close to the wall. She walked up to the harsingar tree, which stood green and proud amidst the detritus of dead bushes and thorny shrubs. It always bloomed out of season, as though it obeyed the laws of some other universe. Under the tree lay a great stone, upon which she set down the steel bowl of milk. She turned off the flashlight. Would the snakes come, as her mother had always said? Usually she'd leave the milk on the stone and go back into the house, but today she wanted to wait.

The fragrance of the harsingar flowers filled her nostrils. The little tree was doing well. It had appeared last winter, the day before the festival of Diwali. She had just gotten back from the market with her mother-in-law. The servant boy did not know who had come into the compound in the afternoon and planted the tree. Susheela's mother-in-law said it must be the gardener who worked in the park—he had been trying to hire himself out in the neighborhood. Or maybe it was the lady from the Big House, the wife of Susheela's husband's supervisor, who had the huge ornamental garden that her mother-in-law had frequently admired. That is what Susheela wanted to believe.

The tree itself was innocent of its origins. She had loved it from the first moment she had seen it. Now it stood partly shading the great stone, beautiful in the moonlight. She shut her eyes and breathed in its scent. There was a sound—a soft, dry, sliding sound, scales against stone. When she opened her eyes the gleam of moonlight on the steel bowl vanished abruptly, and she thought she could see dark, coiled shapes against the stone. Let there be rain tomorrow, she said in her mind. She could not name the nebulous other thing she desired.

Very carefully she gathered half a handful of flowers from the tree and walked back to the house without turning on the flashlight. Inside she put the flowers on the altar in the kitchen. I will put some in my hair tomorrow, she told herself, switching off the light.

That night Susheela fell asleep thinking of her mother's mother, the grandmother she had never known except from old family pictures. This grandmother had brought up six children in a huge, old-fashioned house in the ancestral village. One day the river had broken its banks and filled the emptiness of the big house. The family took refuge on the rooftop terrace. The eldest son was missing—he had been visiting a neighbor. Grandfather had injured his leg so Grandmother went in the little boat, steering with a long pole, in the muddy water full of debris, pots and pans and bewildered river fish. She found her son, delivered him, then went to the aid of her neighbors. She rescued a woman stuck in a tree, several other people clinging to hut-roofs, and a variety of animals, including dogs, goat-kids and muskrats. In the evening she cooked dinner on the rooftop over a coal fire, quite calmly, as though nothing unusual had happened. As dark fell, she told her eldest son, who was still awake, that she had to go do one more thing. She looked on the sleeping, exhausted family one more time, got into the boat, pushed off with the pole, and disappeared over the murky water. She was never seen again.

Stories gathered around the legendary grandmother like moths about a candle flame. She had given herself to the river, people said, so the floods would not come again. Susheela's mother, the youngest child, had been a teenager at the time of the disappearance; she remembered it well, years later, but she did not like to talk about it. Her face would fall slack with the memory. Then Susheela would gaze into her mother's eyes and think she saw what her mother saw: the flood, the dark water, the sole woman in the boat, steering herself away between the drowned houses, under a silent sky.

Her mother was a haunted woman, she knew. Soon after Susheela's marriage she had heard that her mother had gone to visit her ancestral home. At this, Susheela had felt a vague presentiment of disaster. But newly married, and pregnant, she had not been permitted to leave. A month later, Susheela had heard from her brother that their mother had walked to the river one morning, with flowers for worship, and that later that day, her clothes had been found floating some distance down-river from the house. Not long after that, Susheela had received a letter from her mother written a few days before the tragedy; the address on the envelope was nearly illegible and the ink was blurry and unreadable, as though the pages had been left out in the rain. Susheela had felt very clearly then that some intangible thing had passed from her mother's life into her own. For nearly five years it had been a heavy, mysterious presence within her.

She had seen that great river once, as a child. Now it came into her dreams, broad, serpentine, flowing between fragile cities, open fields and wilderness. She dreamed of floods, earthquakes, buildings tottering, the earth heaving, throwing off its old coverings, revealing roots, rocks, darkness. Twice she woke, and lay in the dark, trembling, her eyes wide open, listening to her husband breathe beside her. I must go, she thought, even if it is death that calls me.

Morning filled the house with a pale gray light; a cool breeze came in from the open windows, smelling of dust and anticipation. Susheela, breathless and light-headed, moved from room to room, distractedly applying the dust-cloth. In the kitchen she picked up a few of the harsingar flowers from the altar, hesitated, then put them down the front of her blouse for the fragrance. She did not have the patience to make a flower chain to weave in her hair. When her mother-in-law came into the kitchen Susheela was already rolling paratha dough for breakfast. She fed the family; she herself had no appetite. Her husband pushed away his empty plate with a sigh and unfolded the Sunday newspaper.

Susheela went to the front window in the drawing-room and perched on the cold sill. An army of storm-clouds was poised in the sky, and the breeze rattled the dry leaves on the trees. The raindrops fell, slowly at first, making pockmarks in the dust of the long summer; but in only a few minutes the dust became liquid mud, and the roadside ditches became torrents, and an aroma rose from the earth like a moist, cool breath of relief. All sounds were lost in the music of the rain. Neighbors gathered at their doorways, smiling, watching indulgently as children ran out of the houses and danced in the flooded, sparkling street. Then the clouds rumbled and lightning jagged across the sky. Parents called out to their children. Susheela, watching the rain, tried to decipher what message, if any, lay in its watery speech; what did it sing, as it drummed on the flat rooftops and gurgled in the ditches? She could not bear the thought that after all her waiting it would have nothing to say to her. Listening, she did not at first notice that Kishore was missing.

He'd been sulking; she had not let him go out with the neighborhood children. He must have slipped away while she sat dreaming on the sill. She raised an alarm, feeling her knees beginning to shake. Her husband set down his cup, spilling tea, grabbed an umbrella and went into the storm.

But Susheela knew just where he would be, in the park that sloped down to the lake, their favorite walk. She gathered her sari about her ankles and went into the blinding rain. Her shoes were light and flimsy, they soon filled with muddy water, but she stumbled on. On this day of all days, to lose him like this!

The lake was a blur; the rain fell like thick needles. She looked fearfully around, shading her eyes from the rain. There he was—huddled by one of the neem trees that grew on the lake's edge. He was too heavy to pick up, he bent his head against the rain and sobbed wordlessly, but he let her set him on his feet. She thought she felt or heard something from the direction of the lake, but when she looked back, there was nothing.

She held Kishore to her in a tight grip, half-sobbing in her relief, babbling words of reassurance as she walked him back through the mud and rain to the house. She heard her husband call, saw him running up to them. Kishore looked up at her through a curtain of rain, and she thought she saw wonder in his face, then fear. He left her side and ran to his father, crying. Her mother-in-law was already at the front door with towels, scolding in her relief. Susheela stepped forward to follow her husband and son, anxious to reassure her little boy; what could make him look at her like that? But something made her hesitate on the top step. The rain streamed down her face, running in rivulets down her neck, between her breasts. Her bun had come undone and her hair lay wetly against her neck. Her sari was plastered to her skin. She itched all over. She saw now that there was a faint silvering all along her forearm, spreading rapidly over her skin. A tremor went through her.

She felt it now like a gravitational pull, as if whatever thread bound her to the lake was at last drawing her in. She turned, stumbled down the steps and began to run through the downpour. Behind her she heard her husband cry out her name, but her steps did not falter. Splashing through the water on the street and in the park, she stood at last, panting, on the lake's edge.

She had lost her shoes on the way and the stone paving felt slippery under her bare feet. There was only the sound of rain, sparkling on the lake's surface, drumming on the earth. Susheela put one foot into the water. A great shudder of desire went through her. She stepped into the lake, slipping a little on the stones. Mud squelched between her toes. The water rose to envelop her—it embraced her hips, her chest, her neck. As the water closed over her head she felt the change, like an electric current through her.

Her first feeling was that of sheer terror, as though something alien had invaded her mind and body. She thrashed about, rearing out of the water and falling back again with a splash, trying to see what or who was holding her arms to her sides, drowning her, but the rain fell in great curtains, obscuring everything. A spasm shook her from head to foot; as she lost consciousness she felt warm currents coursing painlessly through her, stretching and squeezing, shaping and molding, as though she were a lump of clay in a potter's wheel.

When she came to, she found herself afloat in the water, conscious only of a great need to fill her lungs with air. She struggled to free herself of her clothes, turning and twisting until she swam out from the limp, wet folds of her sari, raised her head into the rain, and breathed. She turned slowly, and saw that her new body was long, limbless and lithe. Her senses registered a thousand unfamiliar impressions: the agitation of water against her scales; the completely alien sensation of being able to feel, through her skin, tiny reverberations that hinted of life swarming all about her; and the presence, inside her mouth, of a strange tongue, forked and unbearably sensitive. An exultation rose inside her; she became aware of other presences around her, long, sinuous shapes, ancient, powerful, familiar. Their bodies were dark, their heads narrow, their eyes black, beckoning, alive. She turned smoothly in the water and saw that her underbelly was pale, like theirs. Now they were leading her, diving underwater. She took a breath of air and followed them into the depths of the lake, brushing against stone; she sensed she was swimming through the passageways of some underwater structure. Memories that were not her own, yet belonged to her in some mysterious way, came crowding into her mind: warm, narrow spaces in the earth, fluid darkness, the coilings of other bodies beside her. The earth, the womb, shutting out the wide emptiness of the world.

The snakes swam around her, guiding her with gentle nudges. In the dark water they were like slender, graceful ghosts. One touched his head with hers, wheeling around her in an intricate spiral. They went up to the surface together to breathe, and taste the rain. The water was sensuous against her skin, and when the cobra leaned his head close to hers, with bright, ardent, questioning eyes, she felt a small explosion in her chest, as though a dam had burst, letting out all the needs and desires of her barren other life. That life, which she could scarcely remember now, seemed a distant dream; what was real was the movement of scale against scale, coil against coil, the flaring of her partner's majestic hood as they danced, braided about each other in the ancient, intimate rite of procreation. When at last they moved gracefully apart, to lie companionably in the water, spent but not exhausted, a picture came rudely into her mind, an alien intrusion: a small, hot, dusty room, a man asleep, his back to her, unreachable as a distant mountain. It was incomprehensible and disturbing, and she dismissed it sharply. The other snakes were coming up below her, swimming to the surface for air, and she joined them, moving playfully among them, dodging the raindrops. A feeling came to her then that she must have done this before, that this was all familiar, the snakes, the rain, the coupling in the water. That couldn't be—but the seed of a realization took root in her mind, and slowly flowered into certainty: that her mother had once done this. That this was how Susheela had been conceived . . . It was too enormous a discovery to comprehend all at once. When the snakes dived again, calling to her in their wordless tongue, she followed them into the submerged ruins. She understood it was a place of pilgrimage, sacred to her companions, and that they remembered its history in fragments that had been passed on from generation to generation. The pictures that arose in her mind hinted of calamitous events, heroic battles and long, golden periods of peace and prosperity. They were making her a gift of their story, she realized. She had no stories of her own but the memory of her mother and grandmother, which they accepted, she thought, with generosity.

But now the rain was slowing. She swam up to the surface and saw the sun emerge from behind the clouds. The other snakes swam sedately away from her, their farewells echoing in her mind. Until next time, she thought they said, whenever that was, and she had so many questions, so much to ask. But they were already gone, gliding over the ancient paving at the edge of the lake, disappearing into cracks and crevices in the old ruin, and into bushes, tree-holes, and other secret places. All that remained of their presence were wide ripples spreading and crisscrossing on the lake's sunlit surface. Why had they left her alone? Rainwater dripped off the neem trees; in their shade a small emerald-green frog perched on a lotus leaf. She drifted in the middle of the lake, feeling bewildered, abandoned. Then she remembered as if from long ago, the small, heavy weight of her son on her lap, the way he tilted his chin up to her to ask for a story, his upper lip rimmed with milk. She turned and began to swim back to the lake's edge, feeling herself grow heavier and heavier, until she could feel her arms again, and her naked, muddy skin, from which the scales were already fading. Her body felt strange, awkward; at last she stood in knee-deep water, looking at her brown arms glowing in the sunshine, her mud-streaked breasts, the shiny stretchmarks on the slight, taut curve of her belly. The world swam into focus; she felt her head clear a little. She passed her tongue over her lips, and felt the slight notch on its tip that had not been there before. Behind her, under the shimmering green surface of the lake, lay the promise of that other world. She looked around and saw that her sari, blouse and undergarments were floating near her, amidst a sprinkling of harsingar flowers.

For a while she stood quietly in the water, feeling dazed and new, thinking, but not in words, or words she had known before. She knew her mother had stood thus once, filled with excitement and confusion, feeling the new life she had made stir inside her. At last she could stand inside her mother's skin and sense what she had gone through—the dilemma of choosing between two worlds, the prison she had made for herself, of love and guilt. Her brother's wistfulness; like her own son, he had been fathered by a man; he would always hear the call of his mother's kind, but could never transform, never know what it was like to turn underwater in an exquisite dance, to taste the world through his skin, to be life-giver, rain-bringer, death-lord. This new child she carried would be like her, an entity capable of existing in two worlds.

Two worlds . . . Pictures rose in her mind: the warm yellow house, the harsingar tree. She remembered the rhythms of the day, the slow course of the white cow Muniya's morning journey from house to house, the taste of fresh milk. And Kishore . . . No, she was not quite ready to leave it all behind. It was not yet time for that. She would come back to the lake again tomorrow, to begin to learn how to parcel her life between water and earth, fire and shadow, until it was time for the final leave-taking. Slowly, dazedly, she gathered her clothes and emerged from the lake. She went behind a bush and began to squeeze the water from her sari.

Her skin prickled; she sensed the gardener's presence a moment before he came around the bush. His eyes were filled with wonder and desire—he came slowly towards her as though she were a dream that would dissolve with the first stumble. She watched him curiously, without fear, still in the twilight state between her two worlds. He put trembling hands on her bare shoulders. She let him draw her close so that her breasts flattened against his wet shirt; she felt the angular roughness of his chin against her cheek. "Lady," he said, and she tasted his skin, his smell with her tongue, and remembered, with the suddenness of a thunderclap, the old fear and confusion. A bitter taste filled her mouth; as he pulled her down into the wet grass she reached up blindly and bit the side of his neck.

She watched him thrashing about on the ground. After he had stopped she spat and rubbed her face with her hands to try to clear her head. Then she gathered her clothes, squeezed and shook the water from them and dressed. Her hair was wet and tangled, but she managed to comb it back with her fingers and tie it into a bun. She looked once more at the gardener's still body, feeling the beginnings of a vague uneasiness.

She began to walk slowly home, looking about her like a child, letting the sights, sounds and smells wash over her: men on bicycles, ringing their bells, children splashing into rainwater puddles, shouting in their clear, shrill voices, cars all shiny and wet, honking, lurching as they negotiated potholes, the smell of wet earth and the vapors already rising from the moist ground, the drip of rainwater from the tree branches above her. Slowly it came back to her. The way home. It was familiar and strange all at once.

And there, meandering down the street was Muniya the cow. She caught up with the great white bovine matriarch and stretched her arm toward her, but the cow shied away from her as though stung, and began to edge away, fear in her dark eyes. Dismayed, Susheela stood there helplessly, tears welling up in her eyes. She made a small, experimental, cajoling sound, thinking of the way Kishore had looked at her last. The cow let out a breath redolent with the odor of grass and carrot ends, and let Susheela come up to her. She shuddered as Susheela stroked her back, but did not move away.

Susheela felt an urgent need now to see her son. Taking leave of Muniya she began to walk rapidly, knowing that passersby were staring at her, with her disheveled hair and sodden clothes. She had to win back her little boy, to take that look from his eyes. She would do it, she thought in the wordless tongue, with patience, with stories, but—it came back to her now with horrifying clarity: the body of the gardener in the wet grass—how to protect her family from what she had become? What would she tell them? She couldn't even begin to articulate it, she realized in terror. People on the street were talking, laughing, and they might as well have been speaking some incomprehensible foreign language, because their speech had no meaning for her.

Then, slowly, she remembered the words, and understood them. It was Naag Panchami, the Festival of Snakes, and the monsoons had arrived at last. A car went by, fast, and two glittering arcs of water rose in its wake. There was the house; the shisham trees, their round leaves glistening, the trunks dark with moisture. Through the open front window she could see her husband's profile as he waited, reading his paper, one brown hand on the sunlit sill. A picture came into her mind's eye: that brown hand scooping up earth, making a hollow like a womb for the roots of the harsingar tree, patting the soil in place. She trembled, as though a string had been plucked deep inside her. The door was open. She walked into the house as if for the first time.

GROTESQUE ANGELS

GWENDOLYN CLARE

The rain turns the city upside down. In the gutters the water pools and flows, each drop fracturing the surface until the slick streets glitter as if seeded with pavement-bound stars. Low-slung clouds glow orange with light pollution, the night sky lit better than the street below. Not that the street is too dark for her eyes; nothing is ever completely dark in Chicago.

From her rooftop perch, Kelsey waits and watches. The city feels wrong tonight. Something old and hungry lurks in her territory, and the streets moan silently under the unwelcome weight of it. The Old One hides behind the city's glamour—*her* glamour—and she cannot see it. So she waits, wishing shadows were its only disguise, but the Old One is more clever than that.

Kelsey drops off the roof and lands on a narrow ledge part way down the side of the building, her claws scraping the neo-Gothic limestone façade. She crouches, motionless again, and the rainwater runs over her skin and streams from the tips of her wing-feathers as it might from a statue. The sidewalk below grumbles and sighs to her, unsettled by the Old One's passage. It walked this street not long ago.

A muted wail of sirens cuts through the sounds of the storm and the sidewalk's complaints, and Kelsey's head snaps up to catch the distance and direction. The sound lies ahead of her along the path she has already chosen—the path to track the Old One. It could mean nothing.

It's probably not nothing.

The rain stings her face when she flies, and she squints against it. Her nose detects the reek of bad magic from half a block away, vile and sulfurous. It leads her to a narrow alley wedged between a couple of brick four-floor walk-ups. She circles above, evaluating. Police lights paint the old brick in alternating blue and red, and the alley crawls with cops.

She alights on the fire escape above and watches through the black metal grate. The glamour cloaks her from sight. If they were to stare at her hard enough, they might see a shadow shape crouched in her place, but she knows they won't stare; they will not think to look up at all. Humans have an odd deficiency of awareness for what's above their heads. Perhaps their genetic programming is to blame, their pre-historic ancestors never having encountered airborne predators. An odd quirk of human psychology, Kelsey thinks, but convenient.

Below, the flooded alley looks like a biblical curse, rainwater diluting blood until there seems to be much more than a few liters and it flows like a river. Red streaks the side of one building, the evidence already smeared by the weather. Kelsey does not envy the humans as they splash through the remnants of their rapidly deteriorating crime scene. The corpse is a messy pile of ruined flesh likely to win the award for all-time low point in the detectives' careers. Kelsey certainly has no desire to give it a closer inspection.

She has never seen such exuberant carnage before, and it worries her. The Old One's misbehavior is escalating. Time to report in. Perhaps Duncan will know what to do.

A brick-and-glass monolith on State Street, the Harold Washington Library devours an entire city block in downtown Chicago—an impressive feat of architecture, and also Duncan's daytime resting place. Like most grotesques, Duncan has a penchant for dramatic buildings.

Kelsey finds him on the broad balcony that circles the top floor. She lands beside him, drops down on one knee in a quick obeisance, and straightens. Duncan seems pensive tonight, and the rain slicks his shale-gray skin giving him a polished look. The feathers of his headcrest are the color of olivine—a deep greenish hue that darkens to black when wet.

Staring out over his city, he says, "What news of the Old One?"

Kelsey spits over the rail with savage disgust. "It has begun taking human lives, and messily. The police are investigating already. Problematic."

"Find out what they know. Use it if you can."

"And how am I supposed to do that?"

He turns to look at her, meeting her reluctance with a stern command in his eyes. "How do you think? The Change, of course."

She spits again. "Fantastic."

The first time, she was only a child and she thought she was dying. Her claws shrunk to useless, flat nails; her pale gray skin soured to a disgusting pink shade; her silver crest feathers yellowed like old paper and curled into strings of hair. Worst of all her wings melted away, feathers deliquescing and bones softening like hot wax, and the drops of her flesh vanished before they hit the ground as if the limbs had never existed.

She lived, but sometimes wished she hadn't.

The other grotesques called her "half-breed" and "werehuman." It didn't matter that pure bloods were rare; it didn't matter that few if any of them could claim a heritage untainted by humanity. The Change cursed her alone, and so she grew apart from them.

As she takes to wing, Kelsey's stomach clenches with disgust at the thought of becoming that version of herself she has fought so hard to suppress. Duncan sends her forth to the task as if the Change were a gift and not a reason for shame. He knows what it costs her, but it doesn't matter. Anything and everything in service of the city.

Kelsey wonders: if she is not a true grotesque, why does the city still compel her? Surely her human-self would let her sense of duty slide.

The question will have to wait for tomorrow night. Sunlight pales the cloud cover to the east, dull gray light invading the orange city-glow. She already feels the sluggishness of dawn pulling at her, turning her wing-strokes clumsy. She flies south to the university—her beautiful neo-Gothic university—where her own daytime resting place awaits. She takes her post atop the stone archway of Hull Gate and settles down, camouflaged by the city's glamour to look like an architectural flourish, a gargoyle of the inanimate stone variety.

The city sighs relief as somewhere out there the Old One quiets too. Kelsey's eyelids slip closed.

The storm blew off during the daylight hours, leaving the night cold and newly dry. Kelsey stretches her wings in the fading twilight and launches into the air to begin tracking the groans and shivers of the streets. The Old One has awoken, too, and the city hunkers down to endure the long hours ahead.

Tracking is slow business. The Old One keeps to a particular course for several blocks, then suddenly zigzags as if it knows it's being followed and is trying to shake her. She must stop often to listen for the worst creaks and complaints from the pavement below. Perhaps if she were faster, perhaps if she could see her quarry—but "perhaps" is worth its weight in air.

So she keeps moving.

Up ahead the city wails softly to itself, the sound emanating from a spot too ravaged to send out a louder distress call. Another alley, chosen more hastily than the last kill site. Happenstance, or escalation? If the Old One is escalating, this won't be the only body tonight. Kelsey drops onto the edge of a rooftop to survey the damage.

The scene below is a blood splatter analyst's wet dream: the full five liters sprayed in a spectacular starburst that spans the alley and climbs the brick walls on either side. No one is allowed close to the body—or what's left of it—before the photographers finish their work, lest they trample the evidence.

A pair of detectives huddle off to one side, alternately staring and trying not to stare at the bloodbath while they wait for the forensics team to give them the okay. One of the detectives is tall and too narrow at the shoulders for his height, so his trench coat hangs loose on his skinny frame. The other's somewhat shorter, somewhat older, and working on his coffee-and-donuts belly.

Kelsey drops quietly to the ground several yards away from them, landing barefoot on the wailing blacktop. Her clothes will be a problem soon—shorts and a tank top and no shoes in the middle of October—since her grotesque-form doesn't mind the cold. Nothing to be done about it now.

With a deep breath, Kelsey reaches within herself for the closed door, the locked vault, the sealed box—every mental metaphor she used to suppress her blasphemous other half—and she spins the locks, releases the seals, turns the knob and *pulls*.

The Change snaps through her body more swiftly than the first time, the pressure of being bottled up making for a rapid release. She wavers on her too-small human feet with their useless short toes and almost meets the pavement the hard way before her new sense of balance kicks in. The cold starts to seep into her weak human flesh. Time to get this over with.

Twisting a scrap of glamour around herself, Kelsey fashions a fluffy coat and shoes that do nothing to warm her shivering human-form. At least she'll look a little less odd. She lifts the rest of the glamour slowly, sliding into the realm of human awareness as if strolling into view.

The tall detective notices her first and closes the distance in six strides. "Ma'am, I need you to get behind the line. This is a crime scene." He puts a guiding hand on her elbow, though she does not let him pull her away.

"No explosives," she says softly, looking past him at the remains.

He freezes. Then his hand drops from her arm to hang limp at his side. "What did you say?"

"You won't find any traces of explosives," she elaborates. "Just like the last one. Or have there been more?"

Not so subtly he sweeps back his trench coat to rest his hands on his narrow hips, the right one within easy reach of his gun. "If you could come with me, I'll need to ask—"

"No. No police stations, no interrogation rooms. When you're ready to talk, you tell me what you know about the case, and then I'll take care of your problem." She waves a hand in the vague direction of the carnage.

"Look, I don't know who you think you are sweetheart, but this is a homicide investigation."

"You're out of your depth. You need my help. Call me when your ego deflates enough to admit it."

Kelsey tosses a folded scrap of paper between his feet, and his eyes track it. By the time he glances up again, she has wrapped herself in the glamour and faded from view.

After her first Change, she went to Duncan for guidance. Or for penance, or absolution perhaps—she didn't know what she expected from him, but whatever he could give, it had to be a step up from the hollow dread inside her.

She explained to him what had happened, though she doubted he hadn't already heard a secondhand account. Still, he let her speak until she fell quiet, then let the silence stretch for several seconds.

Finally, he answered, "And what would you have me say to this?"

"Well," Kelsey hesitated, knotting her fingers together. "Should I leave the clan?"

Duncan frowned. "I do not know. The city will decide."

She looked away, cautiously persistent. "You could decide."

"If you're looking to me for a way out, for an excuse to run from your duties, you'll not find it here."

"We all know I am an abomination, not fit to serve the city."

Duncan's mouth quirked. "If you truly believed that, you would not need to ask my permission to go."

One body on the North Side, one body on the South Side. Kelsey decides to wait for the detective's call at an intermediate location, or as close as she can get to one. The Tribune Tower just north of the Loop has a glamour relay atop it and comes with additional benefits, such as five hundred feet of gloriously intricate neo-Gothic limestone façade. She lands on the highest peak of the building, with a pleasant view from above of the eight flying buttresses that circle the uppermost floors.

With architecture like that, the Tribune has its own grotesques, but luckily they're away from their roost for the night. Kelsey needs to tap into the glamour relay, and she doesn't want to be disturbed.

The relay consists of a pentagonal brass box and fifteen feet of antenna, and is one of several stations that spread the glamour through the city like an invisible web. Kelsey pops open a side panel and tinkers with the mechanical innards. The number she gave the detective piggybacks on the glamour network. It probably wouldn't please the Engineer who made the network to know she uses it thus, but he's an important being with more important concerns than Kelsey's personal communications.

When she's done tinkering she crouches, motionless. Kelsey is good at waiting, because she has to be. Finally, the air hisses with an incoming call. She places her palm on the slick brass to finish the connection.

She says, "Yes," not really a question.

A male voice thrums through the air. "This is Detective Novak from Chicago Homicide."

Ah, so tall and narrow has a name. "What can I do for you, Detective Novak?"

"You can tell me who you are and how you knew we wouldn't find any traces," he snaps.

"I knew there wouldn't be traces of explosive because explosives weren't used. And I am the person who's going to stop your killer."

He pauses. "Department policy doesn't endorse vigilantes."

At least he no longer seems to have her on his suspect list. "And how far have your policies gotten you on this case?"

He heaves an audible sigh. When he speaks, his words slur with sleep deprivation. "I've been standing in an empty alley for forty minutes, and I'm nowhere. I thought if I went back to the first scene, maybe I missed something . . . "

"You're at the scene alone?" That feels wrong. A place where such destructive power was recently released would still be weak, scarred, and a very vulnerable position.

"I mean, why here?" Novak rambles on, as if he hadn't heard her. "If the murders are about showmanship, why do it outside in the rain where all the work gets washed away before anyone sees it?"

"Listen carefully: you need to get—" A vibration like static suddenly buzzes through the air, the call cutting off. For a split second, the whole glamour network flickers, making her breath catch as surely as a skipped heartbeat would.

"Shit," Kelsey says to no one. Given the size of the network, even a slight fluctuation means a big power drain, and if the interruption wasn't on her end it was probably on Novak's.

It will take her whole minutes to fly to the first kill site. He might already be dead.

She feels the Old One from three blocks away, the city crying and cowering in all directions around it. It is unquestionably active, roiling with a sulfurous heat that chokes her as she approaches from above. For once, the Old One isn't hiding in the glamour. Instead it twists the glamour into hideous malformations that nauseate Kelsey even before she glimpses them with her eyes.

The view of the alley nearly knocks her from the air. At one end, an enormous cloud of black smoke boils and churns, full of glowing eyes and gnashing teeth and other monstrous body parts that smoke should not have.

The smoke cloud seems to pulse and grow, promising horrible agonizing death.

At the other end, Novak is literally stuck where he stands. The pavement has come alive, crawling inexorably over his shoes and up his legs, and—to Kelsey's ears—screeching like a torture victim all the while. Terror rolls off his skin in waves.

The Old One is toying with him, devouring his fear like candy. And it's using the city's glamour to do so.

Kelsey drops down into the alley like a stone, half shifting in mid-air so Novak will recognize her. She keeps her wings, though, to soften the landing.

The Old One's many eyes focus on her and it exudes annoyance at her distraction.

She glares right back. "You think you know glamour, do you? You think you can use my city?"

The Old One huffs disdainfully and gnashes its teeth. Fleshy tentacles curl and whip through the smoke, eager to get on with its horrific business.

"I don't think so."

Kelsey goes down on one knee and places both palms against the wounded pavement. She can feel the threads of abused glamour twisted and knotted within the smoke cloud. Through her palms she senses how the wrongness radiates outward, disturbing the whole city. And if she focuses, she can feel exactly which threads to yank to make it all fall apart.

She yanks.

The integrity of the smoke cloud falters and the Old One lets out a surprised hiss. Then Kelsey flares her wings wide and reaches out through her palms to the pavement, the alley, the streets beyond, and she pulls the citylight into herself. She begins to glow with orange incandescence, the artificial light of a thousand streetlamps growing brighter and brighter until she fills the alley with blinding modernity and the Old One flees.

Kelsey lets go of the light and for a moment all she can do is cling to the blacktop, exhausted and blinded by her own trick. The city should not have lent her such an ability, not in her blasphemous state of being, but she is none-theless glad that it did. With a sigh, she lets go of her wings and finishes the transformation into her human-form.

She stands and turns to face the shell-shocked Novak. The pavement has gone dead again, unfortunately while still wrapped around his legs. Kelsey stumbles over to him, shivering with cold and adrenaline, and she kneels down to coax the pavement off of him. After a minute of her gentle whis-pering, it melts back down and resumes its former shape.

Novak stumbles, almost falls. Eventually he finds his voice again. "A—are you a guardian angel?"

She blinks at him. "Even if I were, I wouldn't be yours."

"But . . . " He leaves his mouth hanging open for a moment before shutting it and looking away. "I don't even know your name."

"Kelsey," she says, with impulsive honesty.

"I . . . need to sit down," he says but makes no move to do so.

Another wave of shivers runs through her fragile human flesh. "Let's find somewhere warm. Come."

It takes Novak three cups of coffee and half an order of cheese fries at an all-night diner before the interrogation instinct supplants the shock. After what he saw, Kelsey doesn't see much use for denial, so she answers his questions more or less truthfully.

"So what are you, if not an angel?"

"A grotesque."

"Are there others like you?"

"I'm unique," she says, which is true though not the answer to the question he meant.

He shakes his head. "Look—it's not that I'm not grateful, but why did you help me?"

"I protect." She shrugs uncomfortably. "Humans, Lorefolk, the city itself . . . from each other. That's what I do."

"Lorefolk?"

"Things like me, and like *it*." The pronoun alone makes her want spit again, though she contains the impulse. "And others like nothing you've ever seen."

"It?"

"An Old One."

He rubs his face with one hand, as if her freely given answers only serve to frustrate him more. "None of this makes any sense."

She shrugs, not knowing what to say to that, and watches the waitress refill Novak's mug.

"Are you sure you don't want anything?" he says for the third time, in between questions.

She shakes her head. "Grotesques don't eat." Her human-form might be able to, but now doesn't seem like a good time to experiment. She feels dizzy and lightheaded, and all knotted up in the midsection.

"You're looking pretty human to me right now. Come on, try some." He pushes the half-eaten plate of cheese fries across the plastic table-top towards her.

Kelsey picks up a single fry and puts it in her mouth. The sensation on her tongue is foreign, overwhelming, and not entirely pleasant. She works her jaw the way she watched him do and swallows it. Her midsection seems to respond, though she can't parse out whether the reaction is positive or negative.

"So? What do you think?"

She frowns, considering. "Being human is problematic."

Novak laughs. "Believe it or not, cheese fries are the easy part."

She pushes the plate back across the table. She does not want to learn how to be human. Not now, not ever. This is a temporary alliance between two protectors of the city and nothing more. The task at hand is all that matters.

She says, "You should know: what I did in the alley with the light just spooked it, didn't get rid of it for good. The Old One's got your taste in its mouth now. It will come back for you."

His hand holding the coffee mug freezes halfway to his mouth. He sets the mug down cautiously, as if afraid his muscles will betray him. "It could be out there killing people right now."

"No, that's not likely." Kelsey shakes her head. "It's you the Old One wants now."

Kelsey rides in his car back to his apartment, and she gives him instructions to turn all the lights on and stay inside until dawn. Just in case, she walks a quick circuit of all the rooms, painting the walls with a subtle glamour of disinterest and distraction. Nobody to see here, move along. She hopes it will be enough. There is work to be done, and she cannot bring him where she needs to go. On the fire escape outside his window, she transforms back into herself and takes to the air.

She approaches Museum Campus from the north, flying low over Grant Park and Lake Shore Drive. The Field Museum, in all its Neoclassical glory, sits atop a well-manicured grassy hill with the Shedd Aquarium nestled against the lakefront some three hundred feet to the left. An expansive flight of steps leads up to the four massive Ionic columns of the museum's north entrance. Kelsey cannot get in that way, of course, not in the middle of the night.

She shims open the latch on a top floor window, slides through the narrow space, and drops down into an empty office room. Peering out into the hall, she checks for cracks of light under the other doors; no one appears to be working this late. Good.

The upper floors, reserved for curators and research staff, are arranged in a disorienting grid of look-alike hallways. Kelsey finds the nearest stairwell and descends into the public-access portion of the museum, and the door at the top of the stairs swings shut and autolocks behind her.

She tried propping the door one time, but the electronic security system tattled on her and a guard fixed the problem before she got back. Funny how it's harder to break out than in.

The second-floor balcony offers a stunning view of the marble-floored main hall below. The hall stretches all the way between the north and south entrances and holds some of the larger items on display, including two taxidermied African elephants and the biggest *Tyrannosaurus rex* skeleton in the world.

The skeleton is named Sue. Kelsey doesn't understand the desire to truss up dead things and show them off, and she especially doesn't understand the need to *name* them. She wishes the humans wouldn't clutter up beautiful architectural spaces.

One hop and she's over the balcony railing, wings snapping open to guide her descent. She lands almost silently, nothing more than a whisper of claws on marble, and darts through a doorway on one side. She runs down a long hallway lined with more crass displays of dead animals. In the back, the hallway opens up into a high-ceilinged exhibition hall wherein her destination lies: a full size replica of a Maori meeting house.

The structure encloses one large, empty room, with a doorway and a single window set into the front wall. Carved mask faces cover the dark, polished wood on the exterior, and the inlaid mother-of-pearl eyes seem to glow in the dimmed lighting. It is a sacred structure, patiently waiting to be used for the purpose it was meant for—a fulfillment that will never arrive.

The Lorefolk, at least, found a use for it, and a respectable one at that. Kelsey steps forward until she can rest her hands on the empty door frame. The wood feels smooth and warm beneath her fingertips. She mutters the Old Words and sends her will down her arms to fill the doorway, and the view of the interior wavers as if no longer confident of its reality.

Kelsey steps through. Her feet land on grass, and a clean, unscented breeze lifts her crest feathers. Behind her, an empty stone archway leading nowhere; in front, the architectural collage of the Engineer's workshop.

The low, sprawling structure shows no respect for right angles. It has three prominent domes—the smallest built of glass and the larger two of wood painted white with stripes of gold—fewer windows than all that weirdly-angled exterior wall space might suggest, and only one door.

Kelsey sidles forward hesitantly, glancing at the rocky humps of small hillocks surround the workshop on all sides, eerily silent and isolated to her city-accustomed mind. She opens the door and slinks inside. The front hallway opens up into a cavernous pentagonal room, three storeys high plus the domed ceiling. Five enormous machines hulk in the center of the room, all shining brass and dark bronze. They hiss and chug in a steady rhythm, filling the air with almost musical sound.

A single door is set in each of the five walls on each floor, and it is from one of these upper doors that the Engineer emerges. He follows a catwalk along the wall to a set of stairs and begins to descend without looking up from the leatherbound book in his hands. The Engineer is a short and squat little man with three sets of spidery arms and an extra joint in each of his too-long fingers. His wrinkled face gives him a look of perpetual squinting, and his ragged robes could be as old as the wrinkles.

Kelsey freezes where she stands, feeling unworthy to ask for his regard. She should go before he notices her.

He reaches the bottom of the stairs and, without looking at her, says, "The Engine Room is not open to the public."

"Sir, I need a moment of your time."

The Engineer adjusts the round set of spectacles perched on his nose. "I'm occupied, as you can see."

"There's an Old One loose in Chicago, and it's using the glamour network."

He makes a motion that might be a shrug. "The network is built for all Lorefolk to use."

"But the Old One isn't just hiding, it is draining power to use during its killing sprees. It's a parasite. It has to be stopped."

"That is . . . interesting." His lowest set of arms folds across his stomach, and his upper arms slowly close the book. "What would you have me do about it?"

"Sir, I know that I impose upon your time, but—"

"To the point, if you please."

Kelsey takes a deep breath and let it out. "I need you to build me a trap fit for an Old One."

Once she slips past the museum guards and regains her freedom, enough night remains for Kelsey to fly back to Novak's apartment and check on him. She alights on the fire escape outside his living room window and peers in. He has fallen asleep in an old armchair, and instead of waking him, she sneaks in and leaves a note: *meet me in Rockefeller Chapel at sundown*. Then she departs to find a resting spot of her own.

Sunrise. The oblivion of sleep. Sunset.

Kelsey launches into the darkening sky, beating her wings to gain some altitude. The campus blurs beneath her, and she lands atop the tower of the university chapel. She takes the spiral stairs down, fingertips running along the brick-lined inner wall of the tower. The chapel sighs comfortably, still warm and calm from the Engineer's daytime visit—she can feel the residue of his presence in every brick.

She cuts through the dim-lit sanctuary past the long shadows of polished-wood pews and finds a side door locked only from the outside. Sticking her head out, she yells for Novak, who comes jogging around from the front entrance. His flashlight rakes her eyes and she squints against the brightness to see him jerk to a halt.

Too late, Kelsey realizes she's wearing her real face.

"It's me," she says curtly.

"You're . . . you're a monster."

"I told you I'm a grotesque. What exactly did you expect?" She spits, angry that for a moment he made her wish for her human face. "If you stand out there all night, the Old One will paint the grass with your innards. Come."

He comes forward again, cautiously now, and slips through the door she holds open. The high, vaulted ceiling of the sanctuary swallows up the brightness of his flashlight, and the scuff of his shoes on the stone floor echoes.

"So, what—ancient cloud demons don't like churches?" He forces out the words, trying not to look at her.

Kelsey shakes her head. "Doesn't matter that it's a chapel, but it does matter that it's *my* chapel. I know these stones well. They'll aid me."

He breathes deep, lets it out, and turns to face her. "Okay. What's my job?"

"Sit on the dais and act, you know, murderable."

"I'm the *bait*?"

She blinks. "Naturally. What did you think I needed you for?"

She turns away and walks the length of the sanctuary on both sides, checking the small brass relays hidden behind each pillar. No long antennas on these pentagonal brass contraptions—the Engineer didn't build them for transmitting in this instance. What Kelsey needs is the opposite. She circles back to the dais and finds that the Engineer left the trigger on the podium, as promised. She picks it up, round and brass like a pocketwatch but singing with the power of glamour.

She says, "Not long now."

"Oh. Great." Novak flops down on the steps of the dais, elbows resting on knees. "I love this plan."

She stares at him, perplexed. "How you feel about it isn't relevant."

"I was being sarcastic."

"The alternative is dying in an explosion of gore."

"Look—I'm in, okay? But I don't have to like it, is all."

Not knowing what to say, Kelsey shrugs it off. Now is the time to focus. She springs up, gives the air two long strokes of her wings, and finds a perch atop the large pipe organ on the right side of the dais. The height and partial concealment give her a comfortable edge. She's ready for it.

They wait.

It comes.

Slowly at first, like the howl of a distant hurricane, the city begins to moan. As the Old One approaches, the calm evaporates from the chapel walls and each stone seems to shiver in terror. Kelsey feels the tremor when the Old One's fluid mass breaks like a wave against the outer wall. It leaks in through the cracks around the front doors, a black cloud thicker than firesmoke pouring into the air.

On the dais below, Novak shifts nervously. Kelsey stares down, willing him to hold his wits together until the Old One has been lured all the way inside. Stupid of her to plan a trap that hinges on a human's help, but Novak stills himself and does not flee.

The Old One literally pulls itself together, black tendrils tucking in to form a sphere of darkness, and begins to glide down the central aisle. It pulses slightly, as if breathing, and the hideous eyes and teeth rise to the surface to gape hungrily at Novak.

When the Old One reaches the center of the chapel, Kelsey pushes off from her perch and snaps open her wings to glide down to the floor, landing in front of Novak. The stones of the chapel quail and shriek beneath the Old One, and she feels Novak's fear, too, like a subsonic vibration. But when she serves the city, she has no fear of her own.

Kelsey kneels to place one palm on the smooth stone floor, the other hand still holding the trigger. She reaches out with her mind and draws in glamour from beyond the chapel, making herself seem larger, more ferocious. Fangs and claws to match the Old One's, eyes that glow with citylight, wings growing spurred and enormous to fill the vaulted space. She shows off for the Old One, goading him to match her skill.

When the Old One rises to her challenge, though, it takes glamour from the immediate area of the chapel. She feels the tension as it draws in more power, as if the relays are springs and the Old One stretches them out to their limits. The web of glamour pulls taut, singing like instrument strings, and when the threads are stretched to the breaking point, Kelsey jams her thumb down on the trigger.

The glamour springs back toward the relays, lightning-quick with elastic tension, and the relays suck it down, devouring the power and storing it. Each relay becomes a point of negative pressure, the energy flow from the Old One firmly established. Mindlessly thirsty, the relays will not stop drinking until the Old One is drained.

The Old One screeches and writhes. Its eyes and teeth and limbs disappear first, then wisps of black cloud begin to siphon off and it gradually shrinks.

The last few seconds are the worst, when the core being of the Old One rends in a dozen different directions, and the very air wants to shrink away from its ancient rage. Then, with a final rip, the relays devour it.

The walls sigh relief at its passage.

Novak stands shakily from the dais steps and walks over to Kelsey. "You saved my life again. That's twice now. Thank you." His eyes are too deep and grateful, with a puzzling lack of disgust.

"Well. Have a nice life," she says and flees the chapel.

With luck, Duncan will never ask her to take on the horrid human-form again. No frailty, no confusion, no illusions of humanity. That is what she wants, yes, she's certain. Never again.

Kelsey flies her rounds, starting at the lake and meandering westwards. The city has been quiet for days, but something is different in the air tonight. Something waits for her.

She lands on the steps in front of Rockefeller Chapel—next to Novak.

"What are you doing?" she says, dropping her cloak of glamour so he can see her.

He jumps at her sudden appearance. "Waiting for you. Took you long enough to show up."

She blinks. "Our business here is done."

"I got this case, see. I think it's up your alley."

The rush of hope and anxiety and desire catches her off-guard, echoes of human-form emotions nothing like the cool certainty of a grotesque's mission.

Novak takes her silence as an invitation to continue. "Today I had a body out behind the River North cineplex that was drained of blood. What do you think? Vampire?"

"There are no vampires in Chicago."

"Well that begs the question—who *did* take the blood, and why?"

She hesitates. "I don't work for you."

"What about my supernaturally blood-free Jane Doe? You willing to work for her?"

Kelsey scowls, knowing he's probably right. This case sounds as if it involves elements he is ill-equipped to deal with, elements that fall into her realm of experience. Her responsibility, even.

"I brought a coat, for when you're wearing your other face." Novak holds the spare coat out to her. "Come on. We can go someplace warm, review the details. And hey, maybe you could give food a second chance."

Reluctantly, she takes the coat from him and lets her wings melt away before wrapping it around her shoulders. The night air chills her human hands, and she shoves them down into the pockets. It feels strangely good—the cold and the coat, the discomfort and the doubt. Maybe it's okay to want this. Maybe her human-self is not a curse, after all.

As they make their way to Novak's car, the sidewalk sighs approval at the touch of her bare human feet. The streetlights flicker their agreement when she passes beneath them. Startled, Kelsey realizes the city wants this of her.

And she always gives the city what it wants.

BLUE JOE

STEPHANIE BURGIS

⟞⟝

Josef Anton Miklovic, Blue Joe, was twenty-one years old and playing the sax in a nightclub in Youngstown, Ohio, when he met his father for the first time.

Joe was on stage with his family band: Karl on keyboard, hunched and intense; Niko on drums, grinning his lopsided, dreamer's grin; and Ivan, as smooth and polished as a Croatian Clark Gable, playing his shining trumpet like a peal up to heaven.

Smoke swirled across the tables, obscuring the waitresses in their Betty Boop outfits and the customers in their sharp suits, with dyed blondes on their arms. Ivan had hooked up with the son of a local mob boss to pull this job, and the rest of the brothers knew how lucky they were to get it. Ivan had big plans, and Joe was happy to go along with them.

Joe soared into his lead break, and at the end of it, as he emerged sweating and victorious, he met the fierce gaze of a hawk-nosed man at the back of the room, through all the smoke and the darkness. Time froze around them, and the music stopped.

"You don't look much like your mother," the man said as he crossed the room. He wore a long black coat from a different era, and it flapped around him like the wings of a crow.

Joe squinted through the smoke, watching the man sidestep frozen Betty Boops and customers' arms flung out in mid-gesture. Joe's brothers were as still as statues on the stage around him, and he thought he probably ought to be scared.

"Everyone always said I took after her," he said mildly.

"All they meant was, you don't look like that lump she married." The man reached the stage and jumped up onto it as easily as if it were only an inch high, instead of four feet from the ground. "You take after me."

Joe looked the man up and down and knew it to be true. They shared the same crazy golden eyes, the same jet-black hair, though Joe's was slicked back into fashionable lines, and the same great, hooked nose, about which Joe's brothers had always teased him.

He turned to look at his brothers now, and the man before him shook his head.

"No. They're not mine. Your mother and I had parted ways by then. But I told her I'd come for you to raise you right, when I was ready."

"And you waited till now?" Joe laughed, despite the shock. "You left it a bit late, don't you think?"

"It took time to make my way over. Do you remember the journey you took?"

Joe shook his head. "I was only a baby when we came over to the States."

"Well, I took a longer route. It's harder to leave the old country, for some."

Some. Joe didn't know exactly what the man meant, but he didn't care to ask, not with the rest of the nightclub frozen around them like stills in a news-reel. Whatever power this man had, it was obviously more than the local mob, and that was enough to scare anyone with sense.

"I'm here now," the man said, "and it's more than time. Your mother hid you too well." He fixed Joe in his hawk-like gaze. "Time to go."

"Hey, I'm not going anywhere." Joe stepped backward, crashing into Karl's keyboard. "I've got family."

"I'm your family."

"Uh-uh." Joe drew strength from his brothers' presence around him, even though they couldn't move. "I'm in a band. We're going places together. Might even break into Hollywood, if we're lucky."

His father snorted. "You're as stupid as your stepfather, if you really think that."

"I'm with my brothers," Joe said. "We're a team." He squared his jaw. "We can have a beer sometime and talk, if you like. But it's too late for you to act like a real father now."

"You'll change your mind," his father said. Anger flared deep and raw in his gaze. "I promise you. You'll change your mind."

Black, choking smoke erupted around him, making Joe tear up. He bent over, coughing . . .

And the music started up around him again, as if it had never stopped.

A black feather lay on the stage next to Joe's polished shoes.

Three days later, his draft papers arrived in the mail. Six days later, Joe shipped out to training camp, carrying his saxophone by his side but leaving his brothers behind.

Joe was on patrol in Germany the next time he saw his father. It was the middle of the night and he was alone on his shift when a great black wolf slunk out of the shadows and shifted into the shape of a man in a long black coat.

"Evening, Joe," his father said.

"Evening," Joe said, keeping his voice even. He kept walking as his father fell into step beside him. "Pleased with yourself?" he asked.

"Not really. It meant another long trip, and I don't care for travel."

"Maybe you should have thought of that before you got me drafted."

"You had to learn a lesson."

"If you mean you've got a nasty temper, I've learned that for sure."

"No," Joe's father said. He stopped walking and stared Joe in the eye as he intoned the words with a street preacher's intensity. "In the end, you're alone. You're always alone."

"Not tonight," Joe said. "Unfortunately."

He started walking again, leaving his father behind.

"You don't know what you're giving up," his father called after him. "I can take you away from all this, boy."

"Too late," Joe called back, without turning around.

His brothers had marched down together to the recruiting office the day Joe's draft papers had come through. That was his family, all over. Sure, Ivan had had big plans, but when it came down to it, they were a team.

They couldn't argue the Army into putting them all in the same unit, but they made a bargain. All of them had joined the army bands, and they saw it as good practice. As soon as the war ended, they'd be back on the road to Hollywood.

When Joe came back on his next rotation to the spot where he'd left his father behind, all he saw was a tuft of long black fur. He shook his head and let it lie forgotten on the ground.

Joe didn't see his father for the next three years, and he didn't miss the old man, either. He marched through days and nights of war, playing his sax for the unit, until the endless German rain rusted his beautiful instrument beyond repair. He played a shoddy borrowed replacement, provided by the army, to cheer the troops as they marched into towns filled with thousands of corpses lying piled on the ground, the aftermath of successful air raids. By nighttime, the corpses had been cleared from the streets with grim efficiency, but their faces filled Joe's dreams, to a soundtrack of the jazzy two-steps he played in the army band.

The day the keys of his second saxophone rusted over for good, Joe thought he'd tasted true despair. But he was wrong. That came later, when he got the telegrams.

Karl, who played keyboard with the intensity of a man possessed by angels, who'd dreamed nothing but music notes since he was a four-year-old kid, had

had his left hand shot off in an accident in the Pacific. Looked like he wouldn't be playing in any band, in Hollywood or anywhere else.

And Ivan, slick, movie star-handsome Ivan with his great big dreams for the family, was dead, killed by a German sniper as he'd marched with his band.

If Joe's father had appeared to him then, Joe might well have killed him.

But his father didn't come.

Joe played a third saxophone, so harsh and squeaky it would have pained him to hear himself play if he'd ever bothered to listen. He was with the army unit that liberated two concentration camps, and the horrors sank deep into his skin and stayed there, like the hollow-eyed stares of the survivors.

The night his unit found out that the war was over, Joe saw his father for the third time.

There was a party in the camp, everyone celebrating with hectic gaiety. Booze flowed hard and fast, as if it could wash away the memories. Joe left after the first round of toasts.

He sat alone in the darkness, smoking one of the free cigars that had been passed around the party. A small black cat crept through the shadows to sit next to him. Joe eyed it warily and didn't reach out a hand to pet it. A moment later, he knew he'd been right, as the cat shifted into his father's shape.

"Well, Joe," his father said.

"Well," Joe said.

It was hard to tell for sure in the dark, but he thought his father looked older and more haggard since the last time they'd met. The black coat billowed out over a skinnier frame, though the golden eyes were just as fierce in the hollow face.

A year ago, Joe would have killed the man on first sight. Now he just kept on smoking, too numb to move or say any more. Faint light and the sound of voices filtered out from the mess hall nearby.

"My condolences," Joe's father said.

Joe stopped smoking and looked up sharply. He couldn't read an expression on his father's shadowed face.

"They wouldn't have been here if it weren't for you," he said.

"Who?" his father said.

They blinked at each other in mutual surprise. Then his father said,

"I was talking about your mother. She passed away two nights ago, in her sleep. I thought that you should know."

Joe took a deep breath. Then he kneaded his fingers over his forehead, closing his eyes against the lance of pain.

He wasn't completely numb yet, after all.

"She was a good woman," his father said, tentatively. "She did her best for you. By her standards."

Joe nodded. He couldn't speak.

"I was thinking," his father said. "I could take you back to see her, if you want."

Joe looked up. "You could do that?"

"I could," his father said. "She would have liked it."

"Did you—?"

"I was with her at the end," his father said. "She'd forgiven me, by then."

Joe tasted a story he'd never know, and let it go. "Fine," he said to his father. "Take me."

That was the night Joe found out what it meant to be his father's son.

They flew some way as crows at the beginning of the journey, but crows weren't fast or strong enough for an ocean crossing. They turned into smoke for part of that, then caught a lift on the wings of a military airplane.

Flying in the cold, thin altitudes, half disintegrated into smoke, Joe felt the wind blow through the pain. Pure, freezing numbness overcame him, and finally, he thought he understood what his father always felt.

Freedom. He could have flown forever, and never had to touch his pain or memories again.

At the end, well past midnight on a dark, cold Ohio night, they shifted back into human shape to jimmy open the window of the funeral home and crawl inside to the room where Joe's mother was laid out for viewing.

Joe touched her cold fingers and tried not to cry in front of his father.

"She was the prettiest girl in Kravarsko," his father said. "She wasn't afraid of anything or anyone. Not even me."

"She turned us into a team," Joe said. He looked down into his mother's face, calm beneath the layers of paint, and for the first time in over a year, he felt a clear point of resolution form underneath the brittle shell of numbness and the swirling, scattered layers of pain that had been hidden underneath. "She's the reason we all take care of each other."

"Well. That." His father cleared his throat. "I heard about your brothers and what happened. So. I guess there isn't going to be a band, after all. No more plans of Hollywood."

"Hollywood?" Joe almost laughed as he looked up from his mother to his father's fierce golden eyes. "You still don't get it, do you?"

"I didn't cause your brother's death," Joe's father said. "But it's been some time since then. I thought you might be ready to move on." He took a breath. "I thought you might be ready to come with me, now. Now that you know what it's like."

At that moment, Joe glimpsed something he'd never expected to see on his father's face. It was fear, pure and simple . . . and there was something else mixed in.

Loneliness.

Flying high above the ground, you could always feel free. Now that Joe had tasted that freedom, he felt the difference himself, standing thick and heavy on the ground, weighted down by human concerns, all the cares and sorrows that his father would never know.

But that wasn't enough.

"I'm sorry," Joe said, speaking to his father gently for the first time since they'd met. "It's too late for me now. It's not your fault. But I need to get back to my unit. I've got responsibilities."

"But—"

"There might not be a band," Joe said. "But my brothers and I are still a team." He hesitated and drew a breath, releasing the anger he'd carried with him for so long. "You could come and stay with us sometime. Anytime, really. I—"

Before he'd even stopped speaking, his father shook his head. The golden gaze shuttered, but not before Joe glimpsed the raw pain hidden behind the fierceness.

"Too late," his father said, and it sounded like the harsh cawing of a bird that knows it's lost all hope. "Too late."

Three of them came back from the war: Joe, without a saxophone, Karl, without a hand, and Niko, whose goofy lopsided grin had turned into a mask of sorrow. They gathered in their mother's house and huddled together, waiting for inspiration.

Ivan had always been the one with the big ideas. Ivan was gone. But the brothers were still a team.

Joe was cleaning out the attic one hot and dusty afternoon when he found his father's final message to him. Buried underneath the rubble of twenty years, he glimpsed the corner of a shining black leather case.

At first, he didn't know what it was. Then he lifted away the piles of old clothing that had covered it and saw its sleek rectangular lines, and his breath caught in his throat.

He undid the clasps and swung the case open.

A perfect, golden saxophone lay inside, gleaming and new.

Joe stared at it a long moment, caught between sharp, prickling emotions.

Finally, he reached out and picked up the saxophone. It fit perfectly into his hands.

As he lifted it out of the case, a black feather slipped out of the bell of the instrument and fluttered onto Joe's knee.

Joe let out a huff of breath that could have been either a laugh or a sob. A box of fresh reeds sat tucked in the case. He took one out and moistened it, even as tears blurred his vision. He fitted the mouthpiece onto the body of the sax and closed his eyes as he lifted it to his lips. He could already hear the wailing tune that wanted to be born.

Within a year, that tune would make his name in the nightclubs of Youngstown and Cleveland.

Five years from then, every jazz fan in the country would know the names of Blue Joe and his backup band—Niko on drums, grinning the loopy, lopsided, visionary grin of a man who's touched despair and been reborn into hope; and Karl, playing the keyboard like a demon with only one hand, worshipped by jazz fans everywhere for the uniqueness of his vision.

But at that moment, as Joe accepted his father's gift, he only knew one thing:

Maybe it wasn't too late after all.

THE WERE-WIZARD OF OZ

LAVIE TIDHAR

━━◆━━

EXT. EMERALD CITY—DAY

Emerald City. A dark and dangerous place. City blocks tower above mean streets and open sewers. The sky is the colour of blood. There are winged monkeys circling slowly in the air, searching for prey. Under a broken street lamp stands OZ, smoking a cigarette, his fedora pulled low over his eyes. His face is in shadow.

                    OZ:
        Emerald City.

                    OZ:
        Shit.

OZ lifts his face. The light of a passing car illuminates them. He is unshaved, and his eyes are red.

                    OZ:
        It's always dusk in the Emerald City.

                    OZ:
        Even in the middle of the day.

━━◆━━

Oz is thirteen, just entering puberty, when he begins to discover the changes to his body.

The way his voice drops several octaves unexpectedly, becomes a growl that makes guests' hair stand on their arms. The way the moon pulls and stretches at his limbs, curves his spine, makes hair grow everywhere.

Learning to shave is embarrassing, the blades break and finally he has to go with a barber's razor, and when he cuts himself the bleeding stops in seconds, the wounds heal—too quickly. At school the kids make fun of hairy boy until he growls and shows them nails like claws and then they stop and after that they mostly keep away from him.

Puberty is confusing, he gets a hard-on every other second, it seems, he has hormones raging through him and on full moon nights he wakes up and doesn't know where he is, and he is naked, and covered in feathers and blood.

Oz lives in a small town where nothing much is going on, somewhere in those featureless plains of a sometimes-Americaland. Mostly, Oz goes to the movies. Alone. He sits close to the screen, in the first or second row where no one else likes to sit, and he watches movies in the dark. There's the smell of popcorn and years of spilled Coca Cola on unwashed carpets. There's the smell of wet hair, and a hint of blood. Kids make out in the back row and the attendant goes around with a torchlight and the smell of grass on his clothes.

Everyone leaves Oz well alone. Which suits him fine.

He watches horror movies and romantic comedies and family dramas, fantasies and sci fi and adventure serials. He watches sequels and prequels and the things that come in the middle. He watches *Wolf* with Jack Nicholson, which is kinda boring (but Michelle Pfeiffer makes him hard), and *Teen Wolf* with Michael J. Fox (an 80s classic, but he secretly prefers *Doc Hollywood*), and *An American Werewolf in London*, but to be honest, even though he won't admit it, he prefers romantic comedies. He loves *Four Weddings and a Funeral*. He just wishes there was someone like him in it. Nobody does romantic comedies about werewolves.

Because that's what he is, he is beginning to realize. He can no longer deny the changes. When he takes on the wolf shape he feels alive, free, strong. He loves to run, for miles and miles, snapping at the wind, scenting for prey. He loves the taste of fear in a chicken's heart when it's taken. He toys with it, listening to its heart beat, smelling its fear before jaws close shut with a snap over the creature's thin neck.

He does okay at school and he does better on the football field but it's not enough, and besides people are beginning to talk. There's mention of pitchforks, not as an agricultural tool but as an instrument of maiming. Nobody likes a teenage werewolf. Especially not the fathers or uncles of teenage daughters.

———◆———

EXT. EMERALD CITY—DAY

OZ stands outside a bar. The sign, in flashing neon light, says, SHIFTER'S CORNER. He growls softly to himself and goes inside.

INT. SHIFTER'S CORNER BAR—DAY

The bar is dark, the lighting red. The counter is long and made of hard wood, scarred by cigarettes and fights. The few drinkers turn to look at OZ, then turn back, quickly. Behind the bar is a solitary figure. OZ walks forward, sits on a stool.

OZ:

Gimme a Jack on the rocks, Billy.

The bartender lifts his head and we get a good look at him. His face is very long and very pale. So are his fingers. His entire body seems stretched, devoid of blood. There are bandages trailing from his arms, his neck. He stares at OZ, not moving.

OZ:

What's the matter, Billy? Missing your mummy?

The bartender's impassive face nevertheless registers a look of fleeting pain. Silently, he points at a sign on the wall. It says: NO MUMMY JOKES. OZ shrugs.

OZ:

Just gimme the drink, Billy. I'm good for it.

OZ slaps some money on the counter. The bartender nods and reaches under the counter for a glass. He makes OZ a drink and pushes it towards him.

OZ:

I'm looking for a girl, Billy. A missing girl. Goes by the name of Dorothy.

The bartender shrugs. OZ takes a sip from his drink and lights up another cigarette. He stares at the bartender meditatively.

OZ:

In this city, we're all lost.

OZ:

Right, Billy?

The bartender shrugs again.

⟞⟝

He loves detective movies and noir and *Casablanca* most of all. He loves Bogie. *Werewolf in a Women's Prison* makes him wake up at night, sweating, with the sheets all damp.

There's this girl at school . . .

She lives with her uncle and aunt. They have a farm. It's not a very successful one. They grow tobacco, but the season's been hard. Her name's Dorothy. She's hard, she has the eyes of someone who knows what poverty is like, and hardship. Her parents are dead. They say her uncle beats her up. For all that, Oz thinks she's radiant. When she smiles—if he can somehow make her smile—it transforms her completely, the way he is transformed. He wants to be her full moon. He wants to watch her when she changes.

They meet secretly. Oz's parents don't approve of farmer trash and her uncle doesn't approve of Oz, or any other boys for that matter. They make plans.

Scram. Leave this town. Disappear. Across the vast featureless plains, towards the coast, east or west it almost doesn't matter, only it does. There is only one place for dreamers, one place that is a magnet, drawing you inexorably towards it.

The city.

The city.

Where everything is possible, and dreams come true.

—⬌—

EXT. THE EMERALD CITY PROJECTS—DAY

There are people sitting outside on stairs, not doing anything. Smoking, talking. Listening to the game on the radio. Boys stand at street corners, dealing. Cars go past slowly. Were-girls in short skirts and hairy legs wait, hopefully.

OZ comes striding into the frame.

> WERE-GIRL:
> Hey, Corn-fed! Wanna have a good time?

OZ doesn't break stride.

> OZ:
> No, thanks, fur-ball.

> WERE-GIRL:
> Fucking were-rat.

OZ goes to a group of boys. They are all half-transformed, and growl when they see him.

> WERE-BOY:
> What do you want here, Daddy-O?

> OZ:
> I'm looking for a girl. Name of Dorothy.

> WERE-BOY:
> Take your pick, old man. Take any girl you want. Or any boy.

> WERE-BOY
> They'll all be your Dorothy, for a price.

OZ reaches over and grabs the boy by the throat, easily lifting him off the ground. He growls, and his face shifts and lengthens, becomes that of a wolf.

WERE-BOY:

Shit, man!

OZ throws him against the wall. The boy crumples down and shifts, becoming wholly human.

OZ:

Well? I'm waiting.

WERE-BOY:

Dorothy, Dorothy... was she hooked up, man? She's that wannabe-actress chick who got hooked on emerald dust, right? Shit, I know her. Everyone knows her. Why didn't you just say so?

OZ growls. There's a growing pee stain on the boy's trousers.

WERE-BOY:

You should ask Tinny. He's dealin' the good stuff. The rainbow dust. If anyone should know it's him.

⸺

Oz runs through the quiet fields on a night of the full moon. His tongue lolls out as he runs. He grins.

Miles and miles of quiet fields, with nothing but scarecrows for company. His wolf-mind dreams of bright lights and crowded streets, a gourmet restaurant and a take-away menu rolled into one, both buffet and a-la-carte. His human mind dreams of the ocean, and the sound of the waves as they break against the shore, and moonlit walks along the beach. He has never seen the ocean—only in movies.

She waits for him at the agreed place. They are on the boundary of her uncle's farm. A barn, and she is waiting outside, in the cold, puffing on a cigarette. His wolf-nose picks up the smell keenly. Her aunt and uncle disapprove of smoking, as they do of most things. It's why she does it, even though he tells her it's no good for her.

But Dorothy doesn't listen to him. She doesn't listen to anybody.

Dorothy is going to be a star.

The city. Their shared dream is joined, entwined. He bounds towards her, jumping over her and they roll on the ground. He changes as he rolls, become a large and naked young man. Dorothy giggles. "You're funny," she says. He licks her face. She pushes him away.

They make out in the hay, in the dark barn. She makes him cum with her hand. Later, they just lie there, in the darkness, and she says, "I wish a tornado would come and take me away from here."

He wants to be her tornado. He says, "I'm saving up. I'm working two jobs."

She laughs. "How much money can you make on a paper round?"

Which hurts, but he doesn't say anything.

"We need to make enough for the city," she says. "It's not a place we can go to just like that."

He is restless. "I want us to go soon!" he says, and she laughs. "Patience, my wolf," she says. But he knows she is equally restless.

❦

INT. BARBERSHOP—DAY

OZ walks into the barbershop. There is one customer, a SCARECROW. TINNY stands above him with shears.

> SCARECROW:
> Just a trim, please, Tinny.

TINNY turns when he sees OZ.

> TINNY:
> What do you want, hairy? A full body buzz cut?

TINNY laughs. The SCARECROW turns around to look.

> SCARECROW:
> Oh shit.

The SCARECROW tries to get up, but TINNY's heavy hand presses him down in his seat.

> TINNY:
> Nobody leaves until the Tin Meister's done with them.

OZ takes in the scene calmly.

> OZ:
> I'm lookin' for a client a yours. Young lady name of Dorothy.

TINNY stands still.

> TINNY:
> What's she to you, furry?

> OZ:
> Enough with the slurs, tin face. She got hooked on your shit,

and she got hooked bad. I know that much. And now she's missin'. And I'm going to find her.

TINNY:

Good luck to ya, pal. Now get out of my barbershop.

OZ calmly puts a cigarette in his mouth. He smiles. He reaches into his pocket and takes out a box of matches. The illustration on the box is of a tall soldier with vivid-green whiskers. Oz strikes a match against one of his claws. He lights the cigarette, puffs out smoke, and tosses the match at the SCARECROW.

SCARECROW:

For the love of Glinda! Help!

The SCARECROW goes up in flame like a bundle of dry hay on a hot summer's day. His screams fill up the shop. The fire spreads. With two quick steps OZ is right beside TINNY. His claws reach out and grab TINNY by the throat. There is the sound of metal being scraped.

OZ:

I'm listenin', metal-face.

TINNY:

You'll pay for this, wolf-man.

OZ:

Spill it out.

OZ's claws tighten over TINNY's throat, easily cutting into the metal flesh.

TINNY:

Okay, okay. Let go!

The flames are reflected in TINNY's face. The SCARECROW burns and screams but neither man pay him any attention.

TINNY:

She got hooked on rainbows and emerald dust, and couldn't pay.

TINNY:

So I sold her.

OZ:

You did what?

TINNY:

She knew what she was doin', man.

TINNY:

No one's innocent in the Emerald City.

TINNY:

Not even you.

OZ:

Who'd you sell her to?

TINNY:

She would kill me if I told.

OZ:

I'll kill you if you don't.

TINNY nods, as if agreeing—then suddenly launches a frenzied attack on OZ. The two grapple with each other in the burning barbershop, with OZ flickering in and out of human and wolf shapes. Finally he subdues TINNY, his claws closing in on the man's throat.

OZ:

Tell me!

TINNY gurgles.

TINNY:

Club Wicked! Look for her at Club Wicked.

TINNY:

If the monkeys don't get you first.

OZ's hands press on TINNY's throat, and press. The man shudders. Then, gradually, he falls still.

⇒

Summer is filled with days that seem to never end, a heat that lies over fields and town, filled with daydreams and unfulfilled desires. Oz is working hard—he had abandoned the paper round for working at the local garage, fixing motorcycles, and walks around in grease-stained overalls. He likes the job. You know where you are with machine parts, the way they fit together, the way they can be cleaned and polished and made good again. But Dorothy won't see him and it's breaking his heart. Sometimes he sees her, going with this boy or that one, in their cars, at night. She's wild and she's never been so beautiful to him. He confronts her one night, and she laughs at him. From her dress, she pulls out a roll of notes. ":This is what it takes to get me to the city,' she said. "You do your part, and don't worry about mine."

Under full summer moons he haunts the fields, his blood aflame. He comes to the place where the cars park at night, where the couples make out. It's just another bit of flat land, with nothing to distinguish it. He howls at the moon and the people inside the cars shudder and lock the doors. He sniffs for her but doesn't find her.

They make up again at the end of summer, and he holds her in his arms and almost cries and she promises she is his and only his, and it was just the summer breeze.

They plot and plan, pooling together their money. Just enough to buy two tickets on the bus going out of town. Just enough to get them to the coast, hire a cheap apartment for a few months. A few months is all it would take, before they make it, make it big in dream town, before they make it big in Emeraldland.

"I love you," he says.

"I love you too."

They kiss, and she runs her hands through his fur.

"I'm going to be a star," she says.

———

EXT. STREET—NIGHT

OZ stands outside CLUB WICKED. The sign, in neon, flashes on and off, next to the image of a girl entwined around a pole. He walks to the doors, where a giant bouncer stands. He has a pumpkin for a head.

                    BOUNCER:
Sorry, pal. You can't go in.

                    OZ:
Says who, friend?

                    BOUNCER:
Don't make it hard on yourself, wolf-boy.

OZ takes out a roll of cash, licks his thumb, starts counting.

                    OZ:
For your trouble.

                    BOUNCER:
Guess you're on the list after all.

OZ smiles. The smile on the BOUNCER's face is, of course, carved in. Money changes hands and the BOUNCER opens the door for OZ. He steps through into the club.

⟞⟝

It's the full moon and his senses are inflamed. He runs through the fields. It is time for them to leave, to go, to abandon this nowhere town behind them, and the plains, and corn fields and tobacco plants. He scents blood, on the wind.

He hears her cry, but softly.

His heart beats fast. He runs, faster than he had ever run.

He finds her in the barn. The barn is locked. The smell of blood drives him insane.

"Go away," she says—whispers—he can smell her fear. Driven mad, he runs at the doors, again and again, until they fall down. The commotion must be terrible. The farmhouse lights come on.

"You have to leave! Quickly!"

He finds her in the hay, half-naked, bruised. She has a black eye, bruised ribs, angry red marks on her back, as if made there by a belt, used as a whip. He howls, in anger and disgust. She hugs him.

'They found out," she said. "They took all the money. Run, before he comes. He has a gun."

But Oz is no longer human, no longer listening. A wolf stalks out of the barn, a giant silver wolf with sour breath and great big teeth and bloodlust.

A man, a short bald man in an old-fashioned dirty-white nightdress, stands framed in the door of the farmhouse. The light is behind him. In his hands he holds a pump action shotgun.

"Get away from here! Filth! Wild animal!"

Oz growls. There is the distinctive sound of the gun being pumped, a bullet being chambered. "Get off my property!"

Oz charges. The figure in the doorway hesitates, then takes aim. There is the sound of a gun shot.

⟞⟝

INT. CLUB WICKED—NIGHT

The club is dark—it is hard to see. there are girls on stage. They are naked. Patrons sit around, drinking. They are mostly winkies, but also some munchkins, humans and weres. OZ stands still, a little disoriented—which is when the MONKEYS catch him.

There are three monkeys, winged, mean, scarred, and grinning. Two grab hold of him while the third lifts a truncheon high in the air. OZ tries to shape-shift but the truncheon comes down, hard, and connects with the back of his head.

FADE TO BLACK.

———

The gunshot takes him in the chest and he drops to the ground. He rolls, howling with the pain as his body extracts the foreign object, spits it out and begins sealing the wound. His opponent recharges the gun.

"You like that?" he shouts, in a voice where fear and glee mix uneasily. "You want some more of that? You want some *lead aspirin*, boy?"

But lead won't cut it, not with a full-grown werewolf, and an angry one to boot. Oz rolls over and stands up on all fours. Growling. Grinning with teeth as large as blades. Yes, he wants some more of that.

Slowly, he advances on the man.

———

INT. CLUB WICKED—NIGHT

OZ opens his eyes. The winged monkeys stand above him, grinning and jabbering in their own, incomprehensible flying monkey tongue. OZ tries to sit and finds that he is trussed up. His eyes focus and he sees a small, elderly woman sitting hunched on a huge throne, her hair in pigtails, an eye-patch over her left eye. In her hands she holds an umbrella.

OZ:
Westerna.

WESTERNA:
Are you really so stupid you thought you could just waltz in
here like this was Munchkin Country? Or Kansas?

OZ shakes his head. He tries to shape-shift, but can't. WESTERNA smiles.

OZ:
Do you have her?

WESTERNA:
Do I have her? Your lady love? Your darling?

WESTERNA laughs.

WESTERNA:
You poor, deluded fool.

WESTERNA:
I guess every wolf needs a bitch.

———

From the barn, a scream. "Kill him!"

Later, much later, when they had gone to the city, when the money ran out, when she began working down in the valley, making the money she had always wanted, getting high on the high life, it occurred to him to wonder which of them she'd meant.

But that was later.

He tenses, jumps. His heavy body sails forward, hits the man in the chest.

The sound of a shot. Yet he feels no pain. His jaws come down and find the man's neck and *tear*.

There's a scream from inside. An old woman, her aunt, crying. Hitting him—he barely feels her. He tears chunks of flesh and chews and the blood fills his mouth. He swallows, and howls, a terrifying, keening sound that makes the old woman cower away from him.

When he is done he goes outside. She is waiting for him, her eyes wide, her lips trembling. She is flushed. She wears only her thin night dress.

"Oh, Oz," she says.

He growls and then he is on her, licking at her wounds, his tongue rasping across her soft, delicate skin.

"Oh, Oz!"

He doesn't know if he is man or wolf. He only knows that she's with him.

⤝⊷

INT. CLUB WICKED—NIGHT

WESTERNA:
I could kill you right now and be done with it.

OZ:
Why don't you?

⤝⊷

He feels sleepy, later, with the feeding and the sex. It's the first time they had gone all the way. "Get up," she says. She is already dressed. "We need to bury him. It's a shame you didn't kill the other one."

"She's just an old woman," he says, shocked. Dorothy shakes her head. "Sometimes I just don't know about you," she says. She had gone through the house, he saw. She shows him what she has—she has taken everything, jewelry and money and the old couple's bank book.

"We have to go," she says. "We have to hurry."

They tie up the unconscious old woman and lock her in the bedroom. They bury the old man in a shallow grave by the barn. With the first rays of light they are at the bus station, waiting.

EXT. EMERALD CITY—DAYBREAK

The three flying monkeys drag OZ outside, onto the street. Wizened WESTERNA follows. Behind her comes a figure he barely recognizes, a woman he had been looking for.

But she is changed.

She wears high-heeled, spiked boots, a short skirt, tank top, gold bracelets, body paint. She's had a boob-job, a nose-job, a tummy tuck and ear reduction and liposuction. She is almost luminous in the light. She looks at him for a long time without saying anything.

OZ:

Dorothy.

DOROTHY:

We had something good between us, Oz, but now it's gone. The city's too big and too wild and no two people can hope to stay together when there's so much to see and do and be. We had something going for a while and it was good—it was very good. But I am not the same girl and you're the same guy you've been, Oz. You're a small-town boy with a small-town mind and you'll never make it big. Go back to Kansas, Oz. Go back to your garage and your bikes and your full-moon runs through empty fields. I've got a future, Oz, a bright and Technicolor future, and you've no part of it no more.

OZ:

Dorothy . . .

DOROTHY:

Forget it, Oz. It's Emerald City.

She turns her back on him and, slowly, walks away, disappearing behind the doors of the club.

WESTERNA looks down at OZ with a look almost of compassion.

WESTERNA:

You'll mend.

>   WESTERNA:
>   Young hearts heal quickly.

She nods to her monkeys and they swiftly untie OZ.

>   WESTERNA:
>   But don't ever come back.

WESTERNA turns to leave, her monkeys following. OZ stares after her, making no move to get up.

>   WESTERNA:
>   Don't come looking for the woman behind the screen.

⎯⬦⎯

As the sun rises over the sleeping town the bus pulls to a stop at the station. It picks up two passengers.

As it drives away Oz look through the window, at the small town receding behind them in the distance. But Dorothy doesn't look back: she looks ahead.

Later, she holds him tight. Her smile is dazzling. "We're going to the city!" she says, almost breathless. "It's going to be so wonderful, Oz, so—so glorious!"

She seems delighted with the word. The world. He smiles. They kiss. Ahead of them the yellow brick road stretches, like a promise, into infinity.

SEVEN YEAR ITCH

LEAH R. CUTTER

—◆—

Mama first put me in a cage when I was seven. I tried to get away, yanking and pulling on Mama's hand, yelling how I didn't wanna be going in there, how I'd be a good boy now. I stopped walking up the dirt path toward dark cave and the wooden bars, sitting back on my butt, but Mama dragged me forward, throwing me into the cage so hard I hit the back wall.

"Mama, why you doing this?" I kept asking as she put the biggest lock I'd ever seen through the loop in the door.

I expected a list of all the things I'd done wrong, like she did when she beat me. All I got was a glare and, "You'll see."

Truth was, that probably would have scared me into being good, at least for a while, if I'd had a chance.

Mama left me then, locked in a hollowed out cave on top of Zeke's hill. I cried and cried, until my head hurt worse than that time Dwight hit me with a bat. I wiped off the tears and snot with my sleeve, then had a look around.

It wasn't much of a cage, not fancy like with metal bars. It smelled of clean dirt, and was cooler than the hot August afternoon sunshine that I'd been playing in. I was pretty sure Pappy had made it: first dug out the hilltop, stolen the wooden slats from a hardware store or a neighbor, then pounded them deep into the ground. I got a splinter when I grabbed one and shook it. It weren't going nowhere, and neither was I.

Mama had left me a loaf of Wonder bread, a jar of peanut butter, some apples and a jug of water. She'd also left me the old pot Grandpa had used to piss in when he'd gotten too old to get up on his own. Under it, I couldn't believe that she'd also stashed two comic books. She didn't approve of that "make-believe shit" as she called it. I'd already read them, of course, standing in the air conditioning of the Big K, but it was still something.

Time crawled. I ate and read and slept but Mama didn't return, didn't let me know how long I was being punished for. It was a strange punishment, here alone, with treats I didn't normally get. I didn't rightly know what she wanted.

I spent the rest of that long summer afternoon calling out to her, certain she was waiting just outside. I confessed to everything I'd ever done, whether she already knew or not, like letting Farmer Gray's horses out of pasture and stealing candy bars from Bobby Holls' lunch. I cried and said I was sorry and begged to please go home now.

My voice grew hoarse as I talked, deeper and gravelly, like Curly the janitor at school who was bald cause he had throat cancer. My hands started hurting and the ache spread to my arms and chest, like I'd taken a bad fall, head first, off Dwight's bike.

"I'm sick, Mama!" I cried. I shivered and couldn't get warm one minute, then had to take my shirt off cause I'd sweat through it.

I don't rightly recall what happened next. I think I dreamed, feverishly, 'cause I saw my boy's hands grow into a man's, with strange dark hair, even on the knuckles. I scratched myself with the long yellowed nails, longer than the old hippy's who lived in Evan's Woods.

I woke up naked, curled on the dirt floor of the cage, cold. I looked worse than the time Bobby Holls and his brother Darren had beaten me up—bruises all up and down my ribs. Not round punch marks: straight lines, like from wooden slats. Sure enough, some of the bars of my cage had been broken through. I could have escaped, gone home, see if Mama had forgiven me yet, but I had no clothes.

I started crying again. The smell of shit was strong, though I was clean. I saw it now, smeared on the walls. My comic books looked like a dog had attacked them, full of claw and teeth marks.

"Drop that," Mama told me when I picked it up. I did as I was told, mostly from being startled.

Mama held out one of Pappy's old work shirts in her hands, big enough to go to my knees. At first I was scared, but then I dove into it, hoping it wasn't a trap. Mama didn't scold me or try to beat me. She turned my face up so she could see it better. "Not too bad," she said, looking at my forehead. When she touched my cheek I realized it was bruised too.

"Mama, I was sick."

She ran her fingers through my hair, smoothing it out. "Yes, you were. But you're better. For now."

I wanted to beg her not to ever put me in a cage again. I wanted to swear I'd be good from then on. However, her look and her words sent a chill through me, freezing everything inside.

I found out later I'd been sick a whole week. During that time, someone had gotten into Farmer Gray's coup and killed all his chickens. His youngest, Mark, had gone out to see what was causing all the fuss, and had been attacked by some kind of wild animal that had torn off one of his calf muscles. He died the following week, never waking up.

We moved the next month, to the far side of town.

The summer I turned fourteen Pappy set me to rebuilding the cage, this time with concrete and bars stolen from the abandoned development down the road. I knew better what would happen: Pappy and I *changed* sometimes. Not like those stupid werewolves on T.V. We didn't care about the moon and shit. We only changed once every seven years, for a whole week. Pappy's time would be in a couple years. My time would come in August.

I didn't know why we changed. Were we cursed? Or was it just something Fuller men did? Pappy said it had just been him and his brother who'd changed, not Grandpa. His Mama had known what to do, though, so maybe it came from her.

I remember holding a rusting pole while Pappy poured concrete, sweat falling out of my bangs into my eyes. The cicada cycled up and down in the grass above the cave. I didn't want to be there, didn't want to be breaking my back or licking the sweet blood off my knuckles when I scraped them *again* on the packed dirt. When Pappy cuffed me, telling me to hold the pole still, I finally snapped.

"Don't know why we're building this thing. I ain't going in it."

I knew it was a stupid thing to say before I said it. Still said it.

Pappy was at the end of his rope too. "You will," he said, growling.

I glared at him. His eyes changed to a strange gold, with long pupils, his forehead grew ridged and his fingernails turned into claws.

I looked down, shaken. Pappy could be mean, hell, the whole damn county was mean. He'd only beat me when I deserved it, though, and never more than I could take. He'd never been a monster to me.

We finished off the afternoon in silence, only cursing the dirt or bars, never each other.

As we walked back to the doublewide, Pappy told me, "After August I'll show you more. Your change is too close, now, to learn any control."

I grunted at him, too tired to reply, but also because I couldn't talk around the rush of joy I felt. Down in my gut I knew a hint of control would mean the difference between being stuck in the Buena Vista Estates trailer park and breaking free.

Pappy was shot the last week of August, while I was still recovering from the bruises of my change. A robbery gone wrong at one of the abandoned houses Pappy "recycled" from. The sheriff said a wild dog had attacked his deputy and he'd accidentally shot my dad. No dog was ever found.

I was going to have to teach myself control, and learn it better than everyone around me.

Mama got remarried and we moved to the city with Stephen, my step-dad. He worked as an engineer for a German software company: Mama reminded him of home and the country.

Turned out I had an aptitude for computers, hacking, more specifically. Just a fancy way of stealing, I told Mama. Just following Pappy's lead.

The summer I turned twenty-one Mama grew more and more nervous. For the first time I felt the beast stirring restlessly under my skin. I gleefully pillaged security sites, laughing at the rumors of an FBI sting. Let them take me. The monster was near.

Mama talked Stephen into building one of those panic rooms, with reinforced steel walls and an electronic lock. She never got around to stocking it though—it stayed an empty room with bare drywall and a door a monster couldn't open.

Just before my change, Mama and Stephen went on vacation. All Mama said was, "Do the right thing."

I spent hours standing on the threshold of my cage. The beast was desperate to run. It remembered the fresh taste of blood, the sudden rush of death.

In the end I walked in, closed and locked the door, hoping the keypad would survive. Because any control was always up to me.

By the time I was twenty-eight I had the best of everything. I lived with Jaslene, feasted on caviar and fine wines, slept on softer than silk sheets. Life was sweet and satisfying, full of sunshine and delights I'd never known existed as a child.

Nights I trolled the internet highways for insecure ports and selfish corporations who put making a buck before building better firewalls. I'd grown rich selling credit cards to other sharks.

Jaslene didn't know what I did, not really. She was willing to believe it was too technical for her, just happy for the cash flowing into her greedy hands. And who could blame her? I wasn't the best catch, unsophisticated and hard edged. But I was rich, and that made up for a lot.

That year, though, that seven-year-itch year, I'd started taking stupid risks. The FBI was on my tail again. I needed to lay low, keep to the shadows, only spend what I already had, but I couldn't stop myself from ravaging yet another system. My famous control was shaky, at best.

Jaslene accused me of being cruel, exposing the soft underbelly of her insecurities, telling secrets not mine to share. She left the week before my change.

Was it me? Or was it the beast? Maybe I'd reached my limit on small talk with Jaslene's friends and smiles hiding sharp teeth. Maybe the monster was hungry for recognition.

Still. Jaslene shouldn't have left. She was my first, my only love, after Mama had died. I didn't have anything soft from the beautiful Buena Vista Estates: everything kind had been sweated out between the heat and the bugs, the broken promises and the dirt. Jaslene had seen that steel and not been afraid to carve out a place between the bars, upwind from the sewer of my heart.

She belonged with me. To me. And now she was gone.

The door to my own panic room stood open. The change was upon me. And she will be here, any moment now. She'd begged me for the truth of my life, accused me of hiding behind my scars.

Come my love. See me. All of me. Be with me forever, blood of my blood, flesh of my flesh, a sweet taste on my tongue and a full belly at the end of my tenure in my room.

Because at the end, the only one I can control is me.

AN UNNATURAL HISTORY OF SCARECROWS

MARIO MILOSEVIC

Straw for guts, as a rule. Also for limbs and general bulk. Other materials will do, but straw is always available so why not use it? For clothes, torn and raggedy cast offs, often patched, often faded. It gives the scarecrow a tough look, like they don't care about getting down and dirty when the occasion warrants such actions. They'll wade into a fight if they have to.

Sticks will do for hands and feet, although neither is truly necessary. Crows have vivid imaginations and they can extrapolate from straw limbs to fingers and toes with little effort.

The head should be sculpted from burlap, again stuffed with straw. The eyes, nose, and mouth painted on. You can make it menacing if you want, but it isn't necessary. Just the suggestion of a human face is supposed to be enough to frighten the crows.

A hat will complete the look. You should have a hat, unless you elect to give your scarecrow a head of hair, but such affectations generally detract from the overall effect. You can make a hat look much more natural than fake hair.

The alert student will note that the scarecrow, as outlined above, does not do what it purports to do. In other words, crows are generally not frightened by scarecrows.

This is no one's fault. All inventions go through stages. At one time, in the distant past, I believe that such avatars did scare crows, but over the years the crows grew accustomed to them and learned that they did no harm whatsoever. We must now apply our intellect and imaginations and concoct the next stage in the evolution of scarecrows. Any suggestions as to how we might go about this?

Ah, yes, you with your hand up.

Pardon me?

You're saying we should interview a crow.

Now class, calm down and save your snickering. It is not such a bad idea.

In fact, I think it might be an excellent idea. Let's begin by interviewing a crow.

Yes, here's one flying by now. Excuse me. Crow. May I trouble you for a few moments?

Excellent, yes, thank you for stopping.

No this won't take long.

What's that?

You say you're apolitical? I understand completely. But you see, this has nothing to do with politics.

No, I'm not asking you to sign any kind of petition or recall effort. I am interested in ascertaining what you are afraid of.

Yes, of course, I understand your suspicions, but I assure my motives are benign. I wish to produce a kind of scare device which will keep you and your kind from our agricultural regions.

I understand you need to eat, but we wish it that you would eat elsewhere.

Of course you can refuse to answer. It is a free country, but I would be remiss if I did not inform you of the fact that if we do not produce a suitable device, we will be forced to take more drastic measures, up to and including the killing of crows.

Oh, dear. Are you all right?

I didn't mean to upset you.

No, it is not that I *want* to kill crows, it is that I may be *forced* to do so, for our own survival. I'm sure you understand.

Oh. You don't understand. Well, that's understandable.

So you will not answer my questions?

Very well.

I wish you the best. Thank you for your time.

And there goes the crow, flying in a decidedly crooked line. That did not go so well at all. Are there any other suggestions?

Yes, the young lady in the back. You wish to offer an idea?

Ahem, well, yes I see where you are going with that. If we were in fact to *become* crows we would, by necessity, be aware of what we feared. But how, may I ask, do you propose to turn any of us into crows?

I thought so.

Any other suggestions?

A show of hands, please. Surely *someone* has some ideas. You are the most advanced class in the academy. Am I to deduce from the general lack of hands showing that my most gifted students are unable to offer a single viable path to success in the present situation? Or are you afraid to look foolish? What have I said about such fears?

Yes, the young man in the front row.

Exactly. There are no foolish ideas, only fools who will not attempt to create ideas.

So let me ask you, one more time, how might we go about creating the next generation of scarecrow?

Nothing?

No one will even attempt a proposal?

Class, what is all that ruckus?

Calm down, please.

What are you pointing at?

Ah, I see. A flock of crows. Yes, and they appear to be heading in this direction. Well, this is fortuitous. Perhaps the pressure of an actual attack will spur you to heights of accomplishment.

Why should we take cover? You do not fear the crows do you? If anyone should, it is me.

Now class, those crows appear to be upset and they wish to unleash their fury on us. Here is your moment. Seize it! How will you scare them away? By what mechanism or sorcery?

No. No. It will not do to run away. Not now. Come back! Class, obey me! Return to your seats this instant.

Yes, my clothes are torn, I see that. My limbs are thin and bent. But why do you point at me so? My head is smooth and bald. What did you expect?

Where are you going?

Come back.

They do not fear me. They will be on me in an instant.

Class.

Come back.

Class, please return. Don't leave me alone. I cannot face them any longer.

THE GAZE DOGS OF NINE WATERFALL

KAARON WARREN

Rare dog breeds; people will kill for them. I've seen it. One stark-nosed curly hair terrier, over-doped and past all use. One ripped-off buyer, one cheating seller. I was just the go-between for that job. I shrank up small into the corner, squeezed my eyes shut, folded my ears over like a Puffin Dog, to keep the dust out.

I sniffed out a window, up and out, while the blood was still spilling. It was a lesson to me, early on, to always check the dog myself.

I called my client on his cell, confirming the details before taking the job.

"Ah, Rosie McDonald! I've heard good things about your husband."

I always have to prove myself. Woman in a man's world. I say I'm acting for my husband and I tell stories about how awful he is, just for the sympathy.

I'll bruise my own eye, not with make-up. Show up with an arm in a sling. "Some men don't like a woman who can do business," I say. "But he's good at what he does. An eye for detail. You need that when you're dealing dogs."

"I heard that. My friend is the one who was after a Lancashire Large. For his wife."

I remembered; the man had sent me pictures. Why would he send me pictures?

"He says it was a job well done. So you know what I'm after?"

"You're after a vampire dog. Very hard to locate. Nocturnal, you know? Skittish with light. My husband will need a lot of equipment."

"So you'll catch them in the day when they're asleep. I don't care about the money. I want one of those dogs."

"My husband is curious to know why you'd like one. It helps him in the process."

"Doesn't he talk?"

"He's not good with people. He's good at plenty, but not people."

"Anyway, about the dog: thing is, my son's not well. It's a blood thing. It's hard to explain even with a medical degree."

My ears ring when someone's lying to me. Even over the phone. I knew he was a doctor; I'd looked him up.

"What's your son's name?"

The silence was momentary, but enough to confirm my doubts there was a son. "Raphael," he said. "Sick little Raphael." He paused. "And I want to use the dog like a leech. You know? The blood-letting cure."

"So you just need the one?"

"Could he get more?"

"He could manage three, but your son . . . "

"Get me three," he said.

I thought, *Clinic. Five thousand each. Clients in the waiting room reading Nature magazine.*

There are dogs rare because of the numbers. Some because of what they are or what they can do.

And some are rare because they are not always seen.

I remember every animal I've captured, but not all of my clients. I like to forget them. If I don't know their faces I can't remember their expressions or their intent.

The Calalburun. I traveled to Turkey for this puppy. Outside of their birthplace, they don't thrive, these dogs. There is something about the hunting in Turkey which is good for them. My client wanted this dog because it has a split nose. Entrancing to look at. Like two noses grown together.

The Puffin Dog. Norwegian Lundehound. These dogs were close to extinction when a dog-lover discovered a group of them on a small island. He bred them up from five, then shared some with an enthusiast in America. Not long after that, the European dogs were wiped out, leaving the American dogs the last remaining.

The American sent a breeding pair and some pups back to Europe, not long before her own dogs were wiped out. From those four there are now about a thousand.

The dogs were bred to hunt Puffins. They are so flexible (because they sometimes needed to crawl through caves to hunt) that the back of their head can touch their spine. As a breed, though, they don't absorb nutrients well, so they die easily and die young. We have a network, the other dealers and I. Our clients want different things at different times so we help each other out. My associate in Europe knew of four Puffin Dogs.

It's not up to me to ponder why people keep these cripples alive. Animal protection around the world doesn't like it much; I just heard that the English RSPCA no longer supports Crufts Dog Show because they say there are too many disabled dogs being bred and shown. Dogs like the Cavalier King Charles Spaniel, whose skull is too small for its brain. And a lot of boxer dogs are prone to epilepsy, and some bulldogs are unable to mate, or are unable to give birth unassisted.

It's looks over health. But humans? Same same.

The Basenji is a dog which yodels. My client liked the sound and wanted to be yodeled to. I don't know how that worked out.

Tea cup dogs aren't registered and are so fragile and mimsy they need to be carried everywhere. Some say this is the breeders' way of selling off runts.

Then there's the other dogs. The Black Dogs, Yellow Dogs, the Sulphurous Beast, the Wide-Eyed Hound, the Wisht Hound, and the Hateful Thing: The Gabriel Hound.

I've never been asked to catch one of these, nor have I seen one, but godawful stories are told.

The only known habitat of the vampire dog is the island of Viti Levu, Fiji. I'd never been there but I'd heard others talk of the rich pickings. I did as much groundwork as I could over the phone, then visited the client to get a look at him and pick up the money. No paper trail. I wore tight jeans with a tear across the ass and a pink button up shirt.

He was ordinary; they usually are. The ones with a lot of money are always confident but this one seemed overly so. Stolen riches, I wondered. The ones who get rich by stealing think they can get away with everything. Two heads taller then me, he wore a tight blue T-shirt, blank. A rare thing; most people like to plaster jokes on their chests. He didn't shake my hand but looked behind me for the real person, my husband.

"I'm sorry, my husband was taken ill. He's told me exactly what I need to do, though," I said.

The client put his hand on my shoulder and squeezed. "He's lucky he's got someone reliable to do his dirty work," the guy said.

He gave me a glass of orange soda as if I were a child. That's fine; making money is making money.

I told him we'd found some dogs, but not for sale. They'd have to be caught and that would take a lot more.

"Whatever . . . Look, I've got a place to keep them."

He showed me into his backyard, where he had dug a deep hole. Damp. The sides smooth, slippery with mud. One push and I'd be in there.

I stepped back from the edge.

"So, four dogs?" he said. "Ask your husband if he can get me four vampire dogs."

"I will check." My husband Joe had his spine bitten half out by a glandular-affected bull dog, and all he could do was nod, nod, nod. Bobble head, I'd call him if I were a cruel person. I had him in an old people's home where people called him young man and used his tight fists to hold playing cards. When I visit, his eyes follow me adoringly, as if he were a puppy.

My real hunting partner was my sister-in-law Gina. She's an animal psychologist. An animal psychic, too, but we don't talk about that much. I pretend I don't believe in it, but I rely on the woman's instincts.

The job wouldn't be easy, but it never is in the world of the rare breed.

My bank account full, our husband and brother safe with a good stock of peppermints, Gina and I boarded a flight for Nadi, Fiji. Ten hours from L.A., long enough to read a book, snooze, maybe meet a dog-lover or two. We transferred to the Suva flight, a plane so small I thought a child could fly it. They gave us fake orange juice and then the flight was done. I listened to people talk, about local politics, gossip. I listened for clues, because you never know when you'll hear the right word.

Gina rested. She was keen to come to Fiji, thinking of deserted islands, sands, fruit juice with vodka.

The heat as we stepped off the plane was like a blanket had been thrown over our heads. I couldn't breathe in it and my whole body steamed sweat. It was busy but not crazy, and you weren't attacked by cabbies looking for business, porters, jewelry sellers. I got a lot of smiles and nods.

We took a cab which would not have passed inspection in New York and he drove us to our hotel, on Suva Bay. There were stray dogs everywhere, flaccid, unhealthy looking things. The females had teats to the ground, the pups mangy and unsteady. They didn't seem aggressive, though. Too hot, perhaps. I bought some cut pineapple from a man at the side of the road and I ate it standing there, the juice dripping off my chin and pooling at my feet. I bought another piece, and another, and then he didn't have any change so I gave him twenty dollars. Gina couldn't eat; she said the dogs put her off. That there was too much sickness.

I didn't sleep well. I felt slick with all the coconut milk I'd had with dinner; with the fish, with the greens, with the dessert. And new noises in a place keep me awake, or they entered my dreams in strange ways.

I got up as the sun rose and swam some laps. The water was warm, almost like bath water, and I had the pool to myself.

After breakfast, Gina and I took a taxi out to the latest sighting of vampire dogs, a farm two hours drive inland. I like to let the locals drive. They know where they're going and I can absorb the landscape and listen while they tell me stories.

The foliage thickened as we drove, dark leaves waving heavily in what seemed to me a still day. The road was muddy so I had to be patient; driving through puddles at speed can get you bogged. A couple of trucks passed us. Smallish covered vehicles with the stoutest workers in the back. They waved and smiled at me and I knew that four of them could lift our car out of the mud if we got stuck.

The trucks swerved and tilted and I thought that only faith was keeping them on the road.

The farm fielded dairy cows and taro. It seemed prosperous; there was a letter box rather than an old juice bottle, and white painted rocks lined the path.

There was no phone here, so I hadn't been able to call ahead. Usually I'd gain permission to enter, but that could take weeks, and I wanted to get on with the job.

I told the taxi driver to wait. A fetid smell filled the car; rotting flesh.

"Oh, Jesus," Gina said. "I think I'll wait, too." I saw a pile of dead animals at the side of a dilapidated shed; a cow, a cat, two mongooses. They could've been there since the attack a week ago.

"Wait there," I told Gina. "I'll call you if I need you"

Breathing through my mouth, I walked to the pile. I could see bite marks on the cow and all the animals appeared to be bloodless, sunken.

"You are who?" I heard. An old Fijian woman, wearing a faded green T-shirt that said *Nurses Know Better* pointed at me. She looked startled. They didn't see many white people out here.

"Are you from the *Fiji Times*?" she said. "We already talked to them."

I considered for a moment how best to get the information. She seemed suspicious of the newsmakers, tired of them.

"No, I'm from the SPCA. I'm here to inspect the animals and see if we can help you with some money. If there is a person hurting the animals, we need to find that person and punish them."

"It's not a person. It is the vampire dogs. I saw them with my own eyes."

"This was done by dogs?"

She nodded. "A pack of them. They come out of there barking and yelping with hunger and they run here and there sucking their food out of any creature they find. They travel a long way sometimes, for new blood."

"So they live in the hills?" I thought she'd pointed at the mountains in the background. When she nodded, I realized my mistake. I should have said, "Where do they live?"

It was too late now; she knew what she thought I wanted to hear.

"They live in the hills."

"Doesn't anyone try to stop them?"

"They don't stop good. They are hot to the touch and if you get too near you might burn up."

"Shooting?"

"No guns. Who has a gun these days?"

"What about a club, or a spear? What about a cane knife? What I mean is, can they be killed?"

"Of course they can be killed. They're dogs, not ghosts."

"Do they bite people?"

She nodded. "If they can get close enough."

"Have they killed anyone? Or turned anyone into a vampire?"

She laughed, a big, belching laugh which brought tears to her eyes. "A person can't turn into a vampire dog! If they bite you, you clean out the wound so it doesn't go nasty. That's all. If they suck for long enough you'll die. But you clean it out and it's okay."

"So what did they look like?"

She stared at me.

"Were they big dogs or small?" I measured with my hand, up and down until she grunted; knee high.

"Fur? What color fur?"

"No fur. Just skin. Blue skin. Loose and wrinkly."

"Ears? What were their ears like?"

She held her fingers up to her head. "Like this."

"And they latched onto your animals and sucked their blood?"

"Yes. I didn't know at first. I thought they were just biting. I tried to shoo them. I took a big stick and poked them. Their bellies. I could hear something sloshing away in there."

She shivered. "Then one of them lifted its head and I saw how red its teeth were. And the teeth were sharp, two rows atop and bottom, so many teeth. I ran inside to get my husband but he had too much *kava*. He wouldn't even sit up."

"Can I see what they did?" I said. The woman looked at me.

"You want to see the dead ones? The *bokola*?"

"I do. It might help your claim."

"My claim?"

"You know, the SPCA." I walked back to the shed.

Their bellies had been ripped out and devoured and the blood drained, she said.

There were bite marks, purplish, all over their backs and legs, as if the attacking dogs were seeking a good spot.

The insects and the birds had worked on the ears and other soft bits.

I took a stick to shift them around a bit.

"The dogs will come for those *bokola*. You leave them alone." She waved at the pile of corpses.

"The dogs?"

"Clean-up dogs. First the vampires, then the clean-up. Their yellow master sends them."

"Yellow master?" She shook her head, squeezed her eyes shut. Taboo subject.

"You wouldn't eat this meat? It seems a waste."

"The vampire dogs leave a taste behind," the woman told me. "A *kami-kamica* taste the other animals like. One of the men in my village cooked and ate one of those cows. He said it made him feel very good but now he smells of cowhide. He can't get the smell off himself."

"Are any of your animals left alive?"

The woman shook her head. "Not the bitten ones. They didn't touch them all, though."

"Can I see the others?" I would look for signs of disease, something to explain the sudden death. I wanted to be sure I was in the right place.

One cow was up against the back wall of the house, leaning close to catch the shade. There was a sheen of sweat on my body. I could feel it drip down my back.

"*Kata kata*," the woman said, pointing to the cow. "She is very hot."

It looked all right, apart from that.

I could get no more out of her.

Gina was sweating in the taxi. It was a hot day, but she felt the heat of the cow as well. "Any luck?" she said.

"Some. There's a few local taboos I'll need to get through to get the info we need, though."

"Ask him," she said, pointing at the driver. "He's Hindu."

Our taxi driver said, "I could have saved you the journey. No Fijian will talk about that. We Hindus know about those dogs."

He told us the vampire dogs lived at the bottom of Ciwa Waidekeulu. "Thiwa Why Ndeke Ulu," he said. Nine Waterfall. In the rainforest twenty minutes from where we were staying.

"She said something about a yellow master?"

"A great yellow dog who is worse than the worst man you've ever met."

I didn't tell him I'd met some bad men.

"You should keep away from him. He can give great boons to the successful, but there is no one successful. No one can defeat the yellow dog. Those who fail will vanish, as if they have never been." He stopped at a jetty, where some children sold us roti filled with a soft, sweet potato curry. Very, very good.

The girl who cleaned my room was not chatty at first, but I wanted to ask her questions. She answered most of them happily once I gave her a can of Coke. "Where do I park near Ciwa Waidekeulu? How do I ask the chief for permission to enter? Is there fresh water?"

When I asked her if she knew if the vampire dogs were down there, she went back to her housework, cleaning a bench already spotless. "These are not creatures to be captured," she said. "They should be poisoned." To distract me, she told me that her neighbors had five dogs, every last one of them a mongrel, barking all night and scaring her children. I know what I'd do if I were her. The council puts out notices of dog poisonings, *Keep Your Dogs In While We Kill the Stray*s, so all she'd have to do is let their dogs out while the cull was happening. Those dogs'd be happy to run; they used to leap the fence, tearing their guts, until her neighbor built his fence higher. They're desperate to get out.

They do a good job with the poisoning, she told me, but not so good with the clean up. Bloated bodies line the streets, float down the river, clog the drains.

They don't understand about repercussions, and that things don't just go away.

The client was pleased with my progress when I called him. "So, when will you go in?"

With the land taboo, I needed permission from the local chief or risk trouble. This took time. Most didn't want to discuss the vampire dogs, or the yellow dog king; he was forbidden, also. "It may be a couple of weeks. Depends on how I manage to deal with the locals."

"Surely a man would manage better," he said. "I know your husband doesn't like to talk, but most men will listen to a man better. Maybe I should send someone else."

"Listen," I told him, hoping to win him back, "I've heard they run with a fat cock of a dog. Have you heard that? People have seen the vampire dogs drop sheep hearts at this dog's feet. He tossed the heart up like it was a ball, snapped it up."

The man smacked his lips. I could hear it over the phone. "I've got a place for him, if you catch him as well."

"If you pay us, we'll get him. There are no bonus dogs."

"Check with your husband on that."

I thought of the slimy black hole he'd dug.

"They say that if you take a piece of him, good things will come your way. People don't like to talk about him. He's taboo."

"They just don't want anyone else taking a piece of him."

We moved to a new hotel set amongst the rainforest. The walls were dark green in patches, the smell of mold strong, but it was pretty with birdsong and close to the waterfalls which meant we could make an early start.

We ate in their open air restaurant, fried fish, more coconut milk, Greek meatballs. Gina didn't like mosquito repellent, thinking it clogged her pores with chemicals, so she was eaten alive by them.

"Have you called Joe?" she asked me over banana custard.

"Have you?" We smiled at each other; wife and sister ignoring him, back home and alone.

"We should call him. Does he know what we're doing?"

"I told him, but you know how he is." She was a good sister, visiting him weekly, reading to him, taking him treats he chewed but didn't seem to enjoy.

We drank too much Fijian beer and we danced around the snooker table, using the cues as microphones. No one seemed bothered, least of all the waiters.

The next morning, we called a cab to drop us at the top of the waterfall. You couldn't drive down any further. In the car park, souvenir sellers sat listlessly, their day's takings a few coins that jangled in their pockets. Their faces marked with lines, boils on their shins, they leaned back and stared as we gathered our things together.

"I have shells," one boy said.

"No turtles," Gina said, flipping her head at him to show how disgusting that trade was to her.

"Not turtles. Beetles. The size of a turtle."

He held up the shell to her. There was a smell about it, almost like an office smell; cleaning fluids, correcting fluids, coffee brewed too long. The shell was metallic gray and marbled with black lines. Claws out the side, small, odd, clutching snipers. I had seen, had eaten, prawns with claws like this. Bluish and fleshy, I felt like I was eating a sea monster.

"From the third waterfall," the seller said. "All the other creatures moved up when the dogs moved into Nine Waterfall."

I'm in the right place, I thought. "So there are dogs in the waterfall?"

"Vampire dogs. They only come out for food. They live way down."

An older vendor hissed at him. "Don't scare the nice ladies. They don't believe in vampire dogs."

"You'd be surprised what I believe in," Gina said. She touched one finger to the man's throat. "I believe that you have a secret not even your wife knows. If she learns of it, she will take your children away."

"No."

"Yes." She gave the boy money for one of the shells and opened her large bag to place it inside.

He said, "You watch out for yellow dog. If you sacrifice a part of him you"ll never be hungry again. But if you fail you will die on the spot and no one will know you ever lived. If you take the right bit you will never be lonely again."

I didn't know that I wanted a companion for life.

As we walked, I said, "How did you know he had a secret?"

"All men have secrets."

The first waterfall was overhung by flowering trees. It was a very popular picnic site. Although it took twenty minutes to reach, Indian women were there with huge pots and pans, cooking roti and warming dhal while the men and children swam. I trailed my hand in the water; very cool, not the pleasant body-temperature water of the islands, but a refreshing briskness.

Birdsong here was high and pretty. More birds than I'd seen elsewhere. Broadbills, honey-eaters, crimson and masked parrots, and velvet doves. Safe here, perhaps. The ground was soft and writhing with worms. The children collected them for bait, although the fish were sparse. Down below, the children told us, were fish big enough to feed a family of ten for a week. They liked human bait, so men would dangle their toes in. I guessed they were teasing us about this.

The path to the second waterfall was well-trodden. The bridge had been built with good, treated timber and seemed sturdy.

The waterfall fell quietly here. It was a gentler place. Only the fisherman sat by the water's edge; children and women not welcome. The fish were so thick in the water they could barely move. The fishermen didn't bother with lines; they reached in and grabbed what they wanted.

Gina breathed heavily.

"Do you want to slow down a bit? I don't think we should dawdle, but we can slow down," I said.

"It's not that. It's the fish. I don't usually get anything from fish, but I guess there's so many of them. I'm finding it hard to breathe."

The men stood up to let us past.

"There are a lot of fish," I said. Sometimes the obvious is the only thing to say. "Where do they come from?" I asked one of the men. "There are so few up there." I pointed up to the first waterfall.

"They come from underground. The center of the earth. They are already cooked when we catch them, from the heat inside."

He cut one open to demonstrate and it was true; inside was white, fluffy, warm flesh. He gestured it at me and I took a piece. Gina refused. The meat was delicate and sweet and I knew I would seek without finding it wherever else I went in the world.

"American?" the man said.

"New Zealand," Gina lied.

"Ah, Kiwi!" he said. "Sister!" They liked the New Zealanders better than Australians and Americans because of closer distance, and because they shared a migratory path. Gina could put on any accent; it was like she absorbed the vowel sounds.

I could have stayed at the second waterfall but we had a job to do, and Gina found the place claustrophobic.

"It's only going to get worse," I said. "The trees will close in on us and the sky will vanish."

She grunted. Sometimes, I think, she found me very stupid and shallow. She liked me better than almost anybody else did, but sometimes even she rolled her eyes at me.

The third waterfall was small. There was a thick buzz of insects over it. I hoped not mosquitoes; I'd had dengue fever once before and did not want hemorrhagic fever. I stopped to slather repellent on, strong stuff which repelled people as well.

The ground was covered with small, green shelled cockroaches. They were not bothered by us and I could ignore them. The ones on the tree trunks, though; at first I thought they were bark, but then one moved. It was as big as my head and I couldn't tell how many legs. It had a jaw which seemed to click and a tail like a scorpion which it kept coiled.

"I wouldn't touch one," Gina said.

"Really? Is that a vision you had?"

"No, they just look nasty," and we shared a small laugh. We often shared moments like that, even at Joe's bedside.

Gina stumbled on a tree root the size of a man's thigh.

"You need to keep your eyes down," I said. "Downcast. Modest. Can you do that?"

"Can you?"

"Not really."

"Joe always liked 'em feisty."

Gina's breath came heavy now and her cheeks reddened.

"It's going to be tough walking back up."

"It always is. I don't even know why you're dragging me along. You could manage this alone."

"You know I need you to gauge the mood. That's why."

"Still. I'd rather not be here."

"I'll pay you well. You know that."

"It's not the money, Rosie. It's what we're doing. Every time I come out with you it feels like we're going against nature. Like we're siding with the wrong people."

"You didn't meet the client. He's a nice guy. Wants to save his kid."

"Of course he does, Rosie. You keep telling yourself that."

I didn't like that; I've been able to read people since I was twelve and it became necessary. Gina's sarcasm always confused me, though.

At the fourth waterfall, we found huge, stinking mushrooms, which seemed to turn to face us.

Vines hung from the trees, thick enough we had to push them aside to walk through. They were covered with a sticky substance. I'd seen this stuff before, used as rope, to tie bundles. You needed a bush knife to cut it. I'd realized within a day of being here you should never be without a bush knife and I'd bought one at the local shop. I cut a dozen vines, then coiled them around my waist.

Gina nodded. "Very practical." She was over her moment, which was good. Hard to work as a team with someone who didn't want to be there.

What did we see at the fifth waterfall? The path here was very narrow. We had to walk one foot in front of the other, fashion models showing off.

There were no vines here. The water was taken by one huge fish, the size of a Shetland pony. The surface of the water was covered with roe and I wondered where the mate was. Another underground channel? It would have to be a big one. It would be big but confining. My husband is confined. I'm happy with him that way. He can't interfere with my business. Tell me how to do things.

At the sixth waterfall, we saw our first dog. It was very small and had no legs. Born that way? It lay in the pathway unmoving, and when I nudged it, I realized it was dead.

Gina clutched my arm. Her icy fingers hurt and I could feel the cold through my layers of clothing.

"Graveyard," she said. "This is their graveyard."

The surface of the sixth pool was thick with belly-up fish. At the base of the trees, dead insects like autumn leaves raked into a pile.

And one dead dog. I wondered why there weren't more.

"He has passed through the veil," Gina said, as if she were saying a prayer. "We should bury him."

"We could take him home to the client. He already has a hole dug in his backyard. He's kind of excited at the idea of keeping dogs there."

Is there a name for a person who takes pleasure in the confinement of others?

We reached the seventh waterfall.

We heard yapping, and I stiffened. I opened my bag and put my hand on a dog collar, ready. Gina stopped, closed her eyes.

"Puppies," she said. "Hungry."

"What sort?"

Gina shook her head. We walked on, through a dense short tunnel of wet leaves.

At the edge of the seventh waterfall there was a cluster of small brown dogs. Their tongues lapped the water (small fish, I thought) and when we approached, the dogs lifted their heads, widened their eyes, and stared.

"Gaze dogs," I said.

These were gaze dogs like I'd never seen before. Huge eyes. Reminded me of the spaniel with the brain too big.

"Let's rest here, let them get used to us," Gina said.

I glanced at my watch. We were making good time; assuming we caught a vampire dog with little trouble, we could easily make it back up by the sunfall.

"Five minutes."

We leaned against a moss-covered rock. Very soft, damp, with a smell of underground.

The gaze dogs came over and sniffled at us. One of the puppies had deep red furrows on its back; dragging teeth marks. I had seen this sort of thing after dog fights, dog attacks. Another had a deep dent in its side, filled with dark red scab and small yellow pustules. Close up, we could see most of the dogs were damaged in some way.

"Food supply?" Gina said.

I shuddered. Not much worried me, but these dogs were awful to look at.

One very small dog nuzzled my shoe, whimpering. I picked it up; it was light, weak. I tucked it into my jacket front. Gina smiled at me. "You're not so tough!"

"Study purposes." I put four more in there; they snuggled up and went to sleep.

She seemed blurry to me; it was darker than before. Surely the sun wasn't further away. We hadn't walked that far. My legs ached as if I had been hiking for days.

At the eighth waterfall we found the vampire dogs. Big, gazing eyes, unblinking, watching every move we made. The dogs looked hungry, ribs showing, stomachs concave.

"They move fast," Gina whispered, her eyes closed. "They move like the waterfall."

The dogs swarmed forward and knocked me down. Had their teeth into me in a second, maybe two.

The feeling of them on me, their cold, wet paws heavy into my flesh, but the heat of them, the fiery touch of their skin, their sharp teeth, was so shocking I couldn't think for a moment, then I pulled a puppy from my jacket and threw it.

Their teeth already at work, the dogs saw the brown flash and followed it.

They moved so fast I could still see fur when they were gone.

I threw another puppy and another vampire dog peeled off with a howl. The first puppy was almost drained, its body flatter, as if the vampires sucked out muscle, too.

"Quick," Gina said. "Quick." She had tears in her eyes, feeling the pain of the puppies, their deaths, in her veins.

I threw a third puppy and we ran down, away from them. We should have run up, but they filled the path that way.

I needed a place to unpack my bag, pull out the things I'd need to drop three of them. Or four.

We heard a huffing noise; an old man coughing up a lifetime. We were close to the base and the air was so hard to breathe we both panted. Gina looked at me.

"It must be the alpha. The yellow dog."

It seemed to me she stopped breathing for a moment.

"We could try to take a piece of him. We'd never be lonely again, if we did that."

The vampire dogs growled at us, wanting more puppies. The last two were right against my belly; I couldn't reach them easily and I didn't want to.

"I don't want to see the ninth waterfall," Gina said. I shook my head. If the vampire dogs were this powerful, how strong would he be?

"It's okay. I'm ready now. I'll take three of them down quietly; the others won't even notice. Then we'll have to kick our way out."

She nodded.

We turned around and he was waiting. That dog.

He was crippled and pitiful but still powerful. His tail, his ears and his toes had been cut off by somebody brave. Chunks of flesh were gone from his side. People using him as sacrifice for gain.

Gina was impressive; I could see she was in pain. Was she feeling the dog's pain? She was quiet with it, small grunts. She walked towards him.

The closer she got to the dog the worse it seemed to get. "I want to lay hands on him, give him comfort," Gina said.

The dog was the ugliest I've ever seen. Of all the strays who've crossed my path here, this one was the most aggressive. This dog would make a frightening man, I thought. A man I couldn't control. Drool streamed down his chin.

He sat slouched, rolled against his lower back. Even sitting he reached to my waist.

All four legs were sprawled. He reminded me of an almost-drunk young man, wanting a woman for the night and willing to forgo that last drink, those last ten drinks, to achieve one. Sprawled against the bar, legs wide, making the kind of display men can.

His fur was the color of piss, that golden color you don't want to look at too hard, and splotched with mud, grease, and something darker.

One ear was half bitten off. The other seemed to stand straight up, unmoving, like a badly made wooden prosthetic.

One lip was split, I think; it seemed blurry at this distance.

He licked his balls. And his dog's lipstick stuck out, fully twelve centimeters long, pink and waving.

Thousands of unwanted puppies in there.

He wasn't threatening; I felt sorry for him. He was like a big boy with the reputation of being a bully, who has never hurt anyone.

But when we got close to the yellow dog I realized he was perfect, no bits missing. An illusion to seduce us to come closer. Gina stepped right up to him.

"Gina! Come back!" but she wouldn't.

"If I comfort him, he will send me a companion. A lifetime companion," she said.

"Come live with me!" I said. "We'll take some gaze dogs, rescue them. We'll live okay."

He reared back on his hind legs and his huge skull seemed to reach the trees. He lifted his great paw high.

Around our feet, the vampire dogs swarmed. I grabbed one. Another. I sedated them and shoved them in my carry bag.

The yellow dog pinned Gina with his paws. The vampire dogs surrounded him, a thick blue snarling band around him.

I threw my last two gaze dogs at them but they snapped at them too quickly. I had no gun. I picked up three rocks and threw one, hard. Pretended it was a baseball and it was three balls two strikes.

The vampire dogs swatted the rock away as if it were a dandelion. I threw another, and the last, stepping closer each time.

The yellow dog had his teeth at Gina's throat and I ran forward, thinking only to tear her away, at least drag her away from his teeth.

The vampire dogs, though, all over me, biting my eyes, my ears, my lips.

I managed to throw them off, though perhaps they let me.

The yellow dog sat crouched, his mouth covered with blood. At his paws, I thought I saw hair, but I wondered: *What human has been down here? Who else but me would come this far?*

I backed away. Two sleeping vampire dogs in my bag made no noise and emitted no odor; I was getting away with it. They watched me go, their tongues pink and wet. The yellow dog; again, from afar he looked kindly. A dear old faithful dog. I took two more vampire dogs down, simple knock out stuff in a needle, and I put them in my bag. A soft blanket waited there; no need to damage the goods.

I picked up another gaze dog as I walked. This one had a gouge in his back, but his fur was pale brown, the color of milk chocolate. He licked me. I put him down my jacket, then picked up another for a companion.

It took me hours to reach the top. Time did not seem to pass, though. Unless I'd lost a whole day. When I reached second waterfall, there were the same fishermen. And the families at first waterfall, swimming, cooking and eating as if there was no horror below them. They all waved at me but none offered me food or drink.

The souvenir salesmen were there at the top. "Shells?" they said. "Buy a shell. No sale for a week, you know. No sale. You will be the first." I didn't want a shell; they came from the insects I'd seen below and didn't want to be reminded of them.

I called a cabbie to take me to my hotel. I spent another day, finalizing arrangements for getting the dogs home (you just need to know who to call) then I checked out of my room.

The doctor was happier than I'd thought he'd be. Only two dogs had survived, but they were fit and healthy and happily sucked the blood out of the live chicken he provided them.

"You were right; you work well alone," he said. "You should dump that husband of yours. You can manage alone."

I'd just come from visiting Joe and his dry-eyed gaze, his flaccid fingers, seemed deader than ever. The nurses praised me up, glad there was somebody for him. "Oh, you're so good," they said. "So patient and loyal. He has no one else." Neither do I, I told them.

A month or so later, the doctor called me. He wanted to show me the dogs; prove he was looking after them properly.

A young woman dressed in crisp, white clothes answered the door.

"Come in!" she said.

"You know who I am?"

Leading me through the house, she gave me a small wink. "Of course."

I wasn't sure I liked that.

She led me outside to the backyard; it was different. He'd tiled the hole and it was now a fish pond. The yard was neater, and lounge chairs and what looked like a bar were placed in a circle. Six people sat in the armchairs, reading magazines, sipping long drinks.

"He didn't tell me there was a party."

"Take a seat. Doctor will be with you shortly," the young woman said. Three of the guests looked at their watches as if waiting for an appointment.

I studied them. They were not a well group. Quiet and pale, all of them spoke slowly and lifted their glasses gently as if in pain or lacking strength. They all had good, expensive shoes. Gold jewelry worn with ease. The doctor had some wealthy friends.

They made me want to leap up, jump around, show off my health.

The young woman came back and called a name. An elderly woman stood up.

"Thank you, nurse," she said. It all clicked in then; I'd been right. The doctor was charging these people for treatment.

It was an hour before he dealt with his patients and called me in.

The vampire dogs rested on soft blankets. They were bloated, their eyes rolling. They could barely lift their heads.

"You see my dogs are doing well."

"And so are you, I take it. How's your son?"

He laughed. "You know there's no son."

He gave me another drink. His head didn't bobble. We drank vodka together, watching the vampire dogs prowl his yard, and a therapist would say my self-loathing led me to sleep with him.

I crawled out of the client's bed at two or three a.m., home to my gaze dogs. They were healing well and liked to chew my couch. They jumped up at me, licking and yapping, and the three of us sat on the floor, waiting for the next call to come in.

SNOW ON SUGAR MOUNTAIN

ELIZABETH HAND

When Andrew was seven, his mother turned into a fox. Snow freed the children from school at lunchtime, the bus skating down the hill to release cheering gangs at each sleety corner. Andrew got off last, nearly falling from the curb as he turned to wave good-bye to the driver. He ran to the front door of the house, battering at the screen and yelling, "Mom! Mom!" He tugged the scarf from his face, the better to peer through frost-clouded windows. Inside it looked dark; but he heard the television chattering to itself, heard the chimes of the old ship's clock counting half past one. She would be downstairs, then, doing the laundry. He dashed around the house, sliding on the iced flagstones.

"Mom . . . I'm home, it snowed, I'm—"

He saw the bird first. He thought it was the cardinal that had nested in the box tree last spring: a brilliant slash of crimson in the snow, like his own lost mitten. Andrew held his breath, teetering as he leaned forward to see.

A blue jay: no longer blue, somber as tarnished silver, its scattered quills already gray and pale crest quivering erect like an accusing finger. The snow beneath it glowed red as paint, and threads of steam rose from its mauled breast. Andrew tugged at his scarf, glancing across the white slope of lawn for the neighbor's cat.

That was when he saw the fox, mincing up the steps to the open back door, its mouth drooped to show wet white teeth, the curved blade of the jay's wing hanging from its jaw. Andrew gasped. The fox mirrored his surprise, opening its mouth so that the wing fell and broke apart like the spinning seeds of a maple. For a moment they regarded each other, blue eyes and black. Then the fox stretched its forelegs as if yawning, stretched its mouth wide, too wide, until it seemed that its jaw would split like the broken quills. Andrew saw red gums and tongue, teeth like an ivory stair spiraling into black, black that was his mothers hair, his mothers eyes, his mother crouched naked, retching on the top step in the snow.

After that she had to show it to him. Not that day, not even that winter; but later, in the summer, when cardinals nested once more in the box tree and shrieking jays chased goldfinches from the birdbath.

"Someday you can have it, Andrew," she said as she drew her jewelry box from the kitchen hidey-hole. "When you're older. There's no one else," she added. His father had died before he was born. "And it's mine, anyway."

Inside the box were loops of pearls, jade turtles, a pendant made of butterfly's wings that formed a sunset and palm trees. And a small ugly thing, as long as her thumb and the same color: marbled cream, nut brown in the creases. At first he thought it was a bug. It was the locust year, and everywhere their husks stared at him from trees and cracks in the wall.

But it wasn't a locust. His mother placed it in his hand, and he held it right before his face. Some sort of stone, smooth as skin. Cool at first, after a few moments in his palm it grew warm, and he glanced at his mother for reassurance.

"Don't worry," she laughed wryly. "It won't bite." And she sipped her drink.

It was an animal, all slanted eyes and grinning mouth, paws tucked beneath its sharp chin like a dog playing Beg. A tiny hole had been drilled in the stone so that it could be tied onto a string.

"How does it work?" Andrew asked. His mother shook her head.

"Not yet," she said, swishing the ice in her glass. "It's mine still; but someday—someday I'll show you how." And she took the little carving and replaced it, and locked the jewelry box back in the hidey-hole.

That had been seven years ago. The bus that stopped at the foot of the hill would soon take Andrew to the public high school. Another locust summer was passing. The seven-year cicadas woke in the August night and crept from their split skins like a phantom army. The night they began to sing, Andrew woke to find his mother dead, bright pills spilling from one hand when he forced it open. In the other was the amulet, her palm blistered where she clenched the stone.

He refused the sedatives the doctor offered him, refused awkward offers of comfort from relatives and friends suddenly turned to strangers. At the wake he slouched before the casket, tearing petals from carnations. He nodded stiffly at his mother's sister when she arrived to take him to the funeral.

"Colin leaves for Brockport in three weeks," his aunt said later in the car. "When he goes, you can have the room to yourself. It's either that or the couch—"

"I don't care," Andrew replied. He didn't mean for his voice to sound so harsh. "I mean, it doesn't matter. Anywhere's okay. Really."

And it was, really.

Because the next day he was gone.

North of the city, in Kamensic Village, the cicadas formed heavy curtains of singing green and copper, covering oaks and beeches, houses and hedges and bicycles left out overnight. On Sugar Mountain they rippled across an ancient Volkswagen Beetle that hadn't moved in months. Their song was loud enough to wake the old astronaut in the middle of the night, and nearly drown out the sound of the telephone when it rang in the morning.

"I no longer do interviews," the old astronaut said wearily. He started to hang up. Then, "How the hell did you get this number, anyway?" he demanded; but the reporter was gone. Howell glared at Festus. The spaniel cringed, tail vibrating over the flagstones, and moaned softly. "You giving out this new number?" Howell croaked, and slapped his thigh. "Come on—"

The dog waddled over and lay his head upon the man's knee. Howell stroked the old bony skull, worn as flannel, and noted a hole in the knee of his pajamas.

Eleven o'clock and still not dressed. Christ, Festus, you should've said something.

He caught himself talking aloud and stood, gripping the mantel and waiting until his heart slowed. Sometimes now he didn't know if he was talking or thinking; if he had taken his medicine and slipped into the dreamy hold that hid him from the pain or if he was indeed dreaming. Once he had drifted, and thought he was addressing another class of eager children. He woke to find himself mumbling to an afternoon soap opera, Festus staring up at him intently That day he put the television in a closet.

But later he dragged it back into the bedroom once more. The news helped remind him of things. Reminded him to call Lancaster, the oncologist; to call his son Peter, and the Kamensic Village Pharmacy.

"Festus," he whispered, hugging the dog close to his knee. "Oh, Festus." And when he finally glanced at the spaniel again was surprised to see the gentle sloping snout matted and dark with tears.

From the western Palisades, the radio tower blazed across the Hudson as Andrew left the city that dawn. He stood at the top of the road until the sun crept above the New York side, waiting until the beacon flashed and died. The first jet shimmered into sight over bridges linking the island to the foothills of the northern ranges. Andrew sighed. No tears left; but grief feathered his eyes so that the river swam, blurred, and finally disappeared in the burst of sunrise. He turned and walked down the hill, faster and faster, past bus stops and parked cars, past the high school and the cemetery Only when he reached the Parkway did he stop to catch his breath, then slowly crossed the road to the northbound lane.

Two rides brought him to Valhalla. He walked backward along the side of the road, shifting his backpack from shoulder to shoulder as he held his thumb out. A businessman in a BMW finally pulled over and unlocked the passenger door. He regarded Andrew with a sour expression.

"If you were my kid, I'd put your lights out," he growled as Andrew hopped in, grinning his best late-for-class smile. "But I'd wish a guy like me picked you up instead of some pervert."

"Thanks," Andrew nodded seriously "I mean, you're right. I missed the last train out last night. I got to get to school."

The man stared straight ahead, then glanced at his watch. "I'm going to Manchester Hills. Where do you go to school?"

"John Jay."

"In Mount Lopac?"

"Kamensic Village."

The man nodded. "Is 684 close enough?"

Andrew shrugged. "Sure. Thanks a lot."

After several miles, they veered onto the highway's northern hook. Andrew sat forward in the seat, damp hands sticking to his knapsack as he watched for the exit sign. When he saw it he dropped his knapsack in nervous excitement. The businessman scowled.

"This is it . . . I mean, please, if it's okay—" The seat belt caught Andrew's sneaker as he grabbed the door handle. "Thanks—thanks a lot—"

"Next time don't miss the train," the man yelled as Andrew stumbled onto the road. Before he could slam the door shut, the lock clicked back into place. Andrew waved. The man lifted a finger in farewell, and the BMW roared north.

From the Parkway, Kamensic Village drifted into sight like a dream of distant towns. White steeples, stone walls, granite turrets rising from hills already rusted with the first of autumn. To the north the hills arched like a deer's long spine, melting golden into the Mohank Mountains. Andrew nodded slowly and shrugged the knapsack to his shoulder. He scuffed down the embankment to where a stream flowed townward. He followed it, stopping to drink and wash his face, slicking his hair back into a dark wave. Sunfish floated in the water above sandy nests, slipping fearlessly through his fingers when he tried to snatch them. His stomach ached from hunger, raw and cold as though he'd swallowed a handful of cinders. He thought of the stone around his neck. That smooth pellet under his tongue, and how easy it would be then to find food . . .

He swore softly, shaking damp hair from his eyes. Against his chest the amulet bounced, and he steadied it, grimacing, before heading upstream.

The bug-ridden sign swayed at the railroad station: KAMENSIC VILLAGE. Beneath it stood a single bench, straddled by the same kid Andrew remembered from childhood: misshapen helmet protecting his head, starry topaz eyes widening when he saw Andrew pass the station.

"Hey," the boy yelled, just as if he remembered Andrew from years back. "HEY!"

"Hey, Buster." Andrew waved without stopping.

He passed the Kamensic Village Pharmacy, where Mr. Weinstein still doled out egg creams; Hayden's Delicatessen with its great vat of iced tea, lemons bobbing like toy turtles in the amber liquid. The library, open four days a week (CLOSED TODAY). That was where he had seen puppet shows, and heard an astronaut talk once, years ago when he and his mother still came up in the summer to rent the cottage. And, next to the library, the seventeenth-century courthouse, now a museum.

"Fifty cents for students." The same old lady peered suspiciously at Andrew's damp hair and red-rimmed eyes. "Shouldn't you be in school?"

"Visiting," Andrew mumbled as she dropped the quarters into a little tin box. "I got relatives here."

He shook his head at her offer to walk him through the rooms.

"I been here before," he explained. He tried to smile. "On vacation."

The courtroom smelled the same, of lemon polish and the old lady's Chanel No.5. The Indian Display waited where it always had, in a whitewashed corner of the courtroom where dead bluebottles drifted like lapis beads. Andrew's chest tightened when he saw it. His hand closed around the amulet on its string.

A frayed map of the northern county starred with arrowheads indicated where the tribes had settled. Ax blades and skin scrapers marked their battles. A deer hide frayed with moth holes provided a backdrop for the dusty case. From beneath the doeskin winked a vole's skull.

At the bottom of the case rested a small printed board. Andrew leaned his head against the glass and closed his eyes, mouthing the words without reading them as he fingered the stone.

. . . members of the Tankiteke tribe of the Wappinger Confederacy of
Mohicans: Iroquois warriors of the Algonquin Nation . . .

When he opened his eyes they fixed upon an object at the bottom of the case: a carved gray stone in the image of a tiny animal with long eyes and smooth sharp teeth.

Shaman's Talisman [Animistic Figure]

The Tankiteke believed their shamans could change shape at will
and worshipped animal spirits.

From the narrow hallway leading to the front room came the creak of a door opening, the answering hiss of women's laughter.

"Some boy," Andrew heard the old lady reply. He bit his lip. "Said he had relatives, but I think he's just skipping school . . . "

Andrew glanced around the courtroom, looking for new exhibits, tools, books. There was nothing. No more artifacts; no other talisman. He slipped through a door leading to an anteroom and found there another door leading outside. Unlocked; there would be no locked doors in Kamensic Village. In the orchard behind the courthouse, he scooped up an early apple and ate it, wincing at the bitter flesh. Then he headed for the road that led to The Fallows."

In the dreams, Howell walked on the moon . . .

The air he breathed was the same stale air, redolent of urine and refrigeration, that had always filled the capsules. Yet he was conscious in the dreams that it tasted different on the moon, filtered through the spare silver ducts coiled on his back. Above him the sky loomed sable, so cold that his hands tingled inside heated gloves at the sight of it: as he had always known it would be, algid, black, speared with stars that pulsed and sang as they never did inside the capsule. He lifted his eyes then and saw the orbiter passing overhead. He raised one hand to wave, so slowly it seemed he might start to drift into the stark air in the pattern of that wave. And then the voice crackled in his ears, clipped words echoing phrases from memoranda and newscasts. His own voice, calling to Howell that it was time to return.

That was when he woke, shivering despite quilts and Festus snoring beside him. A long while he lay in bed, trying to recall the season—winter, surely, because of the fogged windows.

But no. Beneath the humming cough of air-conditioning, cicadas droned. Howell struggled to his feet.

Behind the bungalow the woods shimmered, birch and ancient oaks silvered by the moonlight streaming from the sky. Howell opened the casement and leaned out. Light and warmth spilled upon him as though the moonlight were warm milk, and he blinked and stretched his hands to catch it.

Years before, during the final two moon landings, Howell had been the man who waited inside the orbiter.

Long ago, before the actors and writers and wealthy children of the exurbs migrated to Kamensic Village, a colony of earnest socialists settled upon the scrubby shores of the gray water named Muscanth. Their utopia had shattered years before. The cozy stage and studios rotted and softly sank back into the fen. But the cottages remained, some of them still rented to summer visitors from the city. Andrew had to ask in Scotts Corners for directions—he hadn't been here since he was ten—and was surprised by how much longer it took to reach The Fallows on foot. No autos passed, Only a young girl in jeans and flannel shirt, riding a black horse, her braids flying as her mount cantered by him. Andrew laughed. She waved, grinning, before disappearing around a kink in the birchy lane.

With that sharp laugh, something fell from Andrew: as if grief could be contained in small cold breaths, and he had just exhaled. He noticed for the first time sweat streaking his chest, and unbuttoned his shirt. The shirt smelled stale and oily, as though it had absorbed the city's foul air, its grimy clouds of exhaust and factory smoke.

But here the sky gleamed slick and blue as a bunting's wing, Andrew laughed again, shook his head so that sky and leaves and scattering birds all flickered in a bright blink. And when he focused again upon the road, the path snaked *there*: just where he had left it four years ago, carefully cleared of curling ferns and moldering birch,

I'm *here*, he thought as he stepped shyly off the dirt road, glancing back to make certain no car or rider marked where he broke trail. In the distance glittered the lake. A cloud of red admiral butterflies rose from a crab-apple stump and skimmed beside him along the overgrown path Andrew ran, laughing. He was home.

The abandoned cottage had grown larger with decay and disuse. Ladders of nectarine fungi and staghorn lichen covered it from eaves to floor, and between this patchwork straggled owls' nests and the downy homes of deer mice.

The door did not give easily It was unlocked, but swollen from snow and rain. Andrew had to fling himself full force against the timbers before they groaned and relented. Amber light streamed from chinks and cracks in the walls, enough light that ferns and pokeweed grew from clefts in the pine floor. Something scurried beneath the room's single chair, Andrew turned in time to see a deer mouse, still soft in its gray infant fur, disappear into the wall.

There had been other visitors as well. In the tiny bedroom, Andrew found fox scat and long rufous hairs clinging to the splintered cedar wall: by the front door, rabbit pellets. Mud daubers had plastered the kitchen with their fulvous cells. The linoleum was scattered with undigested feathers and the crushed spines of voles. He paced the cottage, yanking up pokeweed and tossing it into the corner, dragged the chair into the center of the room and sat there a long time. Finally, he took a deep breath, opened his knapsack and withdrew a bottle of gin pilfered from his mother's bureau, still nearly full. He took a swig, shut his eyes and waited for it to steam through his throat to his head.

"Don't do it drunk," his mother had warned him once—drunk herself, the two of them sipping Pink Squirrels from a lukewarm bottle in her bedroom. "You ever seen a drunk dog?"

"No," Andrew giggled.

"Well, it's like that, only worse. You can't walk straight. You can't smell anything. It's worse than plain drunk. I almost got hit by a car once, in Kamensic, when I was drunk." She lit a cigarette. "Stayed out a whole night that time, trying to find my way back . . . "

Andrew nodded, rubbing the little talisman to his lips.

"No," his mother said softly, and took it from him. She held it up to the gooseneck lamp. "Not yet."

She turned and stared at him fiercely, glittering eyes belying her slurred voice. "See, you can't stay that long. I almost did, that time . . . "

She took another sip. "Forget, I mean. You forget . . . fox or bear or deer, you forget . . . "

"Forget what?" Andrew wondered. The smoke made him cough, and he gulped his drink.

"What you are. That you're human. Not . . . "

She took his hand, her nails scratching his palm. "They used to forget. The Indians, the Tankiteke. That's what my grandfather said. There used to be more of these things—"

She rolled the stone between her palms. "And now they're all gone. You know why?"

Andrew shook his head.

"Because they forgot." His mother turned away. "Fox or whatever—they forgot they once were human, and stayed forever, and died up there in the woods." And she fingered the stone as she did her wedding ring, eyes agleam with whiskey tears.

But that night Andrew lay long awake, staring at his Mets pennants as he listened to the traffic outside; and wondered why anyone would ever want to come back.

Howell woke before dawn, calling, "Festus! Morning." The spaniel snorted and stared at him blearily before sliding off the bed.

"Look," said Howell, pointing to where tall ferns at wood's edge had been crushed to a green mat. "They were here again last night."

Festus whined and ran from the room, nails tick-tacking upon the floor. Howell let him out the back door and watched the old dog snuffle at the deer brake, then crash into the brush. Some mornings Howell felt as if he might follow the dog on these noisy hunts once more. But each time, the dawn rush of light and heat trampled his strength as carelessly as deer broke the ferns. For a few minutes he breathed easily, the dank mountain air slipping like water down his throat, cold and tasting of granite. Then the coughing started. Howell gripped the door frame, shuddering until the tears came, chest racked as though something smashed his ribs to escape. He stumbled into the kitchen, fingers scrabbling across the counter until they clutched the inhaler. By the time he breathed easily again, sunlight gilded Sugar Mountain, and at the back door Festus scratched for entry, panting from his run.

The same morning found Andrew snoring on the cottage floor. The bottle of gin had toppled, soaking the heap of old newspapers where he lay pillowed. He woke slowly but to quick and violent conclusions when he tried to stand.

"Christ," he moaned, pausing in the doorway. The reek of gin made him sick. Afterward, he wiped his mouth on a wild grape leaf, then with surprising vigor smashed the bottle against a tree. Then he staggered downhill toward the stream.

Here the water flowed waist-deep. Andrew peeled off T-shirt and jeans and eased himself into the stream, swearing at the cold. A deep breath. Then he dunked himself, came up sputtering, and floated above the clear pebbled bottom, eyes shut against the shadows of trees and sky trembling overhead.

He settled on a narrow stone shelf above the stream, water rippling across his lap. His head buzzed between hunger and hangover. Beneath him minnows drifted like willow leaves. He dipped a hand to catch them, but they wriggled easily through his fingers. A feverish hunger came over him. He counted back three days since he'd eaten: the same evening he'd found his mother . . .

He blinked against the memory, blinked until the hazy air cleared and he could focus on the stream beneath him. Easing himself into the water, he knelt in the shallows and squinted at the rocks. Very slowly, he lifted one flat stone, then another. The third uncovered a crayfish, mottled brown against chocolate-colored gravel. Andrew bit his hand to stop it shaking, then slipped it beneath the surface. The crayfish shot backward, toward his ankles. Andrew positioned his feet to form a V, squatting to cut off its escape. He yelped triumphantly when he grabbed its tail.

"Son of a bitch!" Pincers nipped his thumb. He flung the crayfish onto the mossy bank, where it jerked and twitched. For a moment Andrew regarded it remorsefully. Then he took the same flat stone that had sheltered it and neatly cracked its head open.

Not much meat to suck from the claws. A thumb's worth (still quivering) within the tail, muddy and sweet as March rain. In the next hour he uncovered dozens more, until the bank was littered with empty carapaces, the mud starred with his handprints like a great raccoon's. Finally he stopped eating. The mess on the bank sickened him. He crawled to stream's edge and bit his lip, trying not to throw up. In the shadowy water he saw himself: much too thin, black hair straggling across his forehead, his slanted eyes shadowed by exhaustion. He wiped a thread of mud from his lip and leaned back. Against his chest the amulet bounced like a stray droplet, its filthy cord chafing his neck. He dried his face with his T-shirt, then pulled the string until the amulet dangled in front of him.

In the late summer light it gleamed eerily, swollen as a monarch's chrysalis. And like the lines of thorax, head, wings evident upon a pupae, the talisman bore faint markings. Eyes, teeth, paws; wings, fins, antlers, tail. Depending on how it caught the light, it was fox or stoat; flying squirrel or cougar or stag. The boy pinched the amulet between thumb and middle finger, drew it across his check. Warm. Within the nugget of stone he felt a dull buzzing like an entrapped hornet.

Andrew rubbed the talisman against his lips. His teeth vibrated as from a tiny drill. He shut his eyes, tightened his fingers about the stone, and slipped it beneath his tongue. For a second he felt it, a seed ripe to burst. Then nausea exploded inside him, pain so violent he screamed and collapsed onto the moss, clawing wildly at his head. Abruptly his shrieks stopped. He could not breathe. A rush of warm air filled his nostrils, fetid as pond water. He sneezed.

And opened his eyes to the muddy bank oozing between black and velvet paws.

Perhaps it was the years spent in cramped spaces—his knees drawn to his chest in capsule mock-ups; sleeping suspended in canvas sacks; eating upside down in metal rooms smaller than a refrigerator—perhaps the bungalow had actually seemed *spacious* when Howell decided to purchase it over his son's protests and his accountant's sighs.

"Plenty of room for what I need," he told his son. They were hanging pictures. NASA shots, *Life* magazine promos. The Avedon portrait of his wife, a former Miss Rio Grande, dead of cancer before the moon landing. "And fifty acres: most of the lakefront."

"Fifty acres most of it nowhere," Peter said snidely. He hated the country; hated the disappointment he felt that his father hadn't taken the penthouse in Manhattan. "No room here for anyone else, that's for sure."

That was how the old man liked it. The bungalow fit neatly into a tiny clearing between glacier-riven hills. A good snow cut him off from the village for days: the towns only plow saved Sugar Mountain and the abandoned lake colony for last. "The Astronaut don't mind," the driver always said.

Howell agreed. After early retirement he took his pension and retired, truly retired. No honorary university positions. No airline endorsements. His investments were few and careless. He corresponded with crackpots, authors researching astral landing fields in rain forests, a woman who claimed to receive alien broadcasts through her sunglasses, an institutionalized patient who signed his letters Rubber Man Lord of Jupiter. During a rare radio interview, Howell admitted to experimentation with hallucinogenic drugs and expressed surprising bitterness at the demise of the Apollo program, regret untempered by the intervening years. On spring afternoons he could be seen walking with his English cocker spaniel on the dirt roads through Kamensic. The village schoolchildren pointed him out proudly, although his picture was not in their books. Once a year he spoke to the fifth graders about the importance of the space program, shyly signing autographs on lunch bags afterwards: no, the Astronaut did not mind.

The old man sighed and walked to his desk. From his frayed shirt rose a skull barren of hair, raised blue veins like rivers on a relief globe. Agate blue eyes, dry as if all the dreams had been sucked from them, focused now on strange things. Battalions of pill bottles. Bright lesions on hands and feet. Machines more dreadful than anything NASA had devised for his training. The road from Sugar Mountain lay so far from his front door that he seldom walked there anymore.

The medicine quelled his coughing. In its place a heaviness in his chest and the drug's phantom mettle.

"I wish the goddamn car keys were here," he announced to Festus, pacing to the door. He was not supposed to drive alone. Peter had taken the keys, "for safety." "I wish my goddamn dog could drive."

Festus yawned and flopped onto the floor. Sighing, the astronaut settled onto the couch, took pen and notebook to write a letter. Within minutes he was asleep.

Andrew staggered from the sound: the bawl of air through the trees, the cicadas' song a steady thunder. From beneath the soil thrummed millipedes and hellgrammites, the ceaseless tick of insect legs upon fallen leaves. He shivered and shook a ruff of heavy fur. The sunlight stung his eyes and he blinked. The world was bound now in black and gray

He sneezed. Warm currents of scent tickled his muzzle. So many kinds of dirt! Mud like cocoa, rich and bitter; sand fresh as sunlight; loam ripe with hidden worms. He stood on wobbly legs, took a few steps and stumbled on his clothes. Their rank smell assaulted him: detergent, sweat, city gravel and tarmac. He sneezed ferociously, then ambled to the streambed. He nosed a crayfish shell, licking it clean. Afterward he waded into the stream and lapped, long tongue flicking water into his eyes. A bound brought him to the high bank. He shook water from his fur and flung his head back, eyes shut, filled with a formidable wordless joy. From far away he heard low thunder; he tasted the approach of rain upon the breeze.

Something stirred in the thickets nearby. Without looking he knew it was a rabbit, smelled milk and acrid fear clinging to her. He raised his head, tested the air until he found her crouched at the base of a split birch. He crept forward, his belly grazing the dirt. When he was scarcely a muzzle-length away, she spooked, hind legs spraying leaves in his face as she vaulted into the underbrush. He followed, slipping under grapevines and poison ivy, his dew-claws catching on burdock leaves.

The rabbit led him through a birch stand to a large clearing, where she bounded and disappeared into a burrow. He dug furiously at the hole, throwing up clouds of soft loam, stopping finally when he upturned a mass of black beetles clicking over a rock. Curious, he nudged the beetles, then licked up a mouthful and crunched them between his long teeth. The remaining insects scurried beneath the earth. Suddenly tired, he yawned, crawled inside a ring of overgrown ferns heavy with spores and lay there panting.

The air grew heavy with moisture. Thunder snarled in the distance. How could he ever have thought the woods silent? He heard constantly the steady beat, the hum of the turning day beneath his paws. Rain began to fall, and he crept deeper into the ferns until they covered him. He waited there until nightfall, licking rain from the fronds and cleaning the earth from between his footpads.

At dusk the rain stopped. Through slitted eyes he saw a stag step into the clearing and bend to lick rain from a cupped leaf, its tongue rasping against the grass. Nuthatches arrowed into the rhododendrons, and the bushes shuddered until they settled into sleep. He stretched, the hair on his back rustling as moisture pearled and rolled from his coat. In the damp air scents were acute: he tasted mist rising from the nearby swamp, smelled an eft beneath a rotting stump. Then the breeze shifted, brought a stronger scent to him: hot and milky, the young rabbit, motionless at the entrance of its burrow.

He cocked his ears to trace the faint wind stirring the rabbit's fur. He crouched and took a half step toward it, sprang as it bolted in a panic of flying fur and leaves. The rabbit leaped into the clearing, turned and tripped on a fallen branch. In that instant he was upon it, his paws hesitantly brushing its shuddering flank before he tore at its throat. The rabbit screamed. He rent skin and sinew, fur catching between his teeth, shearing strings of muscle as he growled and tugged at its jaw. It stopped kicking. Somewhere inside the fox, Andrew wanted to scream; but the fox tore at the rabbit's head, blood spurting from a crushed artery and staining his muzzle. The smell maddened him. He dragged the rabbit into the brush and fed, then dug a shallow hole and buried the carcass, nosing leaves over the warm bones.

He stepped into the clearing and stared through the tangle of trees and sky. The moon was full. Blood burned inside him; its smell stung his nostrils, scorched his tongue so that he craved water. An owl screeched. He started, leaping over the rank midden, and continued running through the birch clearing until he found the stream, dazzling with reflected moonlight. He stepped to the water's edge and dipped a tentative paw into the shallows, rearing back when the light scattered at his touch. He crossed the stream and wandered snuffling across the other bank. A smell arrested him: overwhelming, alien to this place. He stared at a pile of clothes strewn upon the moss, walked to them stiff-legged and sniffed. Beneath his tongue something small and rough itched like a blister. He shook his head and felt the string around his neck. He coughed, pawed his muzzle; buried his face in the T-shirt. The talisman dropped from between his jaws.

On the bank the boy knelt, coughing, one hand clutching the bloody talisman. He crawled to the stream and bowed there, cupping water in his hands and gulping frantically. Then he staggered backward, flopped onto the moss to stare exhausted at the sky. In a little while he slept uneasily, legs twitching as he stalked fleeing hares through a black and twisted forest.

Rain woke him the next morning, trickling into his nostrils and beneath his eyelids. Andrew snorted and sat up, wiping his eyes. The stream swelled with muddy whirlpools. He stared as the rain came down harder, slicing through the high canopy and striking him like small cold stones. Shivering, he grabbed his clothes and limped to the cottage. Inside he dried himself with his damp T-shirt, then stepped into the tiny bedroom. It was so narrow that when he extended his arms his fingertips grazed opposing walls. Here sagged an ancient iron-framed camp bed with flattened mattress, hard and lean as an old car seat. Groaning, he collapsed onto it, heedless of dead moths scattered across the cushion. His crumpled jeans made a moist pillow as he propped himself against the wall and stared at the ceiling.

He could come back here every day. It was dry, and if he pulled up all the pokeweed, swept out the dirt and fallen feathers, it would be home. He had the stream for water; a few warm clothes in his knapsack for winter. At night he could hunt and feed in the woods, changing back at dawn. During the day he'd sleep, maybe go to the library and look up survival books. No one would ever find him. He could hide forever here where the Tankiteke had hunted.

It didn't have to drive you crazy. If you didn't fight it, if you used it in the right places; if you didn't care about family or friends or school. He pulled fiercely at the string and held the amulet before his eyes.

They would never know. Ever: no one would ever know.

Howell's treatments stopped that winter. One evening Dr. Lancaster simply shook his head, slid the latest test results into the folder and closed it. The next morning he told Howell, "No more."

The astronaut went home to die.

As long as there was no snow, he could walk with Festus, brief forays down the dirt drive to check the mailbox. Some afternoons he'd wait there with the spaniel for the mail car to pull up.

"Some winter, Major Howell," the mailman announced as he handed him a stack of letters from the insurance company, vitamin wholesalers, the Yale hospital. "Think we'll ever get snow?"

Howell took the mail, shrugging, then looked at the cloudless sky. "Your guess is as good as mine. Better, probably."

They laughed, and the car crept down the hillside. Howell turned and called Festus from the woods. For a moment he paused, staring at the brilliant winter sky, the moon like a pale eye staring down upon the afternoon.

That night he dreamed of the sky, ice melting into clouds that scudded across a ghostly moon so close that when he raised his hands his fingers left marks upon its face, tiny craters blooming where he touched. When he awoke the next morning it was snowing.

The blizzard pounced on Kamensic village, caught the hamlet as it drowsed after the long Christmas holidays. A brief and bitter autumn had given way to a snowless winter. Deer grew fat grazing upon frosty pastures. With no snow to challenge them, school-bus drivers grew complacent, then cranky, while children dreamed of brightly varnished toboggans and new skis still beribboned in frigid garages. In The Fallows a fox could find good hunting, warm holes to hide in; the door blew off an abandoned bungalow and !eaves drifted in its corners, burying a vinyl knapsack.

Beneath a tumbledown stone wall, he'd found an abandoned burrow, just large enough to curl up in and sleep through the bitter days. He avoided the cottages now. The fetid scent of men clung to the forsaken structures frightened him, ripe as it was with some perplexing memory. He yawned and drew his paws under him, tail curving to cover his muzzle and warm the freezing air he breathed. Above him the wall hid the remains of the grouse he'd killed last night. The faint rotting smell comforted him, and he slept deeply.

He woke to silence: so utterly still that his hackles rose and he growled softly with unease. Even in the burrow he could always hear the soft stirrings of the world—wind in dead leaves, chickadees fighting in the pines, the crack of branches breaking from the cold. Now he heard only a dull scratching. Stiff-legged he crept through the tunnel and emerged into the storm.

Stones had prevented snow from blocking the entrance to his den. He slunk through the narrow burrow and shook himself. Snow fell so fast that within moments his fur was thick with it. Everywhere branches had collapsed. Entire pines bowed toward the ground until they snapped, dark trunks quickly and silently buried. He buried his muzzle in the drift, then reared back, snarling. Abruptly he turned and leaped atop the stone wall. As he did so, he dislodged a heavy ledge of snow that fell behind him without a sound.

From the wall he tested the wind. Nothing. It blew his ruff back until he shivered beneath snow so thick that he could not shake himself dry He slunk down, stumbling into a drift, and sniffed for the burrow entrance.

Gone. Displaced snow blocked the hole. He could smell nothing. Frantically he dug at the wall. More snow slid from the stones, and he jumped back, growling. From stone to stone he ran, pawing frenziedly, burying his muzzle as he tried to find a warm smell, the scent of frozen blood or spoor. Snow congealed between his pads, matting his legs so that he swam gracelessly through the shifting mass. Exhausted, he huddled at the base of the wall until cold gnawed at his chest. Then he staggered upward until he once again stood clear at the top. Bitter wind clamped his muzzle. His eyelids froze. Blindly he began to run along the walls crest, slipping between rocks and panting.

The wall ended. A wind-riven hill sloped away from him, and he leaped, tumbled by the storm until the snow met him and he flailed whimpering through the endless drifts.

Howell sat before the window, watching the storm. The telephone lines linking him to the village sagged drearily in hoary crescents. He knew they would break as they did during every blizzard. He had already spoken to Peter, to Dr. Lancaster, to Mr. Schelling, the grocer, who wondered if he needed anything before the store closed. He could snap the lines himself now if he wanted. There was no one else to talk to.

He no longer cared. The heaviness in his lungs had spread these last few weeks until his entire chest felt ribbed in stone, his legs and arms so light in comparison they might be wings. He knew that one by one the elements of his body were leaving him. Only the pills gave him strength, and he refilled the plastic bottles often.

A little while ago he had taken a capsule, washing it down with a scant tumbler of scotch. He took a childish pleasure in violating his body now.

"Festus," he croaked, his hand ruffling the air at his side. Festus shambled over, tail vibrating. "Hey Festus, my good dog. My good bright dog."

Festus licked Howell's hand, licked his chops and whined hopefully.

"Dinner?" Howell said, surprised. "So early." Then wondered in alarm if he had fed the dog yesterday; if he had forgotten that as he had sometimes forgotten the mail, his clothes, his own meals. He stood uneasily, head thrumming, and went to the kitchen.

A moist crust still rimmed the dog's dish. There was water in his bowl. But when Howell opened the cabinet beneath the sink there were no cans there. The tall red Purina bag was empty.

"Oh, no," he murmured, then looked in the refrigerator. A few eggs; some frozen vegetables. There would be soup in the cupboard. "Festus, Christ, I'm sorry." Festus danced expectantly across the planked floor to wait at his dish.

Howell leaned against the sink and stared outside. Schelling's might still be open; if not, Isaac lived behind the store. There was gas in the car. Peter had returned the keys, reluctantly, but Howell hadn't driven in months. If he waited it might be two days before anyone called or checked Sugar Mountain. He rummaged through closets until he found boots and heavy parka, then shoved his inhaler into a pocket. He paused in the kitchen, wondering if he should bring the dog With him.

"I'll be back soon," he said at last, rumpling the spaniel's ears.

Then he swallowed another pill.

Outside, flakes the size of his thumb swirled down and burst into hundreds of crystals upon his parka. The sky hung so low and dark that it seemed like nightfall. Howell had no idea what time it really was. He staggered to the car, kicking the door until snow fell from it and he could find the handle. He checked the back seat for shovel, sand, blankets. Then he started the engine. The car lurched forward.

He had heard the snowplow earlier, but the road was already buried once more. As the car drifted toward a high bank, Howell wondered why it was he had decided to go out, finally recalled Festus waiting hungrily at home.

In a few minutes he realized it was futile to steer toward one side of the road or the other. Instead he tried to keep a few feet between car and trees, and so avoid driving into the woods. Soon even this was difficult. Pines leaned where he had never seen trees. The stone walls that bounded the road had buckled into labyrinthine waves. Down the gentle slope inched the car, bluish spume flying behind it. The heater did not work. The windshield wipers stuck again. He reached out and cleared a tiny patch to see through the frigid black glass starred with soft explosions.

Through the clear spot, Howell saw only white and gray streaks. Smears left by his fingers on the glass froze and reflected the steady green and red lights of the dashboard. His hands dropped from the wheel, and he rubbed them together. The car glided onward.

Dreaming, he saw for an instant a calm frozen sea swelling beneath tiny windows, interior darkness broken by blinking panel lights while, outside, shone the azure bow of Earth. Then his forehead grazed the edge of the steering wheel, and he started, gently pressing the brake.

An animal plunged in front of the car, a golden blur like a summer stain upon the snow. It thudded against the bumper.

"Son of a bitch," murmured Howell.

The car stopped. As he stepped out he glanced behind him, shielding his eyes. Snow already filled the tracks snaking a scant hundred feet to the end of his drive. He pulled the hood tight about his face and turned.

In front of the car sprawled a naked boy, eyes closed as if asleep, skin steaming at the kiss of melting snow. Long black hair tangled with twigs; one fist raised to his lips. A drowsing child. The astronaut stooped and very gently touched his cheek. It was feverishly hot.

The boy moaned. Howell staggered against the bumper. The freezing pain jolted him. He stumbled to the door, reaching for the old Hudson's Bay blanket. Then he knelt beside the boy, head pounding, and wrapped him in the blanket. He tried to carry him: too heavy. Howell groaned, then dragged boy and blanket to the side of the car. For a moment he rested, wheezing, before heaving the boy into the passenger seat.

Afterward he couldn't remember driving back to the house.

Festus met him at the door, barking joyfully. Staggering beneath the boys weight, Howell kicked the door shut behind him, then kneeling placed the bundle on the floor.

"Festus, shh," he commanded.

The dog approached the boy, tail wagging. Then he stiffened and reared back snarling.

"Festus, shut up." Exhausted, Howell threw down his parka. He paused to stare at the blizzard still raging about the mountainside. "Festus, I'm throwing you out there if you don't shut up." He clapped and pointed toward the kitchen. "Go lie down."

Festus barked, but retreated to the kitchen.

Now what the hell is this? Howell ran his hands over his wet scalp and stared down at the boy. Melting snow dripped from the blanket to stain the wooden floor. Tentatively he stooped and pulled back a woolen corner.

In the room's ruddy light the boy looked even paler, his skin ashen. Grime streaked his chest. The hair on his legs and groin was stiff with dirt. Howell grimaced: the boy smelled like rotting meat.

He brushed matted hair from the thin face. "Jesus Christ, what have you been doing?" he murmured. Drugs? What drugs would make someone run naked through the snow? Wincing, Howell let the tangled locks slip from his hand.

The boy moaned and twisted his head. He bared his teeth, eyes still tightly shut, and cried softly. His hand drooped upon his chest, fingers falling open. In his palm lay a stone attached to a filthy string around his neck.

Howell crossed the room to a bay window. Here a window seat served as spare bed, fitted neatly into the embrasure. He opened a drawer beneath the seat and pulled out blankets, quickly smoothed the cushion and arranged pillows. Then he got towels and tried his best to dry the boy before wrapping him in a clean blanket and dragging him to the window. Grunting, he eased him onto the bed . He covered him first with a cotton comforter, then heaped on coarse woolen blankets until the boy snorted and turned onto his stomach. After a few minutes his breathing slowed. Howell sank into an armchair to watch him sleep.

From a white dream, Andrew moaned and thrashed, floundering through unyielding pastures that resolved into blankets tangled about his legs. He opened his eyes and lay very still, holding his breath in terror. The darkness held an awful secret. He whimpered as he tried to place it. Turning his head, he saw a shining patch above him, a pale moon in a cobalt sky. His eyes burned. Shrugging free of the comforter, he sat up. Through the window he glimpsed the forest, snowy fields blued by moonlight. Colors. He glanced down and, for the first time since autumn, saw his hands. Slowly he drew them to his throat until they touched the stone there. His fingers ached, and he flexed them until the soreness abated. New blood tingled in his palms. He sniffed tentatively: dust and stale wood, smoke, his own sweat-and another's.

In an armchair slept an old man, mouth slightly ajar, his breathing so soft it scarcely stirred the air. At his feet lay a dog. It stared at Andrew and growled, a low ceaseless sound like humming bees.

"Hey," whispered the boy, his voice cracking. "Good dog."

The dog drew closer to the old mans feet. Andrew swung his legs over the bedside, gasping at the strain on forgotten muscles. As blankets slid to the floor, he noted, surprised, how the hair on his legs had grown thick and black.

Even without covers the room's warmth blanketed him, and he sighed with pleasure. Unsteadily, he crossed to a window, balancing himself with one hand against the wall. The snow had stopped. Through clouded glass he saw an untracked slope, a metal bird feeder listing beneath its white dome. He reached for the talisman, remembering. Autumn days when he tugged wild grapes from brittle vines had given way to the long fat weeks of a winter without snow.

Suddenly he wondered how long it had been-months? years?—and recalled his mother's words.

. . . they forgot . . . and stayed forever, and died up there in the woods . . .

Closing his eyes, he drew the amulet to his mouth and rubbed it against his lip, thinking. *Just for a little while, I could go again just for a little while . . .*

He had almost not come back. He shook his head, squeezing tears from shut eyes. Shuddering, he leaned forward until his forehead rested against the windowpane.

A house.

The talisman slipped from his hand to dangle around his neck once more. Andrew held his breath, listening. His heartbeat quickened from desire to fear.

Whose house?

Someone had brought him back. He faced the center of the room.

In the armchair slumped the old man, regarding Andrew with mild pale eyes. "Aren't you cold?" he croaked, and sat up. "I can get you a robe."

Embarrassed, Andrew sidled to the window seat and wrapped himself in the comforter, then hunched onto the mattress. "That's okay," he muttered, drawing his knees together. The words came out funny, and he repeated them, slowly.

Howell blinked, trying to clear his vision. "It's still night," he stated, and coughed. Festus whined, bumping against Howells leg. The astronaut suddenly stared at Andrew more closely. "What the hell were you doing out there?"

Andrew shrugged. "Lost, I guess."

Howell snorted. "I guess so."

The boy waited for him to bring up parents, police; but the man only gazed at him thoughtfully. The man looked sick. Even in the dimness, Andrew made out lesions on his face and hands, the long skull taut with yellow skin.

"You here alone?" Andrew finally asked.

"The dog." Howell nudged the spaniel with his foot. "My dog, Festus. I'm Eugene Howell. Major Howell."

"Andrew," the boy said. A long silence before the man spoke again.

"You live here?"

"Yeah."

"Your parents live here?"

"No. They're dead. I mean, my mother just died. My father died a long time ago."

Howell rubbed his nose, squinting. "Well, you got someone you live with?"

"No. I live alone." He hesitated, then inclined his head toward the window. "In The Fallows."

"Huh." Howell peered at him more closely. "Were you—some kind of drugs? I found you out there—" He gestured at the window. "Butt naked. In a blizzard." He laughed hoarsely, then gazed pointedly at the boy. "I'm just curious, that's all. Stark naked in a snowstorm. Jesus Christ."

Andrew picked at a scab on his knee. "I'm not on drugs," he said at last. "I just got lost." Suddenly he looked up, beseeching. "I'll get out of your way. You don't have to do anything. Okay? Like you don't have to call anyone. I can just go back to my place."

Howell yawned and stood slowly. "Well, not tonight. When they clear the roads." He looked down at his feet, chagrined to see he still had his boots on. "I'm going to lie down for a little while. Still a few hours before morning."

He smiled wanly and shuffled toward the bedroom, Festus following him. In the kitchen he paused to get his inhaler, then stared with mild disbelief at the counter where an unopened sack of dog food and six cans of Alpo stood next to a half-filled grocery bag.

"Festus," he muttered, tearing open the sack. "I'll be damned. I forgot Pete brought this." He dumped, food into the dog's bowl and glanced back at the boy staring puzzled into the kitchen.

"You can take a shower if you want," suggested Howell. "In there. Towels, a robe. Help yourself." Then he went to bed.

In the bathroom Andrew found bedpans, an empty oxygen tank, clean towels. He kicked his comforter outside the door, hesitated before retrieving it and folding it upon the sofa. Then he returned to the bathroom. Grimacing, he examined his reflection in the mirror. Dirt caked his pores. What might be scant stubble roughened his chin, but when he rubbed it, most came off onto his fingers in tiny black beads.

In the tub stood a white metal stool. Andrew settled on this and turned on the water. He squeezed handfuls of shampoo through his long hair until the water ran clear. Most of a bar of soap dissolved before be stepped out, the last of the hot water gurgling down the drain. On the door hung a thin green hospital robe, E. HOWELL printed on the collar in Magic Marker. Andrew flung this over his shoulders and stepped back into the living room.

Gray light flecked the windowpanes, enough light that finally he could explore the place. It was a small house, not much bigger than his abandoned cottage. Worn Navaho rugs covered flagstone floors in front of a stone fireplace, still heaped with dead ashes and the remains of a Christmas tree studded with blackened tinsel. Brass gaslight fixtures supported light bulbs and green glass shades. And everywhere about the room, pictures.

He could scarcely make out the cedar paneling beneath so many photographs. He crossed to the far wall stacked chest-high with tottering bookshelves. Above the shelves hung dozens of framed photos.

"Jeez." Andrew shivered a little as he tied the robe.

Photos of Earthrise, moonrise. The Crab Nebula. The moon. He edged along the wall, reading the captions beside the NASA logo on each print.

Mare Smythii. Crater Gambart. Crater Copernicus. Crater Descartes. Sea of Tranquillity.

At wall's end, beside the window, two heavy gold frames. The first held artwork from a *Time* magazine cover showing three helmeted men against a Peter Max galaxy: MEN OF THE YEAR: THE CREW OF APOLLO 18, printed in luminous letters. He blew dust from the glass and regarded the picture thoughtfully. Behind one of the men's faceplates, he recognized Howells face.

The other frame held an oversized cover of *Look*, a matte photograph in stark black. In the upper corner floated the moon, pale and dreaming like an infant's face.

APOLLO 19: FAREWELL TO TRANQUILLITY.

Outside, the sun began to rise above Sugar Mountain. In the west glowed a three-quarter moon, fading as sunlight spilled down the mountainside. Andrew stood staring at it until his eyes ached, holding the moon there as long as he could. When it disappeared, he clambered back into bed.

When he woke later that morning, Andrew found Howell sitting in the same chair again, dozing with the dog Festus at his feet. Andrew straightened his robe and tried to slide quietly from bed. The dog barked. Howell blinked awake.

"Good morning," he yawned, and coughed. "The phone lines are down."

Andrew grinned with relief, then tried to look concerned. "How long before they're up again?"

Howell scratched his jaw, his nails rasping against white stubble. "Day or two, probably. You said you live alone?"

Andrew nodded, reaching gingerly to let Festus sniff his hand. "So you don't need to call anyone." Howell rubbed the dog's back with a slippered foot. "He's usually pretty good with people," he said as Festus sniffed and then tentatively licked Andrew's hand. "That's good, Festus. You hungry—?"

He stumbled, forgetting the boy's name.

"Andrew," the boy said, scratching the dog's muzzle. "Good dog. Yeah, I guess I am."

Howell waved toward the kitchen. "Help yourself. My son brought over stuff the other day, on the counter in there. I don't eat much now." He coughed again and clutched the chair's arms until the coughing stopped. Andrew stood awkwardly in the center of the room.

"I have cancer," Howell said, fumbling in his robe's pockets until he found a pill bottle. Andrew stared a moment longer before going into the kitchen.

Inside the grocery bag he found wilted lettuce, several boxes of frozen dinners, now soft and damp, eggs and bread and a packet of spoiled hamburger meat. He sniffed this and his mouth watered, but when he opened the package the smell sickened him and he hastily tossed it into the trash. He settled on eggs, banging around until he found skillet and margarine. He ate them right out of the pan. After a hasty cleanup he returned to the living room.

"Help yourself to anything you want," said Howell. "I have clothes, too, if you want to get changed."

Andrew glanced down at his robe and shrugged. "Okay. Thanks." He wandered to the far wall and stared a moment at the photos again. "You're an astronaut," he said.

Howell nodded. "That's right."

"That must've been pretty cool." He pointed to the Men of the Year portrait. "Did you fly the shuttle?"

"Christ, no. That was after my time. We were Apollo. The moon missions."

Andrew remained by the wall, nodding absently. He wanted to leave, but how? He couldn't take off right away, leave this man wondering where he lived, how he'd get there in three feet of snow. He'd wait until tonight. Leave a note, the robe folded on a chair. He turned back to face Howell.

"That must've been interesting."

Howell stared at him blankly, then laughed. "Probably the most interesting thing *I* ever did," he gasped, choking as he grabbed his inhaler. Andrew watched alarmed as the astronaut sucked the mouthpiece. A faint acrid smell infused the room when Howell exhaled.

"Can't breathe," he whispered. Andrew stared at him and coughed nervously himself.

Howell sighed, the hissing of a broken bellows. "I wanted to go back. I was queued next time as commander." He tugged at the sleeves of his robe, pulling the cuffs over bony wrists. "They canceled it. The rest of the program. Like that." He tried to snap his fingers. They made a dry small sound. "Money. Then the rest. The explosion. You know."

Andrew nodded, rolling up his sleeves until they hung evenly. "I remember that."

Howell nodded. "Everybody does. But the moon. Do you remember that?"

Andrew shook his head.

"You forget it?" said Howell, incredulous.

"I wasn't born," said Andrew. He leaned against the wall, bumping a frame. "I'm only fourteen."

"Fourteen," repeated Howell. "And you never saw? In school, they never showed you?"

The boy shrugged. "The shuttle, I saw tapes of that. At school, maybe. I don't remember."

Howell stood, bumping the spaniel so that Festus grumbled noisily before settling back onto the floor. "Well, here then," he said, and shuffled to the bookcase. "I have it, here—"

He fingered impatiently through several small plastic cases until he found one with NASA's imprimatur. Fastidiously he wiped the plastic cover, blowing dust from the cracks before opening it and pawing the tape carefully.

In the corner a television perched on a shelf. Beneath it was a VCR, meticulously draped with a pillowcase. Howell removed the cloth, coughing with excitement. He switched the set on.

"Okay," he announced as the flickering test pattern resolved into the NASA logo. "Now sit back. You're going to see something. History."

"Right," said Andrew loudly, and rubbed his eyes.

Static. A black expanse: dead black, unbroken by stars. Then a curve intruding upon the lower edge of the screen, dirty gray and pocked with shadow.

The image shifted. Static snarled into a voice, crisply repeating numbers. A beep. Silence. Another beep. The left side of the screen now showed a dark mass, angular limbs scratching the sky.

"What's that?" asked Andrew. It was all out of focus, black and white, wavering like cheap animation.

"The lander," said Howell. "Lunar lander."

"Oh," said Andrew; the moon. "They're there already?" Howell nodded impatiently. "Watch this."

The mass shuddered. The entire horizon dipped and righted itself. From a bright square within the lander something emerged clumsily like a tethered balloon, and descended the blurred pattern that must be steps. Andrew yawned, turning his head so the old man couldn't see. A voice answered commands. Garbled feedback abruptly silenced so that a single voice could be heard.

The figure bounced down, once, twice. The landscape bobbed with him. Andrew fidgeted, glancing at Howell. The old man's hands twisted in his lap as though strangling something, pulling at the hem of his robe. His eyes were riveted to the television. He was crying.

The boy quickly looked back at the screen. After another minute the tape ended. Angry hissing from the television. Andrew stood and turned down the volume, avoiding Howell's face.

"That's it, huh?" he remarked with hollow cheerfulness, hitting the rewind button.

Howell stared at him. "Did you see?"

Andrew sat back on his heels. "Yeah, sure. That's real interesting. The moon. Them landing on the moon."

"You never saw it before?"

He shook his head. "No. I like that stuff, though. Science fiction. You know."

"But this really happened."

Andrew nodded defensively. "I know. I mean, I don't remember, but I know it happened."

Howell coughed into a handkerchief, glaring at the boy. "Pretty boring to you, I guess." He stepped to the machine and removed the tape, shoving it back into its case. "No lights. Nothing exciting. Man lands on moon."

Embarrassed, Andrew stared at him. Howell returned his gaze fiercely, then Sighed and rubbed the back of his neck.

"Who cares," he coughed; then looked suddenly, helplessly at the boy.

"That's all I ever wanted to do, you know. Fly. And walk on the moon."

"But you did. You went. You just told me." Andrew gestured at the walls, the photographs. "All this—" He hesitated. "*Stuff*, all this stuff you got here—"

Howell stroked the videotape, gnawed fingertips catching on its plastic lip, and shook his head, shameless of tears that fell now like a disappointed child's. Andrew stared, horrified, waiting for the old man to stop, to apologize. But he went on crying. Finally the boy stood and crossed the room, turned to shut the bathroom door behind him, ran the water so as not to hear or think of him out there: an old man with a dog at his ankles, rocking back and forth with an old videotape in his hand, heedless of the flickering empty screen before him.

Andrew made dinner that night, a couple of meals on plastic trays slid into the microwave. He ended up eating both of them.

"I'll bring in some wood tomorrow," he said, pausing in the kitchen doorway to hitch up his pants. Howell had insisted on him wearing something other than the old hospital robe. Andrew had rummaged around in a bureau until he found faded corduroy trousers and a flannel shirt, both too big for him. Even with the pants cuffed they flopped around his ankles, and he had to keep pushing back his sleeves as he ran the dinner plates under the tap. When he finished the dishes he poured Howell a glass of scotch and joined him in the other room. The old man sipped noisily as the two of them sat in front of the cold fireplace, Andrew pulling at his frayed shirt cuffs. In the kitchen he'd swallowed a mouthful of scotch when Howell wasn't looking. Now he wished he'd taken more.

"I could bring in some wood tonight, I guess," he said at last. Howell shook his head. "Tomorrow'll be fine. I'll be going to bed soon anyway. I haven't had a fire here since Christmas. Peter built it." He gestured at the half-burned spruce. "As you can see. My son can't build a fire worth a tinker's damn."

Andrew pushed a long lock of hair from his eyes. "I don't know if I can either."

"That's okay. I'll teach you." Howell took another sip of scotch, placed the glass on the floor. Festus stood and flopped beside Andrew, mumbling contentedly. The boy scratched the dog's head. He wondered how soon Howell would go to sleep, and glanced at the back door before turning to the old man. In the dim light, Howell's cheeks glowed rosily, and he looked more like the man on the magazine cover. Andrew tugged at the dog's ears and leaned back in his chair.

"You got Man of the Year," he said at last.

"We all got Man of the Year. Peter was just a kid. Not impressed." Howell grimaced. "I guess it comes with the territory."

Andrew looked away. "I was impressed," he said after a moment. "I just didn't remember. They don't have any of that stuff now."

Howell nodded. For a few minutes they sat, the silence broken only by the battering of wind at the roof.

Then, "You're a runaway," said Howell.

Andrew stared fixedly at the dog at his feet. "Yeah."

Howell rubbed his chin. "Well, I guess that's not so bad. At least in Kamensic it's safe enough. You found one of the abandoned cabins down there."

Andrew sighed and locked his hands behind his head. "Yeah. We used to go there when I was a kid. My mother and I. Up until a few years ago." He tousled Festus's ears with elaborate casualness. "You gonna call the police?"

Howell peered at him. "Do you want me to?"

"No." The boy drew back his hand, and Festus yawned loudly. "There's no one to go to. My mom died last summer. She killed herself. My father died before I was born. Nobody cares."

"Nobody looked for you?"

Andrew shrugged. "Who's to look? My aunt, I guess. They have their own kids. I did okay."

Howell nodded. "Until the first snow." He coughed. "Well, you must be a damned resourceful kid, that's all I can say. I won't call the police. But I can't let you go back out there alone. It'll snow again, and I won't be around to find you."

Andrew shook his head. "Just leave me alone." He rubbed his stinging eyes. "No one ever cared except her, and she—"

"That's okay," Howell said softly. He coughed again, then asked, "What happened to your father?"

"Dead. He disappeared one day. They never found him."

"The war?"

Andrew shook his head. "Up here—he was up here. Visiting. We had family. He—my mother said he died here in the woods." He stared at the floor, silent.

He wants to leave, thought Howell. In the dimness the boy looked very young. Howell recalled other nights, another boy. His heart ached so suddenly that he shuddered, gasping for breath. Andrew stood in alarm.

"Nothing—nothing—" Howell whispered, motioning him away. His head sank back onto his chest. After a few minutes he looked up. "Guess I'll go to bed now."

Andrew helped him into the bedroom. Not much bigger than the room in Andrew's abandoned cottage, but scrupulously neat, and almost all windows except for the wall behind the double bed. Howell slipped from his robe, leaving Andrew holding it awkwardly while the old man eased himself into bed, grunting from the effort.

"Just put it there—" Howell pointed to the door. Andrew hung the robe on a hook. He tried to avoid looking directly at Howell, but there was little else: the black windows, a bureau, a closet door. Above the bed a framed NASA photo of the moon. Andrew pretended interest in this and leaned over Howell to stare at it. In the white margin beneath the moons gray curve someone had written in a calligraphic hand:

> Come on all you
> Lets get busy
> for the speedy trips
> to all planets and
> back to earth again.

"Huh," said Andrew. Behind him, Festus shambled into the room and, grumbling, settled himself on a braided rug.

The old man winced, twisting to stare up at the photograph. "You like that?" he said.

"Sure," said Andrew, shrugging. "What's it mean? That poem or whatever. You write that?"

Howell smiled. He was so thin that it was hard to believe there was a body there beneath all the smooth quilts and blankets. "No, I didn't write that. I'll show you where it came from, though; tomorrow maybe. If you want. Remind me."

"Okay." Andrew waited: to see if Howell needed anything; to see if he would be dismissed. But the old man just lay there, eyes fluttering shut and then open again. Finally the boy said, "Good night," and left the room.

It took Andrew a long time to fall asleep that night. He sat on the window seat, staring out at the snow-covered fields as he fingered the amulet around his neck. He didn't know why he'd stayed this long. He should have left as soon as he could that morning, waited for the old man to fall asleep (he slept all day: he must be really sick, to sleep so much) and then crept out the back door and disappeared into the woods.

Even now . . . He pulled at the amulet, holding it so tightly it bit into the ball of his thumb. He should leave now.

But he didn't. The wrinkled white face staring up from the double bed reminded him of his mother in the coffin. He had never noticed how many lines were in her face; she really hadn't been that old. He wondered how long Howell had been sick. He remembered the astronaut he'd seen at the library that summer, a disappointment, really. Andrew had been expecting a space-suit and something else: not ray guns, that would be dumb, but some kind of instruments, or moon rocks maybe. Instead there'd been an old man in Izod shirt and chinos talking about how the country had failed the space program. Andrew had fidgeted until his mother let him go outside.

It must have been the same man, he thought now. Major Howell, not really any more interesting now than he'd been then. He hadn't even walked on the moon. Andrew dropped the amulet onto his chest and pulled a blanket about his knees, stared out the window. Clouds drifted in front of the rising moon. At the edge of the woods there would be rabbit tracks, fox scat. A prickle of excitement ran through him at the thought, and he lay back upon the narrow bed. He would leave tomorrow, early, before Howell got up to let the dog out.

He didn't leave. He woke to Howell calling hoarsely from the bedroom. Andrew found him half-sitting on the side of the bed, his hand reaching pathetically for the nightstand where a glass of water had been knocked over, spilling pill bottles and inhalers and soggy tissues onto the floor.

"Could you—please—"

Andrew found Howell's inhaler and gave it to him. Then he straightened out the mess, put more water in the glass and watched as Howell took his pills, seven of them. He waited to see if Howell wanted anything else, then let Festus outside. When the boy returned to the bedroom, Howell was still sitting there, eyes shut as he breathed heavily through his nose. His eyes flick-ered open to stare at Andrew: a terrified expression that made the boys heart tumble. But then he closed them again and just sat there.

Finally Andrew said, "I'll help you get dressed." Howell nodded without opening his eyes.

It didn't take Andrew long to help him into a flannel robe and slippers, and into the bathroom. Andrew swore silently and waited outside the door, listening to the groan of water in the taps, the old man's wheezing and shambling footsteps. Outside, Festus scratched at the back door and whined to be let in. Sighing, Andrew took care of the dog, went back to the bathroom and waited until Howell came out again.

"Thank you," the old man said. His voice was faint, and he trembled as he supported himself with one hand on the sink, the other against the door frame.

"Its okay, Major Howell," said Andrew. He took Howell's elbow and guided him into the living room. The old man was heavy, no matter that he was so thin; Andrew was terrified that he'd fall on the flagstone floor. "Here, sit here and I'll get you something. Breakfast?"

He made instant coffee and English muffins with scrambled eggs. The eggs were burned, but it didn't really matter: Howell took only a bite of the muffin and sipped at his tepid coffee. Andrew gave the rest to Festus. *He* would eat later, outside.

Afterward, as Howell sat dozing in the armchair by the fireplace, Andrew made a fire. The room filled with smoke before he figured out how to open the damper, but after that it burned okay, and he brought in more wood. Then he took Festus outside for a walk. He wore Howell's parka and heavy black mittens with NASA stenciled on the cuffs. The sunlight on the snow made his eyes ache as he tried to see where Festus ran up the first slope of Sugar Mountain. He took off one glove, unzipped the neck of the parka and stuck his hand inside. The amulet was still there, safe against his chest. He stopped, hearing Festus crashing through the underbrush. Would the dog follow him? Probably not: he was an old dog, and Andrew knew how fast a fox could run, knew that even though he had never hunted this spot it would be easy to find his way to a safe haven.

Then the wind shifted, bringing with it the tang of wood smoke.

Festus ambled out of the woods, shaking snow from his ears, and ran up to Andrew. The boy let the amulet drop back inside his flannel shirt and zipped up the parka. He turned and walked back to the house.

"Have a nice walk?" Howell's voice was still weak but his eyes shone brightly, and he smiled at the boy stomping the snow from boots too big for him.

"Oh, yeah, it was great." Andrew hung up the parka and snorted, then turning back to Howell, tried to smile. "No, it was nice. Is all that your property back there?" He strode to the fireplace and crouched in front of it, feeding it twigs and another damp log.

"Just about all of it." Howell pulled a lap blanket up closer to his chin. "This side of Sugar Mountain and most of the lakefront."

"Wow." Andrew settled back, already sweating from the heat. "It's really nice back there by the lake. We used to go there in the summer, my mom and me. I love it up here."

Howell nodded. "I do, too. Did you live in the city?"

Andrew shook his head. "Yonkers. It sucks there now; like living in the Bronx." He opened the top button of his shirt and traced the string against his chest. "Once, when I was a kid, we heard an astronaut talk here. At the library. Was that you?"

Howell smiled. "Yup. I wondered if you might have been one of those kids, one of those times. So many kids, I must have talked to a thousand kids at the school here. You want to be an astronaut when you were little?"

"Nah." Andrew poked at the log, reached to pet Festus. "I never wanted to be anything, really. School's really boring, and like where I lived sucks, and . . ." He gestured at the fire, the room and the door leading outside. "The only thing I ever really liked was being up here, in the woods. Living in The Fallows this year, that was great."

"It's the only thing I liked, too. After I stopped working." Howell sighed and glanced over at the pictures covering the wall, the sagging bookcases. He had never really been good with kids. The times he had spoken at the school he'd had films to back him up, and later, videotapes and videodiscs. He had never been able to entertain his son here, or his friends, or the occasional visiting niece or nephew. The pictures were just pictures to them, not even colorful. The tapes were boring. When Peter and his friends were older, high school or college, sometimes Howell would show them the Nut File, a manila envelope crammed with letters from Rubber Man Lord of Jupiter and articles clipped from tabloids, a lifetime of NASA correspondence with cranks and earnest kooks who had developed faster-than-light drives in their garages. Peter and his friends had laughed at the letters, and Howell had laughed, too, reading them again. But none of his visitors had ever been touched, the way Howell had. None of them had ever wondered why a retired NASA astronaut would have a drawer full of letters from nuts.

"Andrew," he said softly; then, "Andrew," as loud as he could. The boy drew back guiltily from the fire, Festus started awake and stared up, alarmed.

"Sorry—"

Howell drew a clawed hand from beneath the blanket and waved it weakly. "No, no—that's all right—just . . ."

He coughed; it took him a minute to catch his breath. Andrew stood and waited next to him, staring back at the fire. "Okay, I'm okay now," Howell wheezed at last. "Just: remember last night? That picture with the poem?"

Andrew looked at him blankly.

"In my room—the moon, you wanted to know if I wrote it—"

The boy nodded. "Oh, yeah. The moon poem, right. Sure."

Howell smiled and pointed to the bookcase. "Well here, go look over there—"

Andrew watched him for a moment before turning to the bookcase and looking purposefully at the titles. Sighing, Festus moved closer to the old astronaut's feet. Howell stroked his back, regarding Andrew thoughtfully. He coughed, inclining his head toward the wall.

"Andrew." Howell took a long breath, then leaned forward, pointing. "That's it, there."

Beneath some magazines, Andrew found a narrow pamphlet bound with tape. "This?" he wondered. He removed it gingerly and blew dust from its cover.

Howell settled back in his chair. "Right. Bring it here. I want to show you something."

Andrew settled into the chair beside Howell. A paperbound notebook, gray with age. On the cover swirled meticulous writing in Greek characters, and beneath them the same hand, in English:

Return address:

Mr. Nicholas Margalis
116 Argau Dimitrou Apt. No.3
Salonika, Greece

"Read it," said Howell. "I found that in the NASA library. He sent it to Colonel Somebody right after the war. It floated around for forty years, sat in NASA's Nut File before I finally took it."

He paused. "I used to collect stuff like that. Letters from crackpots. People who thought they could fly. UFOs, moonmen. *Outer space.* I try to keep an open mind." He gestured at the little book in Andrew's hand. "I don't think anyone else has ever read that one. Go ahead."

Carefully Andrew opened the booklet. On lined paper tipsy block letters spelled PLANES, PLANETS, PLANS. Following this were pages of numerical equations, sketches, a crude drawing labeled THE AIR DIGGER ROCKET SHAPE.

"They're plans for a rocket ship," said Howell. He craned his neck so he could see.

"You're kidding." Andrew turned the brittle pages. "Did they build it?"

"Christ, no! I worked it out once. If you were to build the Margalis Planets Plane it would be seven miles long." He laughed silently.

Andrew turned to a page covered with zeros.

"Math," said Howell.

More calculations. Near the end Andrew read:

Forty years of continuous flying will cover the following space below, 40 years, 14,610 days, 216,000,000,000,000 X 14610—equals 3,155,750,000,000,000,000 miles. That is about the mean distance to the farthest of the Planets, Uranus.

Trillions, Quatrillions, Billions and Millions of miles all can be reached with this Plan.

Andrew shook his head. "This is so sad! He really thought it would fly?"
"They all thought they could fly," said Howell. "Read me the end."
" 'Experimenting of thirty-five years with levers, and compounds of,' " read Andrew. " 'I have had made a patent model of wooden material and proved a very successful work.
" 'My Invention had been approved by every body in the last year 1944, 1946 in my native village Panorma, Crevens, Greece. Every body stated it will be a future great success in Mechanics.
" 'Yours truly.' "
Andrew stopped abruptly.
"Go on," prodded Howell. "The end. The best part."
On the inside back cover, Andrew saw the same hand, somewhat shakier and in black ink.

I have written in these copy book about 111000 of what actually will take in building a real Rocket Shape Airo-Plane to make trips to the Planets.

There in the planets we will find Paradise, and the undying water to drink so we never will die, and never be in distress.

> Come on all you
> Lets get busy
> for the speedy trips
> to all Planets and
> back to earth again.

NICHOLAS S. MARGALIS
AUG 19 1946

Howell sat in silence. For a long moment Andrew stared at the manuscript, then glanced at the old man beside him. Howell was smiling now as he stared into the fire. As Andrew watched, his eyelids flickered, and then the old astronaut dozed, snoring softly along with the dog at his feet. Andrew waited. Howell did not wake. Finally the boy stood and poked at the glowing logs. When he turned back, the blanket had fallen from the old man's lap and onto the dogs back. Andrew picked it up and carefully draped it across Howell's knees.

For a moment he stood beside him. The old man smelled like carnations. Against his yellow skin broken capillaries bloomed blue and crimson. Andrew hesitated. Then he bowed his head until his lips grazed Howell's scalp. He turned away to replace the booklet on its shelf and went to bed.

That night the wind woke Howell. Cold gripped him as he sat up in bed, and his hand automatically reached for Festus. The dog was not beside him.

"Festus?" he called softly, then slid from bed, pulling on his robe and catching his breath before walking across the bedroom to the window.

A nearly full moon hung above the pine forest, dousing the snow so that it glowed silvery blue. Deer and rabbits had made tracks steeped in shadow at woods edge. He stood gazing at the sky when a movement at the edge of the field caught him.

In the snow an animal jumped and rolled, its fur a fiery gleam against the whiteness. Howell gasped in delight: a fox, tossing the snow and crunching it between its black jaws. Then something else moved. The old man shook his head in disbelief.

"Festus."

Clumsily, sinking over his head in the drifts, the spaniel tumbled and rose beside the fox, the two of them playing in the moonlight. Clouds of white sparkled about them as the fox leaped gracefully to land beside the dog, rolling until it was only an auburn blur.

Howell held his breath, moving away from the window so that his shadow could not disturb them. Then he recalled the boy sleeping in the next room.

"Andrew," he whispered loudly, his hand against the wall to steady himself as he walked into the room. "Andrew, you have to see something."

The window seat was empty The door leading outside swung open, banging against the wall in the frigid wind. Howell turned and walked toward the door, finally stopping and clinging to the frame as he stared outside.

In the snow lay a green hospital gown, blown several feet from the door. Bare footprints extended a few yards into the field. Howell followed them. Where the shadows of the house fell behind him, the footprints ended. Small pawprints marked the drifts, leading across the field to where the fox and dog played.

He lifted his head and stared at them. He saw where Festus's tracks ran off to the side of the house and then back to join the other's. As he watched, the animals abruptly stopped. Festus craned his head to look back at his master and then floundered joyfully through the drifts to meet him. Howell stepped forward. He stared from the tracks to the two animals, yelled in amazement and stood stark upright. Then stumbling he tried to run toward them. When

Festus bounded against his knees the man staggered and fell. The world tilted from white to swirling darkness.

It was light when he came to. Beside him hunched the boy, his face red and tear streaked.

"Major Howell," he said. "Please—"

The old man sat up slowly, pulling the blankets around him. He stared for a moment at Andrew, then at the far door where the flagstones shone from melted snow. .

"I saw it," he whispered. "What you did, I saw it."

Andrew shook his head. "Don't—You can't—"

Howell reached for his shoulder and squeezed it. "How does it work?"

Andrew stared at him, silent.

"How does it work?" Howell repeated excitedly "How can you do it?"

The boy bit his lip. Howell's face was scarlet, his eyes feverishly bright. "I—it's this," Andrew said at last, pulling the amulet from his chest. "It was my mother's. I took it when she died."

His hands shaking, Howell gently took the stone between his fingers, rubbing the frayed string. "Magic," he said.

Andrew shivered despite the fire at his back. "It's from here. The Indians. The Tankiteke. There were lots, my mother said. Her grandfather found it when he was little. My father—" He ended brokenly.

Howell nodded in wonder. "It works," he said. "I saw it work." Andrew swallowed and drew back a little, so that the amulet slipped from Howell's hand. "Like this," he explained, opening his mouth and slipping one finger beneath his tongue. "But you don't swallow it."

"I saw you," the old man repeated. "I saw you playing with my dog." He nodded at Festus, dozing in front of the fire. "Can you be anything?"

Andrew bit his lip before answering. "I think so. My mother said you just concentrate on it—on what you want. See—"

And he took it into his hand, held it out so that the firelight illuminated it. "It's like all these things in one. Look: it's got wings and horns and hooves."

"And that's how you hid from them." Howell slapped his knees. "No wonder they never found you."

Andrew nodded glumly.

"Well," Howell coughed. He sank back into the chair, eyes closed. He reached for Andrew, and the boy felt the old mans hand tighten about his own, cold and surprisingly strong. After a minute Howell opened his eyes. He looked from the flames to Andrew and held the boy's gaze for a long time, silent. Then,

"You could fly with something like that," he said. "You could fly again."

Andrew let his breath out in a long shudder. "That's right," he said finally beneath his breath. He turned away. "You could fly again, Major Howell."

Howell reached for the boy's hand again, his fingers clamping there like a metal hinge. "Thank you," he whispered. "I think I'll go to sleep now."

The following afternoon the plow came. Andrew heard it long before it reached Sugar Mountain, an eager roar like a great wave overtaking the snowbound bungalow. The phone was working, too; he heard Howell in the next room, talking between fits of coughing. A short time later a pickup bounced up the drive. Andrew stared in disbelief, then fled into the bathroom, locking the door behind him.

He heard several voices greeting Howell at the door, the thump of boots upon the flagstones.

"Thank you, Isaac," wheezed the astronaut. Andrew heard the others stomp into the kitchen. "I was out of everything." Andrew opened the door a crack and peered out, glaring at Festus when the dog scratched at it.

Howell motioned the visitors into the bedroom, shutting the door behind him. Andrew listened to their murmuring voices before storming back into the living room. He huddled out of sight on the window seat, staring outside until they left. After the pickup rattled back down the mountainside, he stalked into the kitchen to make dinner.

"I didn't tell them," Howell said mildly that evening as they sat before the fire.

Andrew glared at him but said nothing.

"They wouldn't be interested," Howell said. Every breath now shook him like a cold wind. "Andrew . . . "

The boy sat in silence, his hand tight around the amulet. Finally Howell stood, knocking over his glass of scotch. He started to bend to retrieve it when Andrew stopped him.

"No," he said hoarsely. "Not like that." He hesitated, then said, "You ever see a drunk dog?"

Howell stared at him, then nodded. "Yes."

"It's like that," said Andrew. "Only worse."

Festus followed them as they walked to the door, Andrew holding the old man's elbow. For a moment they hesitated. Then Andrew shoved the door open, wincing at the icy wind that stirred funnels of snow in the field.

"It's so cold," Howell whispered, shivering inside his flannel robe. "It won't be so bad," said Andrew, helping him outside.

They stood in the field. Overhead the full moon bloomed as Festus nosed after old footprints. Andrew stepped away from Howell, then took the talisman from around his own neck.

"Like I told you," he said as he handed it to the old man.

Howell hesitated. "It'll work for me?"

Andrew clutched his arms, shivering. "I think so," he said, gazing at the amulet in the man's hand. "I think you can be whatever you want."

Howell nodded and turned away. "Don't look," he whispered. Andrew stared at his feet. A moment later the flannel robe blew against his ankles. He heard a gasp and shut his eyes, willing away the tears before opening them again.

In front of Andrew the air sparkled for an instant with eddies of snow. Beside him, Festus whined, staring above his head. Andrew looked up and saw a fluttering scrap like a leaf: a bat squeaking as its wings beat feebly, then more powerfully, as if drawing strength from the freezing wind. It circled the boy's head—once, twice—then began to climb, higher and higher, until Andrew squinted to see it in the moonlight.

"Major Howell!" he shouted. "Major Howell!"

To Howell the voice sounded like the clamor of vast and thundering bells. All the sky now sang to him as he flailed through the air, rising above trees and roof and mountain. He heard the faint buzzing of the stars, the sigh of snow in the trees fading as he flew above the pines into the open sky.

And then he saw it: more vast than ever it had been from the orbiter, so bright his eyes could not bear it. And the sound! like the ocean, waves of air dashing against him, buffeting him as he climbed, the roar and crash and peal of it as it pulled him upward. His wings beat faster, the air sharp in his throat, thinning as the darkness fell behind him and the noise swelled with the brightness, light now everywhere, and sound, not silent or dead as they had told him but thundering and burgeoning with heat, light, the vast eye opening like a volcano's core. His wings ceased beating and he drifted upward, all about him the glittering stars, the glorious clamor, the great and shining face of the moon, his moon at last: the moon.

Andrew spent the night pacing the little house, sitting for a few minutes on sofa or kitchen counter, avoiding the back door, avoiding the windows, avoiding Howell's bedroom. Festus followed him, whining. Finally, when the snow glimmered with first light, Andrew went outside to look for Howell.

It was Festus who found him after just a few minutes, in a shallow dell where ferns would grow in the spring and deer sleep on the bracken. Now snow had drifted where the old man lay. He was naked, and even from the lawn Andrew could tell he was dead. The boy turned and walked back to the house, got Howell's flannel robe and a blanket. He was shaking uncontrollably when he went back out.

Festus lay quietly beside the body, muzzle resting on his paws.

Andrew couldn't move Howell to dress him: the body was rigid from the cold. So he gently placed the robe over the emaciated frame, tucked the blanket around him. Howell's eyes were closed now, and he had a quiet expression on his face. Not like Andrew's mother at all, really: except that one hand clutched something, a grimy bit of string trailing from it to twitch across the snow. Andrew knelt, shivering, and took one end of the string, tugged it. The amulet slid from Howell's hand.

Andrew stumbled to his feet and held it at arm's length, the little stone talisman twisting slowly. He looked up at the sky in the west, above the cottage, the moon hung just above the horizon. Andrew turned to face the dark bulk of Sugar Mountain, its edges brightening where the sun was rising above Lake Muscanth. He pulled his arm back and threw the amulet as hard as he could into the woods. Festus raised his head to watch the boy They both waited, listening; but there was no sound, nothing to show where it fell. Andrew wiped his hands on his pants and looked down at the astronaut again. He stooped and let the tip of one finger brush the old man's forehead. Then he went inside to call the police.

There were questions, and people from newspapers and TV, and Andrew's own family, overjoyed (he couldn't believe it, they all cried) to see him again. And eventually it was all straightened out.

There was a service at the old Congregational church in Kamensic Village near the museum. After the first thaw they buried Howell in the small local cemetery, beside the farmers and Revolutionary War dead. A codicil to his will left the dog Festus to the fourteen-year-old runaway discovered to have been living with the dying astronaut in his last days. The codicil forbade sale of the bungalow and Sugar Mountain, the property to revert to the boy upon his twentieth birthday. Howell's son protested this: Sugar Mountain was worth a fortune now, the land approved for subdivisions with two-acre zoning. But the court found the will to be valid, witnessed as it was by Isaac and Seymour Schelling, village grocers and public notaries.

When he finished school, Andrew moved into the cottage at Sugar Mountain. Festus was gone by then, buried where the deer still come to sleep in the bracken. There is another dog now, a youngish English cocker spaniel named Apollo. The ancient Volkswagen continues to rust in the driveway, next to a Volvo with plates that read NASA NYC. The plows and phone company attend to the cottage somewhat more reliably, and there is a second phone line as well, since Andrew needs to transmit things to the city and Washington nearly every day now, snow or not.

In summer he walks with the dog along the sleepy dirt road, marking where an owl has killed a vole, where vulpine tracks have been left in the soft mud by Lake Muscanth. And every June he visits the elementary school and shows the fifth graders a videotape from his private collection: views of the moon's surface filmed by Command Module Pilot Eugene Howell.

AUTHOR'S NOTE: Nicholas Margalis's manuscript is in the archives of the National Air & Space Museum, Smithsonian Institution.

In memory of Nancy Malawista and Brian Hart

THE APHOTIC GHOST

CARLOS HERNANDEZ

◆

Mountain

Sometimes when a body dies in Everest's Death Zone, it doesn't come down. Too difficult, too much risk for the living. Thing is, it's so cold up there, bodies don't rot. They get buried by snow periodically, but the terrific winds of the South Col reliably reveal them: blue, petrified, horned by icicles, still in their climbing gear, always forever ascending. They scandalize the Westerners who paid good money to climb Everest and who don't especially want to be reminded of how deadly the journey can be. But then their Sherpas usher them past the garden of corpses and, weather permitting, to the top of the world.

I am a Westerner, and I paid good money to climb Everest. But the summit wasn't my goal. I was going to get my son Lazaro off of that mountain, dead or alive.

Sea-Level

Lazaro's mother, Dolores Thomaston, taught twelfth-grade biology at the same school where I taught AP World History: Bush High, right on the Texas-Mexico border. Lazaro was born of a dalliance between us almost three decades ago.

Dolores had an Australian ebullience and a black sense of humor and a seeming immunity to neurosis that made her irresistible to me. She could have been twenty-five or fifty-five, and I never found out which. She'd made a splash in the scientific world a few years before coming to Bush with a paper she coauthored on a deep-sea jellyfish that, interestingly, was immortal. After it reproduced, it returned to a pre-sexual polyp state through a process called cell transdifferentiation, and then become an adult again, and then a polyp, and so on. The layman's version is this: age meant nothing to that jelly. It only died if something killed it.

Dolores and I spent the summer together. I really believed we were on our way to getting married. That's why I wasn't worried when she started talking children. In fact, I was surprised to discover how much the idea of children tickled me. I had no idea how much I wanted to be a father until she put the prospect before me. I'd spent all of my adult life contemplating history, and now, suddenly, I was awash with dreams of the future.

She asked me what I would name the child, so I told her: "Brumhilda."

"Be serious," she said.

"I am!"

"Yeah? So what if it's a boy?"

I kissed her, the first of many that night. And then I said, "Lazaro."

Aphotic Zone

Dolores didn't just leave me. She vanished right after we consummated our relationship. She left a note on her pillow that I promptly set fire to in a skillet before reading, then spent the rest of my life wishing I hadn't.

I didn't know she had died during childbirth, that she had opted for an ocean water-birth. Ocean-birthing. Of all the crazy trends. She never left the water.

I found all of this out from a young man named Lazaro Thomaston when he came to meet me. He was twenty-one, already a man. By then I'd missed my chance to be his father.

Sea-Level

An hour since I'd learned I'd been a father for twenty-one years, Lazaro sat on the couch with me, showing me his portfolio. He worked as an underwater photographer and videographer. "It's second nature to me, being in the water," he said. "Really it's the ocean that raised me."

"Looks like the ocean did a pretty good job," I said.

He specialized in ultra-deep dives, descents into the bathyal region, which is the topmost stratum of the ocean's aphotic zone: lightless, crushing, utterly hostile. There he had recorded a score of species new to science; he'd made his reputation before he could take a legal drink. His images were haunting and minimalist, the engulfing darkness defied only by the weak bioluminescence of the sea life and, of course, him. Off-camera, he shined like a sun, illumining the depths like the first day of creation.

"These are incredible," I said. "You must he half fish."

"Got that from Mom," he said. And turned the page.

Mountain

Rather than take a leave of absence from work to climb Everest, I retired early. Lost some money that way, but I had more than enough money to get to the summit, get back, and bury my son. After that, the future would take care of itself. Or go fuck itself. Either way.

I was old to climb the world's tallest mountain, but not as old as some. The ascent from the Southeast ridge is by mountaineering standards fairly straightforward, especially with today's technology. If you died it was because you were reckless, or bad weather surprised you, or your body gave out and you probably should never have attempted it in the first place.

I was in reasonably good shape, but I needed work—strength-training, flexibility, cardio cardio cardio. And yoga: sixty years old, and I'd never learned to breathe. Guess it was time.

I learned to slow my heart. I learned efficiency, repose, elegance of movement. I learned to require less of everything: food, water, air, joy, meaning. I learned to sit.

I bought more gear than I could possibly use in ten ascents, watched every mountaineering video I could find, moved for a season to Colorado where I took a course on mountain climbing specifically geared toward seniors.

I finished top of the class. My instructor said he'd never seen anyone of any age so motivated. But he also said mountain climbing's supposed to be fun. Why so grim? Why was I going to climb Everest if not to have one of the greatest experiences of my life?

I told him my son was lost on Everest and that I was going to find him, but of course it'd been months and I hadn't heard any good news, so he was dead. But I'd be damned if I was going to let my son's body pose for eternity like a movie prop in Everest's death zone so that overprivileged jetsetters could get an extra thrill off of him. I was climbing to claim my son's body—if I could find him, if I could pick-axe his remains free from the mountainside—and bring him home.

But yeah, asshole, I'll try to have grand old time all the way up.

Sea-Level

Lazaro and I had five good years together, during which time he told me almost nothing about his life prior to our reconnecting. I didn't take it personally. He wanted to sever himself from his childhood the way a lizard drops its tail to escape a predator. Whatever his past was, Lazaro wanted nothing to do with it.

I didn't pry. I figured he would tell me when he was ready.

But he never became ready. Instead, he anchored his life to the present, to me. And that happened to be more or less exactly what I wanted. I couldn't go back and be the father he'd never had growing up, but as consolation prizes go, this was the next best thing.

I'm a historian. I should have known better. Histories never stay severed. Like the tail of a lizard, they grow back.

⬥

Mountain

There was exactly one guide who would attempt something as stupid as try to descend Everest with a dead body in tow. He had a Nepalese name but a British accent. To dumb-ass tourists like me he went by Roger.

His main suggestion was that we needed as many Sherpas as I could afford to help search for Lazaro. I could sell all of my extra mountaineering equipment at Base Camp to the rich and underprepared. There's where I'd get top dollar.

"I was hoping it'd just be you and me," I told him. "I don't really want a lot of people around."

He sighed. "Imagine a needle in a haystack," he said. "Now douse the haystack with water, and stick it in an industrial freezer until it's a solid hump of ice. Now remove all the oxygen from the freezer. Now put fifty kilos of equipment on your back. Now go get that needle."

Point taken. But what would I tell all those Sherpas? How could I instruct them what to look for without them thinking I was crazy?

But truly, what frightened me more was the prospect that they'd actually believe me. The Sherpa brand of Buddhism is animist enough that, when I told them what they were looking for, they might accept it as true. Accept it, and then get the fuck off Everest.

Aphotic Zone

I was leaving for Lukla in four days. My equipment had already left. It was too soon for adrenaline but too late to think of anything else. I sat in my living room and didn't read and didn't watch TV and didn't turn on the lights. My own little bathyal region.

Doorbell. I had ordered a pizza. I opened the door and it was Dolores.

She was twenty-five now, if that; there was nothing fifty-five about her. She was dressed for a Texas May: naked as the law allowed. Her body was muscled and sleek, like a gazelle's. Her hair was a corona. And that smile. That tilt of the head.

"Oh my," she said. "It's so good to see you, Enrique."

She was so composed. She was waiting for me to digest what I was seeing. But there was mischief there too, that evil sense of humor, even at a time like this. It really was her.

When I didn't speak, she said, "I told you I'd be back one day. So here I am, love. I'm back."

I didn't respond, and she watched me for a long time not responding. Her face drained of mirth. "In the note?" she said like a question. "You got my note, right?"

"I burned it on the stove," I said.

"Ah." Then she laughed. "Now was that any way to treat me, after what we shared? You wouldn't even read my explanation?"

"Treat you? You left me, Dolores."

"And I explained why in the note, love. It was quite necessary. That's why I left it—so you would understand."

"You're the one who needs to understand. Seeing that Dear John on the pillow, it . . . it ruined me, Dolores. Until Lazaro came into my life I was in ruins."

She came close, then hooked her arms around my neck, and I let her. Hers was not the body my body remembered. It fit foreignly against me.

"Have you been working out, love?" she asked, lips puckered puckishly.

"Apparently not as much as you," I said. And then: "Lazaro. I assume you know?"

"That's why I'm here, love. To help you. To save him."

Oh. Oh no. I suddenly felt tired and old. Whatever my own feelings about seeing her again were, I couldn't let her think her son was still alive, not after he'd been missing for months at the top of Everest. "Dolores, I'm not going to try to rescue Lazaro. I'm going to claim his body. Lazaro is dead."

"No, love."

"Dolores, listen—"

"—He's not," she interrupted. But her expression was not that of a mother in denial; she looked at me pityingly, her mouth sagging with remorse. "There's so much I need to tell you."

She always could be a little condescending. And that helped me remember my anger. I broke our embrace. "What the hell makes you think I want to talk to you? You left me, Dolores. I thought we were going to get married. You left without a trace."

I could see she was about to remind me again that I had burned her note. But instead she metronomed her head to the other shoulder, smiling ruefully. "Do you hate me?"

"I think I do."

"I can tell you don't."

I sighed. "Maybe not yet. I'm still in shock. But I almost certainly will hate you. So let's talk before the hatred sets in and I refuse to ever speak to you again."

She came close again and hugged me to her and stood on her toes, allowing our breath to mix between our noses like a storm front. "Later, love," she said. "First, let's make up a little."

Sea-Level

Lazaro's most recent film, *The Aphotic Ghost*, was nominated for an Oscar in short documentary a year ago. It chronicled a new species of jellyfish over 150cm in diameter, a superpredator by bathepelagaic standards. As it fluttered about the lightless ocean depths, its body took on a vaguely pentangular shape, but with its five points rounded off. It looked almost like an undulating chalk outline, and its blue-white bioluminescence made it positively spectral: thus the name.

Lazaro's footage was gorgeous, unbelievably intimate. Jellyfish usually squirt away from lights and cameras as fast as they can, but the aphotic ghost—enormous, tremulous, poisonous, ethereal—let Lazaro swim along with it and gather images that were not only scientifically priceless but commercially lucrative.

It was me he took to the Academy Awards show. When he won the Oscar, the shot cut to me for three seconds. The caption read "Montenegro's Father." Not Thomaston, but Montenegro. By this point he'd taken my surname.

Mountain

"Why do you want to climb Everest?" I asked Lazaro.

"I'm always in the water," he said. He went over to the fish tank he'd convince me to get. It was a saltwater tank two meters in diameter specially made for jellyfish: a Kreisel model with a constant flow of water whisking the jellies around like a slow-moving washing machine. That's exactly what it looked like: a futuristic upright jellyfish washer.

I looked up from my book. "So now you want to go to the highest point on Earth because . . . it's the farthest place from sea level?"

He smiled ruefully. "Something like that."

"Seems to me like the ocean's been good to you."

He turned back to the tank and watched the jellies spin. Sometimes the tank looked to me like a bird's-eye model of the galaxies. Other times it made me sad, these small, nearly mindless creatures being infinitely jetted around a tiny glass container for my viewing pleasure. They had no comprehension of the forces that governed them. They had no idea their lives were in my hands. And who was I to have dominion over anything?

"It has," he said finally. "The ocean has been my whole life. But it's also defined me." And then, a little softer, he added, "Limited me."

"Still, Lazaro, Everest is one of the most inhospitable places on Earth. You're an expert when it comes to deep-sea diving. But on a mountain you'll be—"

"—like a fish out of water?" he finished.

No mistaking his tone; he was dead-set. So I smiled and turned back to my book and simply said, "Something like that."

⊷

Aphotic Zone

Dolores stayed the night. We made love. Because I couldn't keep up with her, she kindly slowed for me.

After, she asked me to be patient. She said Lazaro was alive, but when she told me how she knew, I wouldn't believe her. But she'd find a way to explain so I would believe, and then I would save Lazaro. I didn't know what she was talking about, but my mind was aswim, awash, adrift. I let myself be overwhelmed by her. We entangled ourselves in each other and fell asleep.

When I woke I found she had disentangled herself. A note on the pillow said, "Read before burning." When I opened it, however, there was just a single word. "Bathroom."

One of Lazaro's video cameras was pointed at the bathtub. Taped to it was a note that read, "View before burning. Full explanation!"

The tub was full. Next to it was the freezer's icemaker bucket, emptied, and a box of Instant Ocean, which I what I used to salinate the jellytank water. It was empty too.

In the tub, its blue-white glow refracting through the ice, filling and emptying like a lung, was a fully mature aphotic ghost.

Mountain

I climbed Everest. More honest: Roger and the Sherpas climbed Everest and hoisted me behind them. They might as well have carried me up on a palanquin for all the effort I expended.

The search began the day after we arrived at the South Col. The weather was cooperating for now, and forecasts were good. If we were lucky we might get two days.

The cold had sunk an inch down into my body, anesthetizing me, preventing both hope and despair. It was the only reason I could function, this close to knowing. If I failed to find Lazaro, I could try again someday. But if I succeeded, he would be alive or dead. The wave would collapse. I would either eject him from his superposition and bring him back to life, or reify his death.

We searched half a day. I saw many bodies, none of them Lazaro. I wondered briefly if I shouldn't make it the work of the rest of my life to bring the dead down and present them back to their families. But let's see if I could succeed on my own mission first.

Roger, with a Rumpelstilskin-like prescience, knew not to pry, but the Sherpas couldn't comprehend that I couldn't care less about the stark and ominous wonders Everest offered. So, thinking I was like every other tourist, they kept trying to show me the sights. Two of them were dying to show me the most curious ice formation they'd ever seen.

I perked up. Ice formation? I followed.

It had appeared out of the ground last season, they said. They exhumed it out of the recent snow for me to see. It was the size of a sleeping dog and looked something like hand-blown Italian glass, impossibly whorling and curling into itself, a hyaline nautilus relentlessly tearing sunlight into rainbows. Deep in its center there seemed to be a dark nucleus, and strange, ciliated phalanges circuited throughout its interior. Climbing gear radiated from it like an explosion.

"Roger!" I yelled.

Roger came. "We need the cooler," I said.

He spoke to the Sherpas and they brought the coffin-sized cooler I had had specially made. It borrowed from ice-cream maker technology, had a nitrogen core lining the metal interior. After I delicately placed the ice formation inside of it, I found I could just close the lid. "Tell them to help me pack it with snow," I said. Soon every Sherpa who could fit around the cooler was dumping snow and ice into it. When it was full I padlocked the lid.

I was weeping, but no one could tell because everyone's eyes cry this high up, and anyway tears freeze before they fall. I took several hits from my oxygen tank, then said, "Roger, this is futile. I'll have to reconcile myself to the fact that Everest will be my son's final resting place. We'll have to abandon the search. Gather the men."

I could see he knew there was more to the story. But all he said to me was "Right." Then he told the Sherpas what I said. A few of them looked at me incredulously—the search had hardly begun, and now I was content to leave with just an ice-souvenir?—but the more experienced among them simply started packing up. Americans were generally regarded as the best tippers in the world, even when an Everest ascent failed. Tolerating their strange ways was a small price to pay.

Sea-Level

It was my fourth date with Imelda. She was a year older than me. She didn't dye her hair and was a retired librarian and said if I ever caught her playing Bingo I had her permission to kill her on the spot.

We had met through Back from Heaven, the nonprofit I founded to recover the bodies of those who died on Everest. She had joined me on our latest mission, our most successful to date: three deceased climbers retrieved, identified, and returned to their loved ones. One ascent and she was hooked; she joined the team as a full-time volunteer researcher.

And now we were seeing each other. And things were moving fast. Just four dates in and we were going back to my place.

I unlocked the door, reached around to flip the lights, then gestured gallantly for her to enter. She curtsied and strolled in.

And saw the tanks. I still had the smaller Kreisel with my original smack of jellyfish eternally smacking into each other, but what stopped her midstep was the new tank. It took up the wall, a tremendous bubbling cauldron of cornerless glass. In it, the two most enormous jellyfish she'd ever seen pulsed with slow dignity through the water, their blue-while auras commingling. A third one, still just a polyp, trailed behind them.

"Jesus!" she said. "Wow. Just wow."

"Do you like it?" I asked, moving behind her, wrapping my arms around her waist.

She leaned against me. "They're so beautiful." And then, searching for a more precise description, "So unearthly."

"My son's an underwater filmmaker. He discovered this species of jellyfish."

She turned to face me, rested her hands on my shoulders. "No!"

"Really. You'll meet him someday. And I'll have to show you his master-work: *The Aphotic Ghost*. He won an Oscar for it." I directed her attention to the mantle.

She looked, then turned back to me and smiled. "You are just endlessly surprising, Enrique." Then, turning herself back to the tank, but belting my arms to her body, she said, "So when do I get to meet the Academy-Award-winning filmmaker?"

"It's going to be awhile, I'm afraid. He's spending time with his mother right now."

"Ah. I see. Let me guess. You and she can't be in the same room together?"

"Not at all. We're in the same room all the time. And she'll always have a special place in my heart. It's just that . . . well, let's just say we come from two different worlds."

"Say no more," she said, squeezing my arm. She turned back to the larger tank and, after a moment's contemplation, she pointed at the polyp and said, "The tiny one's cute. Does it have a name?"

"She does," I said, pulling Imelda a little closer. "Brumhilda."

THE FOWLER'S DAUGHTER

MICHELLE MUENZLER

It was one of those autumn days, late in the season, where the scent of wood-smoke clung to the air like a drowning man. The dry meadow grasses crackled beneath the long stride of my boots, and the cold iron of my dad's shotgun bit through the layered flannels that had also once been his. I'd flushed two pheasants in the far meadow, and now the strung-together pair swished against my back in a halting rhythm.

At the fence, I slipped through an old break. Its wood had been strong once. When I was a little girl, I had clambered along its length and pretended to fly. But that was a different me, a different fence. Given enough time, everything falls apart.

Like my dad, for instance.

I cleared the last hillock, bringing our shack and the pond into view.

"Dammit." My curse startled some quail into flight.

In the brown waters of the pond, my dad was sunk to his waist, floundering after the geese. They cackled and hissed and led him deeper. I slid the gun from my shoulder and set it in the grass along with the pheasants.

"Out of the water, Dad!" I called, hastening toward him.

His slow spiral inward continued. I grit my teeth, splashed into the icy water, and dragged him ashore; all the while, a furious itching staccatoed my calves.

"Where is she?" he asked, his voice the high-pitched whisper of a child. He shivered in my hands.

"Not here." Never here. At least not when we wanted her.

I pulled a handkerchief from my pocket, wiped the blood spittle from the corner of his blue-gray lips, and carried him home. A change of clothes and a triple layer of quilts soon quieted his shakes.

"I'll be back," I said.

His eyes were already gone, lost in old memories. Did he ever dream of me, or had the geese taken even that? I trudged to my fallen catch in the meadow, a light wind pricking my cheeks and warning of colder days to come. As I bent to retrieve the pheasants, a sudden itch crinkled deep in my spine. I turned to the northern horizon. There, a dark wedge of geese pierced the blue glass of the sky like a bullet.

Mother was coming home.

I cleaned the pheasants and dropped them into a pot of yesterday's broth. Over the long afternoon, they disintegrated, flesh splitting from bone, and filled the shack with their fatty aroma. When only a sliver of the sun remained on the horizon, I left my dad wrapped in quilts and marched to the pond's edge, an old dress clenched between my fingers. Mother was waiting, swimming in quiet circles.

She changed as the last rays of red slipped away, her feathers falling into gold-flecked dust, her skin stretching toward the sky. Human again, if you could call her that.

She struggled to her feet, unsteady, and wiped the mud from her knees. "I am home."

Her voice always startled me at first, too quiet for my memory of it and too soft for the hard angles of her face. I squeezed the dress until my fingers burned.

"Where's your father?" she asked.

"Sick." He was more than just sick this time, though.

"Then I must see him."

I pulled the dress against my stomach. "It'd be better if you didn't."

She touched my cheek, and a deep itch fluttered in my shoulder blades. I jerked away and shoved the dress into her hands.

"Don't touch me."

"I am your mother." A shadow flitted across her brow.

"In blood alone."

She stared, her goose-dark eyes unreadable, then pulled the dress over her head and disappeared into the shack. I collected an old quilt from the porch and huddled near the pond to wait for dawn. Whenever the wind bit too hard, I tossed stones at the dozing geese. If I could have no rest, neither could they.

In the gray hour before dawn, Mother emerged, her face tight and pale. I rose from the grass, quilt still drawn tight around my shoulders. A wet hollow marked where I'd sat the night through.

"Satisfied now?" I refused to soften the bitterness in my voice. She'd kill him with her leaving.

"I will come for you in the spring."

After my dad was dead, she didn't say.

"I won't be here. I'm selling the land and moving to the city. There's already a developer lined up."

Her eyes were quiet, but the trembling of her chin told me my barb had struck. She pulled the dress overhead, folded it carefully, and handed it to me. With her eyes on the eastern horizon, she stepped into the pond. I hated her stillness on the edge of change, her calm acceptance. I hated how easily she could let her humanity slide away, like the sloughing of dead skin.

I hated how easily she could leave us, every time.

"Wait," I said, almost biting my tongue. Why should I have to speak if she would not? "You could stay. Until the end at least. Maybe I would feel differently then." Or maybe she would remember what it was to love her family more than a flock of birds.

"They wouldn't stay," she said. "The dream of south is too strong."

"Then let them go."

She did not turn to me, and I almost lost her words as the first raw edge of dawn broke.

"I also dream."

In a glittering rain of dust, she faded. Only the goose remained.

I expected the geese to fly at any moment, and I could see they expected it as well, but she kept them there. They circled the pond restlessly and wandered the meadow with their eyes glued skyward. My dad hid himself the full day, leaving only a brittle shell for me to watch over. His open eyes reflected nothing. When the sun bled into the horizon, the geese were still there. I hurried to the shore where my mother was waiting.

"You stayed," I said, handing her the dress.

"Yes." She pulled it on.

I clasped her hand, ignoring the deep itch shivering beneath my skin, and we walked together toward the shack. My chest was buoyant with giddiness. I could've flown right then.

"I'll make you a warm place by Dad's side tomorrow and make sure you're well-fed and safe during the day. No fox will make it within a thousand feet."

I glanced over, saw the shadows darkening in her eyes, and stopped.

"You're not staying, are you?"

"The south still calls. You will understand. In the spring."

She ran her free hand down my arm. I could almost feel the sickening pop of feathers bursting in her wake.

"No." I pulled myself free and stepped back. "I will never understand."

By dawn, I had settled at the pond's edge, shotgun in hand. Mother appeared, shook her head at the gun, and removed her dress. She held it out for me to take, but I refused. Carefully, she set it in the grass.

"Spring," she said. "Wait for me."

Hadn't I waited long enough already? I wanted to ask her, but the words wouldn't come.

She slid into the water with ease and with the breaking of dawn became the goose again. Ripples fled across the pond, and her flock called out for reassurance against the tang of iron in the air.

"Stay," I said, aiming at the nervous geese. For their lives, surely she would stay.

She circled a moment in silence, then honked, and all the geese but her burst into the air. I pulled the trigger, and lead shot sprayed the scattering flock. Three of them plummeted back into the water.

They were just geese, I told myself. Nothing less, nothing more. Even Mother, black and gray and full of spite like any common goose, was no different. I aimed the rifle at her.

"Stay."

She glared; she hissed. She flapped her wings and hurtled toward the sky. I fired.

Just geese, nothing more, I repeated again and again as her body drifted in quiet circles. Between my shoulder blades, a deep itch fluttered and pressed for freedom.

I pictured the city until it passed.

MOONLIGHT AND BLEACH

SANDRA McDONALD

My mother was the most beautiful werewolf in Brighton Beach. Four legs, sleek silver fur, and a mouth full of well-brushed teeth that could rip your throat out. My father was a Russian immigrant who started a janitorial company that at one time serviced every public school and city building on Coney Island. As their only kid, I inherited the worst of both worlds: my mother's were-curse and my father's ruthless passion for cleanliness. Every month I transform into a magical creature who slinks along the city streets carrying a bucket and a mop.

Yes. I'm a were-maid.

"Like that's the worst thing in the world," Mom used to say, her face beet-red as she scrubbed at pots with steel wool. Until she and my father retired, she did her own housework every day. "Sweetheart, you'll see. A woman who cleans and cooks is a woman who will always have a husband."

She's from German stock, very traditional. She wanted me to be a wife; I wanted to be a career woman. She hoped that I would settle down in Park Slope with my boyfriend Jason after we both graduated from Fordham Law. Instead Jason announced he was dumping me for a public defender in Queens who didn't sneak out of the apartment late at night and return smelling like furniture polish. I told him about the curse. He insisted I had some weird obsessive-compulsive disorder.

"He's an idiot," Mom said when heard the news. "His bathroom will never be as clean as it was with you."

My parents' sympathy is long distance these days. They spend most of each year in Germany, where Mom can run free through the Black Forest when her arthritis isn't acting up. I'm their only child, and by day I'm an ambitious junior partner at the law firm of Sidoriv and Puginsky. I wear nice suits and expensive shoes. Under the full moon, whatever I'm wearing transforms into a black polyester dress, a white apron, and ugly black shoes. The yellow rubber gloves that coat my hands won't come off until sunrise. My hair curls itself up into a bun, tight and impossible to dislodge.

Tonight's one of those nights.

"Hey, baby!" A red car slows down and the driver leers out his window. It's one of those hot summer nights that makes you glad for the miracle of air conditioning. "Going to a party? Want to clean me up?"

I ignore him. The perils of walking around in a maid uniform at night in New York can't be underestimated, but I've got a bottle of industrial grade cleaner in my bucket and I'm not afraid to use it.

He makes some lewd suggestions about sponges and finally drives on. Ten minutes later I reach my destination and knock on the alley door.

"There you are," grumbles my cousin, Alexi, after he opens it. "You're late."

"I had to get ready for a meeting with the D.A. tomorrow," I say.

The smell of chlorine is heavy in the humid air, but the halls are dark and empty. This is one of the smallest, most exclusive Russian banyas in the borough. A banya is a bathhouse to you and me. The bathroom stalls, locker room floors, steam room benches are all prime breeding grounds for germs and grime. It's good, hard work.

Alexi is top masseuse here. He's a big beefy man, and when he has bad news he comes out and says it. "Look, Tania. The customers. The morning after you come, they say it's too clean."

I push my maid's cap higher on my head. "Too clean? What does that mean?"

"Too much bleach. Makes them sneeze. Could you maybe try, I don't know, vinegar?"

"It's not as good."

"I'm just saying." Another shrug, a spread of hands. "Olga wants you to stay in the morning. She wants to meet you, talk it over."

Olga is his boss. We've met before, at business functions, but never while I'm under my curse. "I can't! She'll recognize me!"

"Then you better take tomorrow night off. Find someplace else for a month or two."

It's not that New York lacks places that need cleaning. It lacks *safe* places that need cleaning. Without a haven like this, who knows where I'll end up tomorrow, the last night of the full moon. In desperate times I've broken into hotels and apartments, infiltrated hotels and motels, even hung around bus terminals with a long coat over my uniform. Once I almost got arrested for trying to mop the Brooklyn Bridge.

Alexi holds up one finger. "Good news, though. I've got a guy for you. Needs help."

I squint at him. "What kind of guy?"

"Nice guy," he insists. "Widow. Not a pervert, okay? Just needs a little help."

I trust Alexi with my secret and I'd trust him with my wallet, but you've got to be careful with a curse like mine. Some guys get off on having a woman in a maid's uniform visit them late at night. Leering can lead to groping, and groping can lead to me hitting someone hitting over the head with a mop. I prefer to avoid personal injury lawsuits.

"Nice old guy," Alexi repeats. "University professor. I'll give you his number."

"Fine." It doesn't seem like I have much of a choice. "But first I've got some toilets to clean."

Not only am I the most ambitious junior partner at Sidoriv and Puginsky, I'm the only partner the firm actually has. My bosses are Igor and Boris, two cantankerous old farts with hearing problems, high blood pressure and a fondness for cheap cigars. They've been partners in law for fifty years and closeted gay lovers for at least as long. Or maybe not so closeted. My father used to roll his eyes whenever he saw them, and wring his hands, and then say, "You'd think they could at least marry, have some children. A few seconds of poking and you're done. For appearances."

Most of the firm's work is citizenship problems, workman's compensation and landlord disputes for the economically disadvantaged Russians of Brooklyn. I like most of my clients. They're loud and colorful, on bold new adventures in a foreign land, and the older ones bring us onion and cabbage pirozkhis. I also like being useful. America is full of predators who prey on immigrants the way my mom, during her werewolf nights, is a threat to stray dogs, feral cats, and luckless animals of the forest. Occasionally I do some criminal defense. My current client is an elderly cabbie named Vlad who tried to run over a couple of punks who stiffed him on a fare. I'm dead tired from scrubbing porcelain all night but I make it to the district attorney's office on time for my meeting.

"It was attempted murder," says the prosecutor.

"My client was upset and confused," I reply. "He thought they were trying to rob him."

"He braked, reversed, and then jumped the curb again."

Vlad has big blue eyes that make you want to believe him, but if he ever gives you a hug, be sure to check your pockets afterward. He waves his hands around and speaks rapidly in Russian.

"He thought he saw a gun," I translate.

"Your client is a menace," the prosecutor says.

By the time we leave I have a pounding fatigue headache, and the wretched heat of the day makes my suit cling to me like wet leaves. Back at the opulent offices of Sidoriv and Puginsky—that would be four small ancient, cluttered rooms over what's now an Indian grocery store—I gulp down a giant cup of iced coffee.

"She stays out too late," Igor says, the unlit cigar in his mouth bobbing as high as his bushy gray eyebrows.

"She needs a social life," Boris retorts, shuffling through a mound of folders. Both of them refuse to use computers. "Girl like her, who wants to be alone?"

At times like this, it's best to ignore them entirely.

When I get home to my apartment I feed Alfred, the gray tabby I adopted after Jason left me, and crash for a few hours. The full moon rising in the east calls to me, invokes the change. Like all were-curses, it digs unyieldingly into my sleep. Some were-folk dream of woods dark and deep. I get bleach and moonlight, and oven cleaner that never works as well as it should, and those extendable feather dusters for use with chandeliers and ceiling fans.

It's dark but still searing hot out when I knock on the door of apartment 501 in an old box factory on St. Mark's Avenue. The door to 502 opens instead. Standing there is a handsome guy wearing green shorts and a Fire Department T-shirt. Dark hair, blue eyes, a physique to kill for—he could easily be Mr. January in that charity calendar the FDNY puts out each year.

And here I am, in my polyester dress and dorky flat shoes.

"I thought you were the pizza guy," Mr. January says.

My face heats up. "No pizza here. Sorry."

The door to 501 swings open to reveal a stooped-over old man wearing a baggy black sweater despite the heat.

"Ah, Miss Tania," my client says. "So nice that you came."

I'm waiting for Mr. January to misinterpret the situation and make a snarky remark, but he just smiles. "Hi, Mr. Federov. Thanks for the mushroom noodles. All the guys liked it."

Federov waves his hand. "It was just the extras."

"It was a four-quart casserole dish," Mr. January tells me. What a great smile. "Ask him for some of his fruit cake."

"Off with you." Federov sounds gruff and pleased at the same time. "Come in, girl."

Mr. January leans against his door frame and watches me go into Federov's apartment.

The place is small but has high ceilings and windows from its factory days. The air conditioner rattles but doesn't do much for putting out cold air. Textbooks and foreign novels cover three old bookcases, and bric-a-brac of a long life litter and small tables—photos frames, tiny vases, hundreds of glass figurines. Lots of lovely dust.

"Alexi says you are very good," Federov says, sitting in a lumpy armchair. "That I should not ask questions. That if I ask questions, you will not return. That I should feel free to sleep away the long hours while you toil."

I nod. The raw, pulsing need to clean is making my head hurt.

Federov looks at me shrewdly. "You do this of your own free will?"

"Yes, sir."

"For so little money?"

If I had my way, I wouldn't charge at all. Taking money for my curse just makes it all the worse. But a cleaning lady who only works while the moon is full would raise even more eyebrows if she refused to take any wages for it. My salary here will go straight to charity.

"The money's fine, Mr. Federov. Can I get started?"

"Hmmm," he says. He's thinking about whether to trust me. I might be a harmless housekeeper, or I could be a thief and murderess here to steal his secondhand books about the Bolshevik Revolution.

Finally he shakes his head. "Such a pretty girl, such a situation. Please proceed."

He turns the TV to some late night show with canned laughter and hip young guests. I inspect the premises. The bathroom is tidy enough for a man's apartment, but the grout in the old porcelain tile has gone gray and there's an impressive ring in the bathtub. The bedroom closet is jammed with clothes that smell like old cologne and which need to be thoroughly ironed. In the kitchen I find my true calling: a refrigerator filled with spills and crusted stains, a sink full of dirty dishes and coffee cups, an oven that hasn't been scoured in years. I'm sure there are roaches lurking in the cabinet by the hundreds.

I think I'll pass on that fruit cake.

By dawn Federov is asleep in his chair and his apartment is cleaner than it's been in years. The moon is waning, so I won't see him again until next month. But that means I won't see Mr. January, either. Which is a good thing. I don't need an incredibly handsome complication in my life right now. The district attorney still wants to charge cabbie Vlad with attempted murder; Boris and Igor are feuding daily over Igor's nephew, the no-good trouble-maker who wants to borrow money again; Alfred swallows something which makes him get constipated and feverish, and I have to take him to the vet for two days of X-rays and kitty laxatives.

I've just finished hauling Alfred back into my apartment when my throw-away cell phone rings. It's the one I give to clients but I don't recognize the number.

"Hey," says the guy on the other end. "It's Mike Hennessee. My neighbor Ivan Federov gave me your number."

It's Mr. January.

"Oh, hi." I get Alfred's carrier on the floor and swing open the door. He shoots out like a cannonball, knocks over a lamp, and plunges behind the sofa. The big white lamp breaks into a dozen pieces on the floor. I never liked it anyway.

"Everything okay there?" Mike asks.

"Just one unhappy cat. What can I do for you?"

"I was looking for someone to help me clean my apartment. Ivan said you did great."

Here's the thing: now that the moon is now longer full, I'm about as interested in cleaning as I am in knitting. Which is to say, nice for other people but not for me. I probably won't do my own dishes for a week. Besides which, I really don't want Mr. January—er, Mike—to see me in full blown housekeeper mode.

"I'm really not available," I tell him.

He sounds genuinely disappointed. "Oh."

Alfred makes a plaintive mewling sound from under the sofa.

"Okay," he says. "What if I said I was lying, and I don't want you to clean my apartment, but maybe go out for beer and pizza? Unless you're not a beer and pizza kind of lady. Maybe wine and cheese. Or Thai and whatever goes with Thai food?"

This is a mistake. It can't end well.

"Beer goes with Thai food," I say.

The restaurant is a hole-in-the-wall establishment in what was once a bookstore and which will one day probably be a coffee shop or internet café. Everything in the city changes constantly. Mike Hennessee shows up wearing a blue shirt that matches his eyes and shows off the long muscles in his arms. He probably gets those muscles from carrying children out of burning buildings or lifting wrecked vehicles off elderly pedestrians.

"Most of what we do are medical calls," he says when we talk about his work. "Heart attacks, diabetics, sometimes a woman in labor."

I've bypassed the Asian beer on the menu for an icy watermelon drink. It's about a zillion degrees outside, and if I keep my arms just right maybe he won't notice the sweat stains under my arms. Not that I was worried about this date, but I changed blouses three times before leaving the house and swapped my shoes twice. My best friend Maryanne is on speed dial, ready to show up and help me escape if Fireman Hennessee turns out to be a crackpot or serial killer. So far, so good.

"How long have you been a fireman?" I ask.

He stabs at some basil eggplant. "Four years, three months and a week."

"In my experience, people who count aren't always the happiest at what they're doing."

"When I was growing up I wanted to be an actor," he says. "Three years of casting calls cured me of that. Now I get twenty-four hour shifts, lots of spaghetti dinners, and people who throw up on me. But what about you? The cleaning business is okay?"

Already we're in tricky territory. "It's just moonlighting. I like meeting people."

He nods. But he doesn't look convinced. "It's just . . . look, Tania, I know some cops, some lawyers. You can trust me. If you're in trouble and need some help, they've worked with cases like this before."

Now I'm confused. "Cases like what?"

His gaze is intent and serious. "Your English is very good. I mean, you could pass for a local. And Ivan, he's a good guy. But lonely. I know how these things work. They get you a visa, they promise you all sorts of jobs, you get to America and now you're making house calls that last all night long—"

The realization that this handsome guy thinks I'm part of a sex trafficking ring makes my Pad Woon-Sen go right down my windpipe. Suddenly I can't breathe at all. Before I can make the universal sign for choking, Mike's out of his chair. He wraps his arms around my mid-section and levers his fists under my ribs. He smells nice, but this is not how I imagined ending up in his arms. One Heimlich thrust later, I'm ejecting broccoli and wheezing for breath.

"You okay?" he asks, breath warm in my ear.

"I'm going to throw up," I say. "I'll be right back."

I lurch off to the bathroom, sure that everyone in the restaurant is staring at me, and when I find the back door next to the kitchen it's an opportunity for escape too good to pass by. I feel humiliated and sick and I'm sure I have brown sauce on my face.

So maybe it isn't nice to leave him like that, but I don't know any happy couple who started off with the misunderstanding that one of them was a Russian sex girl. Luckily Mike doesn't know my real name or where I live. I throw away my cell phone, tell Alexi that I need a new client, and spend the next few weeks buried in work. Vlad the murderous cabbie gets a break when the two punks get busted for trying to rob a hack in Astoria. Igor and Boris stop fighting about Igor's useless nephew and instead start arguing about Boris's niece's son, who is in trouble with the IRS for several years of back taxes. My friend Maryanne starts dating a police officer; he's got a friend and we could double-date, she says.

"I'm never dating again," I tell her. It's not worth the trouble. I wish my were-curse turned me into a superhero or asset to society but that's the thing about Old World curses; they're not useful at all. Mom transforms into a wolf but in her animal stage she doesn't drag children from swollen rivers or rescue Alzheimer patients who've wandered away from home. She eats things, and licks herself, and sheds hair all over the carpet. I can mop up a crime scene but not tell you who the perpetrator was; I can scrub smoke stains off walls but I don't save people from blazing infernos. I just clean.

Maryanne sighs over the phone when I turn down the double date. "You have to get over this Jason thing."

"I'm just not interested," I say. It's not like I think about Mike every night, wishing we'd met under other circumstances. Or that I checked with some friends and found out that he's stationed at Engine Company 234, and was honored last year for volunteer work getting homeless people off the streets during the winter.

"Meet us for drinks tonight," Maryanne says. "For me. Just this once."

Tonight's the full moon. I've never told her about the curse, and now doesn't seem like a good time to try.

"Boris is yelling for me," I say. "Bye."

Boris isn't yelling for me at all. He's sitting in his rolling chair, clipping his fingernails. Goodness knows that if all else fails, I could break in here and free his desk blotter from all those yellow pieces of fingernail that have accumulated over the years. I could dust the ceiling fan and venetian blinds, scrub and wax the floor, organize the shelves—but like Mom always said, you don't want to bring your curse to your job. Actually, she said don't piss in your own yard, but it's the same principle.

Ivan is at his own desk, ostensibly leafing through the pages of a Russian newspaper, but his gaze is firmly on Boris and is so obviously affectionate that I start to feel bereft. No one looks at me that way now. Certainly no one will look at me that way when I'm gray and wrinkled and seventy years old.

"Let's get some tea," Boris says to Ivan.

Ivan shrugs without looking up. "Who's thirsty?"

"Tea," Boris insists, and you don't have to be especially insightful to know that's not exactly what Boris has in mind.

I'm depressed and lovelorn, and unless I find a way to lock myself into my apartment tonight, come moonrise I'll be a madwoman roaming the streets with a carpet sweeper. Luckily Alexi calls around three o'clock. He has the name of "a nice old lady in a wheelchair, you'll like her" over in Brooklyn Heights. It's certainly a very nice neighborhood, with views of Manhattan and well-kept tiny gardens. She lives in a two-story brick house and answers her own door. She's seventy or so years old, with a gray braid of hair coiled to her waist and sharp eyes in a wizened little face.

"Alexi said you were pretty." Mrs. Vasilyeva wheels her chair aside to let me in. "I'm afraid it's so messy. I wish I could clean it on my own."

I get two feet inside the doorway before a snarl stops me. Sitting in the shadows is the most enormous dog I've ever seen—a big black hulk of a canine with wary eyes and a mouth of very sharp teeth.

"That's just Rocco," Mrs. Vasilyeva says. "He likes you."

Maybe he'd like me for dinner, sure.

"The kitchen's that way," the old woman says.

The marble hallway leads past a curving staircase and dark library to a modern kitchen that's all steel and granite. The recessed lights cast pools of cool light. The sink is empty, the counters clean enough to eat off, but the white floor is stained and scuffed. Nothing I can't handle. Some soap and hot water and scrubbing, hands-and-knees work that I'm good at, with wax and buffing—

Rocco growls from behind me. He's sitting now next to Mrs. Vasilyeva, who is fiddling with something in her lap.

"Maybe you could put Rocco in another room?" I ask, trying to sound deferential.

"He likes to watch." She lifts up a video camera and gives me a smile of her own. "I like to watch, too."

My throat dries up. "Okay. I need to use the bathroom first."

The bathroom is down the hall. I lock the door behind me, admire the cleanliness of the handicapped-accessible tub, and then shimmy out the window over the toilet. My uniform tears on the sill and I think my bucket cracks the glass. Soon I'm sprinting away from Brooklyn Heights and yelling at Alexi on my cell phone.

"I can't believe you sent me to that crackpot! I was going to be the star of some snuff video on the internet!"

"I'm sorry," he says. "Who knew?"

"You've got to let me into the banya to clean it."

"I can't. I'm in Jersey. Why don't you go see Ivan Federov?"

"I can't do that."

"What are your other choices?"

Clean an alley full of puke and other excretions. Been there, done that. Swab down the steps of Brooklyn Borough Hall. Hard to do since they opened a police sub-station across the street. Hospitals always need cleaning but I've nearly been caught twice—the black dress and tea apron always stand out.

The need to clean something makes my skin itch like there's an army of germs dancing all over me. The compulsion to scrub the world fresh has me strung out like a heroin addict needing a big bad fix.

You've got to do what you've got to do, Mom always says.

I don't have Federov's number, so I go straight to St. Mark's Ave and slip through an ajar side entrance. Up on the fifth floor, I knock on Federov's door. The hallway is too bright, too open, and I feel totally vulnerable. Please don't let Mike be home and waiting for a pizza. A minute of silence passes, and the only sound is the humming of the fluorescent light overhead. I tap on Federov's door again.

Mike opens his door.

"Hey," he says, face neutral. "You're back."

I nod, unable to think of a single thing to say.

He leans against his doorjamb. His hair is tousled and there are sofa creases on his face, as if he fell asleep while watching TV. "Ivan went into the hospital a few days ago. Broken hip, but he's okay."

"Do you have a key?" I ask. Surely beyond Federov's door there are dirty dishes that need scouring, and dust bunnies under his bed, and a coffee filter turning moldy.

Mike's eyebrows go up. "You look—kind of anxious. Are you okay?"

At times like this, my nose goes on high alert. From behind Mike I smell something going bad—old Chinese food, I think, sour with old soy. If he doesn't move out of the way I'm going to knock him flat and storm the apartment.

"Please don't ask questions," I tell him. "It's just this thing. I need to clean something. Your kitchen or your bathroom or anything you want, but please."

He hesitates, maybe cataloging my mental state for the call to 911. But then he says, "Go for it," and steps aside.

His apartment is dark and minimalist, with some old movie posters hanging on the wall over secondhand furniture and bookshelves filled with DVD cases. The Chinese food is right where I expect it to be, and there are some dirty dishes in the sink, but aside from that I've evidently met the cleanest firefighter in Brooklyn. His bathroom has only one stray hair in the sink. The tub looks like it was scoured by magic brushes from some cartoon TV commercial. Even his bed his perfectly made, and smells freshly laundered.

"What are you, a clean fanatic?" I demand of him.

He laughs. "Says the lady in the maid uniform."

My face heats up in a fresh new wave of humiliation.

Mike stops smiling. "Tania, sit down. Please. Tell me what's going on. Is this a bipolar kind of thing? You can trust me. I'm not going to judge you for it."

Trust him. Trust him not. This is how my father met my mother: he was walking by Brighton Beach Pier early one winter morning when he recognized the tracks of a wolf in the sand. Not your usual kind of wolf, he thought. He took to sitting out at night with a scraps of meat. It took months of patience before he befriended the animal, who was skittish and wary of humans. He followed it through the dark streets of Coney Island until it climbed through a bedroom window. In the morning my mother came down to breakfast to find him drinking coffee with her parents, and their courtship started.

"I will tell you everything if you find me something to clean," I vow.

He purses his lips, deep in thought, and then grabs his shoes. "Come on."

Six blocks from Mike's apartment, there's an old building that was once a Jewish hospital. The courtyard is locked off by big iron gates. Mike has a key to the gates and then to a basement Laundromat that must have been the hospital laundry once. He flicks on some of the fluorescent lights and steers me past some old industrial washers and dryers. Dozens of paper and plastic sacks sit piled in the corner.

"How do you feel about doing laundry for strangers?" he asks.

Clothes that reek of vomit, sweat, spilled alcohol, stale cigarette smoke. Sleeping bags and towels with stains of brown and red and yellow. Underwear and clothing with very questionable stains on them.

"What is this place?" I ask.

"Homeless shelter," Mike says. "I volunteer here. There's about two hundred people sleeping on cots upstairs, and none of them can afford a Laundromat."

I can't help myself. I kiss him right there and then.

I'm in heaven.

Mike stays with me all night. I tell him he doesn't have to; he says I owe him a story.

Between soap and bleach, fabric softener and lint sheets, I reveal the improbable tale of my parents and the were-curse, and what drives me to the streets every full moon. He drinks soda from a vending machine and nods in all the right places. He lets me teach him how to fold a fitted sheet, and we have a long conversation about the best way to fold socks (tie them together or invert one into the other), and near dawn he looks at the clock and says, "We better scoot before the day shift gets here."

"What are you going to tell them?" I ask.

"That they were visited by the laundry fairy godmother." He stretches with a grimace; plastic chairs are bad for the back. "I bet they'll beg you to come back tonight."

By the time we lock everything up and go outside, the sky is gray with pre-dawn light. The air is fresh and clean. Or as fresh and clean as it gets in a metropolis of grime. Mike says, "Let me take you home," but that means he'll know where I live. He'll learn my last name. The were-maid's final secrets will be revealed.

"Look, thanks for all you did—" I start.

He puts one finger to my lips to silence me. Uses the other to point at the sky.

"See that? It's beautiful. Like dirty dishwater." He steps closer, a warm smile on his face. "I don't care that you're cursed. I want to spend more time with you. Full moon, half moon, no moon. Maid uniform or blue jeans. Apron or high heels."

It's a risk, trusting people. They can break your heart as surely as lemon rinds make a garbage disposal smell nice. But I kiss Mike anyway. He touches my hair just as the rising sun makes my hair unwind and yellow gloves dissolve. The were-maid is gone for now, and cleaning is the last thing on my mind.

SHE DRIVES THE MEN TO CRIMES OF PASSION!

GENEVIEVE VALENTINE

—❖—

The scene was this: Cocoanut Grove, Saturday night, packed so tight you had to hold your drink practically in your armpit, and the band loud enough that you gave up on conversation and nodded whenever you heard a voice just in case someone was talking to you.

You never went to the Grove on the weekends if you had any kind of self-respect at all—by 1934 all the stars had turned their backs on the Grove and fled to the Sidewalk Café, where they could drink themselves onto the floor without any prying eyes. The reporters had given up trying, and now they came to the Grove to dig up dirt on the third-rate bit players.

It was fine for the bit players, but I had some prospects.

Well, one picture. It hadn't done well. I knew they were talking about putting me on pity duty with the melodramas that shot in four days on the same set. No extras, no stars; nothing to do but come to the Cocoanut Grove and look around at the bit players you were going to be stuck with for the rest of your life.

"You need a friend in the studio, fast," said Lewis. "Come down to the Grove with me. There's bound to be someone."

I nursed my Scotch and grimaced at the crowd for an hour, looking for a studio man I could talk to.

None. Damn Sidewalk Café.

I was on my way across the floor to leave when the music ended, and the dance floor opened, and I saw Eva.

She'd been dancing—strands of her dark hair stuck to her shining brown skin, a spiderweb across her forehead. If she'd been wearing lipstick it was gone, but her lids were still dusted with sparkly shadow in bright green and white that shone in the dark like a second pair of eyes.

I saw her coming and held my breath. I could already see her at the end of the lens—turning to look over her shoulder at the hero, giving him a smile, tempting him to do terrible things.

"You should be in pictures," I said, and it sounded like a totally different line when you meant it.

Her audition alone got me into Capital Films for a feature with her. I knew it would.

There was no point in making her into an ingénue (exotic and ingénue did not mix), so we went right to the vamp. I made her a fortune teller in *On the Wild Heath*. She captivated the lord of the manor, put a curse on him when he scorned her, and got shot just before she could lay hands on the lady of the house.

The Hollywood Reporter called her "Exotic Eva" in the blurb—couldn't have planned it better—and went on for a paragraph about the passion in her Spanish eyes. They wrapped with, "We suspect we haven't seen the last of this sultry siren."

Capital signed me for another flick, and started making us reservations at the Sidewalk Café.

Eva wore green satin that matched her eyes, and as we danced under the dim lights there were shimmers of color across her skin.

"I think I love you," I said.

She said, "You would."

It sounded ungrateful, but I let it go. There was time for all that; right now, our stars were rising.

Capital didn't want her being a heroine yet. ("Keep her mysterious," they said. "The fan magazines can't even tell if she's really Mexican or if it's just makeup. It's perfect.")

I made her a flamenco dancer next, in *Stage Loves*.

The lead, Jack Stone, was nothing much—I was doing the studio a favor just having him—but at least he looked properly stunned whenever she was in the frame.

Originally Stone's theatre patron was going to seduce her and leave the virginal heiress for a life with the variety show, but word came down that Capital was going to start getting strict about the Production Code, so the hero sinning was right out.

So instead Eva seduced the patron, and got strangled by the jealous stage manager in the last reel.

(The poster featured her bottom left, with a banner: "Eva Loba is Elisa The Spanish Temptress—She drives the men to crimes of passion!")

The new script must have worked just as well; the studio asked for two more movies as soon as the film was in.

After the Sidewalk Café one Sunday I drove her home, to some bank of stucco apartments in a no-man's-land north of the city.

"We have to get you a better place if you're going to be worth photographing," I said. "I'll talk to the studio."

"You shouldn't," she said. "I like it here."

"But the cameras don't," I said, and cut the engine.

I helped her out of the car. Her skin was shining in the light, and her sharp green eyes were captivating, and I felt like some poor sucker lord of the manor for letting her get to me like this. I should know better. My head was swimming; I wanted her, I needed her.

Before she was steady on her feet, I pulled her roughly against me.

She took a breath. Then for an instant she was in two dimensions, flat enough for the streetlight to bleed through her like a stained glass window, and before I could even really understand what I was seeing the world had snapped back into place, and there was a flurry of jewel-colored bodies and sharp green wings.

They scattered, and I was left with a satin dress in my hands, blinking at the startling-white impressions of two hundred vanished birds.

My first thought was, *Something terrifying has just happened.*

My second was, *The girl knows how to make an exit.*

Eva was set to play Ruby, the sultry Latin dancer in the musical of the month (*Down Mexico Way*, maybe, or *You're Lovely Tonight*, musicals all look the same to me). I wasn't directing, but it was common knowledge that I was bringing her up the ranks, and if she didn't show, it wouldn't look good for me.

But when I got to the set the next morning she was already there and in costume, practicing the steps on the nightclub set with her partner.

I didn't dare push it with him right there, so I watched quietly from behind the camera all morning, until the director called lunch and the crew scattered.

She stayed where she was, and for a moment I thought about how to keep the cameras rolling in case she did it again. (I couldn't help it; a director's always looking for the shot no one can top.)

"You look like you have something to say," she said, folded her arms.

I kept my distance. If it wasn't on film, there was no point in provoking her.

"Where did you learn to do that?"

She smiled thinly. "It can't be taught. It's just something you are."

"No, I didn't mean—where did you *come* from?"

"Nogales."

That wasn't what I meant, either. "But there had to be some reason you showed me and not anyone else," I went on.

She looked at me, frowning, like I was some kind of idiot instead of the guy who had built her career from the ground up.

"I'm here to be an actress," she said. "I'm not doing any of this for you."

I let it go. It wasn't the time to argue facts.

I said, "We could make a movie about it. I could build the whole plot around you, a leading part. Something from the Arabian Nights!" I paused, overcome with the image of a pasha's throne room and a storyteller who has a trick up her sleeve.

"Just think," I said, "we could show everyone what kind of star you can be."

"No."

That stung. You'd think she'd have taken a starring role from the guy who knew how to direct her. "But imagine it," I pleaded. "Forget the Reporter—this would be history! This town would never top it. We'd go down in the record books with the shot no one could ever figure out."

She narrowed her eyes. "No one would believe it."

Who cared what anyone believed so long as they paid to see it, I thought.

I said, "I can make people believe anything."

Then the crew was filing back in, and the director wanted to see her, so I let her go.

I stayed all afternoon to watch her backstage-at-the-contest scene (I was a better director than the music man), and to think how best to go about getting hold of that moment again.

She was too caught up in the thrill of it to remember who had given her the first shot; she didn't understand how I had built up her audience, that was all.

At least she didn't have much of a part in the musical. When she came back to me for her next contract, I thought, we'd have another talk about who makes a star.

The weekend the musical opened, the Reporter wrote her up as "Eva with the Ruby Throat" (I laughed—what were the odds?), and the studio sent her to the Trocadero alone, without telling me.

Turns out they had engineered a romance for Eva with Paul Maitland over at Atlas Pictures. He was marquee material—his last gig had been Ivanhoe, and they were talking about him for Robin Hood next. He was light in his loafers, though, so someone at Atlas had struck a deal with Capital to get curvy little Eva on his arm but quick.

They had arranged for Maitland to be waiting just under the canopy, so that when Eva slid her arm into his, an enterprising photographer could get a decent shot before they ducked inside.

And plenty did.

The Reporter ran two pictures of them on the front page: one of them arm in arm, and one of him kissing her goodnight at the curb, his arms around her. The gossip column squealed—"Sultry Spanish Siren Seduces Arch Aristocrat!"—and wondered when they'd have the pleasure of seeing them together on the screen.

She really was good at what she did. The way she looked at him in those pictures—if you didn't know, you'd think she'd loved Paul for years.

But now I knew better, and all I could do when I got the paper was stare at Maitland's arms around her waist and wonder what he was going to do when she turned into a flock of birds and vanished.

She didn't vanish.

The contract she signed for the Maitland affair must have been stellar, because her next two pictures went to other directors, and every time I picked up the Reporter there was a picture of her, her jewelry shimmering in the flashbulbs.

At first it was always with Maitland, and I didn't like it, but I could understand. There were terms in her contract she had to fulfill.

But sometimes she was alone. Those I hated, those snaps of her standing in the doorway of the Brown Derby or the Trocadero like she had sprung up there all by herself, like she knew something the world didn't know, like she had made this happen all on her own.

I knocked out two movies that year: a detective picture and a turn-of-the-century romance. The romance took off ("Starmaker Strikes Again!"), and soon I could get into the Trocadero no matter who I had on my arm.

I never went alone; when you had as many movies under your belt as I did, it wasn't hard to find a woman who would appreciate it.

(Eva rarely appeared where I was going. I suspected the studio had arranged things that way.)

I read up on the ruby-throated hummingbird, just on a whim. Turned out she wasn't lying; the Aztecs had used them as talismans because of their power. Maybe that really was just something you were.

I saw the scene unfold in front of me: an ancient stone temple, a hundred wailing warriors, a human sacrifice loved by the gods who exploded into glittering birds. I'd have to put in some explorers (for moral perspective, the Code was pretty clear on that), but it could be a spectacular movie if only she'd agree.

⟞⟝

Capital called me in. They wanted a historical epic, and they wanted me.

Right there in the office, I pitched them *Lord of the Birds*. Exotic siren, cast of thousands, dancing girls and bloody battles and history coming to life.

"I have an effect no one's ever dreamed of," I said. "People will wonder about it for a hundred years."

They upped my budget on the spot, asked me who I wanted most.

"Eva," I said.

The office men loved it, of course. They knew who made a star.

Lewis called from Legal. He told me Eva had a competing contract offer from Atlas Films that she was willing to take rather than be in a movie of mine.

"We don't want to make waves," said Lewis. "You can find another leading lady—they're a dime a dozen, you know that."

Eva wasn't some leading lady, she was a star, but I didn't have to tell Lewis. They knew it. That's why they were cutting me to keep her.

I didn't tell him that she was the key to the whole movie. Best case: he'd think I was out of my mind. Worst case: he'd believe me, and pull my funding.

"I'll look around," I said. "Where should I go?"

I ended up at the Sidewalk Café, watching Eva dancing with a string of men, and hating her.

When she saw me she looked a little upset (I wasn't proud of how happy it made me, but I'd take anything I could get). She sat for three songs, and then she got a light from Maitland and vanished through the crowd.

I went outside after her.

When she saw me she shook her head, ground out her cigarette underfoot, and turned to leave.

"Just hear me out," I said. I hated her for making me beg. I was above begging.

"When I move to Atlas," she said, "you can tell your friends at Capital why."

"You have to understand," I told her. "I promised the studio a special effect like they've never seen. Without your hummingbird trick, the whole movie's a bust."

She raised her eyebrows nearly to her hairline. "My trick?"

"If you don't do it, the studio will make me a laughingstock!" I saw her face and added, "And you! If this doesn't happen, it's going to come back to you, you wait and see."

"I'll live," she said.

And then (just to spite me, I know it) she broke apart, flashes of green and red and the whir of birds disappearing into the dark, and nothing left of her but glimpses of white at the edges of my vision like a scattering of teeth.

A good director films a story that's set in front of him.

A great director can make a story out of nothing.

I stood in the dark outside the club, watching as a straggler fluttered up into the dark, and the rest of her story came to life in front of me.

The next morning I called Lewis and told him that I would find another leading lady.

"I saw Eva last night," I said. "She's not doing very well for herself, it looks like. Looking old. I was thinking we'd do Marie Antoinette instead of that Aztec crap. Everyone loves the French costumes, and then we don't have to worry about making the Code happy."

I was scrabbling, and I knew it, but the only way to get ahead in this town is to lie like you mean it, so I went on, "We can use that blonde instead—you know, the one who can sing?"

(Turned out there were several; that phone call took a while.)

Then I called the publicity office and told them I wanted to offer Eva a part in my new movie; did they know if she was meeting Maitland tonight?

When she left her house that night I was waiting for her, leaning against my car.

Eva was in white silk that looked nearly green in the moonlight, and now I couldn't look at her without looking for a flash of red near her throat.

I knew her so well; it stung that she wouldn't give me credit for it.

"You ruined my movie," I said, casually. "Without you I had to change the whole thing. If that doesn't work, Capital is out a lot of money, and I'm sunk."

"That's because you promised something that wasn't yours to give," she said.

"How do you think movies get made, Eva?"

Now she looked wary. God, her face was exquisite. I realized, too late, I should have brought a camera.

"Do you think this is still just for the movie?" she asked.

She was looking right at me, and I felt guiltier than I had in a long time.

"Someday you'll understand," I said.

Then I yanked the gun out of my jacket and pulled the trigger.

As a director, there were two problems with what happened next.

1) I was a pretty cheap shot—I'd just bought the gun, it's not as if I had practiced—so the recoil surprised me and the bullet went wild, which takes away the power of the moment.

2) When you tell someone "Someday you'll understand" right before you shoot, you're not absolving yourself so much as you are giving them a moment

to prepare, and then what happens is that by the time your shot goes wide you're already staring at the last of the hummingbirds disappearing into the trees.

Still, when I stopped worrying if I'd broken my thumb, I saw that there was a hummingbird hopping around on the dirt in front of me in a panic, one of its outstretched wings suddenly much shorter than the other.

The singed edges were still warm to the touch where the bullet had struck, I noticed, after I scooped it up and kissed it.

The birdcage is an antique, a gift from the studio. It's big enough that the hummingbird could fly around pretty comfortably, if it could still fly.

(I named it Polly for the present, because that was just the best name for a bird. Whenever people come over, they laugh themselves sick when I tell them, and then they try to call her over like it's actually a parrot and can answer to the name. I'm working on getting some more sophisticated people.)

I keep the cage just near enough to the window that when the others come looking they'll see Polly sitting there, and just far enough in that there's no stealing her out without coming all the way inside.

And they will come back; Eva can't become human without all of them, and there are only so many places you can hide two hundred hummingbirds.

("Rising Star Falls," cried the Reporter. "Exotic Eva Disappears—Have We Seen Her Last Film?")

I hope that's not the case. I'm not out to harm anyone. When she comes back to bargain, I'll be happy to bargain.

She knows who makes a star.

COYOTAJE

MARIE BRENNAN

The coyotes of Mexicali were bold. They did their business in cantinas, in the middle of the afternoon; the police, well-fed with bribes, looked the other way. Day by day, week by week, people came into Mexicali, carrying backpacks and bundles and small children, and day by day, week by week, they went away again, vanishing while the back of the police was obligingly turned.

If the people could afford it. "The price is twenty-five thousand pesos," the coyote repeated, and drained the last of his beer. "If you can't pay, stop wasting my time."

Inés bit her lip, looking down at the scratched Formica tabletop. "I don't have twenty-five thousand. I only have—" She stopped herself before saying the number. Mexicali was far from the worst of the border towns, but it was bad enough, if you went looking for the wrong people.

The coyote shrugged. "Try El Rojo. He might take you for less. Especially if you have something else to offer." The quick downward flick of his eyes made his meaning clear.

"Where can I find El Rojo?"

"La Puerta de Oro, in Chinesca. Ask for shark-fin tacos."

Inés nodded and got up. She heard footsteps following her as she left the cantina, and whirled once she was through the door, prepared to defend herself.

Her pursuer held up his hands, letting the door swing shut behind him. "Relax. I only followed because I heard what Ortega said. Don't go to El Rojo."

The sun was like a hammer on Inés' back, trying to pound her into the dust. But it meant she could see the other man's face, broad and pocked with the occasional scar, seamed where he squinted against the light. "If he's cheaper, I have to. Nobody told me it would be this expensive."

The man—another coyote—shrugged and pulled sunglasses from his pocket. "Can't help it. With all the new laws, it's a lot riskier for us, and you need documents on the other side. Look, I'll take you for twenty."

Inés shook her head. "I don't have twenty, either."

"Then stay here a while. There's jobs—not good ones, but if you're patient you can save enough to get across. *Safely.* El Rojo . . . he isn't safe."

None of it was safe; even the honest coyotes could get a migrant killed. "I don't have any choice," she said.

With the man's eyes hidden by the sunglasses, she couldn't be sure, but she thought he gave her a pitying look. "Go with God, then. And be careful."

Caution had gone out the window when Javier died. Shading her eyes against the desert sun, Inés went in search of La Puerta de Oro.

It lay in Mexicali's Chinatown, its garish red and gold faded by the elements. The interior was blindingly dark, after the street outside. "Shark-fin tacos," she said once her eyes adjusted, and the hostess jabbed her thumb toward a table in the back corner.

Two men sat there, both facing the door. The bigger one grinned as Inés approached, licking his lips in an exaggerated gesture, but it was the skinnier one *she* watched. He had a predator's eyes.

She cast her gaze down when she got to the table. "I want to get across the border," she said. Quietly, but not whispering. "I heard El Rojo could take me."

"I can," the smaller man said. He was wiry more than slender, hardened to rawhide by the desert sun. Other Mexicali coyotes took migrants in secret truck compartments, sneaking them across into Calexico or up to State Route 7, then onward to San Diego or Phoenix. El Rojo, according to rumor, went a more dangerous route, through the Sonoran Desert. Less risk of being caught by the Border Patrol, but more risk of dying, whether from thirst or the guns of militia. Or coyotes, of the four-legged kind.

Inés sat, eyes still downcast; the last thing she wanted was for him to take her stare as a challenge. "I can pay ten thousand."

The bigger fellow laughed, a barking sound in the quiet of the restaurant. "That and a bit more will do, girl," he said, laying one hand on her knee as if she might not catch his meaning.

She controlled her revulsion; pulling away too fast would make her look like prey. It was the other man who mattered, anyway. El Rojo, the red one. There were many possible explanations for the nickname, few of them reassuring.

His method of bargaining showed a sharp mind. From money, he would switch without warning to questions about Inés: where she was from, why she was emigrating, what kind of work she thought she would find. She told him she came from Cuauhtémoc in Chihuahua, and had a brother who crossed at Nogales two years ago; if she could get to Albuquerque, he knew a man who could get her a job as a maid. Seventeen thousand, El Rojo said, and if she was coming from Cuauhtémoc and going to Albuquerque, why had she come to

Mexicali? A man had brought her this far, promising help, Inés said, but he'd tried to rape her; she would pay fifteen thousand and no more.

El Rojo smiled, thin, lips closed. "That'll do. Half now, half when we get there, and Pipo here will show you to your room."

"My room?" Inés asked, alarm rising in her throat.

Now he showed a glint of teeth. "I'm your coyote now. Full service, from here until your trip is done. Wouldn't want you getting picked up by the cops."

Or telling anybody about his business. This was his reputation, that he was shrewd and careful, and utterly without human morals. If she gave him reason to cut her throat, he would, without hesitation.

She'd hoped to send a letter, in case she didn't survive this trip. "Do you think I'm stupid? I didn't bring the money with me."

He gestured at his companion. "Pipo will go with you to fetch it. We have a deal, and until it's done, you're mine."

The "room" Pipo showed her to was a basement elsewhere in Chinesca, though Inés, blindfolded, only knew it by the smell of spices. What sort of deals had El Rojo struck, that he chose to do business out of this part of Mexicali?

Maybe the police just paid less attention to the Chinese district. Certainly Pipo felt comfortable enough to lead her blindfolded through the streets, by a very roundabout path. When he shoved her off the last step and yanked off the bandanna, Inés found more than a dozen people in the basement already, sitting in the light of a single dim bulb, watching her with wary eyes.

"Tomorrow night," Pipo said, and left.

Inés brushed her hair from her face, nodded at the migrants, and found a place to sit by the wall, where she leaned against a broken piece of tabletop. Nobody spoke; she didn't expect it. Right now they were all strangers, in an unknown place, taking an enormous risk. Talk would come later, when shared trials created a sense of bonding; then she would hear about relatives on the other side of the border, or the hope of work—whatever dream or desperation sent them on this journey.

She studied them, though, out of the corners of her eyes, taking care never to stare at anyone. Most were a bit younger than her: in their teens, maybe early twenties. A few women, the rest men; three of the women were cradling children too young to walk. One man was substantially older—maybe his fifties, though with his face so wrinkled by the sun, she could be off by ten years. He made no pretense about not staring at her, though when Inés returned the look he glanced away, scratching his fingers through hair like gray wire.

Fifteen thousand pesos, Inés had promised El Rojo. Assume the same for everyone here; some maybe bargained better, some worse, and she didn't know if he charged the same for little kids. Seventeen people in this basement, counting her. Assume that was average. Two hundred fifty-five thousand pesos—more than twenty thousand dollars. How often did El Rojo do this? Every month? Less often? More? However she did the math, *coyotaje* was a profitable business.

One for which many people paid the price.

Javier would've told Inés she was an idiot for coming here, for putting herself into El Rojo's hands. But Javier was gone, and she was the only one who could do this.

She laid down on the hard concrete and tried to get some sleep.

When the basement door slammed open, half the people there were already awake; within seconds, all of them were on their feet, and one mother stifled her daughter's wail. Pipo grinned at them, blunt face monstrous in the dim light, and jerked a thumb toward the door. "Time to go."

Inés sneaked a glance at her mother's old watch, with its extra hole punched in the band to fit her smaller wrist. An hour past sunset. They would make their move in the dead of night.

Last chance to run.

But it was a lie. She'd passed up that chance when she sat down at El Rojo's table—maybe when she came to Mexicali in search of him. Inés followed the others upstairs and into the narrow alley behind.

A truck waited there. Inés didn't see El Rojo, but three other men were helping Pipo, and one climbed into the back with the migrants before the door was rolled down and locked into place. No secret compartment, not here; this was only to get them out of town. Most of the journey would be done on foot.

More waiting, this time in near-total darkness. Inés sat with her backpack in the hollow of her crossed legs, arms wrapped around it, swaying into the gray-haired man or the young woman on the other side every time the truck slowed or accelerated or hit a rough patch of road. The young woman sat in much the same position, only it was a little girl she held, a year old at most. The infant, of course, didn't understand what was going on, and burbled loudly to herself in the darkness.

"Shut her up, already," one of the young men said abruptly, breaking the stifling silence that overlaid the noise of the truck. "That brat's gonna get us caught."

Inés felt the mother shrink back in alarm. "Hey!" Inés said, glaring into the darkness, as if the complainer could see her. "She's happy. Would you rather she was crying?"

By the voice, she guessed him to be one of the younger ones—probably the weedy kid, fifteen at most, and twitchy with nerves. "I'd rather she shut up.

Do you have any idea how far noise like that's gonna carry, once we're out in the desert?"

Better than you do. Instead she answered, "Let her tire herself out now; then she'll be quiet later. The hard part's still ahead of us."

"Nobody asked you," the boy said, but it was sullen rather than threatening. When nobody else spoke up in his support, he made a disgusted sound and fell silent. The mother was stiff at Inés' side, but she made no protest when Inés held her fingers out blindly, for the baby to play with. A bump in the road sent her backpack toppling from her lap, but an anonymous hand pushed it back into place.

Some time after that, the truck slowed, turned, left the paved road. Inés guessed they had been driving for maybe three hours; presuming they were going east, that put them well past Yuma, into the harsh desert of Sonora. So far, at least, the rumors were true.

Knowing still didn't prepare her for what greeted the migrants when the truck rattled to a halt and Pipo let them out. All around was hard dirt and scrub brush, blue and gray beneath the brilliant canopy of the stars. Inés found herself suddenly, irrationally reluctant to leave the truck; it was the only human thing in sight, and once it was gone, they would be completely at the mercy of the coyotes.

Where is El Rojo?

He appeared without warning, from what Inés would have sworn was an empty patch of desert. The coyote sauntered toward them, hands comfortably in his pockets, but she wasn't fooled by the show of relaxation; the wary grace of his movement said he was very much alert. "Any trouble?" he asked.

Pipo bent to murmur in his ear. Inés, straining to hear, caught a scrap about the baby. El Rojo's lip curled in annoyance, and her muscles tensed. But the mother had paid, and a coyote who abandoned his cargo too easily would soon get a reputation that destroyed future business. He waved Pipo back, and turned his attention to the waiting group.

"Listen carefully," he told them, in a quiet voice that raised the hairs on Inés' neck, "because anybody who dies from not paying attention won't be my problem.

"We're going over the fence. Pipo and the boys will show you how. Anybody who makes a sound while we're climbing over will pay for it. Anybody who hesitates gets left behind. When I run, you run until I stop. Anybody who can't keep up, gets left behind. We'll go until midday, rest for four hours, move again. I say 'quiet,' you shut up or pay for it. I say 'hide,' you go straight for the nearest cover, get low, don't move until I tell you. Me and the boys leave, you stay where you are, unless you feel like dying. I give you any other orders, you obey, and don't ask questions. Got it?"

He waited until every migrant had nodded. Nobody dared make a sound, not even to say yes. When he had agreement, El Rojo said, "Let's go."

The fence was a black scar across the desert's face, looming high overhead. No cameras or lights out here, Inés knew, unless vigilantes on the other side had installed their own—but she trusted El Rojo to be canny enough to know if they had. Didn't trust the man any further than that, but to be competent at his business, yes. He had a good system for crossing, too. Pipo made a cup of his hands and lifted his boss to the top of the wall, where El Rojo balanced easily and unfurled a rope ladder, which one of the other men staked down in the dirt. It seemed considerate, until Inés saw how much more quickly people climbed, not having to rappel; and the ladder was more portable than a rigid one, less permanent than a tunnel. It fit everything she knew about him: quick, simple, and above all, efficient.

It was hardest for the women with small children. Mindful of El Rojo's warning, Inés held out her hands wordlessly; after a moment's hesitation, the mother she'd been sitting next to handed over her daughter, then climbed the ladder. When she was at the top, Inés stretched up to give the sleepy infant back. Then she did the same for the other two, quickly soothing the one baby who looked likely to fuss. Pipo glared, but said nothing.

She was the last one over, except for the coyotes. Not letting herself hesitate, Inés balanced on the swaying rope ladder and scrambled up to the top. With her hands braced on the fence's edge, she swung one leg over—and there she paused.

One foot in each world. It felt like it should mean something, like this fence, this barrier dividing one nation from its neighbor, should mark some profound transition. It didn't. The desert on the far side looked no different. It was all borderland, and its inhabitants, regardless of nation, had more in common with each other than with those who lived inside. She had always stood with one foot in each world; only now it was literally true.

Inés swung her other leg over and dropped to the ground below. Now she was just another illegal immigrant, risking her life to enter the United States.

As soon as she landed, El Rojo began to run.

Across the hard-packed stripe of the border road, through the scrubby bushes beyond, not waiting for the coyotes to pack up the ladder and climb down after them. They, Inés supposed, would catch up soon. The pace El Rojo set was steady, but not too fast; they would be at this for a while. She settled her backpack on her shoulders and relaxed into her stride.

The ones with children had it worst. Inés hung back, trying with her presence to give them support; it was easier to run in company than alone. The baby girl she'd played with in the truck, jolted into unhappy wakefulness, started to wail, and the mother clapped a desperate hand over her daughter's mouth. Inés tensed, looking at El Rojo, but it seemed the order against noise had only applied at the fence.

Or perhaps the paying would come later.

She worried about the older man, too. This would be a hard enough journey for her, and she was young, fit, and used to the trials of the desert. How much worse would it be for him? But the man had energy enough to spare her a rueful smile as he ran. Inés wondered what his story was. Everyone who crossed the border had one.

Running, running through the night, El Rojo in the lead, and Inés fixed her gaze on his back, as if he were prey she would wear down and finally catch.

By the time they slowed to a walk, many of the migrants were gasping. Everyone reached for water; the less cautious gulped theirs, thinking only of immediate thirst, and not the miles of desert that still lay ahead. Inés sipped cautiously, trying to estimate how far they'd come. Two miles from the border? To the left, the ground rose in a thin, jagged line. The Sierra Pinta, if she was reading their location right. El Rojo would take them through the San Cristobel wash and south of Ajo Peak, to the Tohono O'odham reservation. The people there had rescued more than a few migrants from death in the desert. Not all of those they rescued were reported to the Border Patrol, either; the Tohono O'odham knew what it was like be split apart by a fence. Some of their kin lived on the other side.

They got a short break at sunrise, among a scattering of saguaro that would hide them from distant eyes. Inés took a hat from her bag, then slipped her hand back in, hunting by touch, until she found the rubber-banded tin tucked inside her one clean shirt. She waited until the coyotes were looking elsewhere, then shifted the tin into her pocket, where she could reach it more quickly.

A scuff of foot against stone made her jump. The older man held up calming hands, then crouched at her side and murmured, "Miguel."

"Inés," she murmured back, keeping a wary eye on the coyotes.

"You seem well prepared."

The practiced lie rose easily to her lips. "My brother crossed a few years ago. Gave me some advice."

He smiled. "Brothers are like that."

Eduardo *had* given her advice, when she showed up on his doorstep in Cuauhtémoc. Much of it had involved swearing. Not that he doubted what Inés had to say; Mother had once sent him out into the desert, too, as she had later done with Inés. But he thought she should let it go. Or let someone else take care of it—as if that had done any good yet.

And she owed Javier too much to let it go.

"If an old man can give you advice, too," Miguel said, even quieter than before, "watch out for that one." He made a tiny gesture toward El Rojo. "He's got his eye on you. But not in the usual way."

Inés' fingers tightened on her backpack. "What do you mean?"

Miguel shook his head. "I don't know. The big one, he wants what you'd expect, but the leader . . . he's watching you for something."

For what, Inés wanted to ask—but El Rojo rose smoothly to his feet, and they had to follow. It wasn't a question Miguel could likely answer, anyway.

With the sun now up, the desert rapidly heated from pleasantly cool to sweltering. Inés and Miguel both took turns carrying the small children, to give their mothers a rest. Why were they crossing now, in the brutal conditions of summer? Couldn't they wait for milder weather? She bit back the desire to yell at the mothers for stupidity. She didn't know their reasons. And it would upset the kids, who out of all those here were completely blameless. Not that innocence would save them, if immigration agents caught their families; they would be deported back to Mexico, with or without their parents.

Inés gritted her teeth and kept walking.

When the noon halt came, people sank down wherever they stood, trembling and drenched with sweat. El Rojo wandered among them, cursing and kicking, until everyone was as hidden as they could get. Even in this desolation, they couldn't assume they would remain unnoticed; the so-called Minutemen rode through here on their self-appointed patrols, and some of them were far too ready to shoot.

Miguel joined Inés in her clump of creosote. The bushes didn't offer much in the way of shelter, not with the sun directly overhead, but it was all they had. The older man offered her beef jerky; Inés gave him chips in exchange, wishing she had brought more. They made her thirsty, but it was necessary to replace the salt lost through sweat, and she could tell that few of the migrants had known to bring their own. She hoped they found a cache of water left by one of the humanitarian groups; some people hadn't brought enough.

Murmurs rose here and there as people made brief conversation, then gave it up out of exhaustion. One curt order, though, made Inés stiffen: El Rojo, speaking to the mother whose daughter had fussed the most. "Come with me."

Miguel's hand clamped down on Inés' arm before she could move. "Don't."

"I can't let him—" Inés growled, trying to rise. El Rojo was leading the young woman to the far side of a cluster of ocotillo.

"Yes, you can," Miguel hissed. "Look." He jerked his chin; Inés, following, saw Pipo watching her. *He wants what you'd expect*, Miguel had said—what El Rojo was about to take from that woman. *Something else to offer*, the coyote in the cantina had said. For all she knew, this was part of the woman's bargain with El Rojo. Which didn't make it right, didn't make it okay—

You aren't here to rescue them, Inés. Not like that. Don't forget your purpose.

She sagged back down, defeated, and tried to sleep. It wasn't the heat and relentless sun that kept her awake, though, but the muffled sounds from nearby.

They rested through the hottest part of the day, then rose to walk some more. Now it was clear that, however hard the night and morning had been, that was only the beginning of their trials; stiff muscles protested, and weariness made everyone clumsy. One of the young men stumbled on his way down a slope, nearly falling, putting Inés' heart in her mouth; if he twisted an ankle, he was dead. Nobody would carry him, not all the way to the reservation. He regained his balance, unharmed, and they went on.

Until the sun set and the desert air cooled, and Inés, stupid with exhaustion, began to wonder if all this risk and effort was going to come to nothing whatsoever, except an embarrassed trek back to Phoenix, and a passport in her mailbox with no stamp marking her return to the United States. *It isn't nothing,* she thought, *you know about El Rojo now, and can tell—*

"Hide," the coyote snarled.

The migrants didn't move fast enough. They'd been stumbling along, one foot in front of the other, like zombies, and now they stared at him; Pipo and the others began shoving people to the ground as distant headlights sliced through the thickening dusk.

Inés remained standing, staring, until Pipo knocked her down, almost into the spines of an ocotillo. Two lights, moving independently: all-terrain motorcycles, not a Jeep. Border Patrol, not vigilantes, and following their trail from the fence.

A low, quiet laugh from El Rojo raised all the hairs along her arms and neck. "Come on, boys."

Making only a little more noise than the desert wind, he and his three fellows loped off toward the approaching motorcycles.

Inés shoved a hand into her pocket, pulling out the rubber-banded tin. When she rose to a crouch, Miguel whispered, "What are you doing?" He wasn't close enough to grab her.

Keeping those agents alive. "Stay here," she hissed back, and ran before he could protest.

She kept low, taking advantage of the scant cover. Already she'd lost sight of El Rojo and the others, but that wouldn't matter for long. She just needed to get far enough away from the migrants. . . .

Good enough. Inés dropped to one knee, stripped out of her clothes, and pulled the rubber band off the tin.

The pungent smell of the *teopatli* inside rose into the dry air. Its scent brought memories swarming around her like ghosts: her first visit to Cuauhtémoc, at the age of fifteen, re-united after seven years with the family she had lost. Her mother sending her out into the desert, with *teopatli* for her skin and *pulque* to drink and a maguey thorn to pierce her tongue, as her ancestors had done for generations before.

Careful despite her haste, Inés dipped her fingers in the paste, and began to dab it onto her body. Legs, back, arm, face, rings and clusters of spots, and even before she was done she could feel the *ololiuqui* seeds ground into the paste taking effect. Her vision swam, going both blurry and sharp, and smells assaulted her nose. Then everything came together with a bone-wrenching snap, and leaving tin and clothes behind, Inés ran once more.

The coyotes weren't hard to follow now. They feared no predators, out here in the desert; Border Patrol, vigilantes, ranchers, all were just different kinds of prey. They ran together for a time, then fanned out, and Inés went after the nearest, knowing she would have to be fast.

He was on his way up a steep rise, aiming for a cliff from which he could leap. Inés caught him halfway, slamming his wiry body to the ground, her jaws seeking and then finding his skull, teeth punching through into his brain. The coyote died without a sound, as in the distance, the barking calls of his brothers pierced the night air.

The motorcycles growled lower at the sound, but they were still approaching much too fast. Inés ran again, the *teopatli* giving her strength she'd lacked before. She was made for the stalking ambush, not the chase, but the lives of those two agents depended on her speed. The second coyote died with his throat crushed. The noise dropped sharply; one of the engines had stopped. She caught the third coyote on his way toward the motorcycles, and this one saw her coming; he twisted away from her leap, yipping in surprise, before going down beneath her much greater weight.

Even as the hot blood burst into her mouth, she heard a scream from the direction of the engines—a human scream.

Cold blue light flooded the narrow valley where the migrants had walked. One of the motorcycles had fallen on its side; the rider lay moaning and bleeding. His partner had a shotgun out, and was pointing it in every direction, unsure where the next attack would come from. If Inés wasn't careful, he would shoot her instead.

Now it was time for the stalk. She circled the area slowly, paws touching down with silent care, nose alive to every scent on the wind. She thought the third coyote had been Pipo—couldn't be sure—but the last was El Rojo. He was the smart one, the subtle one, the sorcerer who had given them all coyote shape, the better to hunt the humans who came to hunt them.

He knew she was out here. Inés realized that when she found his trail looping upon itself, confusing his scent. He'd heard Pipo die, of course—but maybe he'd known since before then. *He's watching you for something*, Miguel had said. Maybe El Rojo recognized a fellow sorcerer when he saw one.

On an ordinary night, she wouldn't have been stupid enough to approach the overhang. But the strength the *teopatli* gave her was no substitute for sleep; Inés' human mind was sluggish, ceding too much control to the beast.

A weight crashed into her back. Pain bloomed hot along her nerves as the coyote's jaws closed on her neck. Acting on instinct, Inés collapsed and rolled, dislodging El Rojo. When she regained her feet, she saw at last the creature she had come all this way to hunt.

His coat was different than the others', more uniform in color along the head and back. In sunlight, it would be reddish brown. El Rojo, the red one, whose jaws now dripped red with her blood. Who had murdered Javier, and Consuela, and David, ranchers and vigilantes, and probably some migrants, too. Coyote attacks, the official reports said; they were suddenly more common than before. But agents of the Border Patrol died more often in the line of duty than any other federal law enforcement division, and the people in charge were more concerned with human killers than animal attacks.

Only Inés suspected more. She could hardly tell anyone it was *nagualismo*, though, even if she admitted to being a *nagual* herself. And so she had gone south, into Mexico, returning as an illegal immigrant, to hunt the coyote who ran on both two legs and four.

They snapped and feinted at one another, El Rojo using his greater speed and agility. But that was a dangerous game for him to play, especially on his own; when coyotes hunted larger prey, they did so in packs, and his was dead. That was why he had ambushed her—and as if he remembered that at the same moment, El Rojo turned and ran.

Inés followed. It might be enough to have killed the others, or it might not. If he could share his *nagualismo* with anyone, it wouldn't take him long to be back in business. But it wasn't pragmatism that drove her; it was the memory of Javier's funeral, and his sister's grief. And her own devastated face, staring back at her from the mirror.

The beast wanted his blood.

And the beast was stupid, forgetting she wasn't the only predator out here tonight. The shotgun blast clipped her right hip, a few of the pellets raking bloody tracks into her fur. El Rojo had lured her back toward the motorcycles, and the agent with the gun. That man didn't know she was a friend. Inés roared, and leaped out of range.

Bleeding, trembling with exhaustion even the *teopatli* couldn't erase, she prayed, as she'd once prayed to the spirit of the day on which she was born. Alone in the desert, hallucinating and exhausted, bleeding from the tongue in the old manner, she'd begged the spirit to come—and the jaguar had answered.

El Rojo was creeping up behind her, not quite silent enough. Inés waited, paws braced against the rocky dirt. Closer. And closer.

When he leapt, she twisted to meet him, with all the speed and power of the jaguar.

One massive paw slammed him to the side. El Rojo yelped, but it cut off as her jaws found his neck. With a single bite, she severed his spinal cord, and his body went limp in the dust.

Panting, she stood over the body of her prey. Not far away, she heard the second engine start up again, and the crunching rush of the motorcycles driving away. The wounded agent was well enough to ride, then, and they'd given up the chase.

For now.

Inés licked her spotted fur clean as best she could. Then, wearily, strength fading again, she padded back along her own trail to her clothes and the tin of *teopatli*. Changing back to human form brought all her previous exhaustion and then some crashing down; she could barely persuade herself to get dressed. The only thing that moved her was the knowledge that sixteen frightened migrants waited in the darkness, knowing only what they heard: motorcycles and guns, coyotes and the roar of a jaguar. She hoped they hadn't run.

They hadn't. It would have been suicide, in desert territory none of them knew at all. Miguel stood up as Inés approached, and a few others followed suit, including the mother Inés had failed to protect from El Rojo.

The silence stretched out. She hadn't thought this far ahead, to what she would tell the migrants. Lack of energy made her blunt. "They're dead. The coyotes."

One of the other women whimpered. Inés stood, only half-listening, as a babble of questions and fear broke out. She didn't come out of her daze until Miguel drew close and said, "Do you know where we were going?"

The Tohono O'odham reservation, probably, where El Rojo would have had some means for them to continue onward. Inés didn't know what that would have been. But she knew some of the Indians protected migrants, and sent them along to others who could help.

Miguel saw it in her eyes. "You'll have to lead us, then."

Inés opened her mouth to answer him, then stopped. She had climbed the fence with these people; she had paid a coyote and gone into the desert, just like the rest of them, and that made them kin. Here in the middle of the wilderness, she could not say to Miguel, *I'm an agent of the U.S. Border Patrol. I don't do* coyotaje. *I arrest those who do.*

She would take them to the reservation, of course; it was that, or abandon them here to die. But when they arrived, she would have to hand them over, to be deported back to Mexico.

Her gaze fell on the young mother, with her infant daughter. Eduardo had been the same age when their mother carried him across the border. He was eleven when they deported him, with no memory of the "home" they were sending him back to; Mamá, caught in the same raid, had gone with him. Inés, born in the United States, had stayed, and lost her family for years.

She'd joined the patrol to fight drug smuggling, to end violence, not to hunt people who only wanted work and a better life. Sneaking across the desert, risking death every step of the way, was no kind of answer—but they had no other. And Inés could not tell these frightened, hopeful men and women and children that the dream was not for them.

"We'll rest for an hour," she said. "Then I'll take you someplace safe."

SWEAR NOT BY THE MOON

RENEE CARTER HALL

The wolf watches us from the far corner of the enclosure as the girl fumbles with her keys to let me inside. I don't bother to call to him; his hearing isn't as good as it used to be, and besides, he won't come near until we're alone.

In the brochure, they called the enclosure an "enriched personal habitat," but it's really more of a pen, a section of grass and trees fenced with chain link. They've tried to make the grounds look something like a forest, but the effect is too neatly trimmed to be convincing. Instead, it looks more like a park—or a zoo.

The only thing that's wild here is him.

In the nearest corner, a three-sided wooden shelter shades two stainless steel bowls. One holds fresh water, changed every hour—a touch I appreciate—and the other is half-filled with a pile of pink beef scraps.

I watch two flies buzz around the meat. It doesn't look like he's touched it at all.

I sigh and turn back to the girl, who has already closed the gate behind me. "Has he eaten anything today?"

She glances at his chart. "No, sir, not today. They tried giving him venison this morning like you asked, but he didn't eat any of it."

"Was it cold?"

Even with the chain link separating us, she blanches under my gaze, and I look away briefly to make her more comfortable. I know, then, that she has no *faol* blood in her. "I don't know," she says.

I try to keep my voice gentle. "He won't eat it unless it's warm."

She jerks a nod. "I'll make a note, sir."

I don't doubt that she will. They love notes at this place: charts and paperwork and orders typed in all caps. But I wonder if they ever bother to read any of them. One shift ends, another one starts, and you might as well have never said anything in the first place.

If it's frustrating for me, I can only imagine what it's like for him. At least I can still speak.

"Thank you," I tell her, though I'm not really sure what I'm thanking her for. "I'll find you if we need anything else."

She locks the gate and hurries away. I wonder how long she'll keep working here.

I double-check that the gate is closed securely, then sit down on the wooden bench under one of the trees. The wolf whines softly as he rises and comes to me. He is thinner than the last time I saw him, and his gait is stiff-legged. If he hasn't been eating, he likely hasn't gotten many pills down for his arthritis, either. He thrusts his muzzle against my hands, and I stroke his silver head lightly, respectfully.

"Hi, Dad," I whisper.

I remember the first time I saw him in wolfshape. He told me not to be afraid, but still, watching the full-body grimace of the change was terrifying to a ten-year-old. It reminded me of the horror movies where you think you're approaching a loved one from behind, until they turn around and the music shrieks and you realize you're seeing the monster instead.

But at the end of it, he wasn't a monster. He was a strong, healthy gray wolf, lean muscle, lush pelt, white teeth. As a man, he had always seemed to me somehow smaller, weaker than the other fathers I saw—although I hated to admit that, even to myself—but as a wolf, he was powerful, he was fierce, and I felt I was seeing his true self for the first time. It was disorienting and wonderful.

As a wolf, I turned out to mirror him in miniature, a fact that pleased me immensely.

He taught me what it meant to be *faol*, to carry a wildness within you. The wolf is always there in your mind, even in human shape, just as the human side of you still lingers in wolfshape. In form, you are one or the other. But in your mind, you are neither, and both. And it is so much simpler, and so much more complicated, than that sounds.

There were no large packs near our home, but he took me to the others within our range. I saw them bare their throats and bellies to him, saw them lick his muzzle. The wolf in me knew what that meant without being told, and the boy in me nearly burst with pride.

Two females ran with that group, both with silver coats and sweet voices, but while they fawned over my father, he never took any special notice of them that I could see. My mother had been gone almost since I could remember, and I asked my father once why I couldn't have one of these for a mother.

He smiled. "The wolf wants to make things easy," he said at last, "but the man knows it isn't that simple. As a wolf, I could. As a man . . . " He didn't finish, and, sensing something in his silence, I never asked him about it again.

Those were star-filled nights, summer-sweet, and like all children, I never imagined they would end.

"Dad," I say now, "you have to eat something. I know it's not what you're used to . . . "

He looks up, his golden eyes cloudy. I can't read his expression, can't tell if he's pleading with me or simply struggling to focus.

"For me, okay? Just a little. I'll bring some liver next time." For one crazy moment I wonder if I could smuggle something alive in here—a calf or a lamb or even a rabbit. He needs hot meat, blood meat, but I don't know if he even has the strength left to make a kill.

The wolf, in the end, is greedy. Bit by bit, year by year, it grows in the mind. Some happily take to the woods for good, as far from humans as they can get. Others hold out as long as they can, until they can no longer change back to human form. Born as men, *faol* die as wolves.

He always swore he would know when that time came. Sometimes he talked of getting to the national park a few hours' drive away. Sometimes he talked about the gun in his nightstand drawer.

That day when I went to his house, when I hadn't heard from him and he wasn't answering the phone, I didn't know what I would find. And so when I saw him lying in wolfshape in front of the old recliner, the TV still tuned to the baseball game, I was glad. Even when his eyes met mine and I could somehow taste the sorrow and defeat that hung about him—even then, I was glad.

I glance back at the gate, but there's no sign of the girl or anyone else. I take my clothes off, carefully arranging them on the bench so they won't get dirty or wrinkled. The change comes swiftly and easily.

I tuck my tail, lower my ears, whine, and lick his muzzle. His eyes brighten, and his tail lifts a little higher.

I long to run, to play the way we used to. But I don't know if he can keep up, and I won't make him feel weak if he can't. In the end, we settle in a patch of shade, with tiny ants tickling our paw-pads. I breathe in his scent, and it makes me feel little again, safe again. He dozes, and I wonder what he dreams about. If he remembers me, is it as a wolf-pup, or his son?

My human mind whispers that I can't stay much longer. I lick his ear gently to wake him up, and as he stretches stiffly and yawns, I get an idea. Tail high, ears up, I trot to his dish. Just as I lower my head to the meat, he growls, and I look up to see him standing with his lips pulled back from yellowed teeth. Instinct has won out over stubbornness.

I back off, allowing him his place. He eats most of the meat, then steps aside, and I finish. The taste of it makes me shudder—I'm used to meat either cooked or fresh, not raw and sun-stale—but I force myself to swallow. Afterward, we wash the juices from each other's faces, just as we used to wash the blood away after a kill.

He whines as I walk back to the bench. I want to stay with him; I want to leave.

The change back to human form is a bit like pushing a wheeled cart over a threshold—a little more force, more of a jolt than the slip into wolfshape. Right now it is still as effortless as breathing, but I know it will gradually get more difficult. And then, one day . . .

I try not to think about it.

He lies down and rests his chin on his paws, watching as I get dressed. Does he still remember how it felt to tuck in a shirt, pull up a zipper, buckle a belt? Or has the wolf-mind carried those memories away, buried them in the scent of dead leaves and the dreams of moon-dappled deer? I don't even know how many words he still understands, but I speak anyway, if only for myself. I speak the words that I couldn't say out loud to the man, the ones I can say only now, to the wolf.

"I love you." I lift the keypad cover on the gate and enter the code to unlock it. "I'll be back soon."

As I close the gate behind me, the low, throbbing howl begins. A moment later, the others join in, the song echoing through the enclosures, and even in human form I can still pick out his voice among the chorus, rising above the others, dying away into a moan, then rising again.

I get to the car, but even with the doors and windows shut, I can still hear them. I put my hands over my ears like a child, rest my forehead against the steering wheel, and weep.

Night falls clear and cool, and I run alongside a white-furred female, our paws skimming the ground. Last night, the two of us shared linguini and red wine; tonight, if the wind is with us, we will feed from an aging doe.

Running is a joy, a song in my blood. I am a pup no longer; I am as fine and strong now as my father was when I first saw him in wolfshape. I am drunk on the night and the run and the she-wolf's scent in my lungs.

And yet.

As I leap to bring the doe to the ground, as I join the tussle of teeth tearing at the hide, as the first hot sweetness of blood tingles in my nostrils, I pray that one day the deer's hard, sharp hoof will find me, a single well-placed blow to blaze my life to its close. Before my eyes dim and my hearing dulls, before the chain-link fence and the stainless steel dish. Before I hold a pistol, or a noose, or the keys to my car, and try to decide. Before it's too late to decide at all. The wolf I am hopes it will be that easy.

But the man knows it isn't that simple.

INFESTED

NADIA BULKIN

—◄═►—

May in the city is the Month of the Missing, and on May 21st the mother of the Cunningham children went the way of a dozen lost teenagers and custody battle babies, as well as uncountable undesirables. She did not come to wake them in the morning, with a shake of the shoulder and a soft "Wakey wakey." Their father said that she had run off with "some son of a bitch" from her office. "No one we know," he said.

It saddened and confused Hazel, because there hadn't been any yelling the night before. Ace was so distressed that he forgot how to tie his shoes and threw up his blue Chemik-O's in the corner trashcan. Hazel had to hold his hand all the way to the subway stop on 84th.

"Maybe she'll come back," Hazel said as they waited for the Red Train. Ace was still pouting, but no longer holding her hand. "Maybe she just had to clear her head." After all there had been times when their mother would pace the apartment with her fingers pressed to her temples, saying she could not hear herself think, saying she had to get out from under these four walls. She always went out to the hall to cry. Their father said it was no way for a mother to behave, but Mom didn't know any other way to be.

"Daddy said no," said Ace. "Daddy said she's just gone."

Daddy had clearly been in pain. He'd sat in the kitchen like normal, with his green coffee mug steaming and his floppy newspaper open to Opinion, but today his fingers trembled as if the ritual was just for show. He said their mother had always been selfish, a quitter, and he shouldn't have expected anything different. Then he said "sorry," which was disconcerting.

On the platform they stood next to a harried man who kept adjusting his tie. A red-haired woman was following him—her eyes were just as bloodshot as his, but her face was rockier, stormier. The man must have known he was being stalked, because he was itchy and jumpy and kept peering down the tunnel, willing the Red Train to come. At first the woman hid behind columns, but she became more brazen as his discomfort grew. When at last he dropped his suitcase and started to choke, she moved into the open.

"How do you like it?" she shouted, although he was too distressed to respond. "Being turned inside out? You see who you are under all that bull? You're scum! Human filth!"

The man was transforming. His hands disappeared up his sleeves, and his height shrank with his shuddering legs. His head withered and twisted like a sweater wrung by a washing machine—for a second, onlookers caught a glimpse of something pale and worm-like where his head should have been, something much like a fetus—and then his entire body collapsed into a heap of clothes. A chorus of shrieks finally broke loose.

The woman's voice was an edict, her finger the only arrow she needed. She silenced the crowd. "That man messed with my little girl! He isn't fit to live!" A murmur spread outward through the platform, as if she had begun a giant game of telephone. "Run, you weasel!"

A brown wriggling animal darted out from under the man's shirt and half-scurried, half-swam toward the edge of the platform. Commuters screamed again, clutching their own clothes as if to keep their bodies from tumbling out. They gave the weasel a wide berth. Rent-a-cops hurried over with BB guns, but the weasel jumped down to the tracks and escaped into the underground, too small to be lit by the green torches on the wall.

"There you go!" the woman shouted. A rent-a-cop tried to restrain her, but his efforts were half-hearted and she shook him away. When she looked around the platform, everyone avoided her gaze. "The police won't help you. The law won't help you. This is what good people have to do these days. This is justice in our city!"

Charlie Cunningham introduced his children to his new girlfriend at the zoo. She was sitting by the large panda statue with her purse in her lap; when she saw them coming she stood and waved. Her name was Paige, and she was skinny and dark-haired. *Almost as pretty as Mom*, the children thought. But up close she looked cold—not cruel, just very cold. Like someone dead dressed up in rouge.

"Paige works for a City Councilman. Theo Robson. Pretty impressive, huh?"

It wasn't, not really—their mother had been a paralegal and after she came home late smelling like cranberry cough syrup she used to tell the funniest stories about city politicians—besides, they could hear the sarcastic bite in their father's voice. Paige lowered her eyes demurely and tucked her hair behind her ear. "It's nothing fancy, I know," she said. Charlie smiled and took her waist.

The shaded walkways of the zoo were quiet—it was late in the season and the day—but the animals were restless for feeding time. Charlie left the children with Paige at the Sea Lion Pavilion. "You know what we need?" he said. "Ice cream." He said "ice cream" as if he meant "bullets."

Paige said, "Don't worry, I'll watch them," and Charlie gave her a tight smile of approval. He was trying to trust her enough to let her into the fortress, but Hazel could see that he didn't look at Paige the way he'd looked at their mother. There was not enough feeling there. Not enough hate.

The sea lions—Goonie and Cha-Cha—tossed and dove in the artificially aquamarine water. It took them four seconds to cross their tank. Occasionally they would stop and look out through the glass with small oily eyes, watching their watchers with glazed boredom.

"Do you kids like monster stories?" Paige asked. "Or are they too scary for you?"

Ace liked zombies; the bloodier, the better. Hazel liked vampires. "Like Bigfoot?" Ace said. "He's not scary, he's just sad. And sea monsters aren't real."

"You're thinking much too big," said Paige. "Have you ever heard of pest-people? They're cursed to live as little tiny vermin. You know, rats and things."

"That's *really* not scary," said Hazel, but Paige's stare made her shrink into her jacket.

"Imagine if you were turned into a skink, and instead of going to the zoo with your daddy, you'd be using your little rubber legs to run away from the whole world, full of predators that want to eat you. Wouldn't that be monstrous?"

"You can do that to people?" For some reason it seemed worth asking.

Paige giggled. "I know someone who can. A sorceress."

Ace crinkled up his nose. "Like the Green Witch in Boxland?"

"Yes, like that." Paige smiled. "Except she doesn't fly. She has an apartment in the Rattle and a magic knee. If you were just a little naughty, she might turn you into something cute and put you in a zoo. But if you were really bad, she'll make a gutter-rat out of you."

The sea lions nipped at each other's fins. They churned like hamsters in a wheel.

Charlie waved goodbye to Paige out by the gift shop after buying her a dolphin-shaped mood necklace. "Say goodbye, kids," he said, and the children shook their new poorly-stitched sea lions. Surrounded by dormant machines, Paige looked even more like a tender will-o-wisp, glowing with dead light.

A flier tucked beneath their windshield wipers advertised a Pest Transformation Service run by a man named Dr. Terry Devine. *Total Transformation Guaranteed, Short 3 Day Turn-Back, All Types of Pests Available! Bring this flier in for a 20% discount.* Ace read it to their father as they drove home.

"I think it's good," said Charlie, nodding. "It's street justice is what it is. Those people that get turned into pests are bad folks, I think that's obvious. Criminals. Assholes. Derelict people. People who've been cheating the system and mooching off everyone else. The thing about life, see, is that everybody gets what they deserve. Call it what you want, karma, whatever. But maybe this'll make people treat each other better."

"And they can't ever turn back into people?"

"They can turn back every once in a while, for a couple of days. Just like shapeshifters change back into coyotes for a day and a half." He glanced at them through the rearview mirror. "Couple guys at work used it to take care of some low-lives. Have you seen that sign at Mr. Lowe's bodega? Act Like Vermin, Get Treated Like One." He laughed. "Good for him."

"What if somebody turns Mr. Lowe into a pest first?"

He gave Hazel a stern look. "Cursing people takes money. Like everything else in life."

After a few blocks of silence, Ace said, "I miss Mom."

Their father's sigh sounded like the whirr of a rickety fan. "I wish she could come back and give you an answer for why she left us, champ, because I sure as hell don't have one."

They passed animals on the street; frogs in drains and blackbirds on awnings and more than the regular number of mice eating out of garbage cans. People came after them with kicks and brooms but being so small the pests vanished into the crevices of the city's architecture, up into pipes and down into tunnels.

A cat appeared on the fire escape outside the children's bedroom while they were practicing mathematics. It looked nearly drowned with stormwater—there had been a big rain the night before. Ace and Hazel eyed each other, twirling their mechanical pencils. Their father was out having dinner with Paige—she had come over to cook for them but had cried into the marinara sauce when she wasn't even cutting onions. Charlie said she'd gotten bad news about Mr. Robson and told the kids to microwave a pizza. He said to keep the door locked, but nothing about the windows.

After they swaddled the cat in towels, they saw it was an orange tabby. Judging by its tangible ribs and dirty fur—still stinking of the world—the cat no longer belonged to anyone. Even so it clung to the children with desperation, as if dangling from a precipice. Its claws poked through their sweaters and drew little teases of blood.

The cat had unusually long canine teeth: unsightly fangs that kept catching on the lip of the dolphin-safe tuna can. Ace christened it Smilodon and the cat looked at him wearily. It humored their play—chased their shoe laces, let them rub its belly, barely yelped when Ace accidentally stepped on its tail—it must have been glad just to be on the inside looking out. Only when they heard footsteps in the hall did the cat become feral again.

Retribution was swift. Retribution was loud. Their father threw the marinara sauce, the coffee maker, and a meat cleaver, though he refused to touch the cat with his hands. Smilodon not only dodged these missiles but hissed back, taking bold jumps toward Charlie and clawing at his socks. Every time the cat shrieked like a howling baby, Paige whimpered as if being socked. "This is bad," she said. "This is bad, Charlie, this is bad . . . "

Hazel tried to gather up the skittering cat while Ace held back their father's arm. Charlie threw another object with his free hand—his green coffee mug—and hit Hazel between her shoulders. She glanced back at him, wounded, and Charlie's arms dropped.

"Do you have any clue what's happening out there?" Charlie was biting his lip and letting his eyes droop like almonds, but every time his defenses slipped he would pound his voice against the ceiling and get the grind back into his face. He had to present a strong front. "You know what kind of danger you're putting us in? This isn't one of your little fantasies, Hazel!"

Hazel and Ace chased the cat into the hall, through the fire door, and down the metal staircase. It looked back at them with wistful, shelter-me eyes. "You can't stay here," the children said, and ushered it out the back door. The cat ran around the corner of the building with its tail to the ground—they tried to follow, to make sure it would be all right, but the alley before garbage day was a miniature city unto itself.

They did not find the cat, but they did find a homeless man in that crack in the great wall of the North Sleeper neighborhood. He was pushing a shopping cart full of rats with gouged eyes and crippled pigeons and squirrels whose tails had been burned to the bone, patients from an animal hospital. Less heavily wounded animals followed the man on foot, circling his bandages, nibbling at debris. The man sang in a voice that was cracked and light as aluminum foil, but the children couldn't understand him. Something about a preacher and a creature?

"Are you one of 'em?" Ace asked. "One of those pest-people?"

"No!" the man shouted. "And they're not either! So you just leave us alone!"

"You should turn them in to Pest Control," said Hazel, reciting what she had heard at an assembly. "Vermin spread disease and consume resources, even the ones that don't start off as people."

The man scowled. "You two can go to hell, and take this damn city with you!"

Upstairs, Hazel hesitated before re-entering the apartment. Her back was still sore. She was afraid that she had been cast out of her father's fortress. Paige and Charlie were shrieking at each other inside—it was almost like old times. "Did you see its teeth? What did she tell you about the cat, Charlie? Is that what she said it would look like?" "Look, you better get a hold of yourself before the kids get back . . . " "Or you're gonna *what*? You're gonna what?"

Ace fearlessly opened the door and grabbed Hazel's hand. He said "come on" and Hazel went in, even though she saw this castle sinking.

In music class, a boy named Abel Farrow shoved Ace so hard that he cut his lip open against a plastic desk. Abel had chosen Ace as a victim back in September—skinny, bug-eyed Ace, out of all the fourth-graders at Independence Elementary. The substitute didn't know what to do—their regular music teacher, whom no one liked, had not been to school all week. Rumors were running rampant that she had been turned into some kind of pest, probably one of the slick black crows that circled the nearby cathedral.

When Hazel saw his bruised mouth, she tried to teach him tricks to stay invisible. But Ace didn't want to be invisible. He wanted payback. "Paige knows where to go," he said.

They got the chance to ask her when their father went out for "supplies"—public health officials were going on about the need for heightened pest control in case of an infestation—and told Paige to put his children to bed.

"Why do you want to know?" asked Paige, leaning against their bookshelf.

"Because I want to curse a kid at school," said Ace.

Paige tipped her head back against the wall, eyes on the smoke detector. "Can I tell you a story first, about the curse?" They shrugged, so she went on. "My boss, Mr. Robson, was running a race—not a *race* race, but a popularity race, do they have those yet at your age?—against a man named Mr. Malachi. He asked me to help. So I went to the Rattle and I said to the sorceress, 'Please turn Mr. Malachi into a rat.' But just before the sorceress started working her magic bone, she said to me . . . " Paige lifted her hands as if to conduct a chamber choir. " 'Magic comes at a price! I hope you're ready to pay it!' I didn't want to believe her. I thought she was just trying to scare me, the way witches do."

They asked what happened next, but Paige seemed distracted. She was running her finger over her little white teeth. "Even little pests can bite," she mumbled.

"Did Mr. Malachi turn into a rat?"

"Oh, yes," said Paige, and then abruptly raised her voice. "Has your daddy ever told you where we met?" No, he hadn't. He just said, *I'd like you to meet someone*, and *I want you to be nice to her*. And then there she was at the zoo, the dead woman in the nice dress—but Hazel didn't mention that. "He was next to me in line to see the sorceress. She warned us both."

"You're lying!" Ace shouted. "My Dad wouldn't curse anybody!"

Paige turned her glacial smile upon him. "You can hope so, sweetie. You know if you wish for something hard enough, you can start to believe it—until you find something else that proves you wrong, of course. Just like you can hope that ghosts aren't real until you meet one under your sheets."

Ace looked at the little blanketed hills—his feet—at the end of his bed.

"Who did Dad curse?" Hazel whispered.

Before Paige could answer, something small darted across the floor of the apartment above theirs. Paige jumped away from the bookshelf and grabbed at her scarf. She was ashen. The children gave her funny looks. "I'm scared of rats," she whispered.

"Why?"

"A rat ate out the neck of Mr. Robson's child. They follow me now, the rats do." She looked from Ace to Hazel. "I shouldn't have brought them here. You have your own vermin to deal with, and anyway . . . yours wouldn't like me being here."

"You're scaring Ace," Hazel said. Indeed, Ace's thumb was back in his mouth. He looked like a baby again, not the boy who'd said something back to Abel Farrow and called a cut lip no big deal. Hazel's memories of baby-Ace always included their Mama, holding him tucked in the crook of her arm. "Dad wants us to stay together."

Paige shuddered as if throwing off a heavy coat. "No," she said, and the despair in her voice made Hazel stop trying. "But you kids should be all right."

Their father came home with bags of pesticides and traps from Safeway. He had already arranged them on the kitchen table—spray cans and bottles in the back, repellent paste and traps and poison pellets in a mandala in the center—before he noticed that Paige was gone, and his children were watching coverage of the infestation well past their bedtime.

"Where's Paige?"

"I don't know," said Hazel. "Maybe the rats got her."

"What rats?" Charlie paused. "Hey, look at me. Something you want to tell me?"

Hazel shook her head. She at last recognized her father's pink, wide-eyed anger as an expression of his fear.

The Channel 8 reporter stood in a building that was silver-plated like a suit of armor, pointing at a small blue door. Pest Control officers in cardboard-colored jumpsuits passed behind her, yelling into their radios. "Shots were shots fired around six thirty this evening—calls started coming in of . . . *bats*, it looks like, several bats the size of dinner plates attacking residents and service personnel starting at three p.m. today."

Charlie sat down behind his children. "What is this garbage," he said, but he couldn't quite turn it off.

"A forty-two-year-old man and a twenty-nine-year-old woman were taken to the hospital with *severe* facial injuries. At least three other people were also injured. Jim, the residents of the Coldhook claim that the bats are actually *pest-people,* former tenants who were apparently *cursed* . . . if so, tonight's events certainly confirm reports that these so-called pest-people are unusually aggressive and extremely dangerous, in spite of their size . . . "

"So Paige left, huh." Charlie sank back into the couch, deflated after all his excitement over the pesticides.

"You can't trust nobody, Dad," said Ace, and Charlie lightly cuffed him on the chin.

"That's right, son. Look at you. Big tough guy."

"Where's Mom?" Hazel asked.

Charlie seemed flustered. "Don't know how many times I gotta tell you. I have no idea."

Maybe he wasn't lying. Their mother could be anywhere in the city's innards by now. On Channel 8, a black bat straight out of a Transylvanian castle swooped out of the basement door—Pest Control officers lifted their guns but the bat had woven itself into the feathery strands of the Channel 8 reporter's hair. The audio feed was quickly cut but they could see the terror and anguish on her face. It was cosmic, sublime; truly something to behold.

Traffic cones made a ring around the subway at 27th Street. Yellow tape and a metal safety gate stretched across its entrance. The children lurked around the corner and listened to sounds of battle—shrieks and bodies falling and flat slams of bone hitting bone—rising from below. "It's the pests," said Ace. "They took over the subway."

"But it doesn't sound like animals, does it?" said Hazel. "It sounds like people."

Ace's high-pitched whine—"Oh, *ma-an*"—drew the attention of one of the patrol cops guarding the subway station. He sauntered away from his post slowly at first, glancing both ways as if to cross the street, before lowering his shoulders and hurrying toward the children. They ducked behind a shuttered newsstand, but he found them there.

"You kids take the Red Train home from school? Station's closed today. It's nothing to worry about, it's just . . . " He was interrupted by a wet underground scream. He looked embarrassed. "It's not safe. Y'all better get along."

Hazel squeezed Ace's hand—it was cold and wet, like an aquarium eel. "There's the stop on 56th," she said to him, but the patrol cop cleared his throat.

"I wouldn't take the subway at all, hon." He whispered this as if he was himself scared, this big tall barrel-chested man in military colors. The absurdity of it almost made Hazel laugh, but she had learned long ago that adults did not want their emotions laughed at.

"We'll take the bus," she said.

"Good girl," said the patrol cop, and left.

They had not taken the city bus for years, not since the winter strike, and the bus shelter looked like an abandoned war bunker now. A glossy perfume poster was hidden behind Missing Pet and Missing Person signs, as well as Beware: Dangerous Pest notices. These came complete with pictures of snarling, bright-eyed rabbits and raccoons, and details of the pest-person's crimes against society: *Thief. Addict. COMPULSIVE LIAR.*

The children sat next to a teenage girl dressed in rags whose bare knees were pulled up to her chest. She smelled of sewage. She was gnawing at herself. An older woman with bursting grocery bags sat down on their left and sifted through her purchases, checking her receipts. Hazel took a peek at the bags and saw the same emergency stocks her father had started collecting during the war—freeze-dry food, cans of peaches, horrible whole grain crackers. "It's gonna get bad," the woman whispered when she saw Hazel looking. Her eyes were gleaming with joy. Hazel could bet she had already hoarded pesticides, and fantasized about introducing her to their father. "You know we're in for a fight. Oh, God, there's one of them there."

The woman's gaze had shifted to the ragged girl with soiled nails on the far end of the bench. "Kids, you'd better squeeze in close to me," she grunted. "She's a *pest*."

The girl was tugging at her matted hair. "I don't—don't—don't know what happened. I don't know how I got here, I just want to get home."

"Oh, I'm sure you know exactly what you did. They'll have boarded those doors when you get home, sweetie, I'll promise you that."

The girl's moan was bloated, like the sound of something rising through layers of mud. She spat up a bit of soap scum: hard to imagine what all she had been eating. It must have angered the woman, because she pulled a can of Home Defense out of her purse and sprayed it in the girl's eyes. The girl yelped—a shocking, harrowing noise—and fell forward onto her hands and knees on the pavement. There her muscles seemed to settle into a familiar, easy space. Her joints locked into position and her fingers caressed the gritty asphalt. The children wondered who she'd been before the change: a rave angel, a shoplifter, some anonymous angry sixteen-year-old that pissed off the wrong person? Whichever—she was something else now. Even semi-blind the girl scurried down the street, scraping the skin off her knees.

The woman settled back proudly, but there were others—shabby, disoriented people who jerked and stumbled down the sidewalks as if searching for something lost. They were side-stepped—with the city so nervous and quiet, this was not hard. Some passers-by did spit at them and hiss things. "Curse you," it looked like; it was what all the kids at school were saying. The returnees always snarled back. Everyone said that pests were twice as aggressive as natural animals, and no wonder, they had more to resent, more to grieve. Ace and Hazel watched this drama from the slow, shuddering safety of the city bus, but whenever they hit a stop light and one of the pest-people stared back at them, they'd duck down, breathing hard. What awful eyes those people had. Naked in their desperation.

Charlie was in one of his slow, smoldering bad moods, so they didn't tell him about the subway. People at work were going AWOL, he said, and he was sick of picking up their slack—but Hazel suspected he was worried.

They ate in silence because the television had become a nightmare-flood of infestation footage: cheap triage, shaky cam, people screaming with fear and rage in the dark. The hall outside their apartment filled this silence, not with rustling shopping bags or jangling keys or the neighbors' usual bitter mumbles—those comforting sounds had been absent for the past week—but with deep, slow creaks that came from right up against the other side of the wall, like an old boatman was rowing through the slate-blue carpet. "Maybe it's the super," said Charlie.

"I don't think so," said Hazel, and then someone knocked on the door. It startled all three—Charlie picked up his knife, Ace pushed away his plate, and Hazel stood. She walked to the door despite her father's yells, looking back over her shoulder once to say, "I'm just going to see who it is," and see Charlie stuck at the table, halfway between sitting and standing. His eyelids were trembling. He looked a little like Ace.

Hazel went up on her tiptoes and looked through the peephole. In the few seconds that she could balance without falling, she caught a flash of blond hair and clammy, dirty skin, like their visitor had been swimming in the Sound. She tasted salt and thought of the time they had gone—all four of them, back when their wounds were still whole—to the Sound and eaten hot dogs on the pier. The water had been too cold to swim in. *Wrong time of year*, their father said. *I told you so.* Dazed, Hazel unlocked the door.

"Hazel!" her father shouted, but it was too late.

The door handle began to turn and Hazel jumped back. After the door swung free of its latches, a pale hand snaked inside the fortress, followed by a pale woman. She had draped herself in plastic. She had no shoes. She smelled a bit like rotten fish—probably all she'd been able to get on good days. Despite all this, she grinned broadly when she saw the children. The corners of her mouth lifted to reveal two long and yellowed fangs.

Here she was, returned. Smilodon. Their mother. The children smiled back. Her expressions had always been contagious, and they had missed the warmth of her burning heart. Charlie sat. He was strangely calm. Maybe some tiny raw place in his heart was glad that she'd come back, even now and even like this, that she wasn't such a quitter after all. Lisa Cunningham pushed her heel against the door as if she was just coming home from the office—*tired, spent, flinging off her purse*—and shut it with a soft, finalizing click. The weight of the old plastered walls finally settled on their bones.

The children did not need to see this last fulfillment of their family saga. Hazel led Ace to a window, and from this vantage point they watched the progress of the infestation on the street below. There was motion in that coiled darkness, the frantic energy of vermin in mid-swarm. This crawling energy swept other things into its chaos: people, cars, the ground floors of buildings. Everything fell. Everything was punctured. Maybe that's what it means to be infested, Hazel whispered. She was holding her brother close, helping him block out the rest. Up and up the infestation climbed, drawing ever closer to their fortress in the sky.

WATCHMEN

AARON STERNS

The illuminated advertisement on the front of the cigarette-machine is a slivered beacon of blue sky and clouds amongst the smoke and strobe lights; a slice of heaven obscured by a couple deep in conversation: the guy all pained mouth and gesturing arms; the woman silent, staring. They are oblivious to the throng around as if enclosed in a vacuum. I stare at them from my post, trying to work out what they're saying—their voices drowned out by the brain-regressing bass pounding up through my feet—but an image of Lisa arguing with me kicks in and I have to flick my eyes away across the dancefloor. I try to suppress a surge of anger.

The straining flux of dancing bodies moves in waves of artfully-ripped faded clothing, bleached hair and pale flesh made gaunt and alien-blue by the overhead fluoros. The sunken dancefloor—the Pit—is huge, nearly fifty feet across, and it's hard to survey its entire length. I glance over at the other black-clad figures on their raised podiums: impassive dark statues almost lost in the belching haze of smoke machines and cigarette smoke, legs spread and hands clasped over their groins as if cupping themselves. They seem like ciphers to me, unsmiling names; protective of their cohesion. I'm still the interloper.

Two girls walk past below, staring up. One is breathtakingly beautiful: tight tan in red lycra, angry auburn hair and clear eyes. She smiles and I reflexively smile back, feeling instantly guilty. She pauses, tracing the neckline of her dress as if considering approaching my podium to stand at uncomfortable groin height and flash her hungry smile up at me, then runs a finger down her perfect cleavage. Unsettled, I'm about to look away when she flicks down the right side of her top to reveal a dusky nipple. She teases it to quick stiffness then disappears into the crowd, hungry eyes melting into the crush of bodies. Her friend follows.

The two-way almost slips from my sweaty hand as I try to track their passage towards the front of the club. I lose them amongst the squawking, impatient drinkers clamoring at the huge main bar for the attention of the bargirls. Disappointed, I glance up at the semi-circular balcony and its darkened tiered couches overlooking the main bar, the figures standing at its edge separated from death only by a thin brass railing. But the massive scale of this cavern has lost its novelty value by now and my gaze drops.

An angry voice pierces the oppressive techno music and I search again through the disorienting sweeping lasers. The man by the cigarette machine throws his hands in the air and stalks off. The girl stares transfixed, tears on cheeks. Just broken up, presumably. I shake my head and start to look away.

But the man can't let this go. He whirls and punches his girlfriend. Hard.

She crumples to the ground. The guy looks at her without expression, then reaches down and grabs her by the back of the neck and the waistband, lifting her off the ground to swing like a battering ram into the illuminated blue cigarette-machine. The crack sounds even above the deafening techno bass. The machine short-circuits and spits flame.

I slam into him too late and we skid through the crowd. His nose smacks into someone's shin in a spray of blood, and when he struggles against me I snap him in the nose again with the two-way, pinning him around onto his front so I can cradle his throat in the crook of my arm and lace the other arm behind his head. He tries to claw up at my arms, my eyes, but I put him out with a vicious tensing of my biceps, cutting off the circulation in his neck. I rest his deadweight on its side and bring the cracked and blood-flecked radio up to my mouth to call the others.

A group of middle-class yuppies ring me, too scared to help but perversely rooted in place by the bloody spectacle. I stare back from my crouch, wondering if the guy has friends here, if someone will launch from the crowd to kick at my face. I can't see the girl past the gathering designer jeans but don't want to risk leaving him alone: sleeper-holds aren't debilitating enough; when they wake they wake instantly, mad and in control—

and then splitting the crowd like huge black-clad figures of death, smoothshaven and short-haired, barely contained. They push the crowd back, striking one guy who won't move with an open hand to the face, sending him beneath their feet. A fury of movement around and then Lucs over me, omnipotent Lucs, always uncannily first on the scene, grabbing the unconscious boyfriend from me, eyes almost gleaming red in the searching light. Raph beside him, staring past me. I follow his gaze to the prone body of the girl: her head split like a melon, open and weeping, curled brains nestled within.

We take the boyfriend up the stage stairs, a warning procession past groping couples on low-slung seating, and shoulder through the milling dancers to a door reading STAFF ONLY. Lucs bursts through the swinging door using the boyfriend's head and dumps him on the corridor floor. The doors close after us like a dampening field. An overhead light glares above and my vision swims as I adjust from the dimness outside, getting a brief glimpse down a corridor extending away in progressive darkness. Raph barks something into his two-way.

Lucs in my face: "What happened?" Angry goatee and sharp slicked crewcut: I'm bigger, nearly six-four, but step back anyway.

"They were arguing—just a domestic—right near me, and he snapped her and . . . and before I could get to him he rammed her into the smoke machine. The sound . . . fuck—"

He grabs my shirt-front, silencing me: "This is what we do."

I shrug him off and nod, straightening my shirt. "I know."

He looks down at the sprawled body; the guy waking now, eyes flitting open and straining at the light. A kick to the side of the head and he is out again. "Take his foot" and we drag him down the corridor and the stairs at the end, the soft thud of his skull on each concrete step keeping beat with the muted, somehow-threatening music through the walls next to us. His head leaves a soft trail of blood. Raph walks ahead and unlocks the door at the bottom of the stairwell. I hear a car pulling up outside, then voices through the wood. A few steps from the bottom my boss pushes me away and reaches down to grasp the shuddering body, standing up with a hand on either side of the guy's head, a raggedy-doll in his grasp. Lucs holds my gaze and then snaps his wrists, sending the guy's arms and legs flailing to flap against the huge chest. A moist crack from the guy's neck and Lucs lets the body slide to the floor. I feel like I'm going to vomit.

Raph opens the door to waiting uniforms and a huge white van. Silent revolving lights on its roof spark blue and red eerily around the alley. One of the uniforms walks up, a cop: "This the fucker?" Lucs drags the body to the van's back-doors and throws it inside. A soft thud. The back hadn't been empty. His partner closes the doors and they drive off, still without the siren, faces swiveling at me as they turn onto the street.

Lucs waits in the doorway, shirt flecked with blood. I look at the empty street and the fading ghostly lights and then back at him, my head spinning. The reek of the alley is like a cocoon. Nausea floods my stomach.

On the way to my post I stop at the staff toilets to scrub the blood off my face. I grip the sink and stare at the mess of flyers pasted above the mirror: amongst them are missing persons photos, a mix of male and female faces, mostly young. Someone has mockingly drawn moustaches on a few. The door opens behind me. Raph's hulking brother Gabe. "We know you get this, David. We wouldn't have let you in otherwise. You think this is any different from what you've done?" He stares at me for a moment then leaves.

The dark figures across from me now seem ominous, always on the periphery of my vision as I scan the Pit. The feeling that they're all watching me, silent, unnerving, is greater than ever and my heart quickens. As much as I want to drop the two-way and rip off my shirt and leave, I can't. The warning in Lucs' eyes as he broke the guy's neck is enough to stop that.

Old Max from the Terminal, where I first started bouncing, had warned me the security at the Metropolis were "hard cunts"; a tight-knit, dangerous crew. When I was still at the ratty Village sports bar I'd see them come in for a quiet drink, these huge refugees from the Meatpacking District dressed in black talking amongst themselves at the bar. I'd tense up, expecting them to cause trouble, but they never did, just stared at any patron stupid enough to come near. They were there the night I lost it, beat the fuck out of this asshole guido: some drunk gangster wannabe who told me he didn't take shit from steroid meatheads telling him when to leave and then tried to pull a piece when I didn't back down. All the shit I'd put up with, all the abuse and violence and threats working as a bouncer, all the shit from my father against Mom and me, became too much and I dropped him with a sharp left—the first time I'd ever hit anyone on the job, the punch feeling like it'd been pent up forever—then grabbed him by the throat and dragged him out to the back alley, and the guy had tried to fight back and I took the hit then splayed his nose across his face—actually *feeling* the cartilage disintegrate beneath my fist—and rode him to the ground, hitting again and again and again until his face was slurry against the cobblestones.

He'd lain there blowing bloody bubbles into the air and as I hunched crouched over his crumpled body I could see nothing in his hand—it'd been a bluff, there'd never been a gun—and I felt my chest constrict, the world spin. I'd gone too far. I'd be going to jail. My life was over. I dropped to my knees, feeling the shock burn through me.

Then someone had grabbed me: one of the Metropolis guys—Mikhaels, Lucs' second—and started pulling me away up the street as two cops ran around the corner. They'd paused and looked at Mikhaels.

Then one had nodded, letting him lead me away—trembling as the adrenalin wore off and the delusions of power faded—as they went on to the barely-alive man.

"This is how it works," Lucs had said when I fronted before him at the Metropolis. "The cops look after us. We look after them. Way of the world. Work for us we make sure nothing ever comes of it."

I'd never seen them go this far until now. They must've been holding back the whole time, waiting until I'd proven myself enough to be accepted into the crew. Until they could trust me. Now they're showing their true selves: the *real* way of the world.

And Gabe's right: it's not like I can throw stones. It's not like what I did's any different.

But I sometimes wonder now how convenient it is Mikhaels'd been there that night, remembering him looking at me from across the bar just before I'd beaten the man; as if he'd instigated it somehow, his presence drawing out the darkness in me.

Maybe I just can't confront the truth: that I'd nearly beaten someone to death. It'd be much easier to blame anyone but myself—

Dammit. There's always too much time in here to think: an endless stretching of seconds, minutes, hours into meaninglessness; aided by the curtains shut against the outside sky, encouraging timelessness and the rejection of reality. Fuck it. The guy deserved it. He killed that girl. Lucs was *right* to snap his neck. The prick would've just bought his way out of it before some bullshit judge in a bullshit courtroom under a bullshit legal system. Weaseled his way to leniency as criminals always did. The system didn't work so what choice is left?

But what's really scaring me—and why I should've run as soon as Lucs turned his back after killing the guy, why I should never have come here in the first place—is that seeing Lucs deal out such justice makes me think of *her*. Of Lisa and that fuck Paul. My hands shake. Sweat rises on my face and across my back. Because I should have fucking—

A drunk is dancing with a chair he has dragged onto the dancefloor as if it's his partner. He clutches it in his arms and pirouettes, then throws it onto the ground and awkwardly leaps over the seat. The crowd around him seem to enjoy his absurd parody of some forties musical star—even the muscle-shirted Greek guy takes the hit in the shins good-humoredly—and I'm roundly booed as I jump off my podium and grab the chair, handing it to Raph who has appeared from across the Pit to back me up. But I need the distraction of work. I push the drunk past the bar to the front door and he gibbers at me: "I was pretty swish out there though wasn't I?" Infectious humor that catches me off guard. His eyes are dilated, oversexed on E's as well: he wants to touch me as I walk him out, feeling my shoulders through my shirt. I just shrug him off. He's harmless.

Then he catches a glimpse of Raph behind me and starts pulling away, seeing something I don't, some revelation his drugged-out brain throws up. "Keep him away from me! Don't you see what he is?"

Raph, following a few feet behind, stares back stonily, eyes drilling into the patron. The drunk gets more and more agitated and I tell him not to worry, to just walk out, but he seems oblivious to me and then tries to run as we enter the foyer, dodging to his left and around a group milling outside the toilets. Raph is already blocking his way to slam him in the chest, and we drag the guy kicking and swearing out the front to dump him on the pavement. He rolls into a ball at Raph's feet, wrapping his hands protectively around his head, and then there is a bark behind me: "That's enough, get back inside." I turn and Lucs stands glaring at us, two doormen behind like twin Cerberus statues at the gates of hell. There are people in line staring at us, elderly couples and families from surrounding cafés, theatergoers passing by. Too visible.

Raph slinks beside me as we head back to our posts, his bleach-blond hair and powerlifter-traps like talismans splitting the crowd before him. He leans in as we reach my post: "These sheep don't understand anything else", then leaves me staring after him.

I continue my watching, unnerved and searching for order in the madness, in the frenetic, restless movement; for some shifting code, some meaning in the faces that coalesce into momentary distinction only to become unformed clay when I look away—brown eyes, blue eyes, blond hair, black hair, blue hair, in an interchangeable melange. I search for joy, for revelation, for knowledge in the faces, for some reason why they come here to waste away their lives with drink and mindless primal movements. All I find is blankness, slack-eyed vapidness. I'm so sick of this.

A hole opens in the crowd and I wonder for a moment if the dancers are ducking someone's vomit. I look closely at those ringing the gap to see if they have that coy disgusted fascination, like dogs trying to avoid their own shit in the backyard. Then I see the swinging arms and sudden surge of bodies across the space and even as I raise the two-way hear a voice, Gabe's perhaps, rattle in my hand: "*Security to Dancefloor, Security to Dancefloor,*" and I jump off to push roughly through the crowd, chest and shoulders hard and unforgiving, distantly savoring the passing looks of dumb shock. I emerge into chaos and grab two of the fighting patrons, tearing apart their clutch by pushing one away, grabbing the other around the neck. The guy I'm holding starts lashing out instead with his feet. "Settle down," I yell with a jabbed compression of his neck for emphasis and he subsides. I look around and Gabe, Mikhaels and Raph are also restraining fighters. We stand each with subdued patrons hanging in our arms searching for further threats, for something missed.

I'm about to turn and haul off my captive when from nowhere comes a fist swung wild and hard to smash into my temple. I hear the disembodied thump rather than feel it—having had much worse before—and swivel to focus in on the terrified tanned face. I drop my forgotten captive and like a berserker lost in fury pummel the face. On the edge of vision I see the other security react as if under fire, choking out their quarry and launching into the crowd with random punches, staining the beer-soaked floor with spatters of blood.

And then I'm sitting on my attacker's chest, yelling at his dazed face: "Why the fuck did you do that? We were breaking it up!"

Spit splays into his mouth as he tries to speak, no air in his lungs. "Be— Because you . . . hit me."

I grab his shirt: "Like fuck I did!" and bring his face up to mine.

He persists: "So—Someone hit me."

I stare into his glazed, convincing eyes and then a hand lands on my shoulder; quick spin and armlock, bending the elbow back to breaking point, my fist cocked—and Lucs stares back at me, a hand raised instinctively to protect his face. I let him go.

He moves in close, goatee like a pointer: "Kill him."

I step back though it's hard to hear him above the music, above the screams of the crowd. "What?"

He surges in again: "Now, while there's still confusion, while there's justi-fication." I push him away, open-handed against the hard solidity of his pecs. "Damn you," he says slit-eyed, "stop fighting it."

I stand over the bleeding kid and, eyes still on Lucs, reach down to haul him up: "Get the fuck out of here." The kid looks at me in disbelief so I slap him across the cheek, bringing sudden clarity to his eyes. I look back at Lucs as he watches the patron disappear into the crowd. Lucs glares at me and walks away, saying something to Mikhaels.

His second looks at me then heads towards the front doors, pushing past the doormen and disappearing outside. I wonder what the hell Mikhaels is doing, leaving the club halfway through the night. I don't understand anything about this place any more.

I watch as Gabe and Raph drag away the injured. But the patrons soon start dancing again, the music an unstoppable Pied Piper-calling to their gyrating and fondling, to the slackening of the vague, drugged faces. Their shoes smear the forgotten blood into the polished floor.

I'm dismissed from my post at the Pit and sent upstairs as punishment. Danteis, who I'm relieving, passes me on the stairs with a nod, grateful to be heading down to the world of the big boys for a change. Heaven, the upstairs bar and club's wasteland, looks much easier to patrol than downstairs: a bar and small dancefloor on one level, leading up to another small bar, some pool tables and a series of isolated grimy couches ringed around a balcony overlooking the Pit. I stand midway up the stairs that split the levels and look out over the sweaty, milling drinkers by the larger bar.

I can't take in anything. I feel strange, panicky. The faces around me, the colors of the lights and bright yellow walls seem to warp and shift. I wonder if it's the cocktail of drugs I'm taking: uppers to get through the night; stano-zolol to maintain my size, my intensity. I feel like I'm tripping.

A girl wearing only a black bra-top and set of tiny shorts walking up the stairs towards me catches me glancing at her. "You want a fucking picture?" She is gone before I can respond, before I can even take offense at her insult. She passes me later, smirking over her shoulder, knowing her allure, as she heads downstairs, tight, arrogant ass rolling beneath the black leather.

"You're not naïve, David." I jump at the voice in my ear; Lucs has sidled up beside me while I've momentarily closed my eyes. He stares out over the drinkers, eyes reflective and distant, silent for a moment. I follow his gaze. "Look at these weak cockroaches," he finally says quietly. "Most of them can't even string two words together; fill them with alcohol and they become zombies, mindless scum."

"And that justifies killing them?"

He turns to me, as if contemplating this for the first time. "This is the way it's always been. You know that. There has always been those like us willing to seek the truth, to unlock the darkness inside."

"What the fuck are you talking about?"

"Think about it, David. Think of how you feel about them. How you feel about your *girlfriend*. Remember that night at the Terminal."

"What do you know about my girlfriend—" I start to demand, having never told them about Lisa. Then he touches my shoulder.

Sudden pain along my chest and arms, as if I'd done a heavy workout, the muscles burning and flaring. I want to recoil but the muscles on my arms and chest ripple in sympathy. I shudder as a wave of pain surges through me; like something opening out inside.

Just like I felt after beating the gangster. Jesus. I'd forgotten that, suppressed that weird feeling as I'd knelt on the cobblestones.

I break his grip and back away, spooked, mouth groping for a reaction. I grab my chest but the pain has just as quickly receded.

Lucs stares at me as I back down the stairs. What the fuck was that? What's wrong with me? He watches me go.

I stumble downstairs, knocking patrons out of the way as if they aren't there. The radio bucks in my hand but I don't hear what's said. Lucs perhaps, telling the others. One of the doormen—that asshole Pēteris who hated me from the moment I arrived, as if I didn't deserve to be here—appears from the foyer near the front door and stands waiting for me. I double back, heading for the back. I traverse the edge of the dancefloor, trying to keep out of sight of the other security perched like gargoyles on their posts.

I reach the Stage unharmed and burst through the double doors into the muted corridor to rest panting against a damp wall, waiting for my smoke-stained eyes and nose and throat to clear. My pulse throbs in my head, keeping complicit time with the music rumbling through the walls.

The one hanging light casts weird shifting sprays of illumination down the corridor. I touch my chest again, recalling that strange pain. I must be going insane, too many late nights, the shock of seeing someone killed. Maybe it's the drugs finally getting to me.

Yet Lucs' words nag at the back of my brain.

I force them from my mind. All that matters is getting out of here and I push off the wall and head for the back door.

I round a corner. Too late realize I'm not alone.

A figure is coming towards me, filling the narrow space. When I see the size of the guy I instinctively put one foot back, planting myself.

Gabe. He's big—bigger even than me—and in the tight corridor he almost scrapes the roof with his head. I tense and wait for him. Then I glimpse over his shoulder another darkened figure bent over something on the ground, something framed by yellow—it is blond hair, it is a woman. Tight black shorts. Bra-top.

There's blood on her neck.

As I stare at it my vision narrows, focusing solely on its dark stain.

I forget about Gabe, about the club, about the patron being killed.

Pulsing sounds in my ears, strong, blotting out everything else. Spit fills my mouth. I can smell the blood. It floods my senses. My head spins at the thought of reaching out and touching it, feeling its dark slick against my skin, of *tasting* it. That feeling of a hollowing-out inside me again, of surging within. Of power. Something related to the blood . . .

I imagine Lisa before me.

I tear my gaze away to look at the hunched-over figure, but the shifting light edging past Gabe's head and shoulders and underneath his arms warps everything and it seems the figure's face is somehow stretched and lupine.

"Thought you were a patron," Gabe says, breaking through my concentration. "Just as well." He points at the blackening egg on my temple. "You got hit before."

Disarmed, I raise my hand to my head slowly and feel the lump. My refined senses dissipate, leaving me feeling washed out and empty. I must be going insane. I look at the other security—it is Raph, his brother—but his face is normal. For a moment I'd thought . . .

"You can't let that happen again," Gabe's saying. "They must fear us."

I stare at him then look at the girl.

"She overstayed her welcome," Gabe explains.

Raph hauls the black-shorts girl up underneath her arms and drags her to the back door. But there is blood on the wall behind, splattered like the blood on Raph's cheek. He waits for Gabe to go down the stairwell and open the door and, as I stand watching, the girl's head lolls to one side on a too-pliable neck and her mouth, split at the corners as if punctured by something, gapes open, drooling a line of spittle onto her top. Raph sees me looking at her face and stares back openly. He reads something in my eyes that satisfies him and dismisses me, dragging the girl outside.

"You should get back to your post," Gabe says.

I hesitate, looking towards the back door. Instead I nod and head back into the club.

When I return upstairs Lucs is still on the stairs. I don't ask how he knew I'd return. He doesn't say anything for a while, then: "You okay?" I nod. He stares at me for a moment, then nods also. "I'll check back soon." He leaves.

I try to watch the crowd but I'm too fucked up, the scene in the corridor still whirling through my mind. In need of air I head up to the top bar to stand beneath the air-conditioning vent jutting from the roof, savoring its cool whisper over my sweating, fevered face.

I open my eyes and see Kelly standing at the bar, the one bargirl I actually liked and would speak to on occasion. But looking now at her tanned shoulders and the tight lycra top hugging her breasts only makes me think of Lisa, remembering the jut of her breasts above the bedclothes when I came home from work, the feel of her skin against me.

We'd met while I was still at the Terminal trying to work as many hours as I could to cover the rent. Some guy had been hassling Lisa in the nearby street as I was heading home for the night and for a moment I'd seen my father looming over my mom and I'd intervened without thinking. The guy—some crazy ex—had trash-talked to save face but when I advanced on him he soon disappeared. Lisa and I started going out soon afterwards. She used to call me her "protector." Things went well for a while and she even moved in, but then it all began to change. She started complaining about my temper affecting the relationship. Or how I was spending too much time in the gym, only concerned with putting on size. How I talked about the scumbag patrons I had to put up with every night, the contempt in my voice never far. How I had no plans for the future, as if working my ass off night after night meant nothing. She started spending more time at the dance studio for what I thought was an upcoming show: her first. I tried giving her space to prepare. But after she found out I beat that guy and was now working at one of the big clubs in the Meatpacking

District without telling her, I returned home one night to find all her stuff gone. She hadn't even left a note. And then I found out about Paul. The other lead. Some lean-limbed, shaggy-haired dancer she must've been fucking for months—she'd mentioned him once or twice but I didn't read anything into it, didn't want to seem jealous. I didn't know the bitch was about to leave me. I eventually found her new apartment and I'd pass by on the way home from work, sometimes sitting outside for a while. I felt stupid, jealous. But I couldn't stop myself. Then one morning, about a week ago, I watched this Paul guy walk out of her apartment with her, intimate hands brushing her face as he left. The shock was quickly overtaken with anger, burning rage. I couldn't believe the fury I was feeling. I wanted to rip them apart. It scared me. I didn't know how far I would go. So I drove away. I chickened out. And now I can't stop imagining what I could have done. Should have done.

I stare at Kelly and feel a rising anger and hatred. She smiles over at me but I turn away and descend past the vomit and beer-stained couches and stand at the balcony looking out over the huge gothic expanse with its sudden three-story drop to the Pit, crisscrossed and bisected by lasers and spotlights like prison-camp searchlights that pierce the hanging smoke. The dancers are a sea of sweaty, jerking bodies, a blind mass of conformity. I feel like jumping, smashing into them from above, shocking them out of their trances. Destroying their oblivion.

It would be so easy.

But I had the chance to run. And I couldn't.

Something distracts me. A frenzy of movement in the far-right corner couch, a couple in oblivious ecstasy, the girl with goth-black hair and raised skirt, her face slackened as she straddles a greasy guy, some mafioso scumbag. As I approach I see the slimy length of his penis jamming up inside her with every raise of her fleshy white cheeks.

I should tell them to zip up, walk them outside.

I wonder if Paul's cock looks like that.

I grab the girl's shoulder and roughly pull her off him, baring her seeping cunt. She tries to break away and stumbles backwards, hitting the brick wall. I let her fall and she lies spread-eagled, blood trickling down her face. I stare at its darkness. Everything shuts down.

Then I'm grabbing her by the throat, leaning in. She smells like metal, copper. Life.

Something on the edge of vision: the guy fumbling for something in his jacket. I swivel as he lunges at me and something wet slices my face, like a spray of cum, like he has opened my face with his cock. I touch the blood on my cheek and the guy stares at me in shock, as if surprised he has cut me, virgin knife held before him like a talisman. I tense and spring and he instinctively arcs the knife back to defend himself. But he is too slow. I grab his wrist then slam the heel of my other hand into the crook of his elbow. His arm jackknifes into his skull and he falls back onto the couch. There's a moment of silence before the girl slumped at my feet wakes up and starts screaming. The guy sits completely still, arms hanging by his side; dripping, alien cock pointing up from his open zipper. The knife is buried to the hilt in his right eye. The socket leaks blood and a clear viscous fluid.

I stare at him, shaking my head in disbelief, in horror.

A figure by my side. Lucs, taking my arm. My muscles burn at his touch and I try to pull away but his grip is iron. Behind him, Raph and Gabe close the area, moving in on the witnesses, silencing the girl. One of the patrons tries to run and Gabe chases him up the stairs, slamming him into the ground.

"You are ready now," Lucs says.

He leads me with his steel grip past the upstairs bar and downstairs. Patrons jump out of the way when they see the blood dripping down my face, staring after us dumbfounded. We head for the stage doors. The club sinks away as the doors close behind. Down the barely-lit corridor and towards the back door.

The outside air is cool on my face. But I don't get a chance to savor it because there's movement in the darkness of the alley. Figures emerging from an alcove: Mikhaels holding a blond-haired girl by the throat, one hand over her mouth. She is dressed in blue silk pyjamas and shivers in the night air.

I look at her face.

Oh God. It's Lisa. She stares at me with terror-filled eyes.

I try to pull away, to run for the street beyond, but Lucs' fingers dig into me like claws. *"You know what to do,"* he says, something wrong with his voice. *"Become one of us. Finish the Change."* I turn and his eyes have become black holes in his face, dilating with darkness. His teeth fill his mouth.

I thrash against him in horror, feeling his fingers sink into my skin like needles of fire, but I have to get away from him, have to escape what he's—

And then the other figures appear: hunched shadows in the darkness of the alley. Gabe, Raph, Danteis, Pēteris, all grinning. Waiting.

I can't look at Lisa, forcing my eyes away from her, searching for a gap in their numbers, some way to escape this. Lucs senses my resistance still in the face of the inevitable. His voice like gravel in my ear: *"Then if you will not kill her, if you can still resist . . ."*

Pēteris reaches back into the alcove, drinking in my despair, and pulls out a struggling man dressed only in tracksuit pants—dragged out of bed also; thin but muscular, like a skinned rabbit, impossibly-defined abs a downward-*V*.

So this is what she wanted. This is who she chose instead of me.

I feel the hatred hit.

"You are a god now," Lucs says. *"Take what is yours."*

My anger surges beyond control. As I stare at Paul the darkness kept deep inside me opens out like spreading wings and a searing pain suddenly runs in rivulets down my arms and across my neck and up my face. Agony floods my throat and I throw my head back to cry out and my jaw dislocates with a wet clicking sound and I can only manage a strangled guttural croak. I feel my nerve-endings fry as my hands and arms and chest ripple and bubble like melting plastic, my back pop and break and fill out impossibly, my fingers lengthen into claws and brow form over and become stretched and lupine and teeth distend my mouth. Then my vision goes black and suddenly all-encompassing as my eyes dilate, the weak moonlight from above sending shards into my brain.

I see the shallows of blood pumping beneath Paul's skin. Can smell its hot, sweet scent. Can smell my girlfriend beyond.

I look at Lisa in Mikhaels' arms and inexplicably a part of me senses I have started crying. Burning tears that score my face. I wish I could tell her I'm sorry, that part of me will be forever destroyed by this. That I loved her.

But when I see her weak, pleading eyes, like an animal at the slaughter, the realization eclipses everything.

She deserves this. They all do. They are only prey.

The growl sounds deep in my throat and is joined by the growls of my Brothers. The man before me pisses himself in fear, the acrid stain blossoming across his track pants. Once I have tasted his flesh, once I have drunk my fill of his life I will kill the woman behind him also.

This is the way it should begin for me. Ending the life I once had. Embracing my rightful place in this world.

Her blood takes me.

AND NEITHER HAVE I WINGS TO FLY

CARRIE LABEN

—◆—

"I'm sorry," Faith says. A lie, but the satellite phone connection is too expensive to argue across. "The only safe thing to do is to stay put. We're well supplied, we're on the sheltered side of the island."

Vivian sighs. It's one with the wind against the porthole. "I wish you hadn't gone. Dad is worried to death."

I hope so. "This is my job. If I only went out when there couldn't possibly be a storm, I wouldn't go out at all."

"Yeah, but . . . "

"I have to go, Viv. Don't call again unless it's a real emergency, okay? I'll let you know as soon as we get back, promise."

"Okay." Faith has the phone halfway back to the cradle when she hears her sister's voice add, "One more thing!" She doesn't hang up.

"What?"

"You'll never guess who I ran into the other day."

"No, I won't." The satellite phone is also too expensive to gossip across, but if she lets Viv have this one moment maybe she'll save in the long run.

"Marika Mendel! Can you believe that? She came into the store, we had a nice chat." Viv pretends to catch herself. Or maybe it's honest, Faith can't know for sure. "But I know you can't talk long. I'll tell you all about it when you come home. Bye!"

Outside, the rain is just getting started, and most of the passengers—five grad students, one professor, two amateur filmmakers, and three die-hard birdwatchers—are still on deck, sucking up as much fresh air as they can, as though it'll last them. One of the filmmakers and one of the grad students have been seasick since they set out from San Diego, and the chop they're likely to get riding this out will be hard on everyone, even the crew. Even Faith.

At night she writes blog posts, even though they can't actually be uploaded until she reaches shore. The blog is her best free advertising, and lots of good you-are-there material is the key to its appeal.

But tonight, even though she should be thinking of adjectives to make the storm sound like a glorious adventure that people would pay for, she's writing about gannets.

The Northern Gannet, Morus bassanaus, is one of the largest seabirds of the north Atlantic. The adult bird is all white and ivory, except its wing-tips and feet which have been dipped in ink. Its beak is a spear . . . no, backspace . . . When it dives, it is a spear, its beak foremost. Flocks of gannets gather over schools of fish and plunge into the water from great heights, like bombs.

She does not write, *My mother is a gannet.* She doesn't put personal stuff on the blog.

Eventually she is done with the gannets, and with the little glass of Laphroig that helps her write. She walks back up on deck, where the rain is now lashing and the waves are sending spray well over the deck. If she had a skin of gannet feathers, it would slide off of her and leave her unaffected. Her Marmot windbreaker is good enough, but the cuffs of her jeans get wet, and then dampen her socks.

But Vivian won't even come out on the boat. She says she's not scared, but Dad won't come—Dad won't even get in sight of the sea, a beach scene in a movie makes him walk out—and she won't leave Dad alone.

Faith suspects she is scared.

At the height of the storm a small yellow-and-black landbird tries to perch in the rigging, then falls to the deck exhausted. The birdwatchers hover over it and identify it as a Hermit Warbler. It would break their rules to touch it, since nature must take its course, but they manage to half-crowd, half-shepherd it into the galley. The cook, Chaz, has been complaining about an infestation of fruit flies since they set out.

Chaz sets out a dish of water and some of the offending peaches. Out of the wind and the wet, the bird soon sheds its sickly, puffed-up look and begins to take an interest in these offerings.

Over dinner, everyone watches their new companion, who seems to have more of an appetite than any human aboard. The sailors and the birders swap stories of other warblers, sparrows, falcons, even a sand grouse that once washed on board an oil rig. The phalarope that flew into a lighted bathroom and swam in circles in the sink. The heron that crossed the Atlantic on a yacht.

When everyone has drifted away and Chaz is washing up, Faith takes a closer look at the bird. It's almost certainly just a bird; still, on the off chance, she waits.

The bird ignores her, hovers to pluck a spider out of the corner, then drops back to the table and drinks. The yellow of its face shines in the slanting evening light. She can understand wanting to touch it, but she can't—can no longer?—understand not knowing that touching it would be wrong.

Maybe she's been hanging out with birdwatchers too much.

The bird stays until the storm has blown itself out and they've started back for San Diego. Then one morning it is gone.

If it headed east, the birdwatchers say, it will probably make it. Or maybe not, but at least it has a chance.

Once they're back in cell phone range of port, Faith calls Vivian. She tries to run through the usual reassuring niceties, but Vivian cuts her off immediately.

"You're back?"

"Less than a day out of port."

"Thank god. We need your help on Wednesday; not tomorrow but this coming Wednesday, I mean."

"That's not going to work, I'm sailing out again as soon as we clean up and take on more supplies."

"I thought that you didn't have another trip scheduled for a month!"

"I didn't. But the director we took out this time got an inspiration bug and is paying us to go out ASAP and get more footage. He wants to do a short feature on birds who get blown off-course and end up . . . "

"We need your help. An apartment in my building opened up and Dad's moving into it. I can't keep driving back and forth across the city twice a day to check on him."

"That's great," Faith says. The idea made her choke, but she'd gotten it through her thick skull at least that other people were other people and had other feelings. "You deserve more free time."

"And this way I can make sure he's actually eating real meals. You know how he is about cooking for himself."

"Well, it serves him right. He's had years to learn." Wrong, wrong wrong time for that argument, but it was too late to back up. "I'm sorry. I think it's a great idea if it makes things easier on you, but I'm heading out again by Monday at the latest."

"Tell the guy you have to wait."

"If I make him wait now, it'll be next year before he get another shot at what he's looking for. And he'll probably go look for it with a different captain."

"We need you."

"No you don't. You'll be fine."

"With just my little car, it'll take two days."

"I didn't even known this would be happening."

"I didn't know that the apartment would be available."

"I'm sorry." Faith would like to think of herself as an honest person, but it's getting harder and harder to do that. Still, she only lies in self-defense and a lot of things are justifiable in self-defense.

"Dad misses you."

There's nothing she can say to that, not even the baldest lie would fool Vivian into thinking that she felt sorry for Dad. The first time Vivian had used the line, back when Faith was in college, she'd tried to lie that she missed him too. The second time she'd been drunk and she'd quoted Star Wars, to the effect that the more he tightened his grasp the more star systems would slip through his fingers. Neither worked, so now she waits. Vivian hears silence, not the slap of the waves on the boat and the chatter of the passengers outside, and her own need to fill that silence will always push her on eventually. That's one of the few ways in which Vivian takes after their father.

"I saw Marika again. In the store."

"How is she?"

"She's fine. I told her you'd be ashore next week, and that maybe you'd want to get dinner."

"Maybe next month."

"She probably won't be in town that long. She's only here to give a lecture at the university." Another pause. "She wrote a book, you know."

"No, I didn't know that. I always thought she was going to be an actress."

"It's about our situation. With, you know, our moms."

"Ah."

"I asked if we were in it, but she just laughed."

"Sounds like Marika."

"She'd probably tell you. If you were going to see her. But I guess you won't."

"I'll have to catch up with her another time."

"You always say things like that!"

"I'm sorry, I'm sorry." It doesn't even feel like a lie anymore, it feels like a mantra. An incantation to protect her sister, and by extension herself.

She doesn't even go back to her own apartment during their brief time onshore, but stays in a small hotel by the dock that normally cater to sport fisherman so that she can more easily oversee the resupply and the minor repairs that the storm made necessary. She knows she should update the blog, at least upload a few photos, but it's a task that's easy to procrastinate on so she does.

On Saturday night, at nine-thirty, Vivian calls again. The temptation to let it go to voicemail is very strong, but it might be an actual emergency.

"Hello?"

"Guess what?" The joy in Vivian's voice tells Faith immediately that no one is in the hospital or dead.

"No idea."

"Oh, come on, guess."

"You got a new job?"

"No, silly. Why would I be calling about a job this late on the weekend?"

"You heard from . . . "

"Mark proposed!"

Faith opens her mouth, but no sound comes out. When she thinks of Mark, she always thinks of the day he came over, drank all her beer, and talked over her with stories about the thirty-foot fishing boat he'd played around on with his dad in Sarasota, before his dad decided that being a bull was better than being a banker and a husband and a dad.

"Tonight, at dinner. He had the waiter hide the ring in my dessert, it was so sweet, I started crying right there." It sounds as though Vivian is crying again.

"Well, congratulations." That's okay. That sounds good.

"Look, I know you and Mark aren't best buddies. But I love him, and he really is a good guy if you'll give him a chance."

"If he makes you happy. . . . I want you to be happy." There. Something true and useful.

"I am! I'm so happy! Listen, here's what he wants to do. We're going to exchange skins. Instead of just him having mine, I'll have his too."

"That doesn't actually make it any easier if you end up splitting up."

"We're not planning to split up!"

"No one plans to split up."

"We won't do that. We both know what it's like, growing up with a parent who took their skin back and just took off. We wouldn't do that to our kids."

"Are you pregnant?" There's no keeping the oh-shit out of her voice.

"No, of course not. I'm just saying, when we do have kids, we have to both be in it for the long haul. And Mark knows that."

Don't say, but what if. Don't say it, don't say it.

"I'd like you to be my maid of honor."

Don't say, but what if.

"We're scheduling the wedding for July or August, you never go out then."

"Of course. Of course I'll be your maid of honor."

Vivian makes a noise of pure delight, and for a moment Faith can feel the lure, the impulse that says, *making this other happy would be easier than making yourself happy. Making this other happy would replace making yourself happy.* But as soon as she feels the lure, she can't help thinking of the hook and how much thrashing it takes to get off of it.

"When you get back, we can sit down and talk about dresses and reception venues and things."

"Absolutely. When I get back." This time, she doesn't want to leave the silence hanging. "I know this is what you've been wanting. Congratulations."

It's the first trip she's ever run where the passengers have complained about the lack of storms. The director says, over and over again, that he know he needs to wait for the right moment, that it's no different than any other documentary, especially when you're dealing with animals, that it's fine. But she can feel his tension, the way he's tallying the cost of each day in his head, and so can his crew. Unlike the birders, or the people she sometimes takes sport fishing, they're not in tune with the kind of waiting the ocean requires. They're antsy.

So when the bird appears on the horizon, the boat damn near explodes. Or at least, some of the passenger do. As it gets nearer, Faith can see that it's not one of the normal Pacific birds she knows, and for a moment her heart rises up—but it's no gannet either, too big, and one of the few birds too white: a gannet would have black wingtips.

It may be the biggest bird she's ever seen. Its long neck splits the air ahead of it as it heads straight for them, its long legs trail out behind it. She's seen the image in a thousand photos and paintings, but she's never seen a real crane, alive and flying free, before.

Without considering, without circling, it drops for the deck and lands among them all. The director's crew scramble to re-aim their cameras and get out of each other's shots. The crane gives an unbirdlike little shrug, shakes its head. It's impossible to see how the feathers start to drop, even if you're watching for it; it's just a sort of rippling motion and then Marika Mendel is standing there in the center of their circle with a slightly sweaty face and a coat of birdskin bunched around her feet. She's wearing a pair of gray slacks and a black silk top, totally unsuitable for salt water, and sunglasses with huge green plastic frames, and the dangling feather earrings that have been her trademark ever since Faith first met her at age twelve. Probably she flew straight from the reading, or whatever kind of reception-type deal they had afterwards, or so Faith imagines.

"Well," Marika says, glancing at the cameras as she scoops up her skin. "Looks like I came to the right place."

Faith shakes her head. "This guy, he only wants birds who are in the wrong place."

"Bummer." Like all of them, she has the trick of folding her skin neatly without any apparent effort; it's now a cube in her hands barely the size of a Kleenex box.

Faith shouldn't stare at it. She should introduce Marika around. She should do a lot of things, and despite her surprise, she does—makes the introductions, shows Marika to an empty cabin and a head where she can wash up, gives her a quick overview of the ship's layout and where the life jackets are and when dinner is served. All the while, she feels as though her brain is drifting somewhere a few feet behind her, still marvelling.

"So, you inherited the skin," she says when her brain finally catches back up.

Marika nods. "And so did Vivian, I hear."

"That's right."

"But . . . "

"But not me."

"Seems like it would have been better the other way around, though."

Faith can't help but smile. "You haven't changed."

"Sure I have. I've gotten taller, for one thing."

"I just heard the Marika who told Dr. Kravitz that her dad was just . . . what was it? . . . just fucked off that he couldn't go around with a Japanese chick on his arm anymore."

"I stand by the accuracy of that."

"How is your dad?"

"Still not talking to me. Somehow, since the book came out, not talking to me even harder."

"Yeah, Vivian said you wrote a book. What's up with that?"

"Half memoir, half cultural survey, all sexy. At least according to Publisher's Weekly."

"Are you allowed to write half a memoir these days?"

"Oh indeed. One of the girls in my workshop was working on a project that was simultaneously about global warming and how her mother died of lung cancer. It was pretty good."

"But not as sexy as yours."

"Nothing's as sexy as mine."

How could she be talking to Marika the way they had at fifteen, without feeling that awful fifteen-year-old feeling again?

And how could the engine choose that moment to make an awful choking noise that demanded any decent captain's attention?

By the time the engine stops hacking, it's dinner time. The director wants to talk to Marika over dinner about how skin-birds cope with the conditions that drive real birds astray, which leads to a discussion of how many skins are rejecting the idea that non-changing animals are more real than they are, which leads to talk about Marika's book, which leads to a short interview on the stern while the sun is setting. Meanwhile, Faith looks at the weather radar, trying to find a pleasing storm to finish off the trip on a potential high note, and talks with Robert, her first mate, about the vacation time he want to take, and works on the blog, and drinks her Laphroig.

Marika disappears to her bed as soon as the interview is over. It must have been tiring, flying so far.

In the morning, Faith sits by the director at breakfast and discusses heading a bit south towards stormier weather, but his budget won't accommodate more than one extra day. Then she goes to check on how the wire-and-duct-tape repairs to the engine are holding up—fine, as they should be. And then she takes a stroll around the lower deck, just to see how things are.

Marika turns out to be inside, talking to Chaz about Indian food. She wraps that up without seeming to, and follows Faith without seeming to out onto the bow.

"So, I didn't ask you how your dad is doing, yesterday. So rude!" She's still wearing the sunglasses and earrings, but she's now in a pair of cargo pants and a green T-shirt. Where these changes of clothing come from is a mystery to Faith; it never occurred to her to ask her mother, until it was too late, and Vivian doesn't ever want to talk about anything to do with having a skin, until this thing with Mark.

She doesn't feel ready to ask Marika, either. "He's still speaking to me. More's the pity."

"That implies that you're still speaking to him."

"Now you sound like Dr. Kravitz."

"She was right sometimes."

"It would upset Vivian if I just cut him out of my life."

Marika nods and pushes her sunglasses up to perch on her head. "Vivian is still making your dad out to be the good guy."

"In her mind it's easy. One person ran away, and it wasn't Dad. Plenty of people agree with her."

"It's the number one question I have to field at readings, you know. Your mom ran out on you. Tell us how mad you are at her, how much it fucked up your life."

"Must make you crazy."

"Nah, I was already crazy, just ask Dr. Kravitz."

"Vivian's getting married soon."

"Yeah, I believe I may have heard a little something about that, when I stopped by to see her Monday night." Fifteen-year-old Marika would have rolled her eyes, and fifteen-year-old Faith would have been mad at her for it, so maybe they have both grown up a little.

"Her fiance's dad was a bull."

"Heard that, too."

"They have some kind of big plan where instead of her just giving him her skin, they're going to swap."

"Let me guess. Then they're going to hyphenate their names."

Faith sighs. "I just don't see how it's going to be any better. I mean, it is better. He didn't outright steal her skin the way Dad stole Mom's. But she's still going to be trapped."

Marika is silent for a moment, the wind ruffling her earrings. A drop of rain hits the upturned lens of her glasses. "And you ran away to sea."

"That I did."

"Are you looking for your mom?"

"No, Dr. Kravitz. Gannets live in the Atlantic Ocean."

"And yet, here you are. In the blue Pacific."

"I just like it out here."

It's raining for real, now, and they retreat inside by wordless mutual consent.

After dinner the rain tapers off. Out on deck, Marika is leaning carelessly against the rail, and Faith has an image of her sunglasses falling off and sinking through the cold water, tumbling, to end up miles below in the silt. Of course they don't.

As she gets closer, she realises that Marika is muttering.

" . . . when my dimensions are as well compact, my mind as generous, and my form as true as honest madame's issue?" She turns, and doesn't even pretend to be embarrassed by Faith's presence. "One of the few good things about getting locked up in an all-girl's boarding school at sixteen is that we got top play all the boys' roles too."

Faith looks at her, at the swing of her hair brushing her shoulder, at her earring.

"So I was Edmund in *King Lear*."

Faith nods. The earring sways in the breeze.

"You know: 'Thou, nature, are my goddess . . . '"

"Sounds cool. The only Shakespeare we ever did in high school was *Romeo and Juliet*. I hated it."

"You never had *King Lear* in college?"

"I mostly took science classes."

Marika shakes her head and chuckles. "All work and no play . . . "

"The ocean is play. The ocean is beautiful."

Faith isn't looking at Marika at all now, but she feels her moving in, feels the air get warmer and moister in the moment before they kiss.

In the morning, Marika isn't in Faith's cabin. Her skin is, though, neatly draped over the chair where Faith sits to write her blog posts, the only place in the room where something that size could be neatly draped, impossible to miss.

Faith hesitates for a moment before even picking it up. The feathers are warm, which doesn't seem like it should be possible. They leave a fine powder on her fingers like a butterfly's wings.

Marika didn't leave it behind by mistake, that's impossible. She must have wanted Faith to see it, to have the opportunity.

Faith folds it—her clumsy inexperienced fingers can only get it down to the size of a bath towel—and takes it to Marika's cabin. No one is inside. She puts the skin on the bed and locks the door so that no one but Marika will find it. Hook evaded.

Maybe she should ask Vivian for a plus-one for the wedding. It would be nice to have someone there who understands.

But that's months away. Today, they'll have to head east.

CONTRIBUTORS

Holly Black is the bestselling author of the Spiderwick series. Her first book, *Tithe: A Modern Faerie Tale*, was an ALA Top Ten Book for Teens, received starred reviews in *Publishers Weekly* and *Kirkus Reviews*, and has been translated into twelve languages. Her second teen novel, *Valiant*, was an ALA Best Book for Young Adults, a *Locus Magazine* Recommended Read, and a recipient of the Andre Norton Award from the Science Fiction and Fantasy Writers of America. Her third teen novel, *Ironside*, the sequel to *Tithe*, was a *New York Times* bestseller. Her new novel, *White Cat*, received three starred reviews. She lives in Amherst, Massachusetts. Visit Holly at www.blackholly.com.

Richard Bowes has published five novels, two collections of short fiction, and fifty stories. He has won two World Fantasy Awards and the Lambda, International Horror Guild, and Million Writers Awards. Recent and forthcoming stories appear in *The Magazine of Fantasy and Science Fiction*, and the anthologies *Digital Domains, Beastly Bride, Wilde Stories 2011, Haunted Legends, Naked City, Best Gay Stories, Nebula Awards Showcase 2011, Supernatural Noir,* and *Blood and Other Cravings*.

Marie Brennan is the author of the Onyx Court series of London-based historical faerie fantasies: *Midnight Never Come, In Ashes Lie, A Star Shall Fall*, and the forthcoming *With Fate Conspire*. She has published more than thirty short stories in venues such as *On Spec, Beneath Ceaseless Skies*, and the acclaimed anthology series *Clockwork Phoenix*. More information can be found on her website: www.swantower.com.

Nadia Bulkin is a writer and political science student. Her short fiction has appeared in *ChiZine, Strange Horizons, Fantasy Magazine*, and elsewhere; more information is available at nadiabulkin.wordpress.com. When she lived in a dorm in New York City not long ago she was her apartment's designated exterminator, but a very bad one.

Stephanie Burgis listened obsessively to 1940s recordings of her own grandpa and great-uncles' Youngstown family band while writing "Blue Joe." She's taken the family immigrant tradition along one more step by moving to Wales, where she lives with her husband, fellow writer Patrick Samphire, their son, and their crazy-sweet dog. Her fun Regency fantasy adventure for kids, *Kat, Incorrigible*, was published by Atheneum Books in April, 2011. To find out more, please visit her website: www.stephanieburgis.com

Seth Cadin lives in Berkeley. He has one daughter, one partner, and sixteen pet mice.

Gwendolyn Clare has a BA in Ecology, a BS in Geophysics, and is currently working to add another acronym to her collection. Away from the laboratory, she enjoys practicing martial arts, adopting feral cats, and writing speculative fiction. Her short stories have appeared in *Asimov's*, the *Warrior Wisewoman 3* anthology, *Abyss and Apex*, and *Bull Spec*, among others. She can be found online at gwendolynclare.com.

Leah R. Cutter is the author of three historical fantasy novels as well as several fantasy, science fiction, and horror short stories. Her most recent published novel, *The Jaguar and the Wolf* (Roc 2005) is about what happens when a group of Vikings encounter the Mayans. Her first novel, *Paper Mage* (Roc 2003) is set in Tang dynasty China, and her second novel, *Caves of Buda* (Roc 2004) is set in Budapest, Hungary. Leah has had odd jobs all over the world, including an working on an archaeological dig in England, teaching English in Taiwan, and tending bar in Thailand. She temporarily lives in New Orleans, doing research for more novels. Her permanent home is in Seattle. She works as a technical writer for a California software firm. Her hobbies include walking, hiking, yoga, reading, drinking single-malt scotch, dancing and goofing off.

Renee Carter Hall works as a medical transcriptionist by day and as a writer, poet, and artist all the time. Her short fiction has appeared in a variety of print and electronic publications, including *The Summerset Review, A Fly in Amber, New Fables*, and the *Different Worlds, Different Skins* anthologies. She lives in West Virginia with her husband and her cat, both of whom serve diligently as beta readers. (If the cat falls asleep on the printout, it's good.) Readers can find her online at www.reneecarterhall.com.

Elizabeth Hand is the multiple-award-winning author of numerous novels and three collections of short fiction. She is also a longtime reviewer for the *Washington Post*, among many other publications. A revised edition of *Glimmering*, her 1997 cult novel of environmental collapse, will be published this year. *Available Dark*, sequel to Shirley Jackson Award winner *Generation Loss*, and *Radiant Days*, a YA novel about the French poet Arthur Rimbaud, will both appear in 2012. She lives on the coast of Maine.

Carlos Hernandez is currently serving as the Deputy Chair of the Department of English at the Borough of Manhattan Community College, CUNY. He earned his PhD in English with an emphasis in Creative Writing from Binghamton University, and is the author of numerous works of fiction, a novella, and the coauthor of *Abecedarium*, an experimental novel published by Chiasmus Media in 2007. He has so thoroughly failed as a blogger he no longer gives out his web address, hoping it might magically disappear on its own. But he will gladly friend you on Facebook. Search for "Carlos A. Hernandez," and good luck. It's a very common name.

Erica Hildebrand loves storytelling and works on illustrated projects in addition to her writing. She has a soft spot in her heart for superheroes, dinosaurs, and the conquerors of antiquity. A graduate of the Odyssey Writing Workshop, her fiction has appeared in *M-Brane SF*, *The Edge of Propinquity*, and *Everyday Weirdness*. Her comics have appeared in *Space Squid* and *Kaleidotrope*. She lives in Pennsylvania.

Justin Howe's fiction has appeared in various online and print publications including *Beneath Ceaseless Skies*, *Crossed Genres*, *Brain Harvest*, and the anthology *Fast Ships, Black Sails*. Born in Boston, he now lives with his wife in South Korea where he teaches English to elementary school students.

Carrie Laben, formerly a lifelong New Yorker, is currently studying for her MFA at the University of Montana. Her work has previously appeared in *Clarkesworld* and *ChiZine* as well as anthologies *Haunted Legends* and anthology *Phantom*. She looks at birds.

Marissa Lingen lives in the Minneapolis suburbs with two large men and one small dog. She loves lakes, snow, hockey, and just about every stereotypical Minnesota thing you can name except mosquitoes. She writes short stories and is working on (surprise!) a fantasy novel.

Nick Mamatas is the author of three and a half novels, including *Sensation* (PM Press) and, with Brian Keene, *The Damned Highway* (Dark Horse). He has also published over seventy short stories in venues such as *Tor.com*, *Asimov's Science Fiction* and the anthologies *Supernatural Noir* and *Lovecraft Unbound*. His fiction has thrice been nominated for the Bram Stoker award, and as an editor for *Clarkesworld Magazine*, Nick has been nominated for both the Hugo and World Fantasy awards.

Sandra McDonald's debut collection, *Diana Comet and Other Improbable Stories,* received a starred review in *Booklist* and is an American Library Association Over the Rainbow book. Her short fiction about enchanted firemen, sexy cowboy robots, and more has appeared in more than forty venues. Her science fiction novels follow an Australian military lieutenant and her handsome sergeant. She earned an MFA in Creative Writing at the University of Southern Maine and teaches college in northeast Florida. Visit her at www.sandramcdonald.com.

Mario Milosevic lives in the Pacific Northwest of the United States in a county which once passed a law making it illegal to kill Bigfoot. His fiction and poetry has appeared in many publications, both print and online. Learn more at mariowrites.com.

Michelle Muenzler was born in the broken pines of East Texas where she fought boys with concrete-sharpened pine spears and mastered squeezing through rabbit trails for quick escapes in the games of childhood war. This particular short story was first published in the third issue of *Shroud Magazine* where the surrounding gore made it seem quite tame in comparison. The rest of her short fiction can be found in publications such as *Daily Science Fiction*, *Electric Velocipede*, and *Space & Time Magazine*.

Cherie Priest is the author of ten novels, including 2010's *Dreadnought* and 2009's *Boneshaker*. *Boneshaker* was nominated for both the Hugo Award and the Nebula Award, and it won the Locus Award for Best Science Fiction Novel. Cherie's other books include *Four and Twenty Blackbirds*, *Fathom*, *Wings to the Kingdom*, and the Endeavour-nominated book *Not Flesh Nor Feathers* from Tor (Macmillan). Her short novels *Dreadful Skin*, *Clementine*, and *Those Who Went Remain There Still* are published by Subterranean Press. She lives in Seattle, Washington, with her husband and a fat black cat.

Vandana Singh was born and raised in India and now lives in the United States where she teaches physics and writes. Her fiction has been published in *Strange Horizons* and numerous anthologies and reprinted in several Year's Best volumes. Her novella *Distances* (Aqueduct Press) is a 2008 Carl Brandon Parallax Award winner and a Tiptree Honor book. The story "Thirst" first appeared in *The Third Alternative* (now *Black Static*) and is also to be found in her collection, *The Woman Who Thought She Was a Planet and Other Stories* (Zubaan/Penguin India). Her website is http://users.rcn.com/singhvan/.

Maria V. Snyder switched careers from meteorologist to fantasy novelist when she began writing the *New York Times* best-selling Study Series (*Poison Study, Magic Study,* and *Fire Study*) about a young woman who becomes a poison taster. Born in Philadelphia, Maria dreamed of chasing tornados and even earned a BS degree in Meteorology from Penn State University. Unfortunately, she lacked the necessary forecasting skills. Writing, however, lets Maria control the weather, which she gleefully does in her Glass Series (*Storm Glass, Sea Glass*, and *Spy Glass*). Readers are invited to read more of Maria's short stories on her website at www.MariaVSnyder.com.

Aaron Sterns' "Watchmen" originally appeared in the tri-country anthology *Gathering the Bones* edited by Jack Dann, Ramsey Campbell, and Dennis Etchison, receiving an honourable mention in the *The Year's Best Fantasy and Horror*. Sterns' first story "The Third Rail" appeared in the World Fantasy Award-winning collection *Dreaming Down-Under* and was shortlisted for the 1998 Aurealis Award for Best Horror Short Story. Subsequent stories appeared in *Orb: Speculative Fiction* and the recent follow-up to *DDU, Dreaming Again*. Sterns served as script-editor for the film *Rogue*, and appeared in Greg McLean's earlier *Wolf Creek* as a nasty truck driver. A former editor of *The Journal of the Australian Horror Writers*, he has also presented papers on *American Psycho* and *Crash* at ICFA (as part of PhD work on postmodern horror), written non-fiction articles for *Bloodsongs: The Australian Horror Magazine* and other publications, and was the Australian correspondent for *Hellnotes: The Insider's Guide to the Horror Field*. Sterns is currently working on a novel based on the dark world of "Watchmen"—*Blood*—and a number of screenplays. He lives in Melbourne, Australia.

Lavie Tidhar grew up on a kibbutz in Israel and has since lived in South Africa, the UK, Vanuatu, and Laos. He is the author of steampunk novels *The Bookman* (2010) and *Camera Obscura*, literary novel *Osama*, and weird SF novel *Martian Sands* (all three in 2011). He is also the author of linked-story-collection *HebrewPunk* (2007), novellas *Cloud Permutations* (2010) and *An Occupation of Angels* (2005 UK; 2010 US), and is a prolific short story writer.

Genevieve Valentine's short fiction has appeared in magazines such as *Clarkesworld, Fantasy*, and *Lightspeed*, and the anthologies *Running with the Pack, The Way of the Wizard, Teeth*, and others. Her first novel, *Mechanique: A Tale of the Circus Tresaulti*, will be published in spring 2011. She has terrible taste in movies, a tragedy she tracks on her blog, genevievevalentine.com.

Kaaron Warren's short story collection *The Grinding House* (CSFG Publishing) won the ACT Writers' and Publishers' Fiction Award and two Ditmar Awards. Her second collection, *Dead Sea Fruit* is published by Ticonderoga Books. Her critically acclaimed novel *Slights* (Angry Robot Books) was nominated for an Aurealis Award, made the preliminary ballot for the Stoker Awards, was shortlisted for the Ned Kelly First Novel Award, and won the Australian Shadows Award fiction, the Ditmar Award and the Canberra Critics' Award for Fiction.

Jen White is an Australian writer of speculative fiction. She lived for many years in the Northern Territory and, although she has now moved to gentler climes, she still finds inspiration in the vibrancy and mystery of Australia's north. Her fiction has been published in various anthologies and magazines, and has recently appeared in the anthology *The Tangled Bank: Love, Wonder and Evolution*. She has a story in the upcoming anthology *Dead Red Heart*.

A.C. Wise was born and raised in Montreal, and currently lives in the Philadelphia area with her husband, two cats, and a very short dog. Her fiction has appeared in publications such as *Clarkesworld, Strange Horizons, Realms of Fantasy*, and *ChiZine*, among others. Along with Bernie Mojzes, she is co-editor of *The Journal of Unlikely Entomology*. For more information, please visit the author's website at www.acwise.net.

Melissa Yuan-Innes likes werewolves (warm, furry) better than vampires (cold, dead). Her fiction has appeared in *Indian Country Noir, Nature, The Dragon and the Stars*, and other fine venues. She practices emergency medicine and dotes on her son and infant daughter outside of Montreal, Canada. Her website is www.melissayuaninnes.net

COPYRIGHT NOTICES

ABOUT THE EDITOR

Ekaterina Sedia resides in the Pinelands of New Jersey. She is the editor of anthologies *Paper Cities* (a World Fantasy Award winner) and *Running with the Pack*. Her critically acclaimed novels, *The Secret History of Moscow, The Alchemy of Stone,* and *The House of Discarded Dreams* were published by Prime Books. Her forthcoming novel, *Heart of Iron,* will be published later this year. Her short stories have sold to *Analog, Baen's Universe, Subterranean,* and *Clarkesworld,* as well as numerous anthologies, including *Haunted Legends* and *Magic in the Mirrorstone.* Visit her at www.ekaterinasedia.com